MOONSET ON DESERT SANDS

SHERRI L. DODD

Black Rose Writing | Texas

This is a work of fiction. Names, characters, businesses, places, events, and incidents are either the products of the author's imagination or used in a fictitious manner. Any resemblance to actual persons, living or dead, or actual events is purely coincidental.

ISBN: 978-1-68513-579-9
LIBRARY OF CONGRESS CONTROL NUMBER: TXu 2-415-006
PUBLISHED BY BLACK ROSE WRITING
www.blackrosewriting.com

Printed in the United States of America
Suggested Retail Price (SRP) $23.95

Moonset on Desert Sands is printed in Minion Pro

*As a planet-friendly publisher, Black Rose Writing does its best to eliminate unnecessary waste to reduce paper usage and energy costs, while never compromising the reading experience. As a result, the final word count vs. page count may not meet common expectations.

PRAISE FOR
MOONSET ON DESERT SANDS

"The suspense, complex plot twists, and mesmerizing display of magical chaos kept me thoroughly engaged and on the edge of my seat."
–Alma Boucher, *Reader's Favorite*

"Sherri L. Dodd's *Moonset on Desert Sands* grips readers with its relentless suspense, intricate plot twists, and dazzling display of magical mayhem. Each chapter brims with chaos and surprises, making it nearly impossible to put the book down."
–*Library Titan*

"From beginning to end, I was engaged, and between the entertaining characters, the multilayered tensions and gradually building suspense, and the wonderful depictions of magick and spellwork and rituals, it was an absolute joy to read."
–J Flowers

"The ending was surprising and, honestly, the entire book felt like this spicy, invigorating concoction brewed under the New Moon to incite growth of the series and plenty more magickal adventures."
–Liljana B.

"The excellent balance of thriller, supernatural intrigue, and psychological growth gives Moonset on Desert Sands a vivid countenance that makes it highly recommended…"
–Diane Donovan, *Midwest Book Review* and *Bookwatch*

Note from the Author

At the back of the book, you will find two sections – For Reference and Inspiration and a Witchy Dictionary, which includes translation for phrases found within the book.

Also, this book includes American Sign Language (ASL). You may enjoy learning the signs. The website used is listed in the For Reference and Inspiration section.

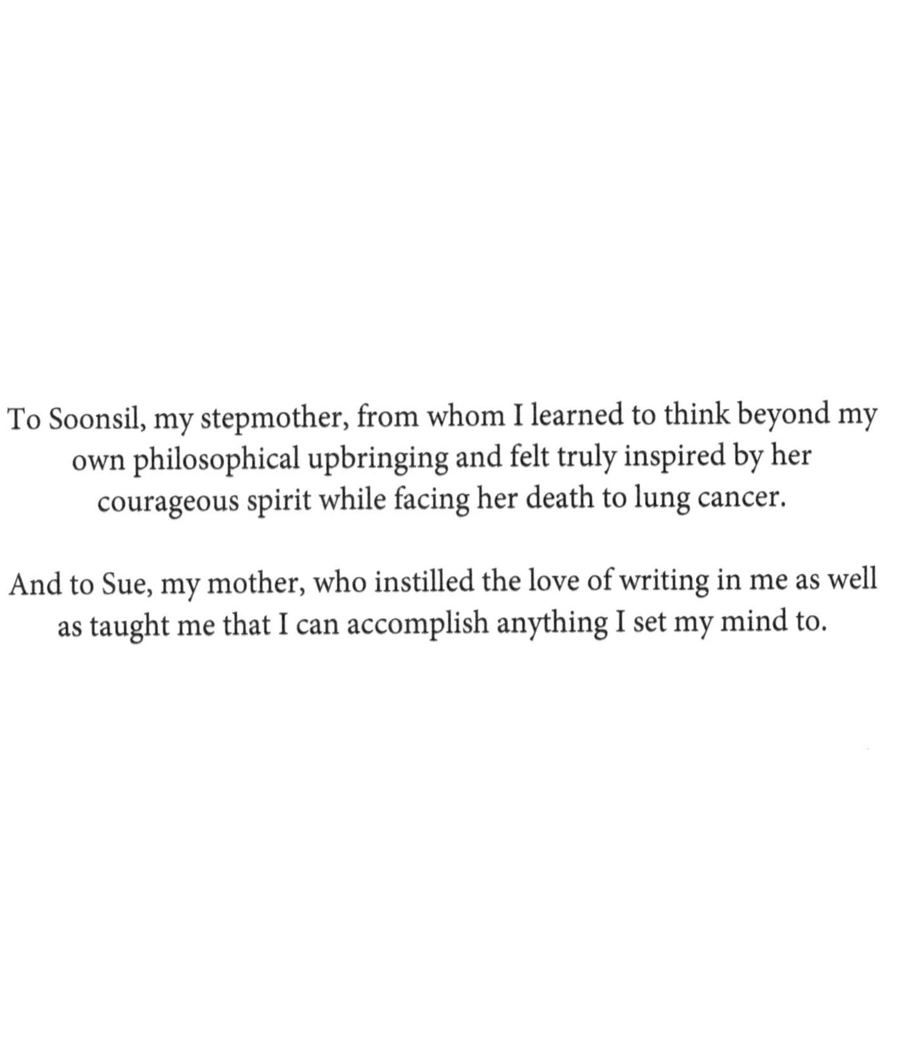

To Soonsil, my stepmother, from whom I learned to think beyond my own philosophical upbringing and felt truly inspired by her courageous spirit while facing her death to lung cancer.

And to Sue, my mother, who instilled the love of writing in me as well as taught me that I can accomplish anything I set my mind to.

MOONSET ON DESERT SANDS

PROLOGUE

"Hey Dustin, I've got to get home. You almost done?"

"Yep, almost done." Dustin continued typing on his terminal. "Thanks for staying!"

"Yeah, no problem. I'm going to make a pit stop while you finish up."

When the deputy disappeared into the hallway, Dustin waited until he heard the bathroom door shut. After seeing the coast clear, he hastily got up from his desk and darted toward the wall unit of keys. He punched in the code, grabbed a small silver key ring, closed the unit, and rushed to the evidence room down the short hallway.

The first key failed.

The second yielded entry, and he stepped inside the stocked room.

While the deputy piddled two doors down, he stared at the partitioned shelving system. He ran his index finger along the file labels—*K … Ke … Kelly!*

He retrieved the small box from the cubby, adrenaline flooding his senses. In sync with the toilet flushing, he secured the sturdy plastic bag containing the athame, noticing it still crusted with Henry's blood. After tucking it into his heavy jacket, he slid the container back into place with sweaty palms.

After carefully closing the evidence room door, he hastened back to the cabinet to rehang the keys.

The sink's running water stopped, and the sound of a ripped paper towel preceded the deputy's reappearance in the hallway.

Dustin had just reached his desk, a lump of guilt in his throat as he shut down his computer with jittery hands.

"Whoa, there, Dustin. No need to hurry *that* much."

"No, I'm sorry. I've kept you here long enough." He swallowed down the anxious lump, grabbed his backpack, and thanked the deputy again for staying late. With his last wave goodbye, he headed out but kept his hand gesture brief knowing by end of shift, the makeup had usually worn off his palm, revealing his inverted pentagram tattoo.

He dove into his car feeling the thrill of success. Victory! The thump of nervousness transitioned to an exhilarated glory. He championed this attainment and reveled in his cunning. Now, the coven would hold him in higher regard.

Trying to calm himself, he took a few breaths and focused on his route to deliver the blade. Knowing of the henchman's impatience, he drove up Felton Empire Grade, taking the mountainous road's twists and turns with the precision of a professional driver. The darkness under the shroud of towering redwoods only gave more awareness to any oncoming traffic well before they veered around the bend, their lights sending beams of forewarning.

But the farther he motored from the station, the more his theft chipped away at his conscience. It ate at him to betray the good people at his new job and the friends he made in Felton.

"It's okay, the payoff will be worth it."

He flipped on the radio to drown out his nagging inner voice.

Still, he chewed the inside of his cheek until finally arriving at the mountaintop's stop sign and a big decision to make. He could continue straight, where he would descend toward Highway 1 and ride the oceanside's sheer cliff until he eventually met up with his recruiter's right-hand man near Davenport. Or he could turn right and drive along the fenced pastures toward his studio in Bonny Doon. He could tell Fergus he had trouble securing the murder weapon and would try again when possible, and tomorrow he would return it to evidence before anyone found it missing.

Home?

Decided. He cranked his wheel right. Rolling only inches, he stopped again.

Fergus would be angry if he did not deliver as promised. Suppose he actually had supernatural power. He had always been a high-strung leader. That was the rumor, anyway. He had only known him a couple years with infrequent face-to-face encounters. But there were plenty of stories. Murderous tendencies, whether by his own hand or his followers who complied without question. He did not want to provoke him.

He huffed out his anxiety and sat in silence on the quiet road, wavering while the car engine idled and the heater blew a warmed gust onto his neck. He looked around at the surrounding darkness, then back at the path toward his house drawn by the headlights.

His eyes caught a subtle movement. He shot a look out his passenger-side window.

Nothing.

His conscience ate at him. What had he gotten himself into? He had worked hard to get his county administrative job, enjoyed his coworkers, and was often recognized around town, sometimes getting his Americano for free at Raven's Latte. This afternoon, the cute barista knew his order the minute he walked through the door and her flirtations had become overt.

He looked over at his notorious passenger, its glimmering steel edge catching hints of moonlight as it peeked out from beneath his rumpled jacket. Mesmerized by the athame's exotic beauty, he could almost feel the awesome power that it must have held during its most infamous moment of taking the life of his old acquaintance, Henry. Rumor had it the possessed blade played a bigger part in ending the life of the notorious serial killer, more so than the young woman's hand that wielded it. Even now, its presence captivated him. Why would he give it to Fergus?

He took one last look in each direction and aborted his mission. This time, he would ride the straight and narrow.

"Not fetching like a dog for you, Fergus. Risk my job for …" He grew tired of even thinking about it. Too much time already spent.

He swept a wide U-turn. Hopefully, he could put it back tonight. He knew the deputy lingered. Rumor had it she and another officer were flinging after hours in the office. No worries. He would slip in and out before they noticed, leaving the package discreetly in his desk and dealing with proper placement when the time allowed. And if Fergus resorted to coercion, he would just threaten to expose the entire plot. Inside information might grant him leniency before the judge.

Satisfied in his decision, he returned to the heart of the mountain, the S-curves lulling him in a rhythmic roll toward righteousness. He turned up his satellite radio, catching the end of a retro eighties hit about fate and how free will has no chance against it. Through the webbed barrage of branches that shrouded the country road, he caught a glimpse of the moon, reminding him of its overarching watch upon him. It was enormous. A Killing Moon, as the song.

As he turned his attention back to the road, a careening pair of headlights rounded the corner. He tightened his grip on the wheel as the car uncomfortably whizzed past him.

"Slow down, for God's sake," he grumbled, angrily looking in his rearview mirror as the car disappeared around the bend.

While usually a lonely road at this later hour, another vehicle approached, making its way up the mountainous turns. A full-size pickup. A behemoth of metal with a grill of bright, glaring lights, golden yellow and searing white. He knew facing them head-on would cause a painful glare.

Sure enough. "Jeezuz!" He squinted and held his hand up, trying to block the glare. He flicked his lights, hoping the driver would lower the beams.

Headed straight for him, the truck blatantly encroached into his lane.

"Okay, asshole!"

Dustin steered toward the cliff wall, hugging it as tightly as possible, allowing more room for his opposition. As he did, the truck veered closer toward him.

A sudden lunge! The truck jerked a hard left, smashing into his front quarter panel.

The shattering of glass and crunching metal united with the sound of exploding airbags all around him. Bright sparks, followed by clouds of white, burst within his cab. Too violent to comprehend. Was his car on fire?

He frantically tried to exit, but the door was jammed. Luckily, it dawned on him. The cloud within his cabin was not smoke, but talc from the deployed airbags.

For a moment, all stilled.

Woozy from the whiplash, he refocused his eyes and realized he faced the rim of the cliff. He pulled himself from his shock. He had to get out! He started to yell, but the effort to rumble up a plea only exacerbated the steady, aching pain in his chest from the steering wheel's airbag. He fumbled to unbuckle, then desperately grasped for the door handle again.

The truck made a cumbersome three-point turn, righted itself, then sped up again, deliberately in his direction.

He tugged and pushed at the door, seeing the truck in his rearview mirror. He felt the impending doom of its fast-approaching headlights. A whimper gurgled within his throat as he thrust his shoulder into the door. Another failed attempt to exit.

SMASH!

Instantly, the explosion of two more airbags further denied his escape. He could not breathe. From the talc. From the stress. The absolute fear enveloped him as his car sat teetering closer to the edge of the canyon, precariously secured by something he could not see.

Through his muddled thoughts, he realized his aim. The bagless shattered back window. But the escape route coincided with the assaulting menace.

The truck backed up a substantial distance, still facing him. It idled in an opposing growl, and its lights flicked from high beam to low, then high again. Repeatedly toying with him.

He sobered to a harsh reality as he eased himself out of his seat—this guy, no doubt a friend of Fergus, was trying to kill him. His life depended upon keeping calm and removing himself from the vehicle. He quieted his panic and looked for the athame, but it had been flung from view. No time. He began his careful attempt toward the back of the car, wedging his upper body between the seats, using the seatbelts for leverage. Carefully, he plopped into the backseat. First clearance—accomplished.

Outside, the rumbling beast revved its engine. In an ironic courtesy, its headlights illuminated the path, inviting him to freedom.

He had little time. He quickly hoisted himself upon the rear dash.

The final blow came swiftly. The steel executioner gunned its engine. With the beacons of light growing larger by the millisecond, he conceded his death. A flash of Fergus's smirking face served a final farewell.

The barging truck inflicted a devastating force, sending the car careening down the canyon. Plunging, it flipped several times over, a rigid impact each time before ejecting Dustin from the window like a lifeless ragdoll tossed into a chasm of darkness.

. . .

The breaking of tree branches and the smashing of metal echoed through the canyon. Porch lights lit upon the densely brushed hillsides as the car settled into its resting place. But by the time anyone looked, the cause of the noise had crumpled in a heap at the bottom of the gulch.

Far above, Conn turned off his engine and lights, avoiding more attention to the previous ruckus. He emerged from the cab, his footsteps grinding the loose shake of the road's shoulder beneath his heavy steel-toed boots. Walking to the canyon's edge, he took out his cell. The light of it became another beacon in the night as he tapped electronic numbers.

"Done," he said with a rasp.

"The athame?" Fergus said.

"Gone."

"Half done. I want that athame."

"No can do. It's down the canyon. But so is he, so it doesn't matter."

"Conn, it matters, and you know it! Get that athame, or you're gone."

Then Fergus's voice was gone, too.

Conn looked around and considered the crime scene. Someone likely called the cops so he would get the hell out for now.

He walked back to his truck, pulled out a cigarette, lit it, and inhaled a bit of cool. Then he grunted, knowing sometime tomorrow he would hoof it down into the treacherous canyon and get that fricken blade.

CHAPTER 1
THE MAGICK QUESTION

~ SEPTEMBER - ONE YEAR LATER ~

Bethie and Pearl, her long-time friend and coven sister, sat in Bethie's cozy southwestern-style living room, surrounded by an appeasing aesthetic of flair—a teal and coral wall tapestry hung against the faux-finished deep-apricot-colored walls, a three-foot-high distressed green terracotta vase, and a variety of potted succulents atop various tables. Outside the picture window, her own front yard displayed a multi-color rock garden and several cacti.

They enjoyed a backdrop of folk music and an ice-cold glass of peach-infused cota tea. Its sweet grass flavor tantalized the taste buds, paired with a lemon scone. The chipper mid-morning conversation between the old friends had them comparing notes on their latest anti-aging potions while Pearl crafted a bracelet of Malachite and Lava beads.

"...and peony, for beauty. I prefer the fuchsia-colored petals, as they turn almost black once dried," Bethie said, quite pleased to be giving the wise tip for a change.

The phone atop the kitchen counter rang, prompting Bethie to freeze. "Who the heck is that?" She sprang up and hustled over to the rarely used receiver, then smiled when she saw the caller ID. "Hah! Will wild wonders never cease?" She answered in a melodic voice. "Hello?"

"Hello, Ms. Spiritbrite, this is Sheriff Michaels. How are you today?"

"Oh, hi, Sheriff. Whew! It's been quite some time!"

"Yes, ma'am. Apologies for not getting back to you sooner."

"That's quite alright. There's no *big* rush, but …" She paused. Would the sheriff volunteer the athame information she had requested several times over the past few months?

"So, how's the weather out there?"

"Fine. Sheriff. So, I know there's a time frame for holding evidence, but we're hoping we can get our family heirloom back."

"Yes, typically that's the case."

"Okay."

"But …"

"Yes?"

"Well, I'm afraid I have some unfortunate news. It's … missing."

"What?!" Bethie squawked like a parrot, stirring her unusually quiet Snow Bengal house cat, Wild Willy Wallace, as he lounged atop his five-story carpeted and hemp-wrapped post. Acquired five years earlier, he had the size of a domestic house cat, yet most times, ran amok patrolling the house, howling out to no one in particular, and climbing the screens and bookshelves when things became too dull.

"What is it?" Pearl asked in a whisper.

Bethie hushed her with a terse wave of the hand.

"We apologize for that, Ms. Spiritbrite. Someone took it from the evidence room out of Felton. Please know that we have been working diligently to recover it."

"Good gracious, Sheriff! That athame has been in our family for five generations. How did it vanish right out from under your nose?"

"Unfortunately, I'm not at liberty to discuss that with you."

His typical emotionless demeanor wore thin. "Do I have to fly back to Boulder Creek to solve this myself? We want that back!"

"I understand how you feel, Ms. Spiritbrite."

The roll of her eyes almost hurt. "Oh, for goodness sake, do not address me like that again! Just call me Bethie."

"Yes, ma'am."

She huffed out her tension. "So, how can I help?"

"Well, off the record … why don't you consult that Ouija of yours?"

"Aack!" *Smoke and mirrors!* He used the Ouija remark to get her off his back. "It does not work like that, Pete Michaels, and you darn well know it. Besides, it's in Boulder Creek, and Arista and I are here in Sedona."

"Okay, I thought it might help. We'll definitely keep you informed on any new developments."

"Fine, please do."

With the formalities completed and the call ended, she took a seat amongst Pearl and Wally, insulted the sheriff had kept the secret for so long. "I didn't see that coming!"

"Are you supposed to call an officer by his name like that?" Pearl asked, peering over the upper rim of her glasses.

"I fed, helped clothe, and oversaw the bath of that man when he was a child. I can call him anything I want. Especially when I'm irritated!"

"I take it the athame—"

"Someone has stolen it right out from under their dip-ding-dong noses! Now I know why we've played phone tag for months."

"So that's it? Hope it comes back. Sorry … not sorry?" Pearl's deadpan expression held, astonished by the news.

"That *is* the magick question!" With anger abating, she eyed Pearl. "In all honesty, I'm not surprised … just disappointed. All the media stories of catching a serial killer have caught his eye. Especially since they would not shut up about that stupid tattoo." She sighed and shook her head. "Fergus has taken our precious heirloom. I hope it's just Felton that drew him because I'd hate to think he knows about Boulder Creek, too. Hopefully, the sixteen-minute drive and the shroud of our forest will still protect us when we finally return. I know Arista longs for her redwoods."

Pearl held her concerned glower.

"And I'm afraid that if he has our athame, he has a plan to go with it."

· · ·

Deputy Hendrickson stepped into the frame of Sheriff Michaels' door, distracting his daze of discontent. "Didn't go so well, huh?"

"Well, she didn't call me a yahoo." He picked up his blue-faced stress ball. "But I understand where she's coming from. Still no sign of our *crafty* Dustin?"

"Not a peep. No car, no arrest … he's been a ghost since his last night at the station."

"Hmph. Something will show. Though going on a year now. Why the hell did it take six months for them to catch on? C'mon! Dustin no shows for weeks—no calls, no *I'm sick*, no *to hell with you and your job*—and it didn't raise any eyebrows? With anyone?" He glanced down at his hand, pumping the hell out of his blue squishie.

"Well, these state employment laws are protective of an employee's rights."

"Are they still an employee if they don't show up week after week?"

"You're preaching to the choir, Sheriff. But you gotta know they're not going to search every evidence file because of a missing employee. And the law protects people's privacy."

He scoffed. "You'd think there'd be some sort of consequences, but it's all about giving people their space, respecting their troubles, and— *no, no*—don't raise your voice at 'em, because it might hurt their feelings."

Hendrickson waited patiently for his ranting to cease.

"Now, I'm left to report that a valuable family heirloom that holds mysterious keys to never-never land has vanished. And I look bad as the messenger … because we didn't even know!"

"I hear ya, Sheriff. You're doing a real number on your stress ball there." Hendrickson pointed at his white-knuckled death grip and snickered.

"Aw, I'm just rankled because my former babysitter reamed me a good one. And I gotta tell you, I felt like a little kid with her sassing me like she did."

"Well … at least she didn't call you a yahoo."

He drew a firm grip around his stress ball and launched it at Hendrickson, who ducked, having already read the signs.

The deputy turned to leave but froze, then turned back toward him. "Oh! Meant to tell you … another incident at the school yesterday."

"Snakes again?" he asked, familiar with the unusual amount of bites at the school since last spring.

"Yeah, Janelle's boy. You know Janelle, that gal from the diner?"

"Yeah, yeah."

"Her kid got bit on the ankle."

"Hmph."

"Between you and me, *that* one was probably poking sticks at it."

The sheriff snorted. "Yeah, I've heard he's an obnoxious sort. Nevertheless, we don't want our young-uns getting bit by snakes … not even the heathens."

"Of course not. But seriously, they need to resolve that."

"You got that right."

His deputy left him with his thoughts. He cocked his head, deliberating. This was the third bite in the past few months alone. Usually, snakebites were few in their neck of the redwoods. He remembered the initial attack had involved Arista's boyfriend and his friend.

"Hmph." He sat back in his chair and crossed his arms tight across his chest. He really didn't want this unexplained crap to keep popping up, but his wants seemed to hold no weight lately. Nonetheless, with the number of snakebites rising, it felt mysterious and kind of … witchy.

CHAPTER 2
WELCOME TO COSMIC PRISMS

Through Cosmic Prisms' windows, Arista watched the sidewalks bustling with the usual flow of tourists. Fingers pointing at the distant monuments, children griping at their parents for something they could not have, and a few smiling couples holding hands while walking with souvenir-laden shopping bags.

On this late summer morning, a random street musician dressed like a makeup-less French mime—black-and-white-striped shirt, red bandana, and a well-worn beret—had set up his electric accordion. Its canned plink farcically entertained right outside of Arista's serene workspace. She tried to ignore the artificial bounce of the musical notes and raised the volume of her ethereal music on the store's speakers. But now, blaring her own soft music took away its serenity.

"This should do it for today," Mrs. Federer said, suddenly appearing at the counter with a colorful array of chime candles. Her petite, elderly hand looked like a child's, holding crayons. She shot an irritated side-eye toward the ruckus outside the shop. "Damn tourists! And they draw these ridiculous performers."

"Aw, they can't help that they love this majestic place. We love it too, right?" A genuine question, as her favor of Sedona had waned from the hellish summer she had just endured.

"I'd say they're a bit too entitled to not actually live here."

She smiled while wrapping Mrs. Federer's candles in glitter-sparkled tissue paper.

"No matter. It's always a pleasure to see your sweet smile, Arista. Thank you."

"Aww, thank *you*. It's always a joy to see you, too."

The transaction finished, she said goodbye to Mrs. Federer, while noticing the two dark brown eyes with tufted brows wearily blinking up from her customer's hip. "Bye little Bruno." Then, the lady and her purse full of Yorkie proceeded toward the door.

"Yes, I quite enjoy this shop. For a minute, it takes all my irritations away," her fussy customer said, struggling to open the door. "Excuse me. Ex-cuse me!" Deftly, she asserted herself into the crowd of gawking faux-music lovers blocking her path.

Before the door shut, a brunette woman with a thick figure entered the shop.

"Welcome to Cosmic Prisms." It struck her. *Wow! I can really see it on her!* Attracted by the radiating glow, Arista took a second look at the woman. "Let me know if I can help you with anything," she added, hoping to entice an engaged response so she could get a better read of the woman's *aura*, her newest metaphysical interest.

The customer gave her a quiet nod and turned away, keeping to herself.

Still struck by her initial impression, Arista exercised her recent study. Softening her eyes and slowing her breathing, she focused on the woman in her peripheral vision and began to see the swelling of a soft orange energy at her abdomen and breasts, with tinges of sharpened silvery contrast. Unfamiliar with the silver aspect, she continued the analysis, noticing hints of red and a thin layer of bright yellow, but she could also see how the blue roiled into a muddy brown.

The woman approached, snapping her out of the analysis and set a Blue Moonstone palm stone upon the counter.

"Oh, Moonstone is such a beautiful crystal! Nice choice. There's so much blue in this one, too." Curious about her reading, Arista politely pried. "I have to tell you, you have such an amazing aura about you. It was prominent the moment you walked in."

The woman smiled and cast a shy glance downward, placing her hand on her stomach. As she did, Arista caught sight of her spinner ring—a thick band filling the space between her middle finger knuckles. A lovely blending of silver and gold metals with a large, smooth, reddish-orange Carnelian at its center.

"Oh, your ring is really pretty, too. Carnelian, right?"

"Right," the woman said, her shyness easing.

"Hi, Trin-eee," Stevie said, poking his head out of the backroom. "I knew I recognized that voice. It's been so long since I've seen you! And my God, Arista is right … you *are* glowing!"

Arista's coworker and Pearl's grandson, Stevie, added a welcome jolt of energy to the conversation. Usually upbeat and full of sassy one-liners, he could elicit a giggle with a simple look or gesture. And he knew it.

Trini's eyes sparkled at the sight of him. "Hey! I didn't know you worked here."

"Hey, Trini … guess what?" Stevie softened into a whisper, eyes wide with enthusiasm. "I do."

Trini smiled.

"Okay, back to work!" Stevie said, sending a flippant goodbye wave to her.

He disappeared into the supply room as quickly as he arrived, prompting a shared laugh between the women.

"Thank you for the *aura* comment. I'll take it as a compliment."

"Of course, life must be treating you *exceptionally* well." Arista felt enlivened by the dose of Stevie's energy.

"Some great things, and … others, not." Trini cast her eyes to the floor, then back up to Arista.

Uh-oh, she has drama. That's the brown. "Well, I hope it's manageable for you."

"Still processing next steps." Trini looked around the shop. "So, I'm fairly new to metaphysical meditation stuff. I also want something for protection."

She had pried enough for their first meeting and re-focused on selling. "Okay, did you want another crystal, or do you want to try a candle?"

"Let's mix it up with a candle."

She walked Trini to the wall, displaying several colorful waxed pillars. "Mental or physical protection?"

"I'd say both."

She grabbed a solid yellow pillar candle. "Okay, this is why I love candles. A lot of times, you will use black for protection. Stones such as Tourmaline, Obsidian, Shungite, etcetera—are all for protection. And I love black! But…" She held up the candle. "… this bright and cheerful baby here is *also* for protection because of the oil blend in its wax. First, take a little smell." She held the stout pillar out for Trini.

Trini took the candle and sniffed. "Nice!"

"Right?" She knew the scent well. "So, it has three citrus oils—grapefruit, lime and bergamot."

"Bergamot?"

"Bergamot. It's shaped like a lemon, green like a lime, but considered an orange."

They laughed at the agricultural irony.

"Anyway, citrus is known for its astringency and cleansing powers. I mean, think about what a lemon does to your teeth if you bite into it."

Trini perked up, nodding her head. "True."

"That same cleansing works on your mind and how you process what bothers you. Basically, *protecting* you from things that hinder you." She paused, then considered the privacy of her customer. "The caveat is, if there's an actual need for protection … like if you're in danger, that's a job for the police." Known all too well since crystals surely would not have protected her from that murdering maniac she and Auntie had endured last year.

Her concern struck a nerve because Trini chose her next words carefully. "I don't *think* it's a police situation." She paused, pondering with a wayward gaze, then snapped present. "So, probably TMI, but this guy … he so frickin' obsessed with me. And I try to be understanding because I think he is special needs. But there's been times when I seriously think he's stalking me."

"Hmm, does he have a caretaker or someone you can talk to?"

"It hasn't gone that far. I really think he's harmless, which is why I'd rather handle it myself instead of going to the cops or rag on his poor caretaker."

"That's cool."

"Anyway, I'll take it." Trini handed the candle back to her as they walked toward the counter.

"Okay. As long as you feel safe …"

At the register, Arista wrapped the citrusy candle and Trini's palm stone in their signature tissue paper. "So, how do you know Stevie?"

"He was the president of our high school's spirit club. Great with everyone, including those who mocked him. He should bottle that energy up and sell it."

"He actually did!" Arista laughed and pointed to a mirrored display on the counter that held a collection of little glass vials with cork tops. Each one sported a different color of hardened wax that dripped from the top, down the sides. Like colorful icing on skinny glass cupcakes.

Trini laughed. "You're kidding me."

"I can hear you two," Stevie said, bellowing from the backroom.

"It's all good fun!" Arista picked up one of his creations and began her spiel. "These are Energy & Happiness spell jars. And, yes, he made them himself. They have Rose Quartz pebbles for opening the heart to self and others. The yellow pebbles are Citrine for joyful energy, and the blue is Blue Aventurine for inner strength and making wise decisions. And, honestly, those crystals cover even more than that, but he chose those aspects as the combo's intention." She momentarily eyed the vial of shiny gems, gave it a little shake, and handed it to Trini.

"Hah, I love it!" Trini gave it back to her. "I'll take it."

"He will *love* that you bought one!"

"I just *love* that you bought one, Trini!" Stevie mocked from the backroom.

Arista kept to her sales pitch. "I will add that this combination is also great for a gratitude prayer."

"Aww, that's cool."

She announced the total and offered the credit card machine. "My name is Arista."

"Nice to meet you, Arista. How long have you worked here?"

"About nine months."

"I'm surprised I haven't seen you before, though I've only been in a couple of times." Trini looked around and then closed her eyes, absorbing their store's music.

"Isn't this song so beautiful? A couple out of Washington. It's more enjoyable at a lower volume, but I turned it up to drown out the sidewalk gig." She pointed to the polka gaiety outside the window.

Trini snickered as the musician bounced along with his notes.

Arista closed out the sale and handed Trini her cache of goodies in a pearlescent-white gift bag. "Here you go."

"Thank you. Now, off to harness the power of being a mother."

With the door closing behind Trini, Arista's mouth gaped in surprise. *Yes! She's pregnant! That's the orange around her belly and I picked up on it.*

Outside, Trini dug through her purse, accidentally bumping into a tall, chubby man on the sidewalk. She corrected herself and apologized but froze upon seeing the man's face. To Arista's surprise, the man reached out and poked Trini's belly, causing her to back away and wince in repulsion.

"Uh, Stevie." Arista rounded the counter, considering Stevie may need to intervene.

Trini and the man turned, each walking in different directions.

"Wow, what a creep," Arista grumbled, now at the window watching the perpetrator lumber away in his ill-fitting tracksuit.

"I beg your pardon!" Stevie feigned a hostile demeanor as he emerged from the backroom. He joined her, peering out the glass. "What's going on?"

"I think it's fine, but that guy …" Arista pointed to the retreating middle-aged man, "and Trini just accidentally bumped into each other, and he touched her on her stomach, and she obviously didn't like it."

"Well, that's forward of him. But he's not who I'm worried about." Stevie pointed in Trini's direction. He drew his lips into a side smirk. "She's always liked bad boys."

"Really?"

"Really."

"Well, she's pregnant."

Stevie's jaw dropped. "No!"

"What do you mean, *no*? She seems really happy."

"Now, I'm *really* worried about her." He walked back toward the counter.

"Oh, come on. She spoke highly of you … said you were quite popular."

"*Moi*? Of course, I was. With this personality?" He proudly looked off to the right, framed his profile, puckered, and paused as if voguing for imaginary paparazzi. Warming to his congenial self, he added, "Anyway, yes, Trini is really sweet, but to be perfectly honest with you, there are secrets she's not letting anyone in on. Now, I'm no gossip, but she hasn't been dating anyone, and now she's with child?" He pursed his lips and raised his eyebrows. "Pret-ty mysterious, if you ask me."

"Really?"

"Like I said … *worried*." Slinging his denim-blue leather backpack over his shoulder, he changed the subject, running down his list of tasks. "Anyhoo, I've taken all the bubble wrap off the new jewelry and arranged them in their pretty little boxes on their little cotton mattresses—lids left open. Bubble wrap is in the bubble wrap cupboard, and I cut down those big-meanie boxes." He lifted his hand to reveal an aqua-maned pony bandaid on his index finger.

"Ouchie. Sorry about that."

"No worries. Now, I'm off to satisfy this ferocious hunger of mine. Thanks for agreeing to hold the shop today. A friend and I are headed to Flagstaff."

"Of course, thanks for coming in to unpack the shipment."

"Always," he said with a chirp, hustling out the door.

The silence from his departure took a bit of her energy, similar to the quiet isolation that remains after all party guests have left. She still had all-day to go.

An hour passed and only a few customers had kept her occupied. In the downtime, she deliberated her growing dissatisfaction with Sedona. At first, the red-rocked monuments had utterly entranced her. She held breathless anticipation at the scenic trailheads that led to a landscape of desert vegetation. They served as a grand escape from her horrible encounter with the serial killer from the past year. Sometimes, she shared the moderate hikes with Auntie. So different from her steep redwood mountain paths, Auntie scaled the less difficult trails with ease. Even at Cathedral Rock, Auntie made it to the *End of Trail* sign. They immortalized the moment with a selfie that still graced both of their phones' home screens. After the quick pic, they explored the trail's lesser-known extension. By cutting left and meandering around a boulder, they left behind a family of obnoxious novice yodelers. Another forty-five feet up, they sat upon a rock platform in a breezeway. Two ascending red walls framed a gigantic, tapered pillar of the same earthen concoction in the middle, like a giant candle before her.

She closed her eyes and let her presence within Prisms fade, remembering the experience.

Perched on the rocky platform, she took in a long, slow breath, then exhaled. The late-afternoon breeze brushed constant and gentle on her face, murmuring intentions of serenity and reassurance. Soothing her angst of all that had troubled her. Present in this moment.

"Excuse me, could I see that Tiger's Eye ring?"

Arista snapped to. "Certainly!" She wished they had a bell for when people entered.

With the customer pointing obscurely into the case, it took three guesses to land the target.

"Yes, that one. How much?" they asked, impatient, with no eye contact.

"This one is ..." She flipped the tag. "One hundred and fifteen dollars. Would you like to try it on?"

The customer winced. "Oh, that's excessive for such a small piece." They turned and sporadically browsed while nearing the door. One last annoyed shake of their head preceded their exit.

Typical. Their prices *were* high. Nearly twice the price you could find online. But Pearl had said the Sedona experience and actually seeing the piece made it worth the markup. And monthly sales supported that notion. The interaction had reminded her of another truth she had decided on Sedona: tourists weren't the only grumps. There were also fellow merchants who judged not only tourists but locals as well. While the crystal merchants were usually helpful, and the Only Girls shop had friendly customer service, The Best of Everything outdoor mall was far from her favorite place to visit. Many shops employed snooty cashiers who did not greet her and appeared put off by her questions—blank expressions and slow to answer. But she had only visited once after she and Auntie had hiked. So, dusty shoes and a perspiring complexion could have given haughty clerks the wrong impression. Still, the treatment was far from the laid-back vibe of Boulder Creek. The longing for her redwood refuge grew stronger.

She waited until closing, then locked the door and gazed out her storefront window. Mime-guy had left, the tourists had thinned and only an occasional passerby walked hastily on their way. The setting sun created a portrait of dusk in the front window. Scattered swaths of blue, magenta, and yellow across the desert sky could have been the inspiration for some of the colorfully swirled, handmade soaps. The sunset also signaled end-of-day duties.

After spritzing the glass and mirrors, she tidied up the displays so they would be perfect for tomorrow's customers. When the time hit six on the shop's gilded agate-slabbed wall clock, she pulled the privacy shade on the front door, double-checked the latch, and turned toward the counter.

BANG! BANG! BANG!

She flinched hard at the aggressive rapping on the shop's glass door. Tension ripped up the back of her neck as she spun around, dreading the instigator. But before she could identify the culprit, a strange sensation washed over her. Dizziness enveloped her, and she found herself in a kaleidoscope of neon designs, swirling and bold, filling her senses … numbing all except sight. Lost in this deepened dimension of shapes morphing into prismatic varietal colors, all thought and sound escaped her. Nothing existed beyond this hypnotic dream. Only here, only now.

Slowly, the designs and colors faded.

She came to, blearily eyeing the wall in front of her with its beautiful silk tapestry of deep indigo. The celestial beauty's ripple of fabric shined beneath the store light, helping her to refocus. She found her breath. Looking behind her, she had landed on the carpet in front of the four-foot set of Amethyst wings. Observing from outside the store, she might have resembled a garden fairy. She found her humor and nervously tittered. Had she fainted?

She firmly stroked and stretched her neck as if waking from a stiff night's sleep. She gazed up at the dozens of hanging crystals wired with a spectrum of fine Czech glass beads that graced the shop's ceiling. The wall clock showed that three minutes had passed since the onset of this odd spell.

"Oh, great. Here we go again. At least no grubby hands or ominous tattoos." She remembered the array of dazzling colors. "And actually, kind of cool."

Once coherent, she carefully stood while realizing the familiarity. It reminded her of waking up to Sheriff Michaels gently tapping her face … finding sticky blood on her hands … and a serial killer dead.

CHAPTER 3
OBSESSED WITH A SHADOW

Stifled in his seclusion, Fergus watched as Fallon gazed into her makeup mirror. She dabbed her cheekbones with the shimmering burgundy powder coating the soft, sable bristles of her brush. The blush added a sharp dimension to her exquisite and hauntingly beautiful face. His apprentice took great pride in that he had made her the interim High Priestess to a flock of practitioners who revered her. She owed it all to him. His failures at finding Arista over the years had depleted his energy. But since the athame had come into his possession, and with the help of this beautiful new image leading his coven, he could let go of his obsession of finding his niece and gaining her prophesied powers … for now.

Fallon hummed along to the heavy metal music before the guitar solo turned shrill through the red, oblong, cordless speaker sitting pert upon her vanity. Adding a third layer of jet eyeliner to her iridescent azure lids, her elegant jaw slightly dropped.

"That's enough. You're already beautiful," Fergus said with assurance. "Don't leave them waiting too long."

"I know, my love." She turned down the volume to hear the murmurings from up the hall. "Yes, my loves. I'll be there soon."

With her lipstick selected, she painted the merlot-color onto her pouty lips, then sealed it with a high-sheen, gold-glitter gloss. She puckered, her smoldering eyes narrowing at her reflection in the mirror.

"You turn fifty this year," Fergus said. "And while you look nowhere near it, time is of the essence to fulfill your destiny. You must gain more power to take your ability to the next level."

With makeup complete, she stood and smoothed her wine-colored sheath dress before re-situating her two-inch Fire Obsidian teardrop pendant between her push-up bra, lined just above her low-cut vee neckline. She scanned her face, body, and butt for flaws. Seamless.

"Enough, Fallon."

Pleased, she winked at herself.

Inside the Rec Center—their month-to-month rented workspace—the temperate breeze of early September blew through the window, keeping a circulative freshness to the otherwise industrial room. It did nothing to settle his anxiety. He was nervous for her.

Fallon seductively slipped into her black bolero jacket.

He need not be. Truth was, *he* lusted for greater command over his patrons, only possible through her. Yet, she remained high on the credibility he had already given her by simply passing the torch. She enjoyed dressing up and putting on a good show. He needed more from her. Where was her thirst for power? Did she possess the heart of the wolf, willing to kill for survival … able to lead the pack to do likewise? It did not seem so. "I wonder if you're hungry enough."

"Fergus, please stop," she said, the poise in her shoulders momentarily sagging.

She was not hungry enough. "The clock ticks."

"Yes, I know, love. But listen to them. Can you hear them?" She paused, listening to the subdued voices behind the closed auditorium doors carrying through the silenced hall. "They adore us."

"They adore only you." With him as the leader, the group had struggled to maintain twenty members. It took only one pivotal moment of him introducing her as leadership to bust through that imaginary obstacle to success. With her svelte, model-esque stature, and confident preaching, a comfortable congregation of nearly one hundred quickly developed. All paying a healthy monthly fee for the benefit of belonging to the coven.

"Don't fret, love," Fallon said, her voice exaggerating as if talking to a child.

It felt patronizing, but he let it slide. "I'm just tired. Very tired."

"Is it any wonder?" she asked, the expression on her painted face softening. She sat down on the edge of her seat and gazed into the mirror, primping her tresses. "You were forever obsessed with a shadow. You couldn't look to the future. Couldn't move on. Your sister, your niece, they consumed you. Yet, admit it. You were terrified to find them."

Fergus froze. She dared not bring up that tortuous beating he endured at the hands of Arista's father, Ian. Maiming him for life, taking away his chance of having children. Yes, he detested kids, but maybe his opinion would have changed.

"And who could blame you, my love?"

He needed to be more encouraging. After all, she was about to perform. "I suppose there's enough time to formally ordain you as High Priestess. Perhaps a grand ceremony for the occasion." In truth, a part of him felt as if his essence had already shriveled to mere existence, anyway. He could not face his flock and had no goals anymore. The regrets of not finding Arista and fulfilling his own blood magick ritual depleted his motivation. His searches always leading to nothing.

Except the athame. Acquired almost a year ago.

Fallon's charm tempered to the calm of an understanding mother. "Fergus—"

"Obstacles have repeatedly slashed my attempt to find her." He felt the words whine out of his mouth, oozing like a weepy sore. He hated how sniveling he had become. He swallowed the pill of insecurity and hardened his voice. "Keira left her somewhere … bolted to the barren desert and retired to her bed. Riddled with disease. Henry had them, though! Santa Cruz mountains, but once again … Arista, nowhere to be found." He looked over at the cracked window with hints of the oncoming color of fall trees framed by the bland, metal-slatted blinds. "But we *do* have the vital weapon held by her, with its first sacrifice executed at her whim. It holds a coarse and dark magick within its steel.

Her spirit, and now, her first kill. Used properly, it could be powerful enough to boost *you* to the next stage of your power."

"Understood. That's why you sent Conn to get it."

"It is." He felt an ounce of relief rouse his last-ditch effort of hope. "With you as leader, I'll continue to contribute behind the scenes. Perhaps a wizened elder in my own right."

"That is you, love." She stood up again, awaiting his blessing.

"Go ahead."

"Be with me tonight," she mewled. "I want you to be a part."

"Just go."

Fallon pouted her lips. "Fergie, my love, are you sure?"

He gazed out the window, imagining the coming season of lightning storms and fallen snow. How the landscape of lushness would wither and die away, and his bones would feel the ache of winter's crushing iciness.

Fallon held strong in her composure. She turned off her speaker, closed her eyes, and absorbed the music building from inside the Rec Center's auditorium. She tilted her head backward, elongating her swan-like neck, and swayed to the music. One last invigorating inhalation curled her lips into a broad smile.

He wanted to hate her, as she gave him no further regard. Focused on herself, she flashed a hard stare at her reflection as if it would cower at the challenge. Then she left him and his thoughts in the lonely room.

But one thought held high above the rest—the end of her, should she falter.

•   •   •

Conn stood gallantly outside the closed auditorium door—chin high, broad, rocked shoulders back and wide chest forward. His usual scowl accompanied the posture as Fallon approached. He swung the door open with a mighty fling, allowing her a clean entrance.

The music ceased, and the room hushed. All the sheep waiting for the whim of their effectual shepherd.

CLICK. Clack. CLICK. Clack.

She relished the sounds of her heels on the wooden floor as she strolled the length of the audience to take her place on the podium. Picturing the bounce of her long, rich brown tresses upon her back, she knew they must resemble the goddess qualities of an un-hexed Medusa.

She stepped on the stage, feeling her body heat rising from adrenaline. She removed her jacket and walked toward the convenient coat rack set back at the curtain. Taking her time, feeling the control, she neatly placed it on the hanger while her audience waited.

Once at the lectern, a broad smile grew upon her lips. "Love begets love, my children. Ask the mother. Is it not her unconditional love from the moment of birth that creates the tightest bonds known to humanity?"

Amidst the blinding glare of the spotlights, she glanced at the few visible faces, projecting warmth and compassion on her entire audience.

"The purest love in the world. Is it no wonder that a child puts all of its trust in its mother? How many of us remember the days of innocence? How we felt when our mother greeted us at day's end? Maybe she dressed in a suit? Maybe she wore a uniform or even a tight skirt and fishnets?"

She paused, letting her hooks of intention sow the seed.

"Our mother's essence glowed the minute she walked through the door. Oh, how our belly warmed at the sight of her. Even those of us burdened with a troubled mother, one of addiction, one of depression, one of violence … as unsure of her as we may have been, did we not, still, hold her in that exulted light?"

She scanned the darkened room, absorbing the sounds of agreement and fervent interest.

"Even more so, those of us who grew up without a mother to call our own … how we *longed* for that love … that bond." Her voice broke, and a tear welled in her eye. She had lost her own mother at a young age, but that fact remained unshared. "The mother gives her child everything she has. And when we grow, it is our turn to reciprocate. We must repay the debt. After all the time that she tended to our needs ... that she sacrificed for us—fed us, bathed us. Blessed us. And even bled for us at our very own birth. After it all, would we not kill for our mother?"

The crowd hissed in encouragement, a viper pit alive in the darkness beneath her. She fed off the venomous energy, and her heart pounded, imagining what they would willingly do for her.

With a warm smile, she gracefully moved across the stage, microphone in hand, orating about her abundant love until the end of her sermon approached.

"When the time comes, when the roles are reversed ... reparations must be made." Her voice grew stronger and louder. "Whatever your walk of life, wherever you have come from, the hardships you have endured ... the *struggles* you have borne ... I am here for you."

A growing murmur of appreciation rose into the air, sending a rush of dopamine the value of a five-mile run.

"I am your *Mother* here. Come to me in your time of need. I will see you through your trials."

She waited for the round of applause to cease.

"Tonight is a dedication to newness as we approach our first anniversary as a group."

She called out to Conn, standing at the back, armed with pens and strips of paper for the ritual, and pointed her long, black-colored index fingernail. "I believe most of you have left your intentions with Conn. If not, he's ready to receive you, and make sure you have your entry stamp. In case you have forgotten, we ask a contribution for tonight's gathering ... or else." Her wicked painted smile of grit teeth lasted only a second.

A rustling of bodies made their way to Conn. She stared into the crowd with a confident smile, pretending she could see them all. After making small talk with those closest to the stage and allowing the energized aims of payment to cede, she raised her arms high, fingers outspread, as if projecting beams of mystical light. She closed her eyes and prayed. "I am here to serve you and commune with you, to guide you to your divinity, to raise collective consciousness and channel you to the frequency of ultimate love … for self and others." She widened her eyes, and her voice boomed. "We are going to change this coven! And may those changes restore unity, balance, and frequency for this earth … for this community … and for each and every one of you—my true children!"

A roar filled the room. She drew in the energetic approval, then held out her hands to hush the crowd. "Let us feel the energy shift toward our goal. For if it does, I promise you as I rise to my ultimate power, you will have a seat at my side because you have been here … with *me* … since inception. This I promise, this I pray … and so, this will be!"

"**So, this will be**," confirmed the many voices.

A musical note set the stage for the onset of celebration. The guitars, ouds, and the hurdy gurdy synchronized, and the music rose, caressing the room and those within it, commanding all to join in a dance commemorating their life as a family. And she, their mother.

She devoured the adoration and descended the small staircase. The voracious love for all her children fed her hunger—the younger participants with their radiant and flawless skin, their physiques and sexual energy. And her older members, graying, self-made and assured, and distinguished with sage spirit.

Amidst her audience, an electronic keyboard engaged, turning the dance hypnotic. The room came alive with writhing movement intermittently illuminated by the colorful strobe light of green and blue adorning flashing specks upon the bodies. Engulfed by a sea of dancing dark figures, she knew her power within this coven. With every meeting, it grew more evident. And poor Fergus continued his spiral into obscurity.

CHAPTER 4
A CHALLENGE WE MUST FACE

Arista awoke to the sound of eight pinging chimes on her triangular wooden alarm clock, but an effect of feline persuasion overtook the pleasantry.

Rawr!

Wally thundered up the hallway past her room, his gallop akin to a pint-sized thoroughbred on Auntie's tiger-bamboo flooring.

Rawr!

And through the hallway again, his distinct voice bouncing off the narrow passage as he dug into his frantic stride, headed back toward the living room.

She heard his claws rip up the length of the cat post.

"Knock it off, Wally! Sssst," she barked out of her room, still raspy from sleep. She figured her Siamese lummox, Royal, received a few punctures in his rear haunch from the activity, so added one more holler for good measure. "Wally!"

Sitting up in her bed, she listened for Royal's response, wondering if she would need to intervene. After a few insulted growls, Wally tore off again.

She relaxed her tensed shoulders. "Jerky kitty."

Not the greatest morning greeting. And a bit of disappointment for the twentieth time that her very missed, fresh mountain air no longer filled her lungs. With the approaching fall, differences became even clearer. While Sedona had plenty of the classic autumn colors in some areas, there would be no cascading rivers nor lush creek banks to sit upon and watch the serene activity of nature's soothing rush. There was no Henry Cowell Park full of its fiery fall foliage and shaded, cool evergreens. And definitely, no vibrant orange newts or yellow banana slugs on the floor of the desert.

She had swapped pines and redwoods for cacti, rock, and scrub brush. Her filtered sunlight streaming through tall, mature trees had been replaced by the relentless shine and heat of a sweltering desert. She stayed indoors most of the time. And while Auntie's Sedona home showed decades newer, more spacious, and better decorated, Arista truly missed the aged feel of her small mountain cottage.

At least summer neared its end.

After tussling her covers to an appropriate neatness, she walked into the kitchen with its white cabinets, white flooring, and mottled white and gray Quartz countertops. Luckily, Auntie had broken up the starkness with splashes of orange—towels, hanging pot pads, a teakettle, and one small still life of citrus wedges on a medium-blue plate. Her theme of oranges also included an always abundant supply of dried rind pieces in a large, clear pop-top jar she used in teas, rubs, and spell work to improve luck, vitality, and even eyesight, the latter her latest gripe of aging.

Even in this hottest of places, the scent of Auntie's freshly made brew soothed her. For this morning, she had created a black tea with the essence of … you guessed it … orange.

However, Auntie was missing.

"Already off on errands …"

She plopped two ice cubes into her sturdy, stoneware mug decorated with a free-running chestnut-colored horse on a desert backdrop. After filling the vessel, she took a sip. "Mmm. A sweet zing to start the day." She inhaled a quick breath through her tightened, puckered lips and smacked her tongue. "A little clove, too."

Cup in hand, she walked toward Royal on the second lowest rung of Wally's cat post, appreciating his ever-beautiful blue eyes against the silky black canvas of a face. Distracted, he still held high alert for a marauding white house leopard.

"It's okay, beautiful." She rubbed his chin, then planted a quick kiss on his nose. "I'm sorry you must endure this. But you're a big guy, so … fight back if you need to."

After encouraging Royal to stand his ground, she settled comfortably upon the velour terra cotta colored couch. Happy the store did not open until ten a.m., she relished this span of time to spend with Royal while sipping tea, munching on crunchy granola nuggets with coconut shavings, and perusing her newest book.

"I'm almost done with aura reading." She picked up the thin, orange paperback and fanned the pages, feeling their breath upon her face. "I figured it was a little more involved than Auntie's philosophy of *'if there's a vibe, you darn well know it.'*" She looked up at Royal. "Wouldn't you agree?"

Mew.

"And aura colors resemble those of the Tarot. The trick is to *see* the colors." She opened to her bookmarked page. "*'Do you feel drained after being around certain people?'* Well … Maddie used to be a little high-strung, but … not as often. Though I haven't seen her in a year, and we've only caught up twice." She curled out her lower lip, missing her friend. "We're both busy. Anyway … *'Have you ever had an instant read on someone's personality?'* Yes. I knew Jaxon wasn't a killer, even though the law thought otherwise. Shane didn't like him much either." She reminisced the thought of his protectiveness at Natural Bridges. "So, yes. Plenty of good intuition there."

After a couple more quizzical questions, she studied the chart of colors and their meanings and considered her reading of Trini.

"There it is! The silver *in* the orange represents the pregnancy!" She looked down at Royal, situating into her lap. "And the bulging aura at her breasts and abs expresses blooming life. Wow, this really makes sense." She felt a bubbling pride in her ability. "I could totally see that on her!"

Further, she read, cuddling Royal with her free arm.

"It's also interesting that while passion, represented by *red*, is high … her happiness—yellow—is really thin. I could barely make that out at all."

Royal's jet-black nose turned upward toward her, prompting her to scratch his chin as he curled into his version of a furry pangolin.

"Does that sound right to you? I mean, it may be right, but it doesn't sound *good*. Happy with being a mom … wants to be a good one, so she sought out the right crystal. Why would someone purchase a beautiful Moonstone to focus on the goddess aspect of motherhood if they didn't want to be a mom?"

She set down her book and observed the rising sun, its brightness attempting to force an unwelcome radiance in between the closed, slatted blinds.

"It's guy problems, Royal." She sighed. "Just like Stevie said. And I can totally relate."

Royal had enough rubs and hopped onto the back of the couch, gazing through the sliver of opened blind. Immediately, his mouth turned into a grand smile. His teeth clicked, and his throat chattered.

She twisted around to investigate. Pulling the blind's string revealed the object of his attention—a desert spiny lizard sunning its ridged backside in Auntie's rock garden.

It jetted away in a flash.

"Oooh, I suppose that's almost as cute as a newt. Sorry for running it off."

She drew a long stroke down his back, then headed for her bedroom. She changed into work clothes, remembering how Shane had also griped of the desert when they acted upon his idea of a couple's vacation after her awful ordeal with the killer. Accompanying her to Sedona during his December break from teaching, they journeyed in his mom's SUV. A comfortable and safe ride. They also packed up her belongings, including a very anxious Royal, knowing she would extend her stay, and killed time with good music and car games.

"D, my name is David, and my girlfriend's name is Danielle, and we come from Denver. And we like Dolphins."

"Okay, I like the dolphin part, but throw in a little more magick," she said, pretending impatience. "For instance, E, my name is Elektra, and my boyfriend's name is Eros, and we come from ... say ... Earthsea. And we like Emeralds. But seriously, I like the dolphin part."

"Earthsea? You could have easily said Egypt," Shane teased.

Their first stop had been the Grand Canyon. It looked fine in pictures, but after they drove up the 64 North and reached the El Toro Lodge, she felt the pull of the distant void as soon as they got out of the car.

"We should get the bags unpacked first," Shane said.

"I just want a quick peek. Come with me."

A quick jaunt around the courtyard, and they found themselves upon grandeur. Standing at the rim, breathing in the power of this world wonder, she realized the location had called to her. No words could truly describe its being. The space in between became the primary, miraculously formed by the softest of elements—water—carving out earth and stone. She inhaled its never-ending vastness, and it filled her with awe.

They had decided someday they would take the fourteen-mile hike down to the river. But the same distance back up, and the horror stories of fit hikers dying from its grueling ascent kept her motivation in check for that day.

"Then, he went home," she said aloud, now fully dressed. She walked into the hall bath and brushed at her hair, still reflecting on the last time she saw Shane. As expected, her visit became a sabbatical, and she stayed in Sedona to study amongst Auntie's Waning Crescent Coven.

Auntie, who had mostly kept up appearances in Boulder Creek for her, happily accommodated her. But that meant Shane returned home alone. Soon, their three calls a week slowed to one, and more often than not, the one became a session of bickering started by Shane asking when she would return home. He wondered if she remained serious about their relationship since she stayed so far away from him. Finally, three months prior, they had broken up in a huff. She expected it to resolve itself, but neither had made the move to reconcile.

She stared blankly at herself in the mirror. Dazed to a blur, she traveled inward to her heart. Sadness. She missed him. How could she have left him? He gallantly stood by her during recovery, driving her to her counseling appointments and showering her with *'I love you's'* and flowers. He was everything she ever wanted, and she left him.

Difficult but she needed the distance. Walking through her old living room was a PTSD trigger, no exaggeration. The visions of the pain she endured and the psychopath oozing his putrefying death blood onto the floor of her cozy cottage had taken a toll.

She forced herself present, applying a spritz of rose water to her face.

Luckily, time had eased her angst.

Outside, Auntie's car pulled into the driveway. Because of schedules, they had missed each other for a couple of days, and she eagerly anticipated catching up.

Soon, the keys jingled at the door's exterior, followed by a fumbling at the knob until, finally, the door cracked and revealed tight red curls. Auntie struggled to free her house key from the lock. "Oh, for goodness sakes," she grumbled, her bony hands gripping with white knuckles at the stubborn silver while balancing three bags of groceries.

"Hiya, stranger! Need help with that?"

"Hiya, back," Auntie responded, handing the lightest bag over to her. "Thank you."

As they unloaded the goods on the kitchen counter, Auntie cleared her throat. "Sheriff Michaels called yesterday. The athame is missing. There's no way to pretty it up. It is what it is."

"What does that mean?" With her uncle and his degenerates roaming, this could be a bad sign.

"I know nothing else aside from the fact that it's missing."

"Okay. Dare I ask if it means—"

"It means we need to get together with my circle and hold a very important session. It also means I don't feel good about it. Not one single bit."

"A full moon circle, I presume … for illuminating shadows?"

"Actually, the waxing half-moon is suitable. This is definitely a bump in the road and a challenge we must face." Auntie lowered her thin-framed tortoise-shell glasses to the tip of her nose and gave a serious stare. "I believe it's trouble at its worst."

She knew the tone. "Oh, great."

"Oh, great, indeed," Auntie echoed, then changed her demeanor. "On another matter, your shift at Prisms today … an envelope. The delivery person may be shy and simply slip it through the door slot."

"Got it."

"I would prefer if you do not open it."

Arista could tell by her lack of eye contact it embarrassed her to place the restriction. "Of course."

Satisfied, a smile grew on Auntie's face as she removed a rectangular cardboard box, inconspicuously tucked into one of the grocery bags. "Would you like an apricot cream scone from Kayla's?"

"Yes!" While not as good as the Danish almond bear claws packed in the black-and-white checkered bags that Shane used to bring her, they still served as a delicious temporary distraction from the athame news.

"Good! I waited almost thirty minutes for it."

"They'll go perfect with your tea."

They each pinched a hunk of their buttermilk pastry, savoring the mildly sweet treat.

"Mmmm," they synced in a resounding appreciation before Auntie added her validation. "Well worth the wait."

CHAPTER 5
QUITE THE TRICKSTER

True to Bethie's word, amongst the milling crowd of morning shoppers, a middle-aged man came up to the door, hunched over, and slipped an envelope through the mail slot. Just as quickly, he whisked away before Arista could break free from her chatty customer. As soon as she completed the sale, she hastened over to the door and glanced down the sidewalks. The dark-haired man with the loose-fitting white shirt was nowhere to be seen.

She picked up the envelope, and a tinge of energy coursed through her forearm, causing the sprigs of her light-colored arm hair to stand on end. "Wow!" Nothing conspicuous, she held it up to the daylight glaring through the window. Light strokes of blue ink scribbled within, jumbled by the folding. Judging by the patterns of numbers and letters, she figured it was an address. But that would be the extent of her nosiness. She lowered the envelope and saw her true *treat-o-the-day*.

Across the street, the slender security guard walked his beat of what she referred to as *Sedona: Part III*, the third cluster of shops, including her own, sitting on the town's sprawling main highway. Crossing the street, he hopped onto the sidewalk in front of her window, prompting her to duck back into her store. She definitely did not want to be seen gawking at him, eyes bugged in *fatal-attraction style*. She dismissed her exaggeration with a humorous snort. Luckily, his attention aimed at scrolling through his cellphone.

Stevie told her his name was Dakota, and he served as the only guy who had lifted her eyebrow since arriving in Sedona. But a chance to formally meet him had been elusive, so she limited herself to sneaky peeks of his good looks through the glass. It mattered not, as she had no desire to date anytime soon.

After he passed, she re-approached the case by the window, arranging the various Moss Agate spheres and Septarian eggs upon their stands. Nonchalantly, she peeked down the walkway.

Dakota had taken a seat on the bench to better slouch while checking his apps.

"So bad for your posture," she mumbled aloud, observing his body shaped like a crescent moon.

Dakota looked up, his eyes darting to the Prisms' doorway.

She froze for a second. *There's no way he heard that!*

She returned to the counter, retreating with a giggle. "Bye, Dakota."

At the register, she stocked the fresh inventory, first picking up one of the neatly packaged Bisbee Turquoise rings from Pearl's recent procurement. Dabbing a soft white cloth with sterling silver polish, she buffed the crevices of the ornate ring. She paused and peered at the stone, which had multiple shades of blue and a rich chocolate-brown webbing.

After a final buff, she set the substantial ring onto the store's Selenite cleansing disk by the register. Finally, she lifted and positioned it properly within its gift box.

"Okay, just for grins …" She flipped the box and eyed the cost. Her eyes bulged. "Six hundred dollars!" She gently set it down and smacked her lips. "I don't think my employee discount will help much with this one."

She should have known. Bisbee Turquoise was rare and had an interesting origin. Auntie had told her that back in the early mining era, the Bisbee Copper mines in Arizona were full of the soft, malleable metal. But they also had an abundance of an odd blueish rock plentifully formed in the Lavender Pit, named as such in honor of Harrison Lavender, who brainstormed the rise of copper ore. A distraction to the miners and an obstacle to the *good metal*, Lavender ordered the Turquoise promptly dumped at the mine's farthest corners. Also discarded were Azurite, Malachite, and other valuable crystals in today's witchy and New Age markets. The workers, possibly thinking that the pretty blue stone would make a sweet gift for the misses or to appease their own interest in geological beauty, took chunks home daily. Lo-and-behold, the stone came into high demand by the sixties and continued to rise in value.

Far from her price range, she placed the valuable ring within the safety of their counter display case, sliding it toward the front so customers could see its exquisiteness.

Two men appeared at the entrance of the store, opening the door, and exposing her sanctuary to the outside soundtrack of gabbing tourists.

"Hi, Albert. Hi, Mr. Tessay!" The latter of the two was a hearing-impaired local artist, vendor, and the store's wholesaler of locally grown sage smudging kits, amongst other inspiring pieces.

She motioned them toward the backroom so they could present the new array of homemade items.

Mr. Tessay set down his boxes. *'Good Morning,'* he signed, bringing his fingertips up to his chin, downward, then up again toward her.

She mirrored the gesture, comfortable with their routine.

Mr. Tessay reached into the largest box to remove a tidily assembled kit while Albert stood by respectfully, waiting for his cue.

'Now,' Mr. Tessay signed, with palms up and the middle three fingers folded back toward him, before both hands dropped downward. Next, he pinched all fingers on both hands together, then merged them as if they were giving each other a quick kiss. *'There's more.'*

Arista watched as he gently slid the tied sage-green raffia ribbon off the box and removed the lid, exposing a vibrantly gorgeous Abalone shell the size of a small dish. Its shiny iridescent-green and blue waves struck her, an explosion of color against its backdrop of the package's ecru grass filling. "So beautiful," she said, mesmerized by nature's work of art.

Mr. Tessay pointed his index finger at a slight angle and gave a quick down-flick of his wrist, prompting Albert to begin translation.

"First, the shells are each an inch larger," Albert said, his eyes fixed on Mr. Tessay's hands and expressions.

Mr. Tessay continued his signing and corrected Albert when he missed even the smallest detail.

"So, you get that much more protection and emotional balance," Albert said, capping the sales pitch.

Mr. Tessay smiled while handing her the shell.

She marveled at the vibrance of nature still alive in color and form. She reverently rotated it, finding a patch of pink sheen as well. "Very pretty." She gently set the piece back into its box.

"Second, he bleached the wood carvings this go-round. You can let him know if those sell better than the natural ones."

Mr. Tessay handed the tripod carving to her.

She ran her fingers over the smooth texture and gazed at the workmanship of the designed, braided pieces of wood. "Both styles are really nice."

Albert continued. "And then, of course …"

Mr. Tessay held up a large, sturdy striped feather, a strong rendition of the majestic bird rivaling a peacock's pride with its fanned tail and puffed breasts of natural colors. He passed it over to her. Then, he folded in his right hand's last three fingers, brought his thumb and forefinger within an inch of each other, and pointed them downward under his chin. He gave a slight wiggle.

She smiled, knowing the sign for *turkey*, the hand gesture representing its wattle. She also knew *chicken*, *rabbit*, and *cat*. The latter of which emphasized a spray of whiskers as its sign.

"And finally, the sage," Albert informed her. "It's fragrant this time."

Mr. Tessay narrowed his eyes at Albert and shook his head. He brought his hand up by the side of his chin as if he were going to claw himself. Then, he shook it vigorously with his mouth in an O-shape and his eyes narrowing as if eating a most heavenly treat.

"*Exceptionally* fragrant this time," Albert corrected.

Mr. Tessay nodded his head, pleased with the clarification.

"This is all really amazing stuff," she said, then looked at Mr. Tessay, brought her fingertips gently to her lips, and dropped her upward-facing palm down in front of her—similar to blowing a kiss without the pucker—thanking him in his language.

Mr. Tessay emitted a proud smile and carefully reassembled the sample package with the precision of a gift-wrapping surgeon. He replaced the cover and the raffia and gave an adamant nod that business was done. Finally, he pulled a pen and his invoice from his inner jacket pocket for her signature.

While usually in an envelope left for Pearl, she noticed the logo in the corner was the same as the tattoo on Dakota's bicep, visible without his security jacket.

"Oh, that's interesting. Your logo is the same as …" She stopped herself before revealing her knack for checking out the ink on the hot guy who passed her shop.

Mr. Tessay looked inquisitively at Albert, who clued him in on her comment.

"My grandson," Mr. Tessay said aloud, his eyes twinkling.

She felt a flush of heat on her face. "Oh … uh …" she sputtered, then diverted her eyes back to the rewrapped box. What could she fixate on?

Mr. Tessay and Albert shared a subtle laugh.

She could not help but smile. They totally caught her.

"Dakota," Mr. Tessay said aloud, verifying Stevie's data. He motioned outside and turned back toward her with a teasing expression. He united his first two fingers, brought them to his right temple, and swept them around his face in a circle.

"He says he's very handsome," Albert said, then translated the rest of Mr. Tessay's comment. "'Like I was at his age.' Meaning, Mr. Tessay *thought* himself handsome at one time."

He gave a humbled laugh at Albert's razzing comment, then winked at her.

She let her smile grow.

"Your age," he verbalized before signing to Albert.

"Bethie says that you're twenty-five?" Albert confirmed.

"Yes."

"Dakota is also twenty-five," Albert said, watching Mr. Tessay's animated hands, "and an early summer baby ... a very sensitive child ... and still very messy."

She laughed at the random dig.

Mr. Tessay chuckled.

"He's just being ornery now. And I don't think Dakota would appreciate he told you that," Albert said.

Mr. Tessay watched his lips, then signed.

"Perhaps he will let him deliver the kits next time," Albert announced on behalf of his elder.

Mr. Tessay gave her a sly grin.

"I think he's enjoying my awkward moment," Arista said, but at this point, no embarrassment remained. Just humor and interest as to where it all may lead.

"I think so," Albert agreed.

"Well, whoever delivers the product is A-okay with me."

The gentlemen set about leaving when Mr. Tessay abruptly stopped. He swung around and signed to Albert in many rapid gestures.

"He almost forgot. He wants to apologize for his youngest grandsons and their friend. I guess their antics made you furious a while back."

Mr. Tessay nodded with genuine concern, his eyes fixed upon her, awaiting reaction.

"Hmm, I'm not sure what you're talking about." She tried to recall an incident where she had gotten mad. "Oh wait, was that them who banged on the door?"

The gentlemen nodded.

"Oh, yeah ... well, it startled me, but I know boys can be that way. I wasn't mad."

"Is that so? They said you stormed over to the door and banged very hard on the glass," Albert said without looking at Mr. Tessay for guidance. "They said you yelled at them with a waving fist and stared like a pouncing puma." He grinned, eyeing her with an air of amusement.

"Oh … no, I didn't do anything like that. I just went back to the register." She felt a little defensive. But truthfully, she did not remember what happened next. Except for waking up on the floor and hoping the brats didn't see her faint.

"That's not what we heard. We heard you gave it right back to them, and they were hoping you wouldn't open the door to come shred them apart."

Clearly, he and Mr. Tessay had already discussed the incident at length based on their amused expressions.

She calmed her rising insecurity and went with a humble demeanor. "Oh, that's weird. I just don't remember it going down like that."

Deciding that he had *stirred the pot* enough, Mr. Tessay gave a last wave as he and Albert headed out into the rising desert heat, its fierceness beginning to emanate through the interior glass.

Watching their departure, she contemplated the conversation. Why did Mr. Tessay have such a different version of the story? While she wished it was just the kids letting their imaginations run wild, there was something quite odd about the whole episode. And up to now, she had not given it much thought. "Weird."

Tasks to be done took forefront—new sage kits to unpack, the box to break down for their oversized alley trash bin, and plenty of inventory paperwork. Hopefully, she could get it all done before the lunch crowd arrived.

"Good, glorious day, Arista!" Stevie's voice rang out in a jubilant proclamation as he barged through the door for his shift.

Perfect timing.

CHAPTER 6
HANDSOME, IN A MOST DIABOLICAL WAY

"I guess I'll see you tomorrow," Trini grumbled, bidding her grouchy store manager goodnight after balancing the store's finances. She walked down the dimly lit stairwell, emerging under rows of bright fluorescent lighting on the main floor. Catching glimpses of acquainted shoppers, she obliged them with a friendly smile as she made her way toward the exit.

"Goodnight, Sydney," she called to the assistant manager on duty.

"Oh, Trini, wait up!" Sydney jogged over and lowered her voice. "Hey, that guy you were talking about … he came in this afternoon looking for you. I didn't tell you 'cause I know you don't want to see him. Are you sure you're okay with all of this?"

"Yeah, I read up on it a little, and it's just irritating more than anything." In fact, she had read several articles that people like her unwelcome admirer are not inherently dangerous but can lack social awareness, which could put them in a poor light with their actions.

Sydney cocked her head and cinched her right cheek. "I don't know about that. He searched aisle by aisle, then asked the new cashier if you were working today."

Trini sighed. "I'm pretty sure he's harmless, but the dude *is* getting a little weird. He actually poked my gut the last time I ran into him."

Sydney frowned. "Not cool. Maybe you should get a restraining order or something."

"Overkill. Seriously. My best strategy is to just keep avoiding him."

"Alright. We'll keep an eye out and give you fair warning if we see him."

"That'll work. Plus, we'll get Kristi on his ass if he gets out of line." Trini laughed, remembering a recent skirmish when their security guard had to strong-arm an unruly customer for harassing a petite stock clerk.

"Yeah, you don't mess with Wholesome Foods's security chick."

Trini smirked, turned, and headed out the door to the far corner of the parking lot. Her small pickup looked tiny in the vast emptiness of concrete, with only a few cars remaining. She chugged along, carrying the extra weight gained from the life growing inside her. Glancing back at the door, she felt slightly unnerved by the solitude. Thankfully, there were plentiful, towering lamps within their lot lighting her path.

Then she saw him. Across the street on the park bench. The same heavyset man, wearing his signature tracksuit. White, on this night. Contrasting against the darkness like a heavyset ghost. Though his suit may as well have been red, signifying the potential issue he could create from his continual stalking. Her gut tightened, more so out of irritation than fear. She picked up her pace.

He saw her, too. He stood up, eyes wide with enthusiasm, and tried to get her attention with an exuberant wave.

"Frickin-A," she muttered, closing in on her truck. She unlocked the door and jammed herself inside the cab. Starting her engine, she kept a wary eye on his presence in her rearview mirror.

The smile left his face. He crossed the street, his lumbering pace full of intention as he entered the parking lot, headed directly toward her.

Thank God he was far enough away. And the way he dropped that smile made her wonder about his true self. Was it all an act just to gain her trust? She shifted to drive, engaged the clutch, and drove to the opposite end of the lot, getting the hell out of there as fast as she could.

•   •   •

Arista sat on her bed in lotus position, her back to the door barely ajar. With Royal's warm body abutting her behind, she focused on her breath, with her light blue Angelite palm stone cupped reverently in prayer hands at her heart line. Relaxing in serenity with an extended, calming hum, she considered her message of the day.

"Arista, we're doing a gathering tonight." Auntie's voice tersely blurted the announcement as she walked past her bedroom toward the kitchen.

She jumped and turned. But Auntie had already left. Her posture deflated. "Okay?" she intonated, loud enough to travel the hallway.

She was as bewildered by the abruptness as she was amused. Since the head injury, Auntie's demeanor had gone beyond the usual spaciness. As flighty as ever, she reminded her of the absentminded, anxiety-ridden professor from the *Back to the Future* movies, but instead of the white-coat, mad scientist look, she presented as a ditzy, red-haired bohemian accompanied by an annoying white, short-haired cat with latte-colored rosettes. The killer's violent blow had made her blunter and more impulsive than ever.

"I thought we were waiting for the full moon," Arista asked.

Unexpectedly, Auntie appeared at the door with Wally in her arms, his cross-eyed light-blues peering at her while his chin received a good rub.

Arista shrank from her overreaching yell. "Oops."

"No, I said waxing was sufficient, so tonight is appropriate." Auntie continued to stroke the silky creature's chin, who appeared calmed by the motion for a change. "We have to search for the athame. I meant it before, but Pearl and I spent the day at Bell Rock, and the masculine energy mixed with our incanting drives us to believe that we have to be decisive in our next move. We walked and meditated, and the energy we received was especially telling. Afterward, we brought our upending visions to light with one another, and both came to the same conclusion ..." Wally squirmed out of Auntie's arms, jumped to the floor, and disappeared from view.

"And?"

"We have to find it," Auntie said, her eyes bugging at the obviousness.

"Oh. I thought there'd be more—"

"Ack! There's so much going on … but too, too much to talk about now! Just get dressed and be prepared. We're on in an hour."

Again, Auntie darted from sight.

"Okie-doke." Arista hopped off her bed and straightened the covers lest the guests mosey past her room. Her new décor was a far cry from her style in Boulder Creek. Here, her bedding shown cheerful and light—a cream-colored background, purple thistles, and leaves of sage. A few other unidentifiable flowers filled out the rest of the botanical ensemble. The one basil-green velvet throw pillow she plopped at the forefront looked paltry compared to the collection she kept at home. But simplicity sure helped when making the bed.

She slipped into a soft, jersey-knit, black sheath dress with a simple black wrap. Her and Auntie's ritual clothing presented much differently from the theatrical outfits they had donned in Boulder Creek. But, since moving to Sedona, they confessed they had only kept up the exaggerated display for the benefit of the other. So, they put the tired habit to rest.

Still, the jewelry remained true. She chose the Labradorite ring Auntie had upgraded for her, now in a lovely sterling silver floral setting after falling and breaking during her melee with the killer. Her cabochon's flash showed its aurorean colors as dazzling as ever.

Ready for action, she straightened up the hall bath of her skin care products, wiped down the mirror, then made one last check that Royal sat comfy on her bed before closing the bedroom door.

A short time later, the Waning Crescent Coven gathered in Auntie's front room. Since privacy held key in their matters, they had closed all the drapes and blinds, as too many neighbors sat home tonight and the trees too few.

Explorative activities within the coven usually started with Auntie's *feelings*, followed by Candace scrying for better insight. With this in mind, Candace used her gift infrequently, not squandering it on menial whims.

A small cast-iron cauldron, the size of your average cereal bowl, rested in the middle of the group as they sat upon their bulky pillowed seats. A whirring air filter ensured clean air, and the sliding glass door remained cracked for ventilation. As the incense appointee, Bridget sprinkled a small pile of black salt into the cauldron, then placed a charcoal tablet atop it. She lit and stoked it until it began the transition to ash, whereupon she positioned frankincense resin upon it to melt and smolder. This, their favored source for visualization and spiritual connection.

Candace pre-gazed into her flawless six-inch-diameter crystal ball, situated atop a gold-plated, sterling silver, three-legged stand that looked like a French Provincial trinket straight out of the Bonaparte empire. No wonder since she had the set imported from France.

"Ladies, we are here to explore Bethie's hunch. A rise of Arista's troubled past. We must find answers so that we can act upon them." Candace paused for effect. "And so, we begin."

With the frankincense resin bubbling, wisps of smoke rose from the cauldron, filling the room with the scent of sweet wood. Energy rose from all but Candace as they chanted in spoken breath.

Hah. Hah. Hah.

The series of three huffs could have been mistaken for broken, unfunny laughter had someone been listening through the walls.

Hah. Hah. Hah.

Candace softened her gaze and looked into the glass orb before her. Her jaw fell slack, and she slowed her breathing to ten-second intervals.

Hah. Hah. Hah.

Candace spoke from a trance of discovery. "I see a woman. A beautiful woman."

Hah. Hah. Hah.

"She has overtaken him." Her facial expression held unmoving, and her tone hypnotic. "He sits in silence."

Hah. Hah. Hah.

"His power wanes. She grows stronger."

Hah. Hah. Hah.

Candace hardened her stare as if grasping at a shadowy vision unidentifiable to her astute third eye. "I see the athame. She took—no, he gave it to her." She paused. "It is unclear."

Hah. Hah. Hah.

"She … no, *he* will come for Arista."

Candace quieted. She sat in a moment of silence, before joining her sisters in the *hah*-chant. The signal that she had exhausted the vision.

They completed the ceremony with a long, intonating hum—a resonance of *a cappella* perfection.

Candace took a deep inhalation, then positioned her body toward Arista, tilting her head and knitting her brows in compassion. "Arista, you will need to take caution again."

She knew this was coming. She turned to Auntie. "I need to know what I'm looking for … *who* am I looking for? I don't even know what Fergus looks like anymore."

"Come," Candace said with outreaching hands. An inviting gesture prompting Bridget to desert her cushion so they could sit closer together.

Candace held her hands palms up, prompting Arista to place her hands upon them. Once she complied, Candace closed her eyes and dropped her hands an inch away from touching, a gap now separating the two sets.

Arista followed her lead on breathing, in through the nose … out through the nose. They synchronized the effort while their audience remained reverently riveted to the outcome.

The warmth percolated within her palms, and she felt the tingle transfer up her forearms. Easily, she released into her mind to a gradual fade-in accompanied by Candace's words.

"Very slim," Candace slowly said. "Large, hazel eyes … beneath thin brows. Cropped graying, and dark brown hair … clean-shaven."

Clearer, Arista could see him in her mind. An indistinct older version of the uncle she once adored. She relaxed her shut eyes to better absorb the visage sent from Candace. His face, the one so long forgotten, now aged with distinguished features. "And unfortunately handsome, in a most diabolical way."

"Do you see the woman?" Candace asked.

Still, Fergus's face held her attention—his chiseled jawline and his prominent nose holding the poise of a dignified noble. "I do not."

Candace grasped her hands, breaking their connection.

Arista opened her eyes, surprised at the abrupt ending to a fascinating experience.

"I apologize. There is great distraction that suppresses my ability to identify who will come for you. I saw him, but I saw the woman too—a tall brunette. What did you see?"

"I just saw my uncle. I actually remember him now, though he's a lot older."

"Yes," Candace said with a satisfied smile. "This was merely an experiment. I wasn't sure that I could transfer the vision to you, but you are very gifted." She looked at her coven sisters. "As we suspected."

Always that expectation of greatness. Just move on. "So, he *is* still after me."

"The details are hazy. But I believe so."

"Does he know I'm here? In Arizona? Or will he go to Cali?"

"I do not know," Candace apologetically said.

She nodded, but felt the frustration of ambiguity. Similar to her ominous visions from the previous year. At least this time, she knew the culprit.

CHAPTER 7
HER RUSHED CUP OF TEA

Bethie awoke at the break of the desert dawn, the sky showing only a hint of the sunny day to come as it hovered dark and sleepy out her bedroom window. Quietly, she hurried so as not to awaken Arista. The final touch of bed-making would not go as planned. After gently tugging her covers to meet the cushioned headboard, she decided to deal with her throw blanket later.

"Well, I guess we must accommodate you, Mr. Wally," she whispered to her lazy Bengal.

Not a single whisker moved in response to her unusual and inconvenient morning adventure.

She hustled to the kitchen and created a new concoction to surprise Arista. One not even she had tried yet. True to the Southwest, it began with dried prickly pear. She opened a jar of crushed hibiscus flowers blended with chamomile, spooned a heap into a small saucepan, then securely shut it again. A couple dashes of chicory root and rose hips created a scent pleasantly swirling about her nose. She lightly tossed the herbs into a chunky, loose tea, then filled her enamel saucepan with instant boiling water from the sink's filtered spigot. Atop the burner, she placed it and ignited the flame to lap at its bottom.

"And now it steeps."

She quickly reorganized her herb jars, wiped away debris, and, within a minute, chomped at the bit for a simmering progress. The day ahead held a monumental discovery, and the sooner she embarked, the better.

A minute later, her anxiety at the ticking clock had her impatiently sighing aloud.

Two seconds after that, she could not wait any longer and poured the brew through a strainer into her tempered glass pitcher to set atop a cool burner. She discarded the used herbs into a small compost bin beneath the sink, already full of lettuce leaves, radish tops, and potato peelings that she gave to Candace for her gorgeous, jet-black Ayam Cemani chickens.

Finally, she poured a generous serving into her mandala-printed travel mug, took a quick sip, and swished it about her mouth. "It will have to do," she said, disappointed by the weak flavor. Too bad. She had already fallen behind schedule. Taking another sip of her rushed cup of tea, she headed out to her small SUV, happy that its hybrid motor allowed a noiseless escape.

Her anxiousness grew as she programmed the destination into her GPS. While only a short day trip, this journey had been years in the making. It was exciting. Stressful. But most of all, it held necessity.

The temperate morning wind blew through her window, allowing for fresh air to calm her already-frazzled nerves. She hit the last stop light within the tourist town, just past Pearl's shop, and thought of the conditions. Undoing this secret, hidden many years, even from her, would require care. Upon returning home and every day thereafter, she would maintain a poker face until the formal meeting occurred.

She brainstormed aloud. "The re-introduction will need to be gentle, and there must be an abundance of compassion for Arista's feelings. Hopefully, she won't feel betrayed." She winced. "She *may* feel betrayed." Stewing, she chewed the inside of her lip, thinking about their joint decision to bring all to the open. "This was necessary for her protection."

She pictured her grandniece receiving the news and envisioned her crying. She could see her angry and lashing out. And finally, she could see her at peace, accepting the sudden presence of her father, whom she had not seen in many, many years. Her mother would be a little harder to endure.

·   ·   ·

Using a soft pink squishy to extract malleable material from between enamel had grown futile. But Sheriff Michaels persisted. Fruitless in his pursuit, he slung open his top drawer and shuffled through its contents—pens, paperclips … Xacto knife? Nah. He opened the second drawer, knowing no toothpick lay amongst the notepads and envelopes. He slammed it shut, the wedged feeling of food in his teeth driving him utterly nutty.

"Fricken chicken sandwich," he said, prying through the corner of his mouth, digging his fingernail at the gum line. Capturing a small edge of the debris, it broke off immediately.

Patty's voice squelched on his speakerphone. "Sheriff, Coroner's on the phone."

"Yep." His last-ditch effort at oral relief achieved as Jo's call rang to the phone. "Hey, Jo! How's it going?"

"Sheriff, I think you're going to like this."

Silence.

He awaited the punchline, rarely amused by the extended delay of Jo's guessing games. "Yeah? Go ahead."

"We've found Dustin."

This was good news!

"Well, a piece of him, anyway."

Oh. "A piece, huh?"

"Yeah. Results are in from that femur found in the grade. We're guessing coyotes must've drugged it up that hillside. Shoot, could have been a mountain lion. Who knows?"

"Mmm-huh. So that was Mr. Rogers, huh?"

"It is indeed Mr. Rogers. Needless to say, scour that canyon and you may damn well find the rest of him."

"Alright, we'll get on it."

"I'm sure that'll take some organization, huh?"

"Yep, but I'm going to call them as soon as I hang up with you."

"Okay, hope you find the rest of him."

"Hope so, too. Thanks for the call, Jo."

Immediately, he phoned dispatch. Permits needed, crews to gather, and drones to hire. "We need a search team over at Felton Empire Grade Road at the hairpin. Possible human body in the canyon."

After giving further details, he set down his radio and pulled up the saved snippet of video from Dustin's infamous night at the station. Fast-forwarding, he viewed the hallway camera's vantage point of Dustin's entry into the evidence room.

"What is your purpose, Mr. Rogers?"

Unexpectedly, he noticed a detail he had missed during other viewings. He set the film back ten seconds and replayed it. As Dustin stuck the key into the evidence room doorknob, he saw a small mark on the heel of his hand. Before, he had dismissed it as a shadow, but now …

"Hunh."

He rewound and played it again. And again. He paused the clip to show Dustin's hand, took a screenshot, then enlarged it. While grainy, he still saw possible similarities.

"Okay, Henry, you former piece of shit … let's see that ink of yours."

He clicked on various folders and pulled up the notorious serial killer's digital autopsy file. In gallery view, he flipped through the photos.

"A dead Henry …" he said, while perusing the grim reminder of his county's worst nightmare in decades, "is a …" He stopped at the photo of Henry's tattooed hand. "Well, he's just a dead Henry."

After comparing the two screens, the sheriff buzzed his officer in the reception area.

"Hey Patty, can you come back here a minute?"

"You bet." Within seconds, her footsteps echoed through the hall and arrived at his door.

"Tell me something …" He motioned to his monitor. "Look at the hands on these two." He enlarged the first window and drew an imaginary circle around Henry's tattoo. Then he pointed to the grainy photo of Dustin's hand. "Is it just me, or do these two idiots have the same tattoo?"

He alternated the full-screen view, enlarging and diminishing each photo, similar to an optometrist helping his patient decipher best sight. Once again, he placed them next to each other.

"Wow, Sheriff, I think you're on to something. It's that point on the lower right. It seems to be the same. Same size, same area. Maybe Dustin covered his full tattoo with some sort of makeup, and that's just a portion of it?"

"Makeup, huh? Okay, I just wanted a second pair of eyes. Thank you."

"Yeah, nice find!" She turned to leave.

"Hey, can you do some investigating to determine the meaning of that tattoo? I'll send you a closeup from Wallish's file. Nothing gory."

"Of course."

As Patty hustled away with a purpose, he diminished both screens. He tidied his desk for the day, knowing he wouldn't be back. Not with the unfolding scene in Felton's deepest canyon.

CHAPTER 8
AN ASSEMBLY OF NON-GIFTED WITCHES

While Conn had the seldom intuitive hunch, he knew himself a mere mortal in an assembly of non-gifted witches. For years, he had served Fergus, hoping that his own ability would reveal itself. It had not. But coasting as his leader's right-hand man was just as easy.

Throughout time, he had become the persuasive force. Big as he was brooding, he had no stops and barely a conscience, all beneath a sun-bleached-blond pageboy haircut that would make anyone viewing him from behind think he was a carefree surfer. But the one who mistook him as a *cool dude* fell sorely disappointed once he turned to face them with an expression of brutish disgust. In addition, he had a wicked scar that ran from between his brows down his left cheek to his jaw, compliments of a clinically psychotic ex-girlfriend with a fancy for sharp objects. Fergus had picked him up from the hospital on the notorious night, solidifying loyalty. To pay homage to his long-time association with Fergus, every couple years, he freshened up the pentagram tattoo sunk into an inked red slit on the heel of his hand. It was the least he could do to honor their friendship rooted in those early SoCal days.

Standing outside in the early-autumn Spokane air, he hand-rolled a tidy cigarette with his thick fingers, stuck it in his mouth, and lit it. The smoke billowed into the breeze as he eyed the bug-spattered grill of his notorious ruby-red Ford Raptor, a gift from Fergus. He carefully pried off the fully intact body of a dead wasp, scrutinized its bulbous stinger, then slung it to the ground.

The buzz of his phone prompted an answer.

"Yup."

"Conn, she wants to see you."

"Yup."

Rarely did Fergus make calls these days. Not since he leaned more on his new high priestess. Even more odd, he had just called on her behalf. There was no doubt about it. Fallon had taken command. But, if that's what Fergus wanted …

He flicked his cigarette ahead of him and squashed it with his boot on the way toward the Rec Center's entrance. Before he stepped through the doors, he checked himself in the glass and stretched his neck from side to side, eliciting a loud pop. He puffed his chest, then struck his lips to a protruding pucker. He looked pretty good.

He entered the unlit hallway and headed toward the office, also known as Fallon's dressing room. "No lights," he said in a grumble, annoyed by the ever-lasting darkness, to help stretch coven funds.

He knocked before entering and found her at her dressing table, brushing her long-curled locks and admiring herself in the mirror.

"Oh, Conn, love. Come in, come in," she said, waving exuberant hands.

He stepped inside the door, keeping a distance, and stood at a soldier's attention with his hands folded at his crotch.

"Conn, I want us to have a special Samhain this year. Let's make it really fantastic!"

She used to be sultry, dark, and mysterious, but as of late, she had become more like an excitable interior designer. Less Melisandre. More Elvira.

"We're less than two months away, so we need to start organizing now. First off, I want it publicized. I want to invite all sorts of people. After all, if people don't know about our group, they won't join. Right, Conn?"

"Yup."

Fallon stood up as she brainstormed. "I want it in the local papers, and I want flyers posted on coffee shop windows. Check with Jameson. I think he does graphic design."

He watched her flailing her arms, more so than he listened to her flapping lips, spewing loads of stupid shit he could barely keep up with.

"And I want it vivid. All the colors of fall, including purple. And signs. And sunflowers … dozens and dozens of sunflowers … pumpkins … corn stalks. All filling our big room. Thematic! Festive! Those are your keywords." Her eyes bugged in enthusiasm.

She spun around, holding her hands as if framing a precious work of art. "We'll call it *Feast of the Dead*!" She paused for effect. "But *dead* doesn't always mean everything has to be dark and dour. I want bright oranges and deep purple streamers. Are you following me?"

He nodded without eye contact. She had definitely changed the vibe of the coven and had become a complete nutbag in the process.

"Dancing as usual, and we'll have little make-out rooms for our frisky guests. Fergus always liked those." She looked at him again, gauging his interest.

"Yup."

"Oh! We'll take the athame and link to the Otherworld. Perhaps Fergus can make an appearance." She paused, considering her own idea. "Yes! Our founder will make a special guest appearance … give some knockout speech, then I'll come out and host the rest of the evening."

The founder and true leader as a guest sounded absolutely ludicrous. And with her railroading everything, he doubted Fergus would appear at all.

"Anyway, let's also have crystal and Tarot stations. Mostly, our people read their own, but newcomers will love it!"

She paced the room, the ideas incessantly pouring out of her fast-talking mulberry lips. Would it ever stop?

"Do you hear me, Conn?"

"Yup."

"You seem distracted."

"Uh, should Ferg—" He stopped himself. Maybe he should not bring up Fergus.

"Should Fergus what?"

He kept silent.

"Should Fergus what?!" All delight had left her face, replaced by a suspicious glare.

"N'up." He shook his head. Why did he have to mention Fergus?

"N'up? What does '*N'up*' mean?"

He re-postured himself at attention, raising his chin and broadening his chest, hoping she would just move on.

Fallon eyed him, and he knew the look well. She was determining whether to indulge in an angry outburst.

Luckily, her demeanor lightened, and she released her annoyance with a roll of her eyes. "Anyway, lots of fun and exciting things. We want to grow, Conn. We don't have to be degenerates anymore. This coven will be reputable, and you can bet there will be much less black magick and illegal doings under *my* watch."

She certainly did not align with the style of his former leader. This was mainstream shallow witchery, not the dark malintent he was used to and preferred.

"I'm not just thinking about the money here. I aim to make a difference. I want people to feel part of our community. Right, Conn?" She eyed him again, a sharp focus bearing down on his response.

"Yup."

"Potlucks and monthly birthday parties, too. Fun stuff. Let's not mull around miserable all the time. Let's grow! We want to be better."

He nodded.

"Okay, I know you have limitations with communication," she flashed him a quick smile and winked, "but I'm going to make you a list, and I want you to get started … *today*! Okay, love?"

He tightened his forced half-smile and gave a quick nod.

"The first thing we're going to do …" Fallon sashayed over to the light switch, "is stop living in the dark."

Click.

A spray of cool fluorescent lighting penetrated the room, exposing even the furthest corner. How odd everything looked bathed in light. He glanced at the illuminated ceiling, then back to her. He had to admit, this was an agreeable change, and he felt a genuine grin escape his lips.

"Well, we don't see *that* very often! I'll take that as a sign you're on board."

CHAPTER 9
ASWIRL WITH AGITATION

Arista loved to shop at Wholesome Foods, Sedona's most health-abundant grocery store. On mornings when Auntie's fridge ran low on homemade lunch materials, she made a quick trip before her shift to create a vibrant salad. The freshly cut selection offered many options, of which she mostly stuck to her mixture of green lettuces, sliced deep-red radishes, purple cabbage shavings, and a slick boiled egg with a sprinkle of pumpkin seeds.

Today, also shopping to appease her sweet tooth, a familiar voice came from behind her.

"Hey, Arista!" Trini said, her face still emitting the prenatal glow.

"Hey!" Now comfortable with their budding friendship, she gave Trini a hug. "How are you doing? How's the baby bump?"

Trini froze, eyes wide like a hare in sudden porchlight. 'No one knows,' she mouthed.

Arista winced, covered her mouth, then awkwardly relented in a whisper. "I'm sooo sorry."

Trini's voice grew a little louder. "It's okay. I'm actually going to tell him later tonight."

"Your boss?"

She said nothing, just gave a half-smile through grit teeth. Going from scared hare to sheepishness with one sentence.

"Ooooooh, got it." *Hmmm, I don't 'got' it. Boss, for time off? Boyfriend, for … whatever?*

"Anyway, he's the least of my worries."

"Oh, no! Don't tell me that guy's still following you."

An abrupt, deep voice called for Trini from behind the adjacent aisle.

Trini rolled her eyes. "Gotta run. I just wanted to say *hi!*"

"I'm so glad you did. I didn't know you worked here."

Trini bellowed out the words, but her feet already had her to the end of the aisle. "I'm in the office. So, no need for the tag or uniform."

"Cool. Okay, well … hi and bye." At this point, she talked only to herself.

She refocused on her shopping, still embarrassed by blurting out such personal information. Hopefully, no one heard.

Onward she meandered, scanning the aisles, grabbing necessities that would get her through the next few days. Finally, reaching the glorious row of colorfully boxed cookies, she set down her heavy hand cart containing two water bottles, a large jar of solid virgin coconut oil for her and Auntie's plentiful spell work, as well as miscellaneous other items.

There it was! The appealing brown-and-green box with a picture of a dark chocolate thin mint. Trying them at Pearl's, she was unaware a processed cookie could taste so good. She scrutinized the ingredients. "Hmmm, not bad." She could already imagine the minty goodness.

Hoisting the handcart, her concentration on clever shopping tactics diverted to an odd feeling. She felt peering eyes, and glanced to the end of the aisle, where a uniformed store worker discreetly watched her. He hid partly behind the promotional display case of unrefrigerated, alternative milks. No denying his hard stare aimed at her.

Does he think I'm trying to steal something? She turned her gaze back down toward the cookie box. *I'm not a thief, just a friendly shopper.*

She flashed a warm smile to him, only to find a very unusual sight. While reading auras had brought a pleasant experience with Trini, this man held quite a different presentation. Surrounding him was a blurry smudge of dark brown, and the gray that accompanied it looked as grimy as a gas station bathroom floor made airborne. For a second, she thought her eyesight faltered and looked at the cookie box—vibrant green accents. With her vision as clear as the sunniest day, she looked back at him and saw an additional element. His eyes shone large and bright white, bringing a shocking contrast against the roiled muck.

Startled, she looked away, stunned by the intrusive reading that she had not initially sought. She blinked and walked in the opposite direction but cast one last glance.

He had left.

"Wow, what an unfriendly guy!" she muttered under her breath. Out of all the Sedonans she had met over the past few months, this guy was the biggest downer of them all.

She warily walked toward the cashiers, keeping an eye out for another sighting of him, but made it to, and through, the checkout line without incident.

At the exit, another familiar sight snuffed the unease. "Hi, Mr. Tessay!" *Good goddess, he's got Dakota with him.*

Mr. Tessay's eyes drew up into a knowing expression. "My grandson," he said aloud and turned to Dakota. "Arista."

She assumed the signing that followed told Dakota she was his customer.

"Hi, Dakota. It's nice to finally meet you. I think I've seen you walking the strip in your uniform. I work at Cosmic Prisms."

"Nice to—"

Mr. Tessay interrupted Dakota's response. "Remember … messy," he said aloud, simultaneously signing.

Dakota narrowed his eyes and surrendered a toothy smile of straight, white teeth. "Nice to meet you, Arista."

She offered her hand for a friendly shake.

Dakota gently clenched her fingers, as if he was going to raise her hand and kiss it. While he did not, the nature of his gesture provoked her to drop her head for a moment before looking into his eyes. He had the same caramel-brown eyes as Shane. Yet long, silky dark eyelashes surrounded them. She looked away, hoping she had not stared too long.

Dakota observed his grandfather's signs before offering an explanation. "We have to get going, but I think he wants me to make the next delivery."

Mr. Tessay motioned to his back, then held his arms out as if a heavy log had dropped into his upright palms.

"His back is not so great, and the boxes are sometimes heavy."

"Great! I look forward to seeing you."

Dakota graciously nodded, and the men journeyed onward into the glare of fluorescent lighting upon shiny apple pyramids.

She felt her steps lighten as she headed outside toward Auntie's car. Dakota smelled so clean. Like he had just washed with rain-scented soap. As she reached her car, she smelled her hand. His scent remained. Then, a thought. She stopped herself and her giddy excitement, imagining Shane's smile, his laughter, and *his* warm-brown eyes. She sighed and plopped inside Auntie's Subaru. No guy would ever measure up to Shane.

Chapter 10
Tainted Perspectives with Idle Hands

Fallon posed on all fours, taking time to straighten her legs, raising her butt toward the ceiling. With heels pressed down, she pulled her stomach tight and, with palms spread wide on the floor, exhaled a long, fluid breath. She released it all the way to the very last peep, her gut concave, then slowly inhaled. "What are you thinking, my love?" Fergus had lingered too long with nothing to say.

"We aren't making enough progress."

She liked him better quiet. "What do you mean, love?" Focused, she brought her pelvis toward the floor as her torso swiveled fully upright, her head aligning with her spine during the continuum. Strength building within her, and body engaged, she pushed the floor away, holding in Up Dog asana.

"You're not hungry enough," Fergus said. "I'm having second thoughts of you leading us."

Less and less did he have anything constructive to say.

She released a solid breath from between her pursed lips and came into a Plank Pose before lowering her torso and face to hover just above the ground. Her elbows now formed into ninety-degree angles at her sides. From her head to her feet, she held a steady horizontal position, solidifying the power of her shoulders, core, and quads.

"Even now, I don't think you realize I'm questioning your ability," Fergus said, his demeanor nagging.

His presence had become grating, chipping away at her concentration.

"Well?" he said in a huff.

She relaxed to the ground and lay still, considering her response. "Fergus, your mind is always taunting you." She had grown tired of his doubt, and his jealousy of her rise in popularity had become problematic.

Fergus persisted, his negativity spewing forth more volatile than ever. "Every meeting … talk, talk, talk. That's all you've been doing. And don't think I don't know about your stupid plans for the coming season. This is not a fucking PTA group!"

"Talking is good for communication. I'm creating trust … forming a bond. What would you have me do?"

He offered nothing.

It was no wonder the group had so little loyalty when he led them. He had not built close relationships with his people. He simply let them brood with no direction, and the tainted perspectives married to idle hands left drug addictions to flourish.

She sat up on the mat and crossed her legs. She *did* have a new vision. "Fergus, I must tell you, I don't believe …well, I really don't think you have a choice anymore."

He sulked, offering no retort.

"In the long run, you'll be glad that I assumed leadership. It will negate any of your past behaviors. People won't look into who you've affiliated with, who you've slept with … or who you've had killed … my love."

She closed her eyes with confidence and breathed in the air of power. The power she held over herself, him, and the coven. Holding it for a moment, she freed it, along with the notion that he had any control left. She no longer needed him. Old news. Dead weight.

Without another word, she stood up and stepped her left foot back at an angle, assuming her Warrior One asana. Hands clasped skyward, she exposed her entire torso. A vulnerable gesture if she had any doubts about her safety and his fascination with that athame. But as she listened to her own in-breath, steady and unwavering, she knew he had already left.

.   .   .

Jeremy sat on his restful bench, already perspiring from the scorch of Sedona's mid-day sun. There was not much shade, but his mother helped him apply sunscreen so he would not get a sunburn. He sat, hoping to see his favorite person, Trini. He had missed seeing her go inside the grocery store this morning, but he knew she was there. Not only by her white truck in the parking lot, but by her schedule, too. Tuesdays and Thursdays were her workdays. Sometimes, she would leave at five p.m., but sometimes, she came back to the store after it had closed.

He knew a lot about her. Her favorite color was white. She wore it a lot. She kinda liked red too, but only wore it sometimes. And she liked to play her truck music loudly and listened to a song called *Jeremy*, just like his name. Maybe she liked him since she sang it really loud. And now that he had touched her tummy, he knew she was soft, too. Her stomach squished when he poked it. And she didn't mind too much.

"Good afternoon, Jeremy," the postman said, his mood cheerful.

"Good afternoon!" he said from his perch with its view of the city street and the Wholesome Foods parking lot.

"Don't tell me you've been sitting in this scorching sun all day again?"

"Only a couple hours. But I'm okay. I don't mind because I take breaks and get water down the street at my house."

"Okay, just don't let this summer heat get to you."

"I won't."

His eyes trailed the mailman as he went about his late-afternoon walking route. He knew his habits, too. He traveled in and out of stores up and down 89A until about four p.m. He took his lunch around noon, either picnicking in his square, white postal truck by the small park at

Arroyo Pinon or getting a strawberry smoothie at the local juicery. He liked those smoothies.

And Barbara, the lady at the smoothie bar, she had a routine, too. She got to work at seven-thirty a.m. and parked in the diagonal parking space farthest from the front door. She would take her lunch at eleven-thirty a.m., but her smoking breaks weren't scheduled at all. No telling when she'd take those. She always looked tired when she left at five p.m.

He returned his gaze to Trini's truck in the parking lot. She was his favorite. She was pretty, and her face and tummy were soft and round, just like his.

He felt a tickle in his crotch and adjusted himself on the bench. Then he stretched out his arms, stifled by the constraining fabric of his dark green tracksuit. Maybe this set had gotten too small because his stomach poked between his jacket and pants like the dough out of a freshly popped Pillsbury container.

The minutes turned to hours. In that time, he had gone home many times to drink his water and snack on peanut butter crackers and cheese sticks.

Finally, in the dusky evening, his beautiful Trini emerged from the store. She was walking kind of funny. And it looked like she was getting heavier because her white shirt stretched against her stomach. That was okay. He was heavy, too.

But Trini did not look happy tonight.

He turned away. Maybe he shouldn't say *hi*. But she was kinda mad every night she left the store. He could tell by her frown.

Hurrying to her little white truck, she disappeared from sight. He stood up to get a better look. Now, he would wait again until she left the lot.

When her car pulled to the exit, he watched her look left. Then right. "Hi, Trini," he said loudly, waving his hand high and fast so she could see him.

Trini *did* see him. Her face became mean-looking. Her eyebrows pinched, her eyes narrowed, and she gripped her steering wheel like Cruella DeVil. She looked really angry now.

"Oh no. I'm sorry." He waved again, hoping that a nice wave might make her happier.

Trini stepped on the gas, and her car bounced from the dip at the parking lot entrance. She revved off down the street.

He sighed and sat down on the bench. She was so pretty, even when she was mad. He did not mean to make her drive away so fast. Hopefully, she could be his girlfriend someday.

CHAPTER 11
ADAM, YOU POOR SAP

The moderate rolling hills of Auntie's neighborhood created a lovely morning walk. The sun had yet to fully rise, and the morning air still left a cool touch to Arista's cheek. Over the past few months, she had taken one solid route to and from Auntie's house to the main road, so hiking through the neighborhood and exploring outer regions with Trini brought novel property designs of which to gander and critique.

Each house had its own style of southwestern feel. Presently, they passed an artisanal blend of brick and adobe with ombre paint from coral to ivory. Waist-high pillars surrounding the property marked its boundary, and that was just the fencing. The house sat farther up the graveled driveway, perched on a desert-flat foundation with three small pine trees blocking a clear view. It looked pretty nice.

"I didn't expect so many hills. Are you sure you're okay?" Arista asked, through puffs of her own exertion.

"Yes! Still good. How about you?" Trini's eyes twinkled.

"I know. I've been sitting too much since I arrived here." She laughed. Go figure the pregnant lady packing a reported extra twenty pounds took the last forty minutes of exercise with greater ease than she did.

"Well, thanks again for the invite. I don't like walking by myself."

"No. Not a fan of putting myself out there all alone, either." She had kept her traumatic baggage to herself, instead sticking to light-hearted talk. "Thanks for coming over here. Next time, we can do your neighborhood, if you want?"

"Actually, I like it here. Nicer scenery with all the landscaping."

Arista looked at the house they were passing—a single, small evergreen tree sat front and center of the yard. Nice, but a fraction of those in California. Beyond that, just more crushed rock. Maybe she took the scenery here for granted, spoiled by the lush redwood forest that awaited her at home. "It is fresh looking."

Finally, they neared Trini's truck parked at the curb in front of Auntie's house.

"Hey, I'll be by the shop later today. That Gaia candle you showed me … I cannot stop thinking about it. And I just got paid, so I'll be picking it up," Trini said with a satisfied nod.

"Oh, cool. Yeah, that one is really lovely." Arista envisioned the chartreuse candle depicting the ancestral mother—a voluptuous pregnant woman sitting in lotus position with long, flowing beeswax hair partly covering her breasts. Her swollen belly, a semblance of planet Earth, and faux-leafy vines twined up one of her folded legs. "Maybe I can get you my employee discount. I'll ask Stevie. I definitely haven't abused the policy. No friends, and my only family—Auntie—has her own discount."

"That would be nice."

After small talk and an agreement to make their walk weekly, Trini left. Arista waved and headed toward the door. The after-effect of her new friendship invigorated her, and she enjoyed the flow of girl talk again—her break-up with Shane, the cuteness of Dakota, comfortable vs. sexy clothes and so on. And while Trini still gave no details of her mysterious pregnancy, she *did* talk about growing up with a single mom, her trepidations of becoming the same, and ways to stay positive in hard times. The latter of which they both shared stories. Arista offered to listen anytime, but there was no need to push Trini into spilling all her baby drama. They had plenty of time to get to know one another.

·   ·   ·

"Hey, you two," Trini said, barging into Prisms minutes before closing time.

"Hey!" Arista set aside her sales slips.

"Trini," Stevie said, throwing a conspicuous look at the wall clock, "you have ten minutes."

"Stevie!" Arista said with an offended laugh.

"I'm *just* kidding," he said unconvincingly before sauntering into the backroom.

"Be nice!" Her remark earned a flippant flick of his wrist. She knew he was only *half*-kidding.

"I know you guys are closing. I know what I want."

"You're not too late. Don't worry about it."

Trini fetched the one remaining Gaia candle from amongst a variety of beeswax designs and brought it to the counter.

"Will that be all for today?" Arista asked in a playful, professional manner.

"That'll do it."

Arista carefully wrapped the candle. "Hey, forgot to ask you about the stalker-guy this morning. Have things gotten quieter?"

"Not really. He tried to flag me down a couple nights back when I was leaving work. He'll probably be there again tonight, too."

"Just be careful," Arista said before quoting the total and offering her the credit card reader.

"It's nothing malicious, so I'll deal with it. One day, he could find another crush, and I'll probably miss the attention." Trini blew it off with a laugh while completing her transaction.

"Well, as long as you think he's harmless." Arista handed over her bagged purchase.

"Yeah, I really do."

"Next week, same day and time for our walk?"

"Yes! It's a plan!"

With Trini's exit, Stevie emerged from the backroom. "How's our Trini doing?"

"She's great." She looked directly at him. "Stevie, our customers need to know they're appreciated … not an inconvenience, and you know your grandmother wouldn't like that." Now, she was only *half-*kidding.

Stevie rolled his eyes. "Well, *our customers* aren't the ones taking inventory for three more hours after closing."

Arista held her unamused stare … but he had a point.

He relented. "Besides, she knows I'm only joking." Sulking from the admonishment, he returned to the back.

With Stevie pouting in solitude, she spent the last couple minutes of their business hours running the small vacuum and reminiscing about meeting Dakota, the story fresh after sharing it with Trini that morning. She looked forward to him coming into the store, and if keeping to his grandfather's schedule, that would mean the coming Monday.

Next, she tidied the books, putting them back in alphabetical order by subject, after many hands had rearranged them throughout the day. Her mind returned to Trini. Who was the '*him*' she mentioned in the store? Was it the father and knowledge of a baby or was it her boss and taking time off work? Or something altogether different?

"Hey, did you know Trini works at Wholesome Foods?" she asked when a renewed Stevie whisked by, holding a freshly unpacked hand-woven mandala in each hand.

"I *think* I knew that." He cocked his head, trying to recall.

"Well, she does. She works in the upstairs office."

"Oh, maybe I didn't know that." He situated the store's step ladder and climbed it to gingerly hang each mandala by its readied hook when a look of contemplation crossed his face.

"What are you thinking now?"

"A few of those staff members … managers *and* workers … can be a lit-tle sleezy."

"There you go again."

"Just sayin' what I've heard. Speaking of such, how far along is she?"

"Six months," Arista cheerfully said, "and she says she's gained twenty pounds, but you can barely tell."

"Well, then, I'm guessing Trini started working there about seven months ago."

She scoffed but could not help but laugh at his sarcastic quip. "Don't be like that."

Arista returned to her literary filing, trying to avoid the gossip. With Trini becoming her friend, she may have to set Stevie straight in the future.

"I'm just saying it's par for the course. And I'm not one to gossip—"

"You've totally become one to gossip. Anyway, what do you say we do a love spell for her after inventory?" Maybe the incanting would clear his Throat Chakra, ceasing his gossiping tendencies. A stretch, but it could work.

Stevie cocked his head and rolled out his bottom lip, considering the proposal. "I suppose. But why?"

"Well, from the sound of it, she hasn't told … *him*." She air-quoted the latter.

"Do you see what I mean? That's crappy business, Arista. She's already six months, and she hasn't even told the guy yet??"

"You've really got this … thing … about dissing her. Stop it!"

Stevie sighed and strolled toward the backroom. "Fine. I don't know what brings the catty out in me. And she *has* always been really sweet." He disappeared, but his voice easily projected. "Shame on me. Yes! Let's do a love spell for her." He emerged with one last acrylic-blue-layered maple plywood mandala, climbed the ladder, and steadied the intricate, laser-cut creation with both hands.

Arista verified it straight. Then, as a team, they quickly worked to fulfill closing duties.

The next three hours dragged by with tedious counting and plotting on pre-made lists. Every stone, even the bins with their two-dollar crystals, had to be tallied as Pearl desired. Jewelry, orbs, candles, and books, all accounted for and recorded. Finally, tasks completed, they pushed aside tables and boxes in the back room in order to secure a small space on the floor.

"Thank you, Stevie. This will bring us good karma. Also, I'm thinking we can use this." She held up an orange-and-blue coverlet with the sun and moon eclipsed as one. "It's a sign of love's greatest possibilities. Appropriate, right?"

"Anyway, we can't resale it because of the snags on the border. So, I'm sure Grand-nan won't mind. And I'll just buy it outright if she gets fussy."

"Thank you, Stevie." He definitely had his thoughtful moments, and he had to be tired by now.

She fluffed out the coverlet, and they sat down, facing one another, before scattering the collected ingredients.

"My, my, my, looks like you're pretty experienced in this particular spell."

"Yes, Auntie has taught me well. Mostly through her grimoires, which I've incessantly studied over the years."

Sprinkle. Sprinkle.

"Though, I haven't used it for myself … and maybe I should have." An image of Shane coming in for a sensual kiss popped into her mind. Frustrated, she shook her head.

"Wow! What was that?" Stevie asked.

"Just clearing my mind."

"In an Etch-a-Sketch sorta way."

She pictured what Stevie must have seen from his vantage and laughed at her own quirkiness. If she ended up like Auntie, the trend of her current path, that would be fine by her.

Sprinkle. Sprinkle.

After scattering a blend of jasmine tea leaves and dry powdered apricot onto a double-folded autumn equinox altar scarf, she unscrewed the dropper from a small vial of botanical oil.

"Wait, what is that?" Stevie put his fingertips on the bottle and adjusted it to his sight. "Adam and Eve oil? Do we carry this stuff?"

"No, it's a special blend Candace gave Auntie. She makes it only for personal use. A secret recipe."

"What's in it?"

"Well, the glass cylinder at home looks to be a blend of minced orange peel … hibiscus flowers … lavender. Here, smell." She held the vial up toward his nose.

"Uh-huh. I smell patchouli … and lemongrass."

"Wow, I didn't catch the lemongrass." She smelled the blend again, inhaling the pleasant natural scents. "Good call. Anyway, I know she puts other roots and herbs in it, too. Funny enough, this stuff is hoodoo, so pretty powerful."

"In-teresting," Stevie said, cautiously pushing her hand away with his eyes cast sideways.

"Oh, also, a few thin slices of apple in my home jar."

"Oh, Adam, you poor sap."

She smirked at his humor. "Well, apple is actually more than forbidden fruit from the Garden of Eden. You use it to send healing energy to a loved one, or in this case, a friend. Trini is worried about something. Why else would she keep the baby news to herself? The good energy will help her worry less … or whatever it is she's withholding."

She usually appreciated Stevie's remarks, but they were beginning to distract her. "Anyway, where was I?" She released a few oily homemade drops onto the herbs.

"One more thing."

"Yes, Stevie?" Maybe she should have done this spell alone.

"Is this black magick? Because Grand-nan said that when you do something that makes someone else do something, it's black magick." He nodded his thirty-something-year-old head like a diligent third grader with an excerpt from the day's lesson. "She did say that."

"Well, I look at it this way. We all have free will. Right?"

"Right."

"So, we … you and I … set an intention for positivity and good will for our friend. It's her choice to receive it or not."

Stevie hesitated. "Still feels a tad invasive to me, especially since she didn't ask for it."

"We don't force it down her throat or anything. Anyway, I categorize this as white or light magick. We send a positive vibe her way, hoping it improves her life. If we're effective … and the spell works."

"Got it," he said, eyeing the herbal mound spattered with oil.

His questions surprised her. "Stevie, aren't you a witch? I mean … your Grand-nan is the high priestess of my Auntie's coven. Isn't she?"

"I think she and Bethie share the lead. And the extent of my witchcraft is meditation with Quartz in front of Buddha."

"Really?"

"Oh, sweetie, I'm too busy to delve into Grand-nan's world of magick. But I'm all for some fun, now and then."

Bowing out now would be too awkward.

"Honest, I'm *totally* into this." He placed his hand on her shoulder and looked into her eyes. "I swear, okay? No more joking. I'd love to help Trini."

"Mmm-kay." The magick of the moment fell flat, but she continued through the motions, tossing the oil and herbs like a miniature garden salad, making it into a loose paste. Working through her deflated energy, she thought of herself as Stevie's teacher, prompting her enthusiasm to return. "Okay, let's do this. Which is your dominant hand?"

He held up his right.

She grabbed the wallet-sized, carnation-pink organza bag she had taken from their surplus and readied it by the herbs. "I owe us two dollars for this."

He dismissively shook his head. "Don't worry about it."

Next, she took a thin, heart-shaped slice of Rose Quartz and held it up. "Okay, this will go between our hands. Press firmly, and don't let up, okay?"

"You got it." An improved attitude and prompt responses confirmed his interest.

She felt her excitement return as she pressed the stone into his right hand, then pressed her left hand onto his, sealing the stone between them. She led them in rotating their joined hands upward, suspending them above the herb mixture.

"Remember, to keep an even, firm press."

"I will."

"Okay, close your eyes, and let's slow our breathing."

She exaggerated her breath's volume so that Stevie could find the rhythm.

"Now envision Trini." She softened her energy. "Our dear friend, Trini, deserves happiness during this most precious time of a woman's life."

"Happiness," Stevie softly echoed.

"She deserves the warmth of being a mother and the joy that new life brings."

"Joy," he repeated.

"And we want to protect her from the woes that make her heart ache."

"No woes."

"Above all, let love flow for this woman, her baby, and her partner."

She waited for Stevie's contribution.

"Lotsa love."

Feeling an amused smirk coming on, she inhaled it away to refocus on her intention. "Feel the warming of the crystal in our hands and let us send it into the universe as true love, uniting for this friend and sending her this blessing. May she receive it at will. So may this be."

She slowly scooped Stevie's hand, rotating it upward. The stone was now securely on top of her flat palm.

"You can let go," she whispered.

He lifted his hand away, and she picked up the heart with her forefinger and thumb and held it for a second in reverence.

Then it fell.

"Oops." *What a rookie misstep.*

Immediately upon landing on the soft pile below, the Rose Quartz heart broke into two large, even pieces.

They stared in silence.

"Uhhh, how the heck did that break?" Stevie asked, cutting his eyes a sharp right.

"I don't know." She felt insecure about the symbolism.

"Well?" Stevie's tone suggested a bit of trepidation for consequences.

"I've never had that happen. And it's a soft landing. Maybe a flaw in the cut?"

"Well, that's a bit of an unclimactic ending. Or maybe *really* climactic! Does it mean our good vibe was checked with an assertive— *Back the eff off!*"

Crystals were supposed to hold their mystical value even if they broke. At least, that's what Auntie had taught her. But what if it happened during spell work, with trouble already hindering the person? Could a flawed spell make things worse?

"Let's just complete it. Auntie says that crystals hold their value, broken or not." She maintained her nonchalance. Stevie would not see her sweat this.

She took the broken heart and put it inside the mesh pink sack, followed by the herbal paste. After tying the pull-strings, the package was ready for placement. "So now we let this simmer." She stood up. "Where to put it?" She clicked her tongue and scanned the backroom.

"How about under the register since she comes into the store?"

"Great idea!"

Stevie led her to the front, taking partnership in their ritual. "It'll be our little secret right there under her nose."

"Yes! I can't wait till she comes in again."

CHAPTER 12
MY LITTLE TREASURE BETHIE

The early morning came too soon after a night of restless sleep. Intrigued by Auntie's announcement of their mysterious trip, Arista had awoken twice in the wee hours, staring into the darkness, wondering if the time had truly come. By the nervousness in her stomach, she knew the trip would be life changing, especially with the mystery Auntie had kept about it. Painfully obvious after a lifetime of upbringing, she trusted Auntie, and knew clarity awaited her.

Ready to go, she stopped in the kitchen to pour herself a travel mug of well-steeped blackberry sage tea when she noticed the spoon holder by the stove top had broken into two large, even pieces. A little nip in her psyche compared the even break to the Rose Quartz mishap during her and Stevie's love spell.

"Auntie, your spoon holder broke," she yelled to Auntie.

Auntie hustled into the kitchen, Wally trotting behind her, his striped tail held high. "I can get another. We've to get moving." Still, she stopped and gave a scrutinizing look to the mama fox and her kit perfectly separated from the break. "It does ring a little odd. Hmph."

"Wally?" Arista asked, eyeing the slim feline below her, thinking of his high-strung antics. At least the consideration of him as a culprit could set her mind at ease of universal messages.

"Hah! If it was Wally, it'd be in pieces all over the floor." She looked down at her pet. "Huh, Mr. Wallace?"

Wally mistook the attention as an invitation to jump on the counter, whereupon Auntie tapped his haunch with a *Psst! Psst!*, sending him back to the floor.

Not the answer Arista wanted, sending her fret bubbling forth. "Auntie, really quick … I'm worried about a love spell I cast for a friend. Toward the end of it, the Rose Quartz we were using broke in half."

Auntie cocked her head. "We?"

"Stevie and I."

"Stevie? Is he doing magick now?"

She did not want to talk about Stevie and his magick dabblings. "No. Not really. But anyway, we did a little love spell for my friend Trini." Her troubled mind needed fast relief that the spell had not been a bad idea … as Stevie had mentioned.

"Did she request this spell from you?"

Oh, no. Arista felt her already-compromised energy quickly collapsing from lack of sleep and now intensifying guilt. "Not really. Don't you and Pearl do spells for people without asking?" She knew they had and remembered the stories well.

"It's best to ask permission first. Even better, let them come to you. Pearl and I learned that the hard way."

Auntie's response vexed her even more, as did the insidious, diplomatic scolding from her long-time teacher. But the story had to be told. "Immediately after the spell, the crystal fell just a couple inches onto a soft bed of herbs and *split* in a perfect diagonal half … like this spoon rest." She looked at the broken illustration of motherhood and dreaded the implications. She felt a small urge to cry, but the lack of tears denied her relief. "Now, I see this image of a mama fox and her kit broken in half, and I wonder if it represents anything." She grimaced, giving in to her reality. "I'm just hoping I didn't make a complicated situation worse."

"Well, I've broken many a crystal by accident over the years, and I don't recall it ever crimping the spell." Auntie dazed, pondering. "Nope." She patted Arista's arm. "Don't worry. It's unnerving when you mar a tool, but it should be fine."

Arista sighed a half breath of respite. Still, it did not feel right.

"Anyway, we need to get going!" Auntie led the charge toward the front door, keys jingling in hand.

Arista grabbed her tea and left the mystery of the halved spoon rest behind her.

The sleepiness of the artsy desert town at dawn made for an uncommon experience. Different from her usual mid-morning commute, the cars on the road were few as they headed down the main strip. While the streets were clear, the sky held *more* activity than usual. Above them, in the distance, rose a bulbous, vibrant, yellow hot-air balloon pushing upward in a slow ascent. Four heads bobbled within its brown woven basket, gawking at all below them. Gradually, it drifted into an air current.

Farther north, they drove. What really surprised her were the tall pine trees. "I didn't know this road was so green. In a way, it looks like California."

"Yes, it is different, isn't it?" Auntie's gaze stayed glued to the road.

As they passed Slide Rock State Park, she noticed little white, rose-like flowers growing out of the crevices of the gigantic blocky red rocks, haphazardly stacked along the highway like a child's building blocks in a messy playroom. "What are those little white flowers called?"

"Not sure," Auntie said without eye contact.

"Wow, it's crazy to think they grow up from between twenty-feet-tall rocks. Where's the water source? Are their little delicate roots that long?" With no response, she looked at Auntie, wondering if she heard what she had said.

And so, it went for miles. Indifferent to conversation, Auntie kept her remarks to soft, disengaged harrumphs.

They emerged from the double-sided canyon, prompting Arista to look out her window and gauge the steepness of the cliff. Unsettling. "Wow. This drop … I know we have our own abyss in the mountains back home, but to actually see it without the distraction of trees gives you no sense of security." She paused and scrutinized the continuing guardrail. "At least that barrier's pretty thick." She looked at Auntie for acknowledgment.

Auntie clutched the steering wheel with a white-knuckle grip.

"You okay, Auntie?"

"Sure," Auntie said, attention to the road intact.

Minutes elapsed as the road hummed. The landscape alternated from cliff to desert to roadside tourist traps and back to a mountainous highway again.

Breaking the trend of silence, Auntie spoke. "Arista … this is a very important trip. I'll tell you now that I knew nothing about it until after your ordeal with that beast in Boulder Creek." Auntie's matter-of-fact demeanor broke into a whimper. "Oh, Arista."

"What?" she asked, alarmed by the desperation in Auntie's voice.

"I'll never forget my adorable eight-year-old Arista," Auntie shot a quick glance over at her, "but I know you're a young woman now … twenty-five, as of last month!"

"A full quarter of a century," Arista said with a chirp. She would ignore the uncomfortable possibilities of what awaited her as long as possible.

Auntie's eyes teared.

In most circumstances, she would immediately tend to Auntie's emotions—asking her what was wrong, handing her a tissue, and duplicating Auntie's tears in her own eyes. Today felt different. She looked out her window, calming her own rising nerves. It would be okay to be reunited with *them*.

· · ·

Bethie navigated the prolonged meandering of the highway until a sign welcomed them to Flagstaff. She noticed Arista had gotten a lot quieter. Surely, as bright and intuitive as she was, she knew the grand surprise that awaited her. Yet, she had kept Arista protected from premature exposure to truth. For this moment, perfect timing mattered.

"Can I turn on some music?" Arista asked, already reaching for the cord.

"Of course. Nothing too crazy."

"Auntie, I listen to mostly our witchy tunes and seventies rock. Not much *crazy* in those genres."

"Hah!" Bethie felt a brief lifting of her anxiety and enjoyed the laugh. She watched Arista plug in her smartphone and make her selection. Keenly listening for those first musical notes, she expected to recognize the selected tune. The bass came first, then the notes. Aah! A rhythmic witchy song by a group she had seen in concert a few times. "Oh! I like this one!"

"I love it! Probably because mainstream didn't burn it out." Arista rocked her shoulders from side to side as the intro built. Then, the words emerged in a controlled contralto voice.

"*Incant … silence…*," Arista sang along.

"Intense."

Arista stopped. "What?"

"She says *intense* … not incant."

"I thought she said '*incant.*'"

"Nope."

"You mind if I start it over?"

"Of course."

She reset the song. Bass. Notes. Lyrics.

"*Intense … silence …* " Arista sang while looking over at her, smiling.

Bethie sang along too, more settled with her nervousness. Still, withholding the mystery was nearly impossible. What if she just blurted out the destination? She felt the bubble of confession rising, then quelled it. Because everything in due time, and she needed Ian to be a part of the reveal. But the struggle she felt with this process had her so anxious. Maybe Henry's blow to her head and the resulting concussion *had* increased her flightiness, as Pearl and Candace had occasionally mentioned.

As the song came to a close, Arista lowered the music. "Are you okay? Do you want to talk about something?"

"Maybe a little jittery from the caffeine." No sense for them both to fret.

Deeper into their trip, Arista's playlist began its second cycle as they arrived at Highway 40. They passed the colorful sign and green athletic fields of Northern Arizona University. Hard to believe it lay covered in snow during the coldest time of year.

Arista eyed the grassy lawns of the sports field. "Maybe I should have gone to a four-year."

"It's never too late. Just depends on your aims."

"I think I like taking random classes at community better."

"Then that will suffice for now."

"So, how far *are* we going today?"

"It's probably another forty-five minutes."

"Wait … are we on Route 66?!" Arista asked, glimpsing a passing road sign.

"Sort of. It's a part of the historic route, but they updated and renamed it in the mid-eighties. The actual Route 66 branches off past where we'll be turning." She appreciated their journey had proven abundant in sightseeing moments for Arista.

Another city disappeared behind them as they drove through more mountains and desolation. Worried about Arista's forthcoming reaction, she looked over at her.

"Auntie!" Arista yelled, her face frozen in terror, eyes wide, looking out the windshield.

Bethie swung her view forward and slammed hard on the brakes as a bushy-tailed coyote bolted directly in front of them. They screamed as the car slid sideways. Tires screeching and skidding uncontrollably until all came to a sudden jolting stop.

The coyote narrowly avoided the hit. Safely across the road, it flung its head to look over its shoulder at them. With Bethie gawking at the creature, it tipped its head back, opened its mouth, and let out a bossy yip, insulted by her lack of caution, before zigzagging its way deep into the desert shrubs.

Bethie relented with a huge huff. Thankfully, she had missed the kill, as neither of them needed to see smashed coyote.

"*Cad é sin*?!" Arista shouted.

Bethie heard the strange words, and they triggered an effect. Though what, she did not yet know. She looked at Arista and was shocked to see her in an upright and rigid posture, emitting a peculiar mannerism.

"*What is it*?!" Arista said in a raspy voice, staring blankly through the windshield.

The voice rumbled out of her grandniece's throat, sounding drastically different from usual. And those initial foreign words she had uttered … the long-forgotten, Irish tongue from Bethie's childhood.

Arista slammed her hands on the dashboard and swung her head toward Bethie. She froze before her expression softened into an odd smile.

"What did you say?" Bethie asked, stunned.

"*Bethie, a stóirín*," Arista said in a gravelly voice. Gradually, the tension in her shoulders diminished as she slowly fell back against her seat. "A *stóirínnn* …" Arista collapsed against her door window, hair tussled over her face.

Bethie could not move an inch. It was impossible. Unheard of! Those words from that voice had not reached her ears since childhood, nor had her beloved grandfather addressed her so endearingly for such a long time.

Beep! Beep!

A car approached them with caution. "You two okay in there?" the friendly man asked, muted by the closed window.

She waved and mouthed a *thank you* to the good Samaritan while pulling to the shoulder. She turned off the engine and took a deep breath to gather her wits.

Arista groggily came to. "Did I seriously just faint again?" Worry filled her face, and she scanned the area around them. "The coyote! Is it okay?"

"The coyote is happily running through the desert. Arista, has this happened before?" Bethie remained mesmerized, remembering the voice of her grandfather coming from Arista's mouth.

"Yes, it happened in the shop a couple weeks back. I told you I thought I had fainted … remember?"

"Yes, but I didn't know you *actually* fainted."

"I did."

"Arista …" Bethie took in a deep breath and held it a moment. "My dear, I believe my grandfather just spoke through you." She sat dumbfounded amid her befuddled emotions struck by that endearing phrase—*My Little Treasure, Bethie*—uttered to only her as she sat on his knee for a root beer barrel or cinnamon disk from his lead crystal candy dish. "What do you feel during these fainting spells?"

"Well, I feel faint, of course, but then this energy surge … happens. Not like my visions last year—those just felt heavy and threatening. These are different. I'm in this realm of abstract lines and … like … neon colors." Arista paused, looking inward, calculating her experience. "There's no sound, and I can't move or anything. I just wait for it to pass. But I remember it really clearly. Very kaleidoscope-y."

"Oh, my …" Bethie felt the stark expression on her face and blinked it away to lighten the mood.

"Is this another power?" Arista asked, her eyes animated after the long ride.

"Let's just say this is shaping up to be a hell of a day!"

Bethie restarted her car and checked the side-view mirror. She exhaled a relieving puff of tension as she gunned the engine back onto the empty highway. "One *helluva* day!"

Chapter 13
Madhouse of Teeming Foodies

Beautiful ocean-side Capitola swarmed with boisterous families, enthusiastic couples, and spry retirees bent on enjoying the good life of a glorious Saturday. Other than a slight breeze drifting in from the fifty-seven-degree salt water, no signs of the colder season to come existed. The sun beat down with a cloudless glare, but the resulting temperature stood satisfactorily to the hothouse flowers of California's central coast, who thrived on perfect weather.

Maddie and Evan strolled along the often-congested parking area abutting the sandy beachfront. Temporarily closed to all vehicles, makeshift booths lined the area, allowing attendees to peruse the quality offerings of art, wines, and miscellaneous wares.

"Oh wow! Is that Pink Umbrella Man?" Maddie excitedly pointed to a person strolling past a booth displaying ultra-clear still shots on aluminum of Santa Cruz Landmarks.

The object of interest stood dressed in a carnation pink dress and shoes beneath a fringed pink parasol. It rang very close to a former local celebrity of sorts.

Striking Evan's curiosity, he looked away from the artist live-painting a version of Capitola's colorful beachside bungalows. With eyebrows lifted, he awaited further clues. "Maybe."

Together, they gawked and waited for the person to turn around, revealing if it was, in fact, the Santa Cruz legend dating as far back as 1999. A self-proclaimed former NASA engineer, he had left the rat race behind and battled his depression by giving downtown crowds a show of his pink-embellished, amusing caricature.

But a slight pivot toward the vendor revealed a woman in her golden years with a head of white, salon-styled hair. A classic bouffant, surely the envy of all her pinocle friends.

"She had me for a minute," Evan said. "Though when I didn't see the pom-pom boa, I kind of figured it wasn't him."

"Whatever happened to that guy?"

"I think he still lives here. A little ahead of his time back then. These days, I don't think he'd get half the attention."

Maddie chuckled. "Definitely not the angry attention. Hey, I'm done here. You ready?"

"Starving!"

They left the hubbub of Capitola's Art & Wine Festival behind them, and trudged up the inclined avenue, passing the police station, and several shops and homes of lucky residents who delighted in the ocean, walking-distance from their front door.

Finally, they arrived at a four-way stop sign, their destination just across the street. Home to the black-and-white checkered bags that could contain any combination of delicious ready-made foods—Chicken Diavolo, twice-baked potatoes, penne d'alba, a slice of Princess cake or, as everyone knew, Arista's favorite bear claw.

Inside the madhouse of teeming foodies, Maddie cranked the free-standing red lever to reveal her number. She showed it to Evan. "Sixty-four." She grimaced, looking at the digital counter. "They're on forty-one. This is gonna take for-ev-er."

"It goes fast," Evan consoled, already eyeing the delectable possibilities.

"Oh … my …. Gawd."

"What?" Evan asked, yet remained focused on the cold case.

"He's already dating!" Though emphasized, Maddie's voice stayed hushed to avoid a scene, but she felt her anger rising.

Outside on the patio, Shane sat across from a maddeningly gorgeous blonde. Her shoulder-length beach-swept hair lay perfectly mussed against her evenly bronzed skin, and her shining smile was almost as white as the macrame halter top that came to a point just below her breast line, exposing toned abs and a gold belly ring.

"Are you fricken kidding me? Bitch."

Evan looked up, surprised by the profanity. He grit his teeth when he saw the source of her disquiet, then relaxed. "Okay, let's not jump to conclusions. There's obviously two other people. Look at the place settings."

"Lame excuse. And where are they?"

"I don't know." He scanned the strangers milling around them in the disorganized crowd, awaiting their number to be called. "Maybe they decided they wanted something else to eat."

Miffed by the entire episode, she looked at the digital counter. "Good Gawd, Evan, they're only on forty-five. I don't want to wait another minute. This is totally awkward and actually ... terrible. It's going to crush Arista."

Evan's eyes bugged. "Why would you tell her? You don't even know the whole story."

"Of course, I'm going to tell her!"

Evan scoffed. "What if you're overreacting?" He returned his interest to the golden halved baguettes filled with ham, salami, and cheddar cheese.

She flashed a quick look, only to make eye contact with Shane. "Dammit! He just saw me."

"I think I'm getting the Italiano Ficelle."

"Evan! Shane saw me."

"Cool! After our order, we can go say *hi* before we leave. He'll probably introduce us, and we'll see it's no big deal."

"No way." She wadded the number and took it to the trash. "Please, let's just go."

"C'mon! What happened to your hunger? Mine's still raging."

"*Please!*" she said with utter restraint between gritted teeth.

Evan rolled his eyes.

His irritation held no clout, and he could get Shane's input on his own time. She barged toward the back door.

Evan followed, lagging behind like a kid dragged from the toy section by their parent, grousing with every step.

As they exited through the narrow hallway, a man emerged from the restroom, separating them and bumping into Evan. She kept going but heard the conversation.

"Oh, hey, Mr. Stoddard!" Evan said with renewed energy.

"Evan, great to see ya, son!" Shane's dad gave him a firm smack on his arm. "Shane's on the patio!"

She listened to Evan apologize for his current rush, and that he would catch up with Shane later. When he arrived outside, she greeted him with crossed arms. "'Bout time."

"That was ridiculous. What's your problem? Why couldn't you at least say *hi* to Shane's dad?"

Now, Evan sounded like a scolding parent with his rapid-fire admonishment, and that pissed her off even more. "Are you kidding me? I can't talk to him right now. Arista's heartbroken and Shane's with some blond chick having a good ol' time."

"As I said, you don't know the whole story."

"Oh, do you?"

"No, but—"

"I know he sure looked entertained." She held her indignant stance and solid stare, daring for a counter remark. "Anyway, let's just grab Dairy Queen."

Evan deflated. "What? Leave the gourmet deli for fast food?" He whined his contempt. The child again.

She paid no attention and led them across the street, looking back with one last context. "And seriously, wouldn't you want me to let *you* know if I found Bree lunching with some hot guy?"

That shut him up.

•   •   •

Another forty-five minutes landed Arista and Bethie at an industrial-sized welcome sign designed upon a massive slab of the rose-colored sedimentary rock—*Welcome to Ashfork, Flagstone Capital of U.S.A.*

Arista sighed at the heat, her sore butt, and the burrowing wedgy from their never-ending ride. The songs had grown tiring, yet she had no interest in changing them. With the anticipation diminished, all she wanted was to be home in jersey pajamas with Royal on her lap. At this point, even Sedona sounded good.

"It's just down this road. I know you're anxious," Auntie said, then huffed. "I am, too. I gotta say my heart is thumpin' a mile a minute."

She looked at their vastly barren scenery, the flat desert, and the very distant mountains. Even the usual cacti and scrub brush became sparse, looking like leftovers from a warehouse plant sale.

In the far distance off the highway, she noticed a small block of four houses on extra-large parcels. An oasis of life amongst the miles of aridness. Before she could inquire, Auntie cleared her throat.

"Okay, that's it." Auntie pointed to the distant house.

"Mmm-huh. I see it." Arista's stomach turned. As a thought of its meaning came to mind, she snuffed it.

A couple turns later, Auntie pulled up to a small gate connecting the scant effort of barbed wire fence that surrounded the property. The little home sat another eighty feet up the makeshift driveway. Auntie hoisted herself out of the car and rolled the gate's combination lock to an appropriate order, then opened the entryway to the day's mystery.

Arista's heart thumped, and she felt its vibration in her throat. She attempted to swallow the discomfort. Obviously, Auntie's nervousness had meaning. Nothing really stirred her other than serial killers and villainous uncles, of course. But this was something else. If not common sense, intuition dictated there remained only one thing they needed to face together. If it was the uncle, Auntie would be spitting venom, heavily stirred, and downright pissy. But she held an air of excitement and anxiousness, like a child waiting in line for Santa—wary of the odd stranger in a brash red suit but looking forward to the gifts he brought.

Auntie hopped back in and drove through the gate. "Can you clasp the lock behind us … and scramble the code too, please?"

"Sure." Arista got out of the car and enjoyed the stretch while discreetly readjusting her cotton thong. The temperate autumn desert breeze held a welcome distraction to her rising anxiety and cooled her heated limbs and face.

She looked farther up the property. True to the town's sign, an abundance of tan and light beige flagstone created a small yard in front of the house, similar in size to her own cottage in Boulder Creek. However, it appeared modern with artisanal detail and a rich maple stain rather than the charm of the mid-1900s. In front, two maple-stained patio chairs and a chiminea shaped like a genie bottle overlooked the property.

She walked toward the car, glancing at the home's many wind chimes made from various materials—glass and different weights of metal—hanging from the eave. There was also a surrounding deck that looked like loving, wooden arms hugging the home and its occupants.

Back in the car, she felt Auntie's stare upon her. She tried to avoid the look and felt uncomfortable with the expression's meaning. Finally, she turned to Auntie. "What?" she asked, immediately feeling guilty for her spark of irritation.

Auntie drove her Outback in a crawl and stopped in front of the house by a colorful planter box with cacti boasting incoming blooms of a vibrant pinkish-red.

Then, out of the front door, walked a hauntingly familiar man.

CHAPTER 14
SELF-CONTROL FADING BY THE MOMENT

Cough. Cough.

Fresh from the gym, Mike's exertion, blended with the damp city air created havoc for his lungs. No matter what the season, his recent move to San Francisco had proven a chance of hovering fog above the city on any given day. The moist air would send him into bouts of coughing that had people glaring at him. No, he was not spreading the post-pandemic C-word. His hack signified the pulmonary inflammation he still carried from a former five-year stint of smoking.

"Get that cough checked, man."

He already had, and it made no difference.

Mike and his friend strolled toward his house, where they would fill the weekend afternoon with video games and a few brewskis, priming themselves for a night of partying at the clubs. Before long, they arrived at the small neighborhood cemetery.

Out of the corner of his eye, Mike saw a flash of white. Just in time, he witnessed a child dressed in white slip behind a headstone.

His friend shot a glance over to the source of his interest. "What is it?"

"There's a little kid in the cemetery." Mike stopped and stared.

"Probably lives around here." His friend threw a dismissive wave in the general direction and kept walking.

Mike scanned the cemetery, then looked up at the many second and third-story windows surrounding them to see if anyone stood watching.

His friend scoffed and said, "I'm telling you, there's all sorts of feral kids around this city. Some parents just don't care. Let's go."

"Pfft, that's messed up, man."

Swiftly, the child shot from behind one headstone and hurried to another.

"You see that? Doesn't feel right." He led them into the peaceful setting of the greenest grass and lushest trees that, on a much smaller scale, could rival the city's Golden Gate Park. Picking up to a small jog, he scanned the serene backdrop that housed many headstones adorned in fresh-cut flowers and silk floral arrangements well past their purchase date.

Another flash of white.

Mike looked in the vicinity she had just run. "Hello?"

The child darted to another stone farther from them than he calculated.

Carefully, he walked the grassy lawn, not stepping upon forbidden areas of those who had left this lifetime. One after another, he peered around each grave, looking for the elusive kid. A tall marble obelisk held the prize. He found … *her* sitting against the stone structure. He looked at his friend and conveyed his worry. "It's a little girl. I'm telling you, she looks lost. Don't you think?" He squatted down, feet away from her, held out his hand and calmly spoke. "Hey … are you okay?"

His friend tugged on his shoulder. "Come on! If her parents see this, they're gonna think we're harassing her!" He paused. "Then again, she's seriously got that feral look."

Mike glared at his friend, pissed at the boldly rude behavior right in front of her. He mouthed for him to shut up, then quietly uttered, "Not cool. This could be my niece."

"Oh, come on. No way."

Mike eased the tension in his face after dealing with his friend's jadedness and re-approached his question while keeping a safe distance. "Do you need help?"

She cast a glance up at his friend.

His friend peered down at her, then blew out an exasperated raspberry and crossed his arms.

She glowered, lowered her chin, and looked back at Mike.

"It's okay," Mike said. Slowly, he reached out his hand, but another bronchial tickle overtook him.

Cough! Cough.

In a flash, she launched up and bolted farther into the cemetery.

His friend snickered from behind him.

Mike stood up, pissed. "That was you. Look at that look on your face. She doesn't feel safe."

His friend's eyebrows incredulously lifted. "Me? Like hell! That was *you* coughing in her face." He punctuated his declaration with a laugh.

Mike shook his head in disappointment. "You better hope there's not an Amber Alert for her!"

"I didn't say anything."

"You didn't have to. Your bitch-ass look said it all."

•   •   •

Arista sat in the passenger seat, feeling the man's gaze upon her, but refused to look at him. The subtle butterflies in her stomach became agitated bees. Where did this angst come from? She knew what the visit entailed. Had felt it in her bones, like the assuredness of a coming storm. And she *had* felt fine … even confident about meeting them. But every mile farther from Auntie's house brought on a pebble of insecurity. And resentment. What made *now* the right time, and why did they get to choose? Now, all her pebbles held a boulder's weight.

From her peripheral, she saw him step off of his porch. She sat in silence, her stomach churning.

Auntie walked around the car and opened her door. She gently pulled Arista from the car. "You ready?" She draped her arms around her and walked them toward the house.

Arista kept her gaze down and avoided eye contact with him. The stranger.

"Arista, I love you," Auntie said in a murmur. "I haven't said that often enough, but you know I do. Today is going to be an experience. But, at this point, it is important to just rip this Band-Aid off."

"I know," she conceded. But hardly able to breathe, she changed her mind about meeting him.

Reaching the first level of flagstone, she finally glanced at him, the one who abandoned her. She felt annoyance at his growing smile.

"Hello," the man said, his voice kind.

No! Not that voice. She hoped for words from Auntie, something to provide guidance … anything to take away her anger or quell the rising resentment.

Or was it heartache?

"I'm so happy to see you, Riss." He cocked his head, trying to make eye contact.

Maybe it was love, a missing love that ached to her core.

"We finally made it," Auntie said.

As Auntie made small talk with the man, she felt her tears forcing their way through her attempted, hardened exterior. Her eyes swelled, and her body felt an internal tremble. As logic and rationale turned surreal at the sight of him, she felt her face scrunching, ready to release an awful sob. She *had* to hold it together.

"I'm sure it was quite a drive," he said.

Every word out of his mouth made her cringe. His voice, painful to hear.

As they walked up to him, her self-control felt flimsy, like waterlogged paper. Finally upon him, his arms reached out in a welcoming invitation.

A current of emotion rose from her stomach into her throat and exploded behind her eyes. The tears released like a mountainside's hydro dam, drenching her as she continuously wiped at them. Sniffling brought no relief, and to hold in the volume of her sob took great effort. Her head pounded.

Gently weeping, Auntie guided her into his hug.

The stranger … her father … squeezed her so tightly, so securely, that she felt the tension sapped from her body and collapsed her head onto his shoulder. The love. Strong, plentiful, and finally free to flow. Along with her shuttering sob.

He cupped his hand around her head.

This comfort, along with his scent of pine, bay leaf, and cedarwood, brought back childhood memories of consolation. These arms and their scent had hugged her many times—in happy-birthday and apology hugs, way-to-go and loss-of-a-pet hugs. Hugs that greeted a morning hello and had accompanied a last goodbye.

"I've missed you so much, Riss," he said in a broken voice.

And that name! She realized Shane was not the first to address her like this. Her father had called her *Riss*. How could she have forgotten this?

Her father pulled Auntie in to join in their hug.

"It's good to see you, dear nephew."

He smiled at both of them before his expression turned serious. "Your mother's upstairs. She knows you're here."

Her mother. His tone hit heavy. How sick was she? As they walked the distance of the makeshift driveway, her angry bees settled into butterflies once more. Upon the porch, she looked down at the cheerful coconut fiber door mat painted with white-spotted, dark red mushroom caps. A cute distraction from her aching heart.

"Riss, I have to tell you … she's very sick."

She nodded, then looked back at Auntie, who dabbed her tears with a well-worn, pocketed tissue.

Auntie reached into her skirt pocket and handed her an extra tissue, scented with eucalyptus.

Entering the home, she found it serenely quiet, save for the sixty-gallon aquarium that gurgled against the farthest wall. A magickal underwater kingdom shone beneath the fluorescent lighting—black pebbles mixed with sporadic purple nuggets covered the tank's base, and Amethyst spears spiked up from the manmade hills. Charoite boulders and Lepidolite slabs further accessorized the aquatic environment, and throughout the tank, a jungle of grasses, leafy plants, and frilly, waving moss brought a rich, green contrast. Two large angelfish swam near the front glass, their bodies reflecting like silver dollars, and a small school of lively red-and-blue neons darted around, dodging an occasional run-in with a blue-spotted gourami.

Self-soothing her distress, she observed the aquatic pecking order with subtle amusement and grounded herself.

Her father took the lead up the stairs.

She hesitated. The path to her dying mother lay right in front of her, illuminated by the home's skylights. For her mother's sake, she thought of it as a natural path to the Summerland—or perhaps this is what Shane would call a true stairway to Heaven.

At the top of the stairs, her father took her hand and led her into the master bedroom. Her mother faced the window, tucked under a blue-and-white patchwork quilt as if a chilly winter day.

"Keira, Arista's here," her father said in little more than a whisper.

When her mother did not respond, he approached her and lightly placed his hand on her shoulder.

Arista followed suit and felt the lack of solidity in the skin stretched over bone. "Hi, Mom." The gentle ease of greeting her mother surprised her.

Keira made no movement other than the shallow, labored breathing that proved she was asleep.

"I'm so happy to see you," she said. Understanding the frailty of this person who remained but a fraction of the mother she once knew, she kept her volume low and gentle.

Her father gave her a little smile and motioned for her to follow him back to Auntie waiting at the door. Once out of the room, he quietly debriefed them. "Her mornings and nights are mostly sleep, but she may talk a little later this afternoon."

Arista took a huge inhalation, hoping to nourish her lungs after holding her breath for so long. Possibly since she had gotten out of the car. And inside her mind, questions began to accumulate.

As her father led them downstairs, she felt unstable, almost dizzy. How did this fit into an established life? Her entire world felt shaken, even crumbling, and all the stability she had created, now toppled by a schism of upending discovery. She longed for the familiarity of Boulder Creek, for Maddie, Evan, and even Shane. How she would love his hug right now. Above all, she longed to erase the entire past year, including the last twenty minutes.

At the foot of the stairs, her father said something, eliciting a laugh from Auntie, but she did not hear it, nor engage. How could she face this reality? A father, alive and well, and a mother, sick and dying. Had she been in a state of denial her whole life? Maybe she wasn't the *feel-good* person she had perceived herself to be because digesting this massive revelation truly sucked! "Have you been here the whole time?" She let the words blurt out as soon as they entered the living area.

"No." He kept a collected manner. "We have lived many places since we had to say goodbye to you. I'm sure you have many questions. First, would you like some tea? It's fall, and I have a killer chocolate chai. What do you two think? Do you like tea?" He looked over at Auntie for confirmation. "Black tea with a little cocoa, cinnamon, cardamon … cloves?"

"Yes, Ian, that sounds delightful. Thank you," Auntie said, jumping in to offer courtesy in the troubled moment.

He flashed Arista a quick look before jetting off to the kitchen.

Auntie motioned for her to come sit beside her on the puffy dark brown leather sofa arranged cozily by an unlit wood stove.

She obliged, taking the opportunity to further study her parents' dwelling. The surprising touches of witchcraft caught her off guard. For so long, she and Auntie were the only ones to practice the arts, but of course, her parents each had a special supernatural gift. Auntie had told her just last year.

Across from the fish tank in the great room stood a solid, dark walnut altar accented with familiar items: heart-healing, green candles, herbs, and crystals. It also displayed a Labradorite orb as big as a bowling ball. Even at ten feet away, she could vividly see the casting of its orange iridescence.

"You like Labradorite?" she called out to him, surprised they favored the same crystal.

"I do," he said from the kitchen, the sound of a clinking spoon accompanying his voice. "I hear you have a favorite ring of it as well."

How did he know that? She turned to Auntie. "How long have you known they lived here?" Though she released the question with annoyance, she needed to keep respect for the only family member who *had* stuck with her.

"I started searching in December, just before we moved. We finally connected by phone a short time back, and last week, was our first meeting. Remember, dynamics sparked the whole exodus, and they still exist. So, please … just be patient, and let it unfold." She ended the statement with a reassuring expression—pursed lips and a slight flicker of her eyelids. And after all these years, she still trusted Auntie's process.

Her father reentered the room with a tray bearing the same solid stoneware mugs that Auntie had, though different in designs. He handed her one imprinted with a blue cat.

"I hear you have a Siamese now … finally got that kitty you always wanted, huh?"

Irritated, she flinched at his knowledge of Royal while she knew little about him. "Yes, Bethie got Royal for me when I graduated high school."

Auntie flashed a surprised look at her, probably triggered by the rare usage of her first name. After a brief side eye back to Auntie, her rising testiness became averted by the scent of chocolate chai. Its rich, delicious aroma wafted up to her face within the rising steam. She kept the appreciation to herself and thought of how ill her mother looked upstairs. Why hadn't they created this reunion when she was healthier?

"Nice move, Bethie," he said while handing her a mug with a great horned owl. "And how's Margaret been?"

"She's as reclusive as ever … but a tough ol' bird," Auntie said with a wry smile and chuckle.

He snickered and took the remaining mug—a white snowman against a navy-blue canvas dotted with snowflakes—then set the tray aside.

"A little unseasonal, don't you think?" Arista said, her seldom-experienced sarcasm exposing itself.

He looked at the mug and smiled. "Well, it's just me and your mother, and we have two regular mugs and two Yule mugs."

"Hmph. So, whose is whose?"

"I got the owl, and your mother got the cat because it reminded her of you. You have always loved cats."

Her mother. Her frail and sickly mother. Feeling a jolt of guilt for her testy behavior, she put the mug up to her nose, then took a sip. "This is really good. Thank you." She let the warmth of her beverage melt the iciness she felt toward her father. Time had come to let go and embrace the valuable lesson to be learned.

"So, your mother has struggled with cancer over the past two years. They killed it once, but then it came back. Again, it went into remission. But this time, it's—"

"Is she going to die?" she asked, shunning the emotion.

"Arista," Bethie said, gently scolding, her head atilt in disappointment.

Another tinge of shame. "I'm sorry. I don't mean it rudely … I'm just asking." Her principles. She had to maintain her principles.

"I'm afraid this may be her final …" He looked away, choking back tears.

"How long does she have?" She felt a renewed gentleness rise within her.

He hesitated. "Not long at all." He cleared his throat. "Riss, we are so very sorry for all the years we've been gone. I know Bethie has filled you in on the reasons. That we trusted your uncle, but he betrayed us all."

"Yes." Removing herself from hurt, pain, resentment, and even sadness, she objectively considered his words.

"Even now, he has the ability to find her. For your safety, we had to find another way … which led us to Bethie."

"Yes, I know."

"I hope you know it was *only* to keep you safe." He peered at her, unflinching in sincerity.

"I do."

"I wish we could have kept you close, but we couldn't risk it."

She sighed and took another sip. Auntie had talked with her about the details, and how no better option existed.

"When we left Boulder Creek, we went to Taos, but they found us. So, then we moved to Carson City, and they found us there. Finally, we settled here in a trailer, determined to stay put." He scanned the room. "It took me quite a while to build this home for us."

She looked at the ceiling, the walls, the stairwell. A momentary reprieve from emotion. "You built this? Wow, it's really artisanal and … quality. Nice job."

"I appreciate that, Riss. I think it's important I get this story out … okay?"

She nodded for him to continue.

"When we first got here, he sent his people to harass us. At least once a month, your mom would run into them."

"Bastards," Auntie muttered, turning her head away in disgust.

"And I wanted to kill him, Riss. I really did." He adamantly nodded. "But I couldn't justify taking a life based on a dream I had. And the law surely wouldn't honor it. We agreed that my committing murder and going to prison or being on the run was not the legacy we wanted for you or a good life for your mother."

She intently listened with her heart open to the honesty. Time to let her anger go. It served only as an impulsive reaction to the initial shock. Her true self held kindness.

"But once we settled here, your mother got sick. Oddly enough, the tailing stopped shortly thereafter. I think … in a way … she either

sacrificed herself to keep you forever safe," he twisted his mouth, "or …
it was guilt … for leaving you behind." His lips disappeared into a tight,
thin line. "But she doesn't talk much now. So, her reasons remain with
her."

Arista did not know how to respond. How carefully they had
calculated all the angles. And her mother's ultimate sacrifice humbled
her.

"I also decided, after we built this house, that if they came again, I
would kill him. I would not let him harass her anymore, not in her
condition. Sadly, it took finality to bring a resolute answer." His mood
lightened, and he looked at Auntie. "However, when I learned Bethie
had a place in Sedona and wanted us to reconnect, it seemed like the
right time."

Arista felt fully grounded and herself once again. "I'm really sorry
for her. I don't get … this uncle. Our witchcraft embraces good … with
crystals and herbs …," she looked down at her cup of chai, "and tea! It's
loving nature and … cats!" She felt the anger boiling again and, this
time, placed it upon the true cause. "I hate him for ruining our family,
for putting her in this position, for—"

Auntie placed her hand on Arista's knee, stopping the spiral.

She relaxed with a sigh. "But I also can't imagine life without
Auntie. And honestly, I have absolutely loved my life! Auntie is
everything to me."

"We knew she'd be good for you." He looked at his aunt with a
warm smile. "She was always my favorite, especially when my folks
were taken from me. Even adults need their parents … parental figures
… and she stepped up mightily."

Arista knew well of the car accident that claimed her grandparents'
lives. She set down her tea and eased back into the sofa, feeling the
comfort of its pillowy leather like the loving arms of a classic, portly
grandmother.

"This has been a lot." Her father stood up and took the empty mugs
and wadded tissues from in front of his guests. "Why don't we step out
for some fresh air? I'll show you the place, and we can re-approach your
mother a little later."

CHAPTER 15
AS FAINT AS A FLICKER

Forty-five miles from where Arista adjusted to the idea of her long-forgotten parents, a group of shady characters gathered.

Because of their migration habits, it was unusual to see the crimson-skinned heads and nostrils of circling turkey vultures. In case it was anything beyond an unfortunate desert animal, the highway patrol officer radioed her intent to dispatch, then traveled down the isolated fire road to investigate.

As she approached the area of interest, she spotted the rocky mound of a shallow, unmarked grave. Two black-and-brown scavengers bounced atop the heap, insufficient in masking the scent of carrion. These senior members of the committee already staking their claim. Half a dozen more hopped and squabbled at its perimeter, taking turns nearing the crude grave, pecking, then jumping away when another jabbed at its tail feathers.

"This doesn't look good." She radioed for backup, secured her walkie-talkie and baton on her belt, and exited the cruiser. A careful scan proved the area clear of armed villains and dangerous wildlife. Closer, she walked toward the heap, the smell turning harsh. She could see the inept burial, a failed attempt from someone unprepared for the resistance of the hardened desert ground.

"Get! Yahhh!" she hollered, waving her baton to disperse the birds.

The pecking had turned the sandy shake into a mixture of terrain remnants with pasty clumps of blood and torn pink flesh, and wisps of brunette hair blew from between the stacked rocks.

She rounded the small hill and noticed a hand protruding from the stones. She squatted down for a closer look. It appeared to be a woman's—French-manicured, callous-free, and wearing a thick-banded gold and silver ring with a large, reddish-orange stone in the center.

• • •

As the mid-afternoon approached, Ian suggested they attempt to talk with Keira once more. Auntie took a seat at the end of the bed as father and daughter huddled beside Keira.

Her father softly spoke, "Keira, Arista is here to see you."

She touched her mother's shoulder as she stirred. "Hi, Mom."

Keira listlessly turned her head toward Arista, revealing two hollowed eyes with grayish-blue bags beneath them. Her skeletal face showed thin of skin, wan and blue-tinted. She struggled to swallow.

Arista gifted a smile to her mother, feeling love in her heart as their eyes met. The cancer had horribly transformed her, but she would not look away, nor would she let her mother know how it frightened her to see such anguish.

"My … beau … ti-ful … girl," Keira said, breathy and straining for volume.

Instantly, the wetness revisited her eyes. The voice! She remembered that voice from her childhood. As labored as it was, she could hear traces of her mother that she had long kept in memory. She leaned toward her and gave her a soft hug. No bitterness remained. All feelings of being unloved and abandoned diminished.

"She loves you so much, Arista. She wants you to know that," her father said.

Keira tightly closed her eyes as if enduring years of accumulated regret in the single moment. She opened them again. "So … much …

love." She tried to lift her hand toward Arista's face, but her arm could not fulfill the movement and fell back to the bed.

Arista cupped her mother's hand. "I love you, Mom."

Suddenly, Keira froze. Despite her weakened state, her eyes widened with energy as if staring at an inevitable death they could not see.

"Keira, what is it?" her father asked.

Without a word, she closed her eyes in defeat. She struggled with her movement, prompting Arista to release her hand. In a pained, gradual process, and with a bit of her father's help, Keira re-situated herself back toward the wall and closed her eyes.

A hush fell over the room as their eyes locked. What did it mean? If her father thought it surprising, it must be something very unusual.

"I love you, Mom," Arista said again, feeling the threat of finality. Startled by the sudden conclusion of their visit, she was at a loss for words.

Her father draped over his love, holding her in his arms, and talked into her ear with the benevolence and tenderness of one's closest soulmate. "Keira, what is it?"

They all waited for the answer, but her mother remained disengaged.

He looked puzzled but offered an excuse. "It's the disease. Talking is very difficult." But the shiftiness in his eyes suggested his own confusion. He looked at Arista and took her hand while placing his own on Keira's shoulder. "Seeing you today meant everything to her."

Arista stood up and stroked her mother's long, gray hair. It felt like straw. She let her hand linger, then walked toward the door.

Unexpectedly, an odd sensation washed over her. Like the feeling you get as you descend stairs in a spooky house. Someone watched her. As her father and Auntie walked past her toward the door, she stopped and glanced at her mother facing the wall, then a quick scan of the room as they departed.

Auntie noticed her distraction and lifted her brows in question but kept quiet as they paraded out and down the stairs in a solemn hush.

At the front door, the three embraced.

"I don't think I'll let you go this time," her father said during his bear hug.

She endured it, even relaxed into it with a child's acceptance. However, she didn't want to rely on him too heavily. What if she was to lose him again? Inevitably, time neared of her mother's last breath.

He released her and hugged Auntie, who was quick with her plan. "We'll get here weekly. Or anytime you need us."

"Thanks, Bethie."

Arista glanced up to the second level, picturing her mom beneath the blankets and sent her a blessing of comfort. Then she gave her father one last genuine smile before they walked to the car. She hated to admit it, but she was glad to be leaving. She needed to reconcile all of this with Auntie and then alone.

"Just leave the gate open. I'll get it later," he said, leaning on the deck's railing.

"Will do," Auntie said as they lowered into their seats.

And with their farewell, the most extraordinary reunion of deep sentimental value came to an end.

•   •   •

Fergus sat in his hand-carved, high-back mahogany chair, feeling his importance in a room of one. From the large office window, slivers of sunlight struggled to stream in at the border of his blackout blinds. Like a vampire hiding from daylight hours, he tapped his fingernails on the arm of his chair, impatient for when *she* might decide to appear. She, with her laissez-faire whims.

Suddenly, a recognizable sensation washed over him. His heartbeat rose hollowly in his chest. His pulse quickened, and the urge to motivate rushed through his body. What could bring this energy? It had been many years since he felt this high.

He sat forward in his chair.

A notion arose.

"You've *got* to be kidding me." He closed his eyes and held his nose high in the air, inhaling like a wolf detecting a wounded deer. "No." Incredulous of the mere thought, he cried out. "Could it be?"

The door opened. Conn wore an inquisitive scowl, his suspicious eyes implying an offer of help if needed.

"It's okay," Fergus said, energized for the first time in years. "I'm fine. Although, wait … or nevermind, just wait outside." He dismissively waved, remembering he remained in charge. "In fact, shut the door behind you."

Alone again, he hastened to his antique chest, sitting atop two archaic metal file cabinets. He marveled at the possibility while removing its top sectional tray to uncover his sixteen-inch Obsidian obelisk that had sat unused for years.

At the room's center, he sat on the floor, the obelisk before his folded legs. Sitting tall and with steadied breath, he pressed his palms firmly upon the obelisk, he brought it to his chest. Focusing. *Fo-cus-ing.*

With his heart rate rapid from excitement, he could also feel the pulse thump within his thumbs and found the rhythm within the reading.

> *May the opportunity be open, and the glimpse be designed,*
> *May the facts reveal themselves in concept to this mind.*

His eyes rolled behind closed lids. Again, he repeated the chant, delving deeper into concentration. After a brief pause, he opened his mind's eye and found himself in a desert yard. Keira's yard. Drawn through the door and ascending the stairs, he saw her. How deathly she looked. And yet, her spirit soared. So much that it brought him to her. What motivated her long-dormant ambition?

Fergus gripped the cold stone structure in his hands. His blood coalesced within his veins, and the ambiguity thrilled him. A long-forgotten connection made again as he engaged within her mind. Through her eyes, he observed the room and its occupants.

Ian, that hateful bastard.

He hesitated, intimidated by his brother-in-law, but resisted the urge to abandon the vision.

An old bag with ginger, curly hair. Interesting. Perhaps the one Scout reported years ago in the Santa Cruz area. Betsy ... Bessie, something like that. Definitely a witch, based on his sudden obsession with hummingbirds.

Then he saw her. The young woman. He fixated on her, sharpening the focus. But as he honed the visage, as faint as a flicker, he heard Keira's weakened voice and felt the flow of her emotion.

"So ... much ... love."

It was Arista! All the years he had waited, he could clearly see her—youth he no longer had, a natural beauty that he coveted, and an adoring love in her compassionate eyes ... one he felt a desire to destroy. Then, the connection terminated.

Chapter 16
The Dustin Riddle

Sheriff Michaels tapped on his keyboard, wrapping up protocol for his latest DUI arrest. *"Signs of intoxication included breath odor, slurred speech, bleary eyes …"* He paused. The best way to put it? *"… and Mr. Griffin vomiting on my shoes during the Horizontal Gaze Nystagmus sobriety test."*

A ring from the front desk. "Sheriff, I have the Coroner for you."

"Go ahead."

He saved the file for later as another ring announced Jo's call.

"Sheriff, you're gonna love this! I now have a fully assembled Dustin puzzle here on my exam room table, and it's quite the bone collection."

"Yeah?" *Here she goes.*

"Got a random rabbit skull too, but I guess you don't need that." Jo laughed, before bringing forth her best impression of a professional. "Anyway, the body proved quite shattered, though the trunk and skull were intact. Of course, a few neck fractures … and believe it or not, almost all teeth present, so easy to identify him, thanks to that alone. That, and the fact his ID was in the pants pocket of his, literally, bony hips."

For a minute, he thought she could pull it off and grunted in acknowledgment of her twisted humor.

"We still have work left to complete the formal reports, which will take another week."

"Right."

"I've been doing this a long time, Sheriff, and the Dustin puzzle seems to fit together."

"Alright. Any reason I need to come down there?"

"Not unless you miss bio-lab."

"Not in the least."

"Then, you're clear. Just letting you know we have him, and no foul play is evident. Maybe he hit the turn wrong?"

"Hit the turn wrong, huh?" *Maybe* his irritation was primed from the wet, though cleaned, shoes on his feet from the DUI's bodily fluids, but Jo's flippant dismissal after too many poor attempts at humor peeved him. "Mr. Dustin stole evidence, had ties to a serial killer, *and* went off a cliff. Apart from his broken body, they also found dark-red paint chips on his crumpled car at the base of the canyon ... on the bumper and quarter panel."

"I don't know, sheriff. Maybe foul play, or maybe he got too hasty on the getaway, but from what I see, his own car and the terrain beat him to death."

"Okay, Jo ... got it. I gotta go." Futile to discuss the possibilities with Jo, but good for her and her contribution to the Dustin case.

"You bet, Sheriff."

He hung up, sat back in his chair, and tucked his bottom lip up into his gumline. Crinkling his nose, he repeated, "Hit the turn wrong." He snorted at the ridiculous assumption and dialed the front desk. "Patty, have we gotten the security footage from the gas station at the base of Felton Empire Road yet?"

"No. I'll ping 'em again."

"Thank you."

"You got it."

· · ·

Upon returning to Sedona, Arista stared out the car window, alternating between wild thoughts of a life with her parents and befuddled emotions about the importance of them leaving.

Overwhelmed by the incessant musing, she numbed and absorbed mindlessly into a building dust devil whipping around brittle tumbleweeds off in the distance. Her eyes burned, reminding her to blink, so she squeezed them shut, then opened them again, watching the barren desert zoom past. Giving her mind a rest, she had one goal—spot a coyote, a rabbit, or anything to stop thinking.

After miles of silence, and no wildlife, her rumination began again. This time, it came accompanied with stable rationale.

"I cannot believe how much they sacrificed for me."

With her voice breaking the drone of the road noise, Auntie released a breath, then threw her a pleased smile. "I'm so glad you can see that. I hope you're not angry with the way we sprang it on you. I've just been so anxious and thought it important your father be there, too."

"I understand. As for my parents, I see it was their only option, and maybe I always knew that." She looked at Auntie, her heart begging for validation. "Maybe that's why I never asked. You were my family, and that was enough." She felt the assembly of her character—a child of selfless parental love, reared by an amazing woman who took full ownership. "It could be why I look for the silver lining in everything. Poopy times have their purpose? Using manure to make compost? I don't know." She shook her head, trying to resolve a lifetime of questions in this sole moment.

"You're very intuitive, and that sounds about right to me."

"I knew they loved me, and they were in a no-win situation … for all involved. So, I just dug into the family I had." She took a breath of appreciation. "And that was you, Auntie."

Auntie flinched, then fanned at her face, holding back tears to see the road. She reached over and squeezed Arista's hand.

They sat in a comfortable silence as they neared home.

Her mood turned. "I'm *incredibly* angry with this uncle of mine! Where is he?"

Auntie opened her mouth to answer.

"Wait a minute! Don't tell me you know—"

"No! None of us do, and we don't want to. We hope he stays in the hole he's crawled into. But as I've said before, not knowing is like sticking our head in the sand and hoping everything's fine."

Arista twisted her mouth as she pondered. "I'm thinking I *want* to meet this a-hole." She remembered the vision Candace had sent her—a caricature of an older, sickeningly attractive man—but it had not been clear. More of an AI version or a scientist's prototype. "At least I have an idea of what he looks like. Hopefully, I would recognize him if he stood right next to me."

"Arista, every part of me believes you would know. Do not underestimate your gifts. But please, don't go looking for trouble."

Auntie had so much faith in her abilities. What if her so-called powers were exceptional enough to give Fergus a well-earned comeuppance?

"Please," Auntie said again.

She laughed. How did Auntie know her so well? Because she was the one who raised her, that's why! "I'm sorry for snapping at you today. I would not be a fraction of the person I am without you, and I shouldn't have been rude to my father. I'll have to apologize next time."

"You weren't as bad as you think. And ... just know, it has been my pleasure being your guardian. I didn't know if I was up to the task, but you, my dear, made it pretty darn easy ... and a lot of fun."

Arista thought about how fast the past couple years had gone and the amazing talents she had picked up in her craft. "I think all these powers I'm *supposed* to have are finally showing up."

Auntie nodded confirmation. "Yes, indeed."

"I guess ever since last year, there have been ghosts ... visions, and I'm honing my aura reading, which is different. And we've kind of talked about this before ... but I don't think I killed anybody. More like a portal for my ghost? So, channeling, too?" She paused, remembering the ruckus on the drive to her father's and Auntie's shocked expression. "Oh! What were you saying earlier about your grandfather?"

Auntie pondered the question, then said, "You have taken in so much today. Just give yourself time to process it, and in the coming days, we'll talk more about your fainting spells."

"Ugh. Nothing bad, I hope." She looked at Auntie hoping to gain a better read of her thoughts, but reconsidered. "They don't feel like it."

Auntie briefly scrunched her face, then said, "We'll figure it out." Her attention diverted to the distance. "Uh-oh, trouble ahead."

Before them, strobing red and blue lights flashed off the main highway, their vibrance crisp even in the glaring desert sunlight. The source—a cluster of emergency vehicles.

"Oh dear," Auntie said, decreasing her speed.

As they drew nearer, Arista scrutinized the gathering of first responders and tried to determine the cause. Away from the road, deeper into the desert, a group of officers stood by a blue-tarped mound.

An oncoming ambulance approached from behind, drawing Auntie's focus back to the road and prompting her to speed up to make way.

Arista strained her neck, looking back at the dramatic spectacle.

"They don't give that much attention to a dead coyote," Auntie said.

"Yeah, that's sad."

Chapter 17
Intense Psychological Showdown

"Fergus and I need a moment," Fallon said, gesturing for Conn to exit.

"Yup."

But Conn did not give them a moment because the maniacal look in Fergus's eye, and the precarious situation concerned him. Instead, he sat down on the chair situated right outside the closed door and eavesdropped. Although loyal to Fergus, he grew fond of the new lights-on policy and Fallon's promise of a higher room temperature come winter. Whatever. He would follow either way because he had grown tired of the ambiguity. He settled in to listen.

"I got full sight of her in Arizona! They're together again, and the location is clear. Out of Flagstaff."

It had been a while since he had heard Fergus speak with such conviction.

"Fergus, this is a dead end for you. No matter what you see now, it's fleeting, as it has been. It's the main reason you took to me. Don't you realize this?"

"It's a solid lead this time."

"It was solid many times before. Yet numerous times we flew south, only to root around the countryside for nothing."

"It doesn't matter. She's there now, and we have to move."

Conn found enjoyment in the argument's escalation, electrified to hear Fergus speaking as his true self again. The reemerging strength of his leader more than compensated for losing office comforts.

"You said she was in the Bay Area, too. Yet, how many times did you send our people to California? Wasting money and getting nowhere."

"She's in Arizona! I know it, for sure! Before, I had only seen Keira. But I saw *her* this time!"

"Scout came back hexed … transfixed with hummingbirds, and Henry *never* came back. In fact, with Henry, you just sent a hungry dog in the vicinity of raw meat, hoping for the best. A shot in the dark that resulted in the deaths of innocent women."

"I'm telling you, it's real this time. I saw the old bitty who raised her, too. I saw them all."

"You turned on that poor kid, too!"

"I knew Dustin would waver. That had to be done."

"People die because of your obsession, Fergus! When will you stop?" Fallon's voice softened. "Think of our new direction."

"This time, I'm going to have Conn kill Ian, too! Once and for all. I'm sick of his existence!" He spit out the words in a venomous spite.

Conn stood up and grunted. Of course, he would kill for Fergus. He felt his adrenaline rising, assuming the power of predator and imagining his weakened prey. He paced as the pressure intensified behind the closed door, and their volume grew.

"Fergus, listen to me. Even when you *knew* they lived in the redwoods, she had moved before you got there. Now you say Arizona, where you have already traveled … so many times! It's no-win! Let it go."

"I'm going."

Conn heard a calm return to Fergus's voice. He knew it well from decades of their friendship through street warfare with rivals to shady underground drug dealings to the day he disclosed his intentions of bringing Fallon on as leader. Now, his true leader, his brother-by-spilled-blood, had shut down, and it no longer mattered what Fallon said.

"When will you wise up? There's no catching her. It's delusion at its worst! No matter the energy you put in, it's divine intervention that prevents you from attaining it." She, too, calmed. "Fergus, my love … let it go."

Quiet ensued. Had Fallon gotten through? Or, as suspected, had Fergus already decided? Hopefully, he would just silence her forever and be done with the theatrics.

"Please, love, we are creating a beautiful life here. We're growing as a community, and we have great people who love us."

"You! They only love you!" Fergus cried out, spiteful and angry.

"It will always be *our* dream, Fergus. You and I are one."

"I'm going for her."

Conn chewed his bottom lip. All previous strategies from both these personalities had expressed cunning against the other. Now, it all boiled down to this pivotal moment in Fallon's stint as leader. He would not interfere unless Fergus beckoned him or if she screamed out in pain. Listening to the final showdown created the worst kind of inner conflict, not only for him but for Fergus as well. He questioned the mental stamina of his leader and wondered who would prevail in their game of mastermind.

"Fergus! Listen to me! It's—"

"I'm done with charades!"

Conn heard the sudden clang of something thrown against the wall. The conflict had reached its face-off. With the rising heat in their profane argument, a sudden effectual sound. Conn heard the tinkling of many small bottles tumbling to the floor. He paced. Should he intervene? It had never gotten to this point.

"Please, Fergus—"

"Shut up! You stupid bitch! JUST! SHUT! UP!"

Fergus's voice lingered, the force of it bouncing off the door to which Conn's ear stayed glued. But the sudden shattering of glass brought him to full attention. He bolted upright, then pushed his ear closer to the door, trying to decipher the slightest peep.

Silence.

He waited, hoping for the sounds of cooperation … an apology. An acceptance? At this point, he didn't care who won.

With nothing apparent, he knocked on the door.

No answer came.

"Fergus," he called, knocking harder.

Still nothing.

He cracked the door. "Fergus?"

Makeup bottles, lipstick tubes, and artsy eye shadow compacts littered the floor. Glittery debris from their broken clumps—blue, dark pink, and starlight-white—created a colorful palette on the floor. He pushed open the door to find the dressing mirror shattered to bits, its shards adorning the low-pile commercial carpet in a sparkling array of reflected light.

He surveyed the damage, then looked at Fergus standing next to his dressing table. Eying him, Conn held his breath, hoping his leader had something to say.

But Fergus remained quiet with his eyes bugged, jaws clenched in anger, and his chest heaving in agitation. His heavy feminine makeup shown smeared, obscuring its usual perfection, and in the tight wad of his fist, single tresses hung down from his brunette wig. Small, fresh nicks on his face seeped blood, all distorting his former persona of Fallon.

"Conn," Fergus said, in rigid, psychotic calm.

"Yup."

"Get us two tickets to Phoenix, leaving this week."

"Yup."

CHAPTER 18
I LIKE YOUR INK

True to Mr. Tessay's words, Dakota walked through the door toting the next box of wares from Coyote Totem. With all the astounding drama Arista had endured having her parents come back into her life, not one butterfly attempted flight within her stomach. Instead, this felt novel, easy, and kind of fun, and she indulged in her role as shopkeeper, offering a professional greeting with a pinch of charm.

Dakota peered from behind the bulky box. "Hey, how's it goin', Arista?" He looked around, unsure of next steps.

"This way." She led him to the back and looked forward to inspecting the day's mystical pieces.

"So, I guess I'm supposed to present all this stuff to you," he said with a shy smile.

"Yes!" *This one needs encouragement.*

Dakota popped open the flaps and reached inside the box. He briefly deepened his voice as if to mock a seasoned sales rep. "*Mr. Tessay says this is an improved combination ...* and he thought you'd like it. Smudging, of course, but he's wrapped the desert sage in rose petals, so it's supposed to clear negativity and promote love and peace ... and a bunch of stuff like that."

So cute, pitching for his grandpa.

Dakota set down the sample, then pulled out an item enfolded in newspaper. He carefully unwrapped it to reveal a small trinket of pottery, and handed it to her, before wadding the paper and tossing it in the box.

"Wow, beautiful … and cute, at the same time." She fawned at the iridescent painting on the small medallion.

"It's Raku pottery. Apparently, it's created in a blazin' high-heat kiln before being crammed into a pile of something flammable … sawdust … wood … something like that before it smolders for hours."

She gazed at the medallion's image of a sleeping feline on a crescent moon. "I love it! It's like capturing a bit of a brilliant sunset and making it metallic." She gazed at it, then looked into Dakota's eyes. "I am definitely buying this. Please tell your grandfather I *know* they'll sell."

"Will do. Anyway, there's a bunch of designs in there—incense holders, a couple coasters, but mostly the little tiles."

"Does he make these himself?"

Dakota laughed. "He told me to say *'yes'* if you asked, but he's joking. His friend JD is the artist."

"Just lovely!" She set the piece down on the table.

Dakota dug through the box for the next item.

"I like your ink," she said, pointing to the tattoo peeking out from beneath his t-shirt.

He brightened and lifted his sleeve to expose a thin yet toned, golden-brown arm with an admirable tattoo. "Yeah, my coyote. It's my family thing."

The tattoo showed a lovely coloring, much unlike the small photocopied, black-and-white rendition on the Coyote Totem invoices. It comprised a vibrant desert backdrop complete with a classic Saguaro cactus, a cow skull, and a sunset of red, yellow, and purple. Front and center, the coyote stood in its most spirited stance—high on hind legs, front paws pulled in toward its chest, and its body curved similar to a crescent moon. Cute and playful to the human eye but surely menacing to the rodent beneath it.

"Oh wow! I love it! So, the coyote is your family totem?"

"Yeah, we're tricksters, especially the old guys. My grandpa is the craftiest of the bunch."

"Aw, he's always been sweet in here."

"Well, he's nice to the ladies, but watch out if you're his grandson—endless harassment, humiliating pranks, and no peaceful rides. Not to mention he loves to embarrass me and my cousins in front of the opposite sex."

She giggled. "Well, I can relate a bit, but Auntie doesn't realize when she's embarrassing me." In truth, Auntie did no such thing, but the importance of relatability mattered.

"Hey, you like horses?" His eyes lit up, and his enthusiasm beamed.

"They're pretty, although I've never been riding. But, yeah, I love all animals."

"Well, my grandpa has a few of them, and his friend owns a large chunk of property. Let me know if you want to go ridin'."

And there it was, but *it* came way too soon. Super cute, and glad to be talking with him, but the chance of starting a new relationship felt taxing. Already, she had so much on her mind with her parents, and what about a reconciliation with Shane? With Sedona not her forever home, she longed for Boulder Creek. "Aww, thank you, but things are hectic for me right now—"

"It's cool," he said, nodding.

His deflated posture and sudden loss of eye contact reflected the rejection as *anything* but cool. She had to give him something. "I think in a couple weeks, things should lighten."

He perked up, and responded, "Right on."

Stevie barged into the store with chin high and stride, graceful. "Hello, everybody. Sorry I'm late, Arista." He sashayed past her and Dakota into the backroom, not needing their response.

"Okay, I've got to head out for my shift," Dakota said.

"Thank you so much for bringing the goodies."

She walked him to the front and busied herself at the register while he ambled out the door. Once out of sight, she wilted like a water-starved flower. Had she made the right choice? The horseback ride on scorching desert sounded daunting, and she wondered how long she could postpone it without hurting his feelings.

Stevie emerged from the back. "What's up with you, Miss Miserable?"

"I've been fixated on Dakota for months, and he just asked me out."

"Good! That's good. Right?"

"I kind of turned him down."

"Why?"

She threw her forearms atop the counter and dropped her head in defeat. "Too much happening in my life right now." The muffled words ricocheted from the glass countertop back into her face, breathy and hot.

Stevie patted her back. "There, there, drama queen."

What did he just say? She rose and looked at him. Triggered by his ignorance, the rant began. "I will forgive you for saying that because you are unaware that, *one*, my mother is dying from cancer about two hours from here. *Two*, I had not seen her, nor my father, since I was eight years old … until a few days ago." She paused, considering the topic, but could not suppress it. "And *three*, I killed a guy strangling me in my living room last year, around this time, and I don't even remember it!" With her voice raised and close to tears, she added, "And I miss the love of my life, who is at my true home, in my beautiful mountain sanctuary and not this dry … hot … full-of-rude-people desert!"

Stevie stared at her.

She stared back.

A moment lapsed.

"Feel better *now*?" he asked in a smug tone, with his head bobbling like a desktop doll.

She burst out laughing with dewy eyes. "Yes, I think I do."

"Good! At least you're not the woman they found in the desert."

"So, it made the news? Auntie and I saw the scene when returning home the other day."

"Yeah, you're safe and alive and have plenty of potential." He grimaced while scanning her face. "Though, you need to go freshen up with water, as you're a little blotchy from your tantrum." He gave her a guided shove toward the backroom and went to greet an incoming customer.

She checked the mirror. He was right about the blotchiness, prompting her to splash a couple handfuls of water on her face, leaving the sink looking like baby ducks had enjoyed an aquatic playday. She lightly paper-toweled her face, then the rim of the basin. The distraction had helped her recover from her emotional outburst, so now she could start working on all the unpriced merchandise scattered about the tables.

Within a few moments, her cohort blared his great salesmanship, fists pumping in triumph. "I just sold the Bisbee ring! Most expensive thing in the house, y'all!"

"Nice work. Check this out." She held up a small pewter figurine. "Did you know we're carrying Christian stuff now?"

"You mean the archangels?"

"Yes," she confirmed, eyeing the semblance of St. Michael and his accompanying papyrus card with plenty to read.

"Angels are not bound to a specific religion. Grand-nan says they're prayed to by Jewish people, Muslims, Catholics, and even little witches like you." His eyebrows lifted in arrogance. "We are an *all-in-clusive* store."

"Well, that's kinda cool. My boyfriend would like that ... well, ex-boyfriend ..."

"You mean Mr. Shane? Yes, that's why I added the Catholic bit."

To hear Shane's name in conversation made him real again, and this savored feeling was *exactly* why she was reluctant to start anything with Dakota. They could get back together, especially when she moved back to Boulder Creek.

"Well, Mr. Shane would also appreciate that the Celtic goddess, Brigid, became a Catholic saint. In fact, the poor woman shucked all her suitors and became a nun, though I'm sure I'm preaching to the choir right now."

"I knew the Catholic church used—"

"Canonized ..."

She smirked. "*Canonized* her to appease the old pagan ways. But I think you're making up the nun part."

"Hah! I figured you knew, you little Celtic goddess, you."

"My ancestors may have been Celtic, but I'm eclectic, and Auntie's primary lesson was to be a good person." She laughed it off while thinking how, when she and Shane reunited, the topic of his saint and her goddess being the same could make for great conversation. "But seriously ... that nun part ..." She shook her head.

"Well, Miss Arista, don't quote me on the stuff. I'm working in my grand-nan's crystal shop, not as some prestigious, tenured Theologian at the university."

"I know."

"But don't you forget I *do* have my masters!" He wagged his finger, feigning contempt.

"Yes, You're a rocket ... I mean, *geo*-scientist."

CHAPTER 19
THE POSTURE OF A NOON-TIME DUEL

Raow. Raoooow.

Distracted from dialing Sheriff Michaels, Bethie watched Wild Willy Wallace engage in his usual antics, zipping around the living room, ripping across the top of the couch, bounding over the ottoman, up his cat post, and out of the room within seconds. A white blur with a dark-striped tail. She knew he found difficulty in being sequestered to the house, thus, he created his own chaos.

Royal watched with focused eyes, awaiting the impending burst of pandemonium on his bottom rung of the cat post.

"What is his gripe now?" Arista asked, pretending annoyance as she walked in the door from work.

"He's bored. How was the shop today?"

"Good! Gonna go shower."

"Okay. The sheriff left a message. Hopefully, he's got good news."

"Hopefully." Arista's voice trailed off down the hall.

Waiting for the sheriff to answer, Bethie tapped an anxious finger on her cheek, anticipating an update on the athame.

"Sheriff Michaels."

"Hi, Sheriff, it's Bethie. I'm hoping you have good news for me."

"Well, I think we're making progress, but I do have some questions for you."

"Ask away."

"Do you know a Fergus—"

Bethie cringed and interrupted. "Stop right there. That's Arista's estranged uncle, and I absolutely detest that man … and his name. Please never say it again." She snorted in objection. "But yes … I know him."

"Are you aware he was affiliated with the same gang as our perpetrator from last year? They had the same tattoo on their hand."

Bethie sat in stunned silence. Of course, she knew, but how the heck did the sheriff find out? "Well, pfffft, I don't remember if I knew that or not. Why do you ask?"

"Because *he*—let's call him *DM* for *detested man*—seems to be the ringleader of a gang, and that gang may have your heirloom. So, I've tracked down DM in Spokane, Washington. Were you aware of any of this?"

"No, we don't keep track of him." And it was damn good hearing he lived four states away.

"Well, it may behoove you to get interested in his whereabouts because I believe he may have your heirloom."

"Ack! Well, how the heck did he get it if he's up in Spokane?"

"Based on the recent discovery of a former employee … who went to great lengths and failed miserably doing DM's dirty work, I think your athame is with him."

She grunted. His knowledge barely scratched the surface of their family drama, and to enlighten him now felt burdensome. Anyway, he was *the law,* so finding out that Ian had beaten the living daylights out of Fergus may turn him sour to the Kelly clan and their methodologies. "Well, Sheriff, what shall I do with this information?"

He paused, no doubt calculating her lack of interest. "Well, Ms. Spiritbrite, find out if he has it. Albeit distant, he is family. Check-in, and ask him how his summer went or if he's come into any family heirlooms."

They sat quiet in the moment.

The controlled posture of a noon-time duel.

"Sheriff, I think sometimes you rile me on purpose," she said, oozing wryness.

"I do not."

"Well, I'm very interested in knowing how … DM figured out that the athame was in Boulder Creek."

"Well, he did not take it from Boulder Creek. It disappeared from Felton."

"Okay, Santa Cruz County! Whatever the case, it's a fragile situation with our bunch." She changed her demeanor, her voice projecting in a light and respectable manner. "Let me poke around."

"That's fine. You let me know when you're ready to divulge more."

"I will, indeed."

After hanging up, she phoned Pearl.

"Yes, Bethie," Pearl answered, expecting her call.

"I need to call a meeting. Matters are growing … complicated."

• • •

In Arista's room, another chat between old friends occurred. With her yellow, fuzzy-socked feet propped on the wall above her headboard and pillows, she took in all Maddie's local news from back home.

"So, Jalen and his family moved to Sacramento to open a new family law firm, and now Kenny moved, too?"

"Yep!"

"I guess it's no surprise since they already had the property."

"Yep, and truthfully, he was always the weakest link in our group on personality anyway. So, I'm left with lovey-dovey birds—Bree and Evan."

Interesting. Auntie didn't think too highly of Kenny either, but neither she nor Maddie had endured a nitpick session from a group of mean girls freshman year only to have him pass in the nick of time and stop the mental assault by assertively criticizing their nastiness. "So, how *are* Evan and Bree?"

"They had planned to get a place, but Rose was unwilling to let him go, so now Bree lives with them. Of course, he put a ring on it first."

"Engaged at twenty-five?" She considered her own lack of suitors but abandoned her self-centeredness. "I'm happy for them. Evan deserves someone special, and Bree seems sweet."

Maddie groaned and changed the subject. "Oh! Danger at the school again! Little kids gettin' bit by rattlers, left and right!"

"Are you serious? That's awful." She remembered Shane's incident the year prior.

"Yeah, two boys and a girl this year."

"Can't they do something about that? Animal control or something?"

"They do! By the way, this is hearsay from Uncle Pat, who heard it from a customer, who heard it from a summer school parent. I mean … there's not much in the news. Anyway, I guess it happens so fast that the snake retreats to the brush, and that's the end of the story. They lay traps, but nothing."

"Oh, that's awful. Poor little kids."

"Can *you* do something about it?"

"Me? I don't think so. I'm more of a make-it-better-afterward kind of person. I don't have general foresight, just normal intuition … I think." Except for those elaborate visions of Psycho Henry months before the final showdown.

"You had visions about the serial killer."

Arista paused. Surely, Maddie knew she did not want to relive that right now.

Maddie read the cue. "Never mind, what about you? How's stuff in AZ?"

Thank goodness. "Hot … dry … very dry here." The words croaked out of her throat as if the desert dust had settled on her tonsils from a morning hike. She adjusted her attitude. "But the cacti is green, and the fall colors are in, so it's got its charm."

"Okay, I'm picking up vibes of no sex."

Arista laughed.

"Kidding! I know how much you miss our beautiful redwoods."

Enough positive fluff. This was her bestie, and she needed to vent. "In all honesty, when I first came here, I *loved* the natural monuments, but at lunch with Auntie the other day, I noticed a change." She searched for the right words for her disillusionment. "I see them differently. They're unmoving, solid ... and overbearing, like emotionless godheads. I don't know how else to explain it."

Maddie hummed in understanding.

"I'm stuck indoors with a little window of time to go outside before the sun and heat kick up. Miss that window, and I'm smothering hot and burnt to a crisp, even though I go through sunscreen like crazy. It's just so—"

"Arista, come home! If you don't like it, why do you stay?"

"I think about it a lot ..." She took a deep breath and released the bombshell. "I met my mom and dad."

"What?!" Maddie's voice reverberated through the speaker.

Arista spent many minutes recounting the poignant reunion with her parents, the fragility of her mother, and the relationship-building she expected to accomplish with her father. She felt nourished by Maddie's understanding and well wishes. Then, after plenty of detail, she grew tired and changed the topic.

"I met a guy after gawking at him through the window for months on end."

Maddie laughed. "Do tell!"

After explaining her interest in Dakota, she added, "But he's not Shane, and I don't think I'm ready. Plus, I'm not planning to stay here forever. In fact, I know I'm coming back, and when I do, I know Shane and I will reconcile because we have true love, break-up or not."

Maddie remained silent.

With no comment forthcoming, she knew Maddie held a different opinion. "Hello?"

"Um ..."

"What?" She held her breath, staring at her witch-inspired dream catcher—a set of five separate weavings on one branch holder embellished in feathers, moon, and stars. When Maddie remained quiet, she fixated on the stark white wall beside it, barren of color and form. "Never mind, I don't want to know."

"It's about Shane."

From Maddie's tone, she felt oncoming dejection, leading her legs to collapse at the knees, creating a diamond shape on her headboard.

Maddie sighed. "I questioned whether to tell you. And Evan told me not to. I saw Shane with someone else." She paused. "I think his dad set him up with a friend or coworker's daughter because they were all together."

She righted herself on the bed and laid her head on her pillow. All energy left her body as Maddie's voice faded in and out with unwelcome words.

"… I know you are still hanging on. But he isn't." Maddie's tone lightened to reasoning. "Just because you two date others now doesn't mean you won't get back together later."

She squeezed her eyes shut, willing the news to be different.

"It's a very long-distance relationship, and you guys broke up months ago—"

"Only three months ago." Why did Maddie have to exaggerate everything?

"Three months ago, but you live nowhere near each other, and there's no chance to run into him at the park … or store …" Maddie softened and slowed her tone. "Listen, I pride myself on being your best friend, and I'm giving you an honest and realistic opinion that you must move on."

She did not want to hear this.

"This guy, Dakota, sounds totally hot! Go for him! You don't have to do anything, just get out and date other guys. It's important for your healing. That's something you would tell me, and you know you would!"

She pressed on the single tear, struggling to emerge from each eye. Stupid tears, again.

"Arista, it's going to be okay—"

"Yes, I know." She took a deep breath to ease the clutch of heartache so thick in her chest.

"What about Royal? How's your fluffball?"

"He's good." She looked over to Royal, licking his paw and rubbing his brow. "He's tolerating Wally pretty well."

"Good!"

The friends wound down their hour-long call and promised to talk soon.

Now sitting alone in silence, Arista could hear Auntie clinking metal on glass in the kitchen. Perhaps it was a fresh pot of tea, or maybe she was making a tincture. It didn't matter. She flopped back on her bed, watching a swirling array of dust poof up into the sunbeam that streamed into her room.

How could Shane be dating someone already? Had they already slept together?

She buried her face into her accepting pillow. Everything had shifted, and while she knew she had to flow, lest the tides of change overtake and drown her, she could not deny the accompanying pain. Each day's newness only increased the discomfort. Everyone had moved on with their lives, while hers became lonelier and more dramatic, not to mention threatening, with her mother's illness and a wicked uncle looming. Her current reality had strayed so far from the happiness and ease of her upbringing in Boulder Creek. The movie reel of woes waterboarded her senses, leading her anxiety to turn to tears. This had to stop.

"Sick of crying!"

She bolted upright, appalled by her reflection in her dresser mirror—her face mottled red and scrunched up like the Christmas Grinch. She rubbed her eyes and cheeks. If Stevie could see her now … his expression … and comments!

"I can handle this. Another lesson learned, but I'm better off!"

"What was that?" Auntie hollered from the front room.

"Nothing. Just thinking out loud."

She launched herself out of bed and went into the hall bath to splash her face with hot water. She looked in the mirror to see her skin shining a solid pink, the blotchiness gone. She ran her fingers through her straggly hair, sprucing up the wallowed mess, then marched back into her room and picked up her phone.

She had dialed this number many times before—to set appointments, place orders, and pay invoices—but this afternoon, she called Coyote Totem for a different reason.

The voicemail beeped, and she kept her message brief.

"Hi, this message is for Dakota. This is Arista, letting you know my schedule has cleared, and I'd *love* to go horseback riding."

CHAPTER 20
GAME OF CRONES

The chattering crones milled around Bethie's kitchen counter, filling their plates with a sampling of the aromatic fall hors d'oeuvres. Creamy sausage mushroom caps with drizzled aioli of garlic, rosemary, and thyme; whipped feta and avocado atop a crisp, buttery crostini with four pomegranate arils atop each; five green beans wrapped in a half-piece of pan-seared Black Forest bacon then roasted in butter, mustard, basil, and seasonings; and a crudités platter full of bright and colorful, raw seasonal vegetables.

Bethie's contribution had filled her home with the warmth and sweetness of the autumn season, negating the need for scented candles. The spiced pumpkin bread, which included pecan pieces and dark chocolate shavings, never lasted the night.

Plates stacked high, they readied in the backyard for the night's meeting. The cooler temperature had prompted shawls, wraps, or extra-long, roomy sweaters. Starting this session with a bit of light humor, Bethie went first.

"Okay, sisters, what do you call a witch from Texas?" She looked at the blank stares and applied an appropriate wait. "A hexin' Texan."

A round of cackling ensued.

Hoping to coast on the laughter tailwinds of Bethie's joke, Pearl interjected, "Okay, what's a witch's favorite TV show?" Pearl awaited a knowing chime in, but none came. *Game of Crones.*

Louder, they laughed, and as one Pearl joke hinged upon another, they laughed at each other, laughing.

"Candace, you're up." Bethie giggled and took another sip from her finely etched crystal flute.

"Okay. My granddaughter told me this one. Why can't male witches have babies? Because they have—"

"Wait, wait, wait, you need to let the suspense build," Bethie counseled, her joviality beaming.

Candace flinched and tucked her lips tightly shut. She waited until the chortling subsided.

"Well, now, you've let it die out," Bethie said with contrived impatience.

"—crystal balls and hollow weenies!"

A moment of pause while they recollected the initial joke, then a round of howling laughter filled the Sedona night.

"Okay, Bridget, give us our R-rated joke," Bethie said, taking another sip.

Bridget wiped at her happy, moist eyes. "Let me think. Okay, what did the oversexed witch doctor say to his hot assistant?"

Candace's eyes grew wide while Pearl and Bethie nodded the go-ahead.

"I just need a little head."

And the breathtaking hilarity took off again. If anyone in her neighborhood asked later, Bethie would say the uproar had been from the cumulative effects of a single glass of prosecco imbibed by lightweight and alcohol-intolerant women.

"Oh, my goodness!" Candace crowed through breathless laughter.

The antics abated as they nibbled on nourishing bites, and all settled into an informative note.

"So, my sisters, we have a situation, and tonight, it's important that *we* talk first before I pull Arista into the mix." With all eyes fixed upon Bethie, she continued. "It has become apparent that my grandniece did not just channel the ghost of her cottage. She has, in fact, been possessed by said-ghost. Further, this ghost is no ordinary ghost. It's my grandfather."

Three mouths dropped open in awe.

"Bethie! How on earth did this come to light?" Candace asked, eyes fixed upon her.

"The spells seem to happen when she is very frightened. Arista told me she had one at the store after some kids had banged on the glass door. It jarred her, and she woke up on the floor moments later."

Candace winced.

"The second episode happened right in front of me. On our trip to see Ian, we almost hit a coyote—damn creature ran right out in front of me! Luckily, I was only going sixty, or I would've creamed him. Poor thing. And the car repair … ugh! … if it could even be repaired—"

"Bethie," Pearl said in a firm tone. "Stay on track."

"Oh … Yes! Anyway, during all the screeching and spinning, Arista fainted, and, lo-and-behold, his raspy voice came right out of her mouth! Then, she … he … turned and looked at me. He called me his little treasure. He knew it was me! '*A stóirín … my little treasure*,'" she said then paused, astonished by her recount.

"That is a marvelous story, Bethie! What a wonderful treat for you," said Candace.

"Amazing," Bridget added.

Pearl brought back the logic with a sharp rebuttal. "Maybe, but Arista doesn't need her great-great-grandfather popping up every time she startles."

Bethie squished her lips into a suppressed smile. "True, and it's our key topic for the night."

"I'm sorry, Bethie. I know you loved that dear man. I remember all the stories," Pearl said, finding her sensitivity.

"Of course, it's better we fix it, but I do declare it was a treat. Ages go by with no sign of them, then—Bam! They reach out to you. Not in some dream or your imagination, but it's truly them … their voice!" Bethie sighed. "But I also imagine he wants to go home."

Candace spoke in consolation, "What a blessing to receive such a gift, but yes, he wants to go home."

"Right," Pearl said. "My guess is that he could not properly transfer back into his realm. I'm sure it was an extraordinary effort for him to help Arista in her darkest moment, but somehow, his return faltered. Add to that the fact Arista moved here … far from his dwelling. Bethie, you've told me he built that house himself, did you not?"

"He sure did!" She straightened her posture upright, proud of his accomplishment.

"And even before that, she moved into your cottage."

"She did."

"Then he's waiting for you and Arista to take him home. His home. In the meantime, dear witches, we have a job to do. Turmoil rises for this young woman again—she's got a madman, maybe a woman, on the hunt for her; her mother is in dire straits, struggling to take even a single breath, and her father will be distraught once his beloved passes. And even though she just met them, she needs to return to Boulder Creek."

Pearl's statement rang true to Bethie. "That is what I dread. Keira does not have much time. How can we take Arista from her? Or her from Arista! Worse, what if she passes while we're away? I'm worried for Arista, as she's endured so much."

Pearl stood firm. "Bethie, Keira will die. It is a sad fact, and it will affect Arista in any which way. But I tell you this. It's crucial to get her back to Boulder Creek for the coming Samhain, which is barely a month away. It is the ultimate liminal timing needed in order to make sure the transference is successful."

"I'm sorry, Bethie. While Pearl's delivery is tough, she is correct," Candace said, then turned to Pearl. "Will she need all of our help?"

"I'm not sure. It will depend on what we're able to do from here. Candace, we need your scrying again. Has enough time passed since our last session?"

"A week more of recovery, then I should be ready."

Pearl looked to their newest member, "Bridget, you can offer insight into our town of constant strangers—who's a sightseer appreciating our spiritual community and who is here for malintent. Our madman may have an accomplice."

Bridget nodded in compliance.

Pearl continued her appointments. "Bethie, your job is spell work and taking care of Arista. I know you're good with that. Stay in tune with her and feel your own intuition at the same time. How close is danger? This is where a little distance, even separate rooms, will provide better clarity."

"What about Arista? What shall I have her do?" Bethie asked before feeling the reality within her. "I believe the weight of all this is affecting her."

"The situation with her parents and the fact that your grandfather possesses her puts her in a tenuous state. Tonight, you tell us that her boyfriend has moved on. Give her nothing to do. Well ... maybe some kitchen magick. Baking and creating delight in the realm of food and drink. Otherwise, she needs to be well-rested, grounded, and readied for an outrageous autumn ritual."

Chapter 21
No More Buck

Arista sat upon sturdy horseback and embarked up the hill. Perhaps she was a descendant of her favorite goddess, Rhiannon. She sat taller but remembered that Rhiannon's horse was white and hers, not. Maybe she was an ancestor to Áine, with her reddish-brown mare closer in color to her ride, as long as gender did not count.

"This is fun." She adjusted her posture upon the flaxen chestnut gelding, whose color-name she had just learned from Dakota at the stables.

Dakota rode beside her on a taller gelding with a light-golden coat and a jet-black mane, tail, and legs. His *buckskin* resembled the movie she had watched as a young girl—*Spirit*. Noticing the similarities of one she held dear, she made her observation. "Buckskin, huh? How about a Siamese horse?"

Dakota gave a genuine chuckle and glanced back at the comfortable distance that his Grandpa Tessay and Albert kept behind them.

"Though, I guess Siameses aren't tan … they're more cream-colored. Or, like my Royal, he just turned really dark." Yes, she knew *Siameses* was not a word, but she would pull out all the stops in keeping a fun conversation flowing since Dakota seemed to be light on talking.

The steady climb up the scrub-brush-lined pathway became an experience she had not imagined. The smooth rhythm of the horse's gait felt like a slow dance or like being lulled to sleep in a gliding rocker.

However, the strength of the equine chariot beneath her also felt intimidating, if not for its solid broad shoulders, alone.

It became a grand distraction from personal issues. Thoughts of Shane faded, as had the dread of an envious uncle and even the sadness of her terminal mother. The novelty of this outdoor activity felt exhilarating, and Dakota's company made it even better. Even the heat did not feel so bad.

"How long have you been riding?" she asked, studying Dakota's posture and doing her best to mirror it.

"I think I rode horses before I walked."

"Cool. This is my first time … it's very spiritual." She settled into the soothing rhythm of the horse's stride.

"Yeah, it is." Dakota held the rein one-handed as he gazed at the surrounding scenery.

So, he does *have a spiritual side.*

She studied their mounts, walking side by side. "They really cooperate with each other. Like, they know their place and happily abide by it."

"Pretty much, but don't let 'em fool you. A good horse will take care of their rider above all else. They won't bicker with you on their back, but later, at feeding or simple turnout, they'll kick and bite if they have a score to settle."

She chuckled at the mental image of squabbling horses, imagining their large, rubbery lips and blocky teeth nipping at each other.

Farther they climbed, up the rolling hills of parched land toward the top of the ridge. Along the way, Arista noticed an increase in flora. Unlike her greenery back home, the vibrant blooms still possessed a vivid allure.

"What are these little hot pink flowers called?"

"That is the hedgehog cactus."

"Aww, cute name … and so pretty! What about that one?" She pointed to a tall stalk of delicate white flowers, almost orchid-like, rising out of a spiky pompom of a bush.

"Yucca."

"That's the yucca?" She examined it, feeling the stride of her horse through a gentle forward thrust of her shoulders. She kept her gaze on the yucca until they were completely past it. "Hunh, this area has way more flora than the tourist trails."

"Yeah, you're getting the last show of the season. Pretty much nothing blooms past September."

"Cool." She looked around them. "Oh wow. What's that monstrosity?"

"That is agave tequilana," Dakota said with a rolling tongue annunciation. "It's a base in tequila."

"How funny. I've always heard about the agave plant. I've only seen the little starters in tiny terracotta pots at my old nursery."

"Yeah, that one's about sixteen feet. Pretty much their max."

She noticed the crimson-red tips and added more humor. "It looks like they've already done a job on their victim."

"Yeah, that's funny." Dakota's smile held a little longer than her other jokes.

"So, tequila … and its spiked … tentacles?"

"I think they're just called leaves, but they *should* have a different name, huh?"

"Tentacles work." She smacked her lips, self-assured in her declaration.

Dakota laughed.

"And it's kind of like my process with lavender, but instead of a delightful tea that calms the nerves, it's something alcoholic that fuels aggravation." Ridiculous analogy, but someone had to keep the dialogue going.

He laughed but kept focused on the trail. "We need to be careful up ahead. The terrain narrows, and it's a little unstable. Don't worry though, the horses just need a little extra reassurance. I'll lead us through."

She trailed behind him, following his direction. A real hottie in his cowboy hat. Maybe she would get one, too.

As they rode through the compromised section, she felt the instability of her horse's footing. She looked at the drop, and while gradual in steepness, it was a long way down.

A short distance and the path widened again, and with it, her original impression of the red rocks returned. Prominent, majestic, and magnificent. Perhaps it was the new company she kept. Better mindset? "I have to say my favorite part of Sedona is the beauty of the monuments."

Dakota nodded.

"What's *their* story? Iceberg or something?"

"Uh, let's see." Dakota reflected, blinking his eyes, gears churning to recollect. "Millions and millions of years old … not an iceberg, and sculpted by the sea that used to be here, plus sand and lots of wind."

"Like a giant sandcastle or mud pie?"

They laughed together.

"So, it's sand. What about clay … because of red color?"

"From what I remember, red wall limestone and seashells."

"It's interesting that Arizona has seashells in its mountains. That's like finding a coffee bean in your tea."

Dakota did not laugh. Instead, his eyes became keenly fixed on something.

I think he's tiring of my jokes. She followed his gaze. "Oooh, a Monarch, we have—"

Without warning, her horse began tossing its head and jerking on the reins, forcefully yanking and causing her to feel as if her arms could be pulled from their sockets.

"Whoa. Whoa!" Dakota said, reaching out toward her horse.

The agitated beast moved out of his range, jostling her. "What do I—"

"Just hang on," Dakota warned, trying to gain control of her mount.

The butterfly fluttered closer.

Arista's horse jerked its head, a quick right, then left, pulling the reins out of her hands.

Dakota tried to reach for the fallen reins as the orange-and-black insect with its stained-glass pattern fluttered right up to her gelding's nose.

The horse reared, sending Arista to the back of the saddle.

She screamed out while instinctively grabbing the saddle horn.

And they were off! In a whirlwind, running at full speed, back toward the most precarious part of the trail.

"Hold on!" Dakota yelled from behind her, hot on her heels.

The galloping sounded deafening in her ears, and the pace felt utterly terrifying. She had no control as the horse charged back to the unstable ground. And amidst the flurry of jarring movement and her own screams, her eyesight faded. She swept inward to a kaleidoscope of neon shapes and a soundless realm of spinning spirals and pulsating strobes.

·   ·   ·

Hunkered down and galloping at full speed, Dakota's body lay aerodynamic against his horse's neck. He could not believe his luck, and he'd never hear the end of it—invite the cute girl out for a ride, and she leaves with a broken leg, or worse, ends up in the hospital after somersaulting down the hillside. He had to make this right!

"*A Dhia dhílis!*" Arista hollered in a raspy voice, her hair flying in the wind and her horse clouding him with fine desert dust.

"Just hold on! I'm right behind you!" he yelled, his throat scratchy from sucking down her dusty wake.

The notorious, narrowed pathway known for taking life and limb neared, and weighed heavily on his mind. He grit his teeth and dug into the stirrups.

Arista shouted out, angry and gruff, audible even through the thundering hooves. "*Damned horse!*"

Her horse struck hard into the treacherous passageway, the rocky ground crumbling beneath its hooves. It faltered, its legs struggling, and slid down the hill. But only a short distance before it regained footing and bolted back up onto the trail, holding strong and quickly passing through as Dakota closed in behind them.

With the danger of the precarious area efficiently navigated, the possibility of Arista being thrown still existed. He galloped up beside the runaway horse, reaching out and grasping for the swinging, loose rein.

His grandfather and Albert approached head-on, but Arista's horse made a sharp right, avoiding all of them, going off trail, and bolting straight up the hillside.

He stayed on them, with the horse's turn bringing them closer together. Making headway, hooves a thunder, he caught up and again swiped at the flapping rein.

Contact! At last, he seized his target and gently tugged. "Whooooaaa. There ya go. Good boy, whoooaa." The horse slowed enough that he reached over and stroked its neck while trotting beside them back to the trail. "You're okay," he told Arista, hoping to settle her fright.

Arista did not respond, but sat rigid, fidgeting in the saddle, and grumbling in an incoherent rasp.

He worked to console her and her gelding as their pace slowed to a walk. Hopefully, her agitation would not stir up everything again. "Hey, it's okay. You're safe."

Instead of her usual bubbly self, she stared ahead, trancelike. And that voice …

At a full stop, she turned to him, her pupils dilated into black orbs, her brow deeply furrowed, and her usual fresh expression, a sour scowl.

He stared back at her, hesitant about what he faced.

Suddenly, her body buckled, and her shoulders sagged.

"Hey!" Seeing her about to faint, he swung his leg over his horse in a swift, acrobatic move and dismounted in true cowboy fashion, catching her in the nick of time.

"Goddamn," he sputtered, now juggling two sets of reins with his arms full of an unconscious Arista. "Whoa … whoa," he coolly spoke to the horses while gently setting her to the ground and propping her against a convenient boulder.

His grandfather and Albert rode up and dismounted. Albert handed Dakota his hat, blown off in the melee. "What the hell just happened?"

"Butterfly. The horse spooked and took off. And she's a beginner." Dakota paused. He did not want to badmouth her but struggled to convey the baffling behavior he had just witnessed. "She was acting really weird, like possessed … speaking some language I've never heard."

Albert translated Dakota's agitated summary to his Grandpa Tessay, whereupon the elder acknowledged with a nod, then squatted down in front of Arista. He placed his palm two inches from the crown of her head and closed his eyes.

"He's reading her spirit," Albert said.

Grandpa Tessay gently ran his palm down to the space between her eyebrows. He dropped his head and softly hummed with his chin low. Slowly, he opened his eyes and looked up at his companions. With a glint in his eye, he gave a knowing smile.

"She okay?" Albert asked.

Grandpa Tessay stood and pinched each forefinger to thumb, then joined them together, one atop the other. Fingers still pinched, he raised the right hand upward in a small shimmy.

"Ghost," they said simultaneously.

"It's in her," his grandfather said aloud.

·   ·   ·

Arista struggled to open her eyes. She blinked herself coherent and found three grown men hovering above her. With immediate humiliation, it mortified her to imagine what had happened during her fainting spell. Yet another incident, this time under the worst scenario—on a horse, with a date, whose friend and family were present, and far from the comfort of home.

Dakota and Albert backed up to give her room, while Mr. Tessay squatted down and gave her a warm smile before inquiring aloud, "Does Bethie know?"

His gentle inquiry settled her rising angst. "Yes." She *had* told her of the fainting spells. But Auntie had implied it had something to do with her grandfather. *What on earth did they just witness?* "Ugh, I'm sorry, but I just want to go home." She felt all the joy of the day slide off her face, leaving her in a disenchanted sulk.

Mr. Tessay stood up, and he and Dakota offered their hands to hoist her to her feet.

"Just glad you're okay," Dakota said with a cowboy's politeness, walking beside her as the other men got upon their awaiting horses.

Now, *he* seemed fully engaged, making the small talk about who knows what because all she could focus on was how the entire scene must've went down and how much she wanted to be home. She could not look at him.

"You need to ride back with one of us—unless you want to ride Buck."

She groaned. How could she have missed that name? "No, thanks. No more Buck for today."

The guys could not help but laugh, and it eased the tension even in this humiliating moment. She really liked to make people laugh, and she released her own snort at the audacity of it all.

While Dakota helped her on his horse, he educated her. "Buck's a good horse. It happened too fast to tell you, but horses typically don't like butterflies. They'll check out most snakes with curiosity, but butterflies, plastic bags … ridiculous stuff … set 'em off."

"I thought you'd say it *was* a snake! Butterflies? Why butterflies? They're harmless."

"Yeah … Buck doesn't know that."

•   •   •

Still feeling awkward but trying to keep it light, Arista found solace in the vibrant blue sky, soothing her major fail at horseback riding. She anticipated a steamy, hot shower and candlelit meditation after this escapade.

"Hey, did you see they found that lady up by Flagstaff? She was a Sedona local."

"Yeah, Stevie told me. Auntie and I actually drove past the scene. Have they given the name yet?"

"I don't think so. Probably have to notify next of kin first."

"That's awful." She had known of Henry's coming for months prior. Maybe she or Candace could help solve the mystery? But first, they would need a name.

Dakota turned up the country tune, twanging out a bouncy rhythm.

She did not listen to country much, but this lady's voice and happy lyrics of being *in love with the boy* felt like a sunflower, personified. Lifting her spirit, she broke the silence. "On a positive note, thank you for today! It *was* fun … at the earlier points." She laughed it off.

"Yeah. We obviously have supernatural stuff in my family, too."

"Wait, what do you mean?" They'd just driven forty minutes and had no discussion of *supernatural.* Sure, she fainted, but what did that have to do with it? Once home, she had to learn more about Auntie's *'grandfather'* remark.

"Your ghost."

"My ghost?"

"Your ghost. My grandpa says you have a ghost … or spirit within you."

"I don't know much about that. So, what happened after I fainted?"

"You were talking in some language I've never heard. Then my grandpa—you know he's a mystic—he more or less said you're possessed."

"Possessed!?" That sounded awful! Sure, Auntie had said her grandfather had talked through her, but that just sounded temporary … loving. She blew it off for Dakota's benefit. "Yeah, we're looking into that."

They pulled up to Auntie's curb. "Well, good times! Great to have you. Sorry 'bout the horse going crazy. Just let me know if you want to do it again."

"I think I do." She laughed, figuring she must not have been too wacky since he just asked for a second date. She leaned over, gave him a sweet peck on his clean-shaven cheek, and exited before he could respond.

She hustled up Auntie's walkway a safe distance and turned around to give him a broad smile and a friendly wave goodbye. In her heart, she knew Dakota would not be the one to replace Shane, especially given her intent to move back to Boulder Creek. In the meantime, they could have fun. He smelled enticing, even after the rigorous ride.

As soon as she opened the door, she heard the oncoming thunder of Wally's speckled paws. He emerged at the living room entryway, his light blue crossed-eyes upon her. Quickly, he turned and jetted off again.

"Weirdo," she mumbled, realizing his quirkiness had amusingly grown on her.

She put her satchel on the kitchen counter and searched for signs of fresh tea, thoroughly parched from the day. "Auntie?"

Despite all the chaos, she could not wait to report her time with Dakota and the wild horse ride. Most important, she wanted to discuss the ghost revelation in further detail. "Auntie?" Her car was out front. Bathroom, maybe?

She snooped the refrigerator and pulled out an apple and almond butter. She ran water over the apple, cleaning its red, shiny skin.

Auntie's footsteps sounded up the hallway.

"Auntie!" She cheerfully turned to greet her.

Auntie's somber expression dispelled all excitement.

"What is it?" she asked, aware of the answer the minute the question left her mouth.

"It's your mother, Arista. I'm so sorry."

CHAPTER 22
ALL CHANNELS HAVE BEEN CUT

Fergus hated flying. The thought of cramped bodies shoved into a metal tube, sharing recycled air, and being trapped for hours was repugnant. Hopefully, he would not get sick. The bunchy feel of his sport coat and dress shirt added to the problem, so he passed the time trying to distract himself by perusing the *SkyMart* magazine. He flipped through pages of frivolous crap—a giant red inflatable slide, a seven-in-one wireless weather station, and a kayak storage rack for the kayak he might get one day.

"Ridiculous." He slapped the magazine shut before cramming it into the back of the seat in front of him and attempted to straighten his cramped, long legs, one by one. Disgruntled by the necessity of a sixth desert trip in the last few years, he eased the inconvenience by recalling Keira's view of Arista. Despite previous dead ends, this blessed new vision showed promise, and it did not matter that Keira had turned away from Arista, attempting to thwart his view. She was too late.

"You know, the glimpse was brief, but sickening. I looked through her eyes upon her body, and nothing but bones under thin, blue skin." He shook his head. "Wretched woman."

"Huh?" Conn jolted from the sudden engagement after an hour and a half of silence.

"Now, all channels have been cut."

Conn grunted.

"My sister's dead. I don't feel anything as of yesterday. I felt the drop like a sobering cold shower. The lights just … went out." He clenched his jaw and gazed out the window.

"Sorry."

Fergus harrumphed. True, it should have been a moment of sadness, but he endured nothing—no remorse, no emotion whatsoever, only the hope that he could catch Arista. "You know how much I detest the desert—arid, blistering, and ruinous to my dress shirts. Tropical would have been better. Maybe too many tourists. Another country? Anyway, it makes no sense that after the many times we searched the desert, I find her there. I gave up too soon."

"Mmh."

"Long have I waited for this moment, Conn." He glanced over into the eyes of his grunt, making sure he sat riveted. "You've supported me and will be the only one left when I succeed. Other than Jameson, of course, but he's administrative."

"Yup."

"I've studied antiquated scripts, and I'll have the supplies." He stared into Conn's eyes, lowering his voice. "You know what comes next? You and I are going to pay a visit to the Flagstaff post office, where I have set up a PO Box. Do you know what awaits us there?"

"No."

"I've shipped the athame. When the time is right, I'll drain the blood, life, and power from that little bitch. It's going to make me everything I've worked hard to attain and greatly deserve! Woe be the one who gets in my way."

Conn snickered, his go-to response.

"That's right, laugh about it. Time turned out to be on my side since my problematic obstacle—my dear sister—is now gone. But not before she revealed her little secret of Arista's whereabouts. I'll tell you, they're bound to be hosting a ritual, and *that* will take days to organize."

Conn raised his chin, scrunching his lips, and gave a forward nod as if rocking out to a favorite song.

Fergus looked at the strange acknowledgment, his concentration broken. The irritation brought up another bone to pick. "You know, I was a little put off by your poor planning." He eyed him. "The way you sat on my request to leave. Jameson would have jumped on that immediately. Now we've lost a couple days since we're getting there at night and tomorrow's Sunday. I need to count on you, even for admin tasks, when Jameson is away. You got me?"

The scolding wiped the amused look right off of Conn's face. "Yup. Sorry."

"I accept your apology." Fergus sat back, took a breath, and gazed out the window. "Anyway, I can see it now. With Keira dead, they'll all be there. They have to be."

"Yup."

He looked around, ensuring their privacy. "In fact, I want you to be sure and gut that bastard, Ian, who maimed me. I think we'll finish the old biddy, too, since Henry—ha! Henry—turned out to be the useless sack he'd always been." He reflected on his former devotee. "Ugly man."

"Loser," Conn said with a sneer.

"What do you think, Conn? Do you believe a ritual blade with the lifeblood of three witches will yield an unholy power?"

"Yup."

"Precisely, so, this inconvenient trip … to an inconvenient desert holds great reward."

CHAPTER 23
A BLACK-FEATHERED HEN

The service for her mother ran brief, and the mourners few. The coven had departed, leaving the three of them standing in a moment of silence with their heads lowered in a room that looked like a typical doctor's office—white vinyl floors, walls, and ceiling. Clean and stark, except for the stainless exam room table that held her mother's casket.

The funeral home director mumbled to her father, prompting a nod. Then, the man tapped onto a digital screen, sending the casket into the brick-lined cavern. The steel door shut, and she turned away as the flames ignited, heading for the door with Auntie close behind her.

A solemn walk to the car had Arista fiercely praying, working to suppress her grief. No tears today. Instead of succumbing to the sadness, she seized upon her anger as the lifeline to propel her forward. To keep her energy stoked.

They said much over the past three days while waiting out the transitory period. With few friends, there would be no funeral, and Keira had asked Ian that her ashes be scattered in Arista's childhood forest so there would be no burial.

"She selected A Finer Place. We'll know more about it when we get there, but she'll be in Santa Cruz County," her father said, on the car ride back to Auntie's. "They give you a license to spread the ashes. She'll be by a tree of our choosing, and we'll put it as close to your house as we can." He craned his neck, looking into the backseat at her.

She heard his encouraging words, but his tired, bloodshot eyes held her attention. She nodded and set her gaze out her window. Within two weeks of meeting her mother, she had died. They had planned to visit her the following day, but too late. The more she thought about it, her mother had died when she was eight, and that seemed a lifetime ago.

"Arista," Auntie said, capturing her lost gaze, "we're going back to the house to clean up and rest. Then, we'll wake up to a nice cup of tea. Your dad is going to run to Ash Fork, but he'll be back tonight, and we need to talk."

She knew what the talk involved, and she welcomed it. All the innuendos about her great-great-grandfather's spirit within her would be addressed, and getting him back home seemed to be the logical resolution. That meant leaving Sedona. She suspected her dad might go with them, especially since he just said he was taking the ashes to the mountains.

Before the killer's arrival last year, the mountains were her sanctuary from Fergus. Auntie had said Fergus remained unaware of their actual location, or he would have come himself. If the sheriff's claim of him living in Spokane was true, maybe the threat had lessened. Could her mother's death have overridden Candace's vision of him coming for her? Had fate gone another direction?

She let out a relieving breath and embraced the idea of going home.

•   •   •

When they got to Auntie's house, Arista found it surprising the coven had congregated in the backyard. Although she politely waved at them through the glass, her spirits sank. She did not realize they were going to be part of the talk and had no energy for the company nor the role of friendly co-host.

She made a stop at the cat post and rested her head on Royal, feeling his body rise and lower with each breath. As he purred, she nuzzled into his fur then gathered her strength to ready for their guests.

Never had a hot shower felt so foreign as it thrashed upon her bare skin. To find grounding, she inhaled the expanding cloud of steam. She remembered her mother's drawn face and deathly expression upon her pillow. *Stop.*

She shook away the vision and mindlessly stared at the white ceramic squares that encased the shower while lathering herself in her Earth & Ocean chai soap with its sluffing coconut shell fragments. Its spicy scent and the abrasive grain against her skin insulted her senses today. She saw the flames consuming her mother's casket and all turning to ash. *Stop!*

She drew her name in cursive script on the steamed glass of the shower door and enclosed it in the shape of a heart like she had done a thousand times before. She stared at it, unthinking, as the water crashed down upon her in its loud, explosive force.

A rage built inside of her. Angered by the semblance of cutesy happiness, she slashed her fingers through the misted design. She smeared it to oblivion until not a trace nor the surrounding steam remained. Consumed, she wiped at the beaded water—up and down, across and in circles, to the point of madness.

Stop it!

She whimpered and cupped her face into her hands, but no tears came. She surrendered to her hopelessness. "Everything around me leaves, dies … goes to ruin!"

She could usually snuff self-contempt, but this time she let the loathing sink its sharp teeth into her. Her lack of tears and sadness gave way to bitterness, and she felt displaced from her true self. Not only the pressure of her changing life but also the constant reminders of her growing potential from Auntie and the witches made her resentful of the expectation. In fact, she hated everything. Most especially, herself.

"Freak!" She showered in the anger. For the first time, she embraced her shadow self—heavy black makeup, a wicked black ensemble complete with a raven-feathered headdress and shouldered cloak, brewing a concoction of poison for malice upon whomever crossed her path.

A knock, then Auntie's voice. "Arista, did you call me?"

Startled by the interruption, her imagined wickedness dispersed, leaving only the jet-black-colored lips, her sharp voice coming out of them. "No!"

"What?"

Once more, the whitened steam accumulated on the glass, and the remnants of her shadowside vanished. "No, I didn't call you."

"Okay, just checking. I thought I heard you call me." Auntie paused. "Everything okay in there?"

This had become irksome, too. The constant checking. She forced out another huff, took a final rinse, and killed the flow of noisy water. "Yes, I'm fine." Her words bounced off the glass enclosure and back at her. *Liar.*

After toweling off, she threw on her robe. Today, it did not feel soft or cozy. Still miring over her involuntary duty to co-host the meeting, she hustled through the hallway to avoid the sight of any witches. She did not want to hear how sorry they were nor see their saddened eyes or frowny faces of compassion. She wanted to be left alone. But *no*, she had the big ol' get-together when her father returned. So, not only did she have to entertain the whole damn coven but also him, and he may as well have been a stranger.

She barged around the corner and came face to face with a pear-shaped Royal sitting at the edge of her bed, his piercing blue eyes upon his black satin face staring up at her.

Mew.

She froze. For a second, she wanted to hate him, too.

He blinked his frosty blue eyes.

She could never! She shut the bedroom door behind her and laid down beside her trusted companion, who had just broken the vicious spiral. "I love you," she said, giving him long strokes of appreciation the length of his body. "You were so comfortable out there on your post. How do you know when I need you most?"

Taking another breath, she focused on the feel of his soft fur. She soaked in the beautiful sheen of his face and listened to the vibrating whir coming from deep within his chest. She released her last bit of anger and allowed the loss to return. Sadness. A motherless child, once again. Finally, her tears released.

Grabbing a pillow from the top of her bed, she laid at the opposite end so she could stare up at her feline, her forehead touching his hip. For this moment, she would sink into her soft pillow and breathe … long … slow … breaths to ease her angst. A mindful present, calm, and settling.

"Arista, what are you doing asleep? Get up! Everyone is waiting," Auntie said with impatience.

She snapped to, noticing a dark night had replaced the sun. "Sorry! I must have fallen asleep."

She hopped up, but her robe got caught beneath her hand and yanked downward, exposing her bosom. She screeched, quickly pulling up the cover.

"Oh, it doesn't matter. Just get dressed and hurry out."

Auntie's intolerance hit harshly. How could she be so abrupt after everything that happened today? The head injury excuse had worn thin. Nonetheless, Arista hastened into her gray jersey pajamas, thick enough to pass for street wear, yet soft enough to wear to bed, and hurried to the living room.

Her father had returned. Noticing the strange addition of an extra-large, pot-belly cauldron atop Auntie's backyard firepit, she figured that the cumbersome spectacle must be his discipline. But it sure begged the question. "What are we doing?"

Auntie came from the kitchen and kept at her like a chihuahua nipping at a stranger's heels. "Just hurry up. We wondered what was taking you so long."

Arista stopped at the sliding door, feeling uneasy. Why were the witches staring at her like that, and where *were* the saddened eyes?

"Come on, dear," Auntie prodded her toward their circle.

Her father stood by the cauldron with dark, red-rimmed, puffy eyes. He looked like he had been crying for hours. "Riss, our family has long held that you are the promised one. And you have honed quite a few skills since we left you with Aunt Bethie." He motioned for her to come closer.

"Go on. It's okay," Auntie said, her guiding fingers pressed into Arista's lower back.

Didn't they realize the complexity of emotions she had dealt with today? So much rushing and so little compassion.

Her father beckoned with his hand, flicking it toward himself in gentle invitation as Bridget and Pearl closed in behind her. She stepped up to the cauldron and felt the heat emanating from the cast iron's bulging sides. The temperature strengthened, prompting her to back up, but the witches blocked her.

With love in his eyes, her father spoke. "Riss, your mom and I want you to know this is all your fault."

The shock rendered her speechless. The feeling intensified as she peered into the cauldron to find a horrific discovery of her mother's body crammed into its burning gut. The tips of jagged leg bones protruded at her folded knees. Her blistered flesh bubbled into a red goo, while other parts remained rotted, decayed, and blackened, and the area of her face that resembled her humanity bore the same drawn and withered look she had witnessed at the house.

"It's your fault, Arista," he said again, his tears gone, his eyes clear, white, and piercing.

Within the cauldron, her mother's eyes shot open, then immediately rolled back into their sockets while the rest of her face singed to ash.

Knock. Knock.

"Arista?"

Her mother's head knocked against the wall of the cauldron, mouthing Arista's name as her entire body became flame.

Knock. Knock.

Arista awoke with a heaving gasp and sat upright, profusely blinking. She looked at her window and saw a dusky sky. She calmed her thumping heart, took a breath, and noticed Royal on high alert, staring at her from the far side of the bed.

"Arista?" Auntie called from the hallway, the source of the timely knocking.

"Yes." She turned to Royal, reached out her hand, and wriggled her fingers whispering, "I'm so sorry. Come here."

"Are you about ready?"

"Yes … coming."

With her abrupt awakening and Auntie's loud response, Royal had enough and jumped off the bed.

She laid back down on her pillow. While relieved that her encountered horror was only a nightmare, the lingering images kept their hold.

"It was just a dream," she said, reassuring herself. She gasped out the exasperation and got up with a renewed appreciation for Auntie's constant checking. Life was manageable. Being stuck in that nightmare was not! She had the support of people who loved her and would not take these awful events out on them. Yes, it would be nice to have the night to herself, but she could endure whatever had to be said. It was a hell of a lot better than what her anger, self-deprecation, and negative psyche had just created.

•   •   •

With nightfall upon them, the effects of Sedona's Dark Sky policy exposed the stars as bright and plentiful. The speckling of celestial diamonds on deep, midnight blue set a bold contrast to the orange, glass-pebbled fireplace that animated before the collective group. Even without an extra-large pot-bellied cauldron, the warmth of the lapping gas flames helped to relieve the gentle nip of the autumn desert night.

The last to arrive, Arista sat down with a cup of spiced caramel apple herbal tea in hand and kept her ghastly dream to herself.

After a loving round of support for her loss and apologies for the inopportune announcement, Auntie dug into the topic. "Simply put, you're possessed, and you probably have been since that awful day your hand put an end to that murdering monster."

She sat back in her seat and drew her legs up onto the cushion. She already knew their destination. Was it growing intuition or common sense?

"We need to get you back to Boulder Creek and perform a Releasing Ritual on Samhain."

Okay, didn't think about a special ritual. "That's less than two weeks away."

Bethie nodded with bright, energized eyes. "Yes, we need to plan, pack, and go!"

She nodded in agreement, playing it cool when what she really wanted to do was screech out like a giddy schoolgirl. If anything could lift her grief, it was the thought of seeing her evergreens, smelling the scented evening breezes, and returning to a town of friendships that provided the nourishment she so missed. Though she would miss Trini … in fact, it was weird she had not checked in for their upcoming walk.

Pearl asserted herself. "Arista, we believe the ceremony should not be too difficult."

"Pearl, let Bethie …" Candace said in a gentle reminder.

Pearl abruptly shut her mouth and sat back while looking at Candace.

Candace kept her gaze on Auntie.

Inside, Arista chuckled at the discreet squabble but turned to Auntie and gave a quick bounce of her shoulders, awaiting the next directive.

"I truly believe my grandfather has possessed you. I had not spelled it out quite that way, and I'm sorry you had to hear it from Dakota. With all that was going on, I didn't want to burden you with more."

The reminder of her humiliation in front of Dakota stung, but with all that had happened since then, the embarrassment felt insignificant. "No worries. You had said he spoke through me, so at least you gave me warning."

"Ooh. Do you see why I love her so much?" Auntie clasped her hands at her heart, then continued. "So, from what I've gathered, he's triggered when he senses you are very fearful or in serious danger."

"And you cannot have that happening at inappropriate times," Pearl interjected.

"Agreed. I already dealt with that ... three times now."

Bethie regretfully shook her head. "As you know, Mr. Tessay sensed the spirit in you. He felt that it was an elder, even before I mentioned my episode with you in the car. He's more gifted than I thought. You know, his story is similar to Margaret's, though instead of being mute, he lost his hearing when he was young. Since that time, he's been blessed with many gifts. Which goes to show the universe compensates for what it takes."

"Bethie, let's stay on track," Pearl said.

"Oh, for goodness sake!" Candace said with a snap and side-eyed Pearl.

That had to be the wickedest look she had ever seen on Candace's face. She coughed down an emerging chuckle and looked at Auntie, hoping she would just keep talking.

"Anyway, we need to take the spirit back to Boulder Creek. My grandfather needs to be back in his home, which he built and loved so much. And, as Pearl said, you don't need that kind of trouble lurking in your psyche."

"Agreed! When do we leave?" She looked at her father. While she had a lifetime of happiness awaiting her, her dad would go to scatter painful memories. "Are you coming too ... to do Mom's ashes?"

"Yes, the three of us will leave in a couple days," he answered.

She nodded, subduing her excitement in reverence for her father's feelings, then looked at Auntie's coven sisters, wondering why they were present.

Auntie took the cue. "So, you're probably wondering what my sisters are doing here?"

"I come with a gift, Arista," Candace said with a soft smile. "I have something unique from my extended beliefs." She pulled out a black silk pouch and untied its drawstring to reveal a talisman. "You may recognize this."

"It's a chicken foot." A little gross. Hopefully, they didn't sacrifice the chicken solely for this amulet. She hated to think of life taken for magickal purposes.

"Yes, it's hoodoo. A chicken foot from a black-feathered hen. In the farmyard, a chicken will kick, scratch, and scrape its claws into the dirt. While they are looking for food, they are also cleansing the earth by the action, bringing the base up to the surface, circulating settled dirt, and also weeding out and devouring the pests. I will let you draw your own symbolism from those facts. I am giving this to you so you can ritually cleanse your home space. May it bring you blessed protection."

Candace tucked the trinket back into its pouch, drew the string, and handed it to her.

"Thank you." She had always loved Candace.

"Also, I know how much you love animals—as do I—so please know that we blessed, defeathered, and gave reverent thanks before we consumed her in a most delectable way."

Sustenance works too! This night turned out easier than expected. She felt comforted, safe, and part of something greater.

As Candace walked away, she passed Pearl, and they touched hands. Peace amongst the coven sisters.

Pearl approached her. "I'm here to smudge you tonight. As you know, Mr. Tessay and I have long been colleagues, and while there will always be those who disagree, he feels that the medicine wheel teaches us that Mother Earth's four nations are equal upon this earth. With great reverence, we can all use the methods that unite us in sacredness and destroy fear in the process."

Pearl is thoughtful when she puts her mind to it. Arista nodded and waited for direction.

Pearl gestured to her father.

"Riss, it's birth rite to receive a family member's power, and Mom and I considered her giving you the ability to attune to Fergus. We wondered if knowing where he was might make you safer. But in the end, she took the only power he's known to have and let it die with her. So, I don't have a *power* or trinket, but I packed some things in the trailer outside. We can go through it, and you can keep mementos of your liking. Meanwhile, Bridget is going to fish and plant-sit while I go on sabbatical with you. I'll work on long-term plans as time goes on."

"Sounds good," she said. He could stay as long as he wanted.

"I'll stay with you and Bethie until we head back to California, and I hope you're open to me being part of your life."

A tinge of warmth filled her heart. She felt the love as he took her in his arms for a fatherly hug.

"I love you so much," he said, his voice muffled within her hair.

"Love you," she peeped out, a little awkward saying those words in return. As her dad released her, movement from Bridget caught her attention.

When their eyes met, Bridget threw her hands in the air and shook her cappuccino-colored mane. "I'm just here to learn. Sorry ... but thank you for allowing me that!"

The group united in a laugh at her modest honesty.

"No worries," Arista said, smiling.

The assembly disbursed and left Pearl and her in the backyard. The smudging would only take a few minutes. Then, at last, she would find comfort with a furry feline, soft bedding, and a dreamless good night's sleep.

CHAPTER 24
A CONSEQUENCE OF ILL WILL

"Turn here," Fergus said from the reclined passenger seat, his eyes closed.

Conn cranked the wheel of the rented SUV, causing a raucous screech as he made the last-minute right onto Quarry Road.

Fergus concentrated on his vision of the house that had held Keira and Arista, as the smooth pavement turned bumpy. "We're almost there."

A couple minutes later, he sensed the familiarity. "This is it." He opened his eyes and raised the seat to see where his guidance had led them. Once upright, he peered past the flimsy closed gate to a small house defined by unique workmanship.

Conn held the car idling at the gate, staring out the windshield.

Too long. Fergus swung an indignant look over to him. "Well? Get the gate."

Conn jerked back to his grunt role. Once outside, he tugged at the secure lock, then looked at Fergus, puzzled.

Fergus groaned at the bother and reached down to the floorboard to grab the athame in its makeshift sheath he had fashioned after picking up the package from the post office. He tucked it in his waistband and hoisted himself out of the car. Immediately, the blade slid beyond the crude rendition of a covering and pricked his groin. He re-situated it as he neared the gate.

"Try 0-8-1-9. It's my niece's birthday." He would never forget the random baby announcement Keira had sent him despite resisting attunement.

Conn scrolled the numbers into the lock, then yanked.

It held tight.

"I'm not dressed for this. Go kill the engine." Waiting for Conn, he eyed the barbed wire. He dared not snag his Zegna dress shirt.

When Conn returned, Fergus had him take the lead in jumping the flimsy gate. It withstood his weight. Seeing it possible, he followed, working to avoid another blade mishap.

They strode up the flagstone walkway and looked through the glass door into the home's foyer. Fergus stilled and listened, hearing nothing but the faint gurgle of water. He relaxed his shoulders, closed his eyes, and relished in one long breath, remembering the stairwell in his vision. When compared to the one just through the door, the familiarity rang true. "Do it."

Conn raised his knee toward his chest. With his heavy boot, he kicked in the door's sizeable pane, creating an effectual pop followed by shattering glass.

Fergus scanned the surroundings and saw nothing but desolate desert with a few scattered houses. No one around.

Conn reached inside and opened the door.

With caution, they stalked into the house, aware that it could harbor a consequence of ill will. Soon enough, they found themselves alone. Fergus felt the same old feeling of previous fruitless searches nipping at his psyche but reassured himself he was not up to facing Ian today anyway. Instead, he'd root around and see what he could find.

Conn walked into the kitchen. He opened and shut the many cabinets and drawers while Fergus checked behind closed doors to find a laundry closet, storage room, and a hot water heater.

"I'm going upstairs." He motioned for Conn to investigate the downstairs living area, then scaled the pine-logged staircase. The vision of his walk to Keira's bed came present as he entered the convalescent room. He could smell her. He could smell her death, and it made him feel even more predatory. Arousal filled him with a renewed enthusiasm as he creaked across the floor toward her bed—a tidy ensemble of a thin blue-and-white floral quilt with nary a wrinkle and two stark white pillows, puffed in invitation.

"Pathetic," he said with a sneer. It was. How she let herself succumb. All for nothing. A life given to save another and not even around to appreciate it. Sheer idiocy at its finest.

A few slips of paper in the small waste basket caught his eye. Once retrieved, he saw the first to be a list of grocery items. He wadded it up and tossed it. But the second became a little treasure to behold. He chuckled aloud, tonguing the inside of his cheek and tucked the paper inside his shirt pocket.

He felt the rise of confidence in spite of his sister's vindictive act of running away and hiding for so long. It begged a response, and he obliged. "Looks like that loving adoptive upbringing of yours served you no better than my own nightmare. Sick before me. Dead before me." He snorted at the irony, then tightened his jaw. "Just know that I will find your darling Arista, and when I do, your sacrifice will have been for naught … and she *will* feel pain." He pictured his sister's sickly head upon the pillow. "Goodbye, Keira."

Shock! A burning sensation rose from his crotch and shot into his heart, its throbbing pain taking his breath. He grabbed at his chest, grimacing from the ache, and doubled over, only to be stopped by the athame's rigid reminder. He adjusted, while massaging his chest, hoping to force relief. Harder he pressed, catching his breath.

In a gradual release, the pain subsided. He slowly stood up straight and surveyed the room. Stagnant. Stilled. But, startled by the drastic effect after his malicious words, he hastened his exit.

Halfway down the stairs, he caught sight of Conn sprawled on the sofa. One arm rested high on the couch's back while the other hand dug into a bag of pretzels. With his jaws grinding away, he looked to have not a care in the world as his thick leg and dirty boot sat propped atop the cushions.

"What are you doing?" Fergus asked, irritated by the untroubled appearance.

"Resting."

"We've been sitting on an airplane and in the car for hours. Why do you need to rest?" He stared at his idiot, the anger bubbling, as he reached the foyer. He could have died upstairs, and Conn is sitting on his stupid, oblivious ass. "Get up!"

"Yup," Conn jumped up and heeled at the foot of the stairs.

Just as quickly as it came, Fergus's agitation faded. Other than the nasty brief episode in Keira's room, his streak of good fortune continued. Everything had gone his way since the vision, and the little slip of paper gave yet another clue. He pulled it from his pocket, held it up, and looked Conn in the eye. "Do you see?"

"Yup."

"Read it."

"*Deliver to Arista. Crystal shop ... Sedona strip,*" Conn read aloud.

"Do you—"

A sudden whirring noise came from the far end of the living room. After a minor startle, they realized it was the automatic fish feeder delivering flakes for the day.

"He's gone for a while." Fergus folded the paper into a neat square, tucked it back into his pocket, and led them out the door. He fiddled with his map app as they walked toward the car and offered the plan. "Sedona is less than two hours from here. We should get there three-ish. I count seven crystal shops lining the strip. But we have time. She's within reach, Conn."

Conn snickered.

"Yes. This is getting fun."

They hustled into the car and began their drive up the long, bumpy road. Once they reach the highway, Conn waited for a break in traffic.

Fergus noticed an oncoming car slowing to turn onto the road. "Wait." He stilled for a glance at its occupant, but as the driver awaited a break in traffic, he could see she looked to be in her forties, with a lush cappuccino mane similar to his Fallon-wig. Not Ian nor Arista, so of no consequence to them. "Alright, let's go."

CHAPTER 25
THE BAD MAN

Regardless of their delay, the ladies wanted to say goodbye to Pearl and Stevie. Uncertain of her return, Arista wanted a farewell hug from her high-spirited co-worker. It would have also been nice to give Dakota a delightful hug goodbye, but he had left for a family affair, so they texted their *farewells-for-now*. Trini was another story. Despite her efforts, Arista could not reach her, but Stevie had said before she could be a procrastinator.

Her father dismissed himself to grab more water from the mini-mart for their trip. Auntie and Pearl kept to the front of the shop, while Stevie and she reminisced about good times and unruly customers. But soon Stevie grew preoccupied, and his upbeat demeanor flattened.

"Hey, what's up? I can tell something's vexing you."

Stevie groaned, pursed his lips, and stared at her.

"What?" This concerned her. He would talk about anything, and right now, his eyes reflected regret.

"Have you heard any *news* over the past twenty-four hours?"

"No."

His body sagged in defeat. "Arista, this is going to be difficult, especially with all your other challenges."

She whimpered. "I can handle it." However, her mind flashed to the hectic scene she and Auntie had come across in the desert and Dakota relaying a local's deathly news story. Then, images of a love spell gone wrong—the broken crystal and spoon rest—and the first day she met Trini and her maternal aura. "No! *Please* don't …"

His expression said it all.

"It was Trini! That's who they found in the desert," she said glancing at him, hoping to be wrong.

His expression held before he lowered his head.

The thought of Trini's painful end crushed her, and her body felt the blow as its own.

"I'm sorry, Arista." He rested his hand on her shoulder.

"No!" No time to despair. She had to do something. "It was that guy at her store … the worker. I know he did it. I saw his darkness, and I did nothing!" She felt the guilt ripping at her from her apathy and its consequence. "I said *nothing* and now's she's gone! Do they have the murderer yet?"

"I don't think so."

"Stevie, we have to call the cops." She fumbled to unlock her phone screen and could not dial fast enough.

"What are you doing?" Stevie asked, his brows knitted in confusion.

After the emergency operator transferred her to the local police, she gave her personal information before offering a tip on Trini's murder case. "I know this is going to sound weird, but I know it's someone she works with. I don't know his name, but he's about six feet tall and has dark hair. Please, you have to investigate her co-workers."

After answering a few more questions, she hung up. The guilt returned, thick inside her, feeling the size of a mooring rope knot. Lost in her own woes, she had failed to act on her aural reading, a gift still so new to her. She whimpered. "That spell we did … what if—"

"Hey, don't do that to yourself!" Stevie said with a hug. "Your plate has been full, young lady. Remember, she also talked about a stalker. We don't know who did this, but you calling and trying to help is something."

She squeezed him back, then released. "No, I saw the stalker, and other than a quick poke at her belly, he did not *feel* malicious. Even Trini said his vibe was more irritating than threatening."

She cast her sight on the indigo wall hanging—stars and moons, and squiggles of gold—losing herself in its pattern. She envisioned the scene. A thrilled mother-to-be and a man who had no intention of her carrying it to term. A chill ran through her. "She worked with the killer. I know it."

In an instant, they heard the door swing open and her father jabbering at Auntie in a panicked tone.

"Go see! I've *got* to go to the restroom." Stevie disappeared behind the small door.

Stepping to the front, she found her father's face glaring with alarm—skin pale and eyes wide.

"We need to leave now! Fergus is here. I swear it's him! He's got some big goon with him, and they're walking the strip."

"How did he find us?" Auntie asked as Pearl's phone rang in Bridget's dial tone.

"They always knew Keira and I were in Arizona. He must have attuned to her, and that's why she clammed up." He waved his arms in frustration. "It doesn't matter! We've got to go! We need to get back to California and pray the sanctuary of the mountains still exists."

Pearl's expression froze from the news in her ear. "It's Bridget. She said someone has broken into the house and shattered the front door glass. She had stopped at your closest neighbor's house to introduce herself, and they offered her lunch. When she finally got to your home, she found the damage." Pearl stopped and listened. "She said not to worry about the mess … they're helping her clean it up and she just wanted us to know."

"I'll try to get back soon," Auntie said in a rush. "Please give my Wallybear lots of love."

"Of course! Stevie and I will take good care of him. Call me when you're safe in Boulder Creek, and let me know if you need us. Just remember I'm leaving for that crystal show today, but I'll have my phone with me."

"Got it! Also, since Margaret is in Shasta, I'm going to consult with Iris about the Samhain ritual."

Pearl's expression soured before settling into acceptance.

"I know," Auntie said with a consoling nod, "but she has a superb reputation in ritual. If we need more, I'll be in touch."

The fleeing trio rushed to the door. Her father pushed it open and vigilantly looked down the sidewalk, holding them at bay. When he saw the coast clear of their nemeses, he hustled them into the confusion of the crowd.

·   ·   ·

Jeremy stomped down into the asphalt beneath him, pounding out his anger into the soles of his Adult Keds. Maybe he was afraid before, but he had to be brave. The bad man had to pay for what he did.

"Jeremy," called out his bewildered mother, trailing behind him. "Slow down." She held her cotton visor closer to her head so the breeze from rushing would not blow it away.

"He's a bad man!"

"Jeremy, son, please slow down."

"No!"

Past the hardware store, beyond the bank, and into the Wholesome Foods parking lot they trudged, dodging the cars sharking for the few-available front spaces.

A crisp greeting of air-conditioned coolness welcomed them into the brightly lit shopping center. Colorful donuts and decorated cookies sat in organized rows within the acrylic glass case on their right, and large, brown cardboard bins of dried beans, granola, and nuts rested lower to the floor on their left.

"He's a bad man!" Jeremy hollered, walking past the registers full of gawking shoppers.

Customers stopped perusing labels and shopping lists, interrupted by the oversized man-child and his alarming accusation.

"Jeremy, inside voice," his mother sheepishly reminded him, embarrassed by all the eyes upon them.

But he was used to that and did not care. "Where's the bad man?!"

"Ooooh, dear," his mother sniveled.

Nearing the stairway to the management office, two workers descended.

"Sir, you need to calm down," said a man named Joe, evident by his nametag.

"We'll call the police," warned Sydney, her nametag adorned with colorful pins and flower stickers.

"Joe and Sydney," he said, reading their tags, "there's a very bad man in here, and he's got a very bad secret!"

Joe and Sydney looked at each other as if they had a crazy person on their hands. He could tell they did not believe him by the look on their face, the same look he got from many people. But it was true, and he needed their help. The memory came back to him, and he began to cry. "He hit my girlfriend."

"Who hit your girlfriend?" asked Joe.

"My girlfriend, Trini, he hit her! And I won't keep it a secret anymore because I'm not afraid anymore."

"Wait a minute. What about Trini?" Sydney asked, her focus now upon him with narrowed eyes.

"He hit her really hard over the head, and she fell down. I saw it. I was waiting for her after work."

Sydney's eyes grew large. "Who hit her?"

"The man who works here."

Joe and Sydney exchanged glances as heavy footsteps descended the stairs. The owner of the effect appeared—shoes, legs, and a shirt with a bigger name tag adorned with a red stripe and a gold metal pin.

"You! You're a very bad man!" Jeremy cried out.

"Calm down, sir," said the store manager, his face twisted in aggravation from the ruckus.

"I'm telling on you! Your name is …" Jeremy carefully read the nametag. "Patrick James McGish and you're the bad man. You hit—" He cried out, and tears ran down his cheeks. "You hit my pretty Trini so hard she died."

"You need to leave—now!" Patrick said with authority, his chest puffed with boldness.

"No, you're going to jail!"

Patrick's eyes grew shifty. "Somebody get this freak out of here. Where's Kristi?"

Sydney eyed Patrick. "We should just get the cops here. You know … just in case …"

"On it," said Joe, already making the call.

Jeremy wiped at his falling tears, his mother at his side.

Patrick became angrier. "Hey! I said stop! You're scaring everyone with your crazy stories."

"No, you did it! I saw you! I saw you hit her!"

Patrick clenched his jaw, rushed, then shoved Jeremy to the ground, sending a gasp amongst the growing crowd around them.

His mother shrieked and reached for him. She tried to help him stand, but their difference in size proved too much.

On his own accord, Jeremy struggled to his feet while eyeing Patrick. It was embarrassing to fall in front of people, but it was more important to get the bad man arrested for what he did.

Patrick glared at Jeremy, then looked at Joe talking with the emergency operator and over to Sydney, who stood staring at him.

In a flash, Patrick took off running.

The crowd parted to avoid a collision.

He ran fast! Straight down the aisle.

The further he got, the customers started yelling.

"Stop him!" yelled a young mother as she rolled her cart toward the check stands, her glassy-eyed toddler mesmerized by all the action while gnawing on a bright orange carrot stick.

On his feet again, Jeremy lumbered after Patrick.

The security lady, triggered by the chaos, came sprinting from the far-left of the store, her determined focus set on the escapee, keys swinging at her hip and muscular arms pumping.

As Patrick hit the electric door pad, the security lady launched herself up and over the metal guardrail, arms open wide. She clamped onto him like a steel trap, knocking them both to the ground. She tussled around until she had him face-up on top of her, his neck in the bend of her elbow. With teeth gritted, she cranked her wrist as he struggled to free himself from her grip. It looked like his head could pop off. His movement slowed, then stopped, as he relaxed onto her thick arm.

In an instant, the security lady shoved him aside and sprung up. "Stand back, everyone," she ordered while keeping a close eye on him. "I saw it on the cameras. Have the cops been called?"

"On their way, Kristi," said Joe, staring down at Patrick.

Jeremy studied the bad man. He did not look so mean now.

"I frickin' knew it was you," Sydney said in her nastiest voice to the sleeping bad man. She turned toward Kristi. "She told me the baby was his, and she wanted to keep it. I'm guessing he didn't want his wife and kids to find out."

Kristi looked down at him, sneered, and shook her head.

"Are *you* okay?" Sydney asked.

"Oh yeah, I'm good," Kristi said, still a little breathless. She licked the blood off the slit on her bottom lip and smiled. "I love it when they run, and grappling's even better."

•   •   •

Restless, Arista fidgeted in the backseat, scanning cars and pedestrians, dreading the sight of her uncle. "Why is he in Arizona? I thought he was in Spokane. Are we sure he doesn't know about Boulder Creek? I mean, Henry was there as his associate."

"I don't think he told him, or he would have gone himself," her father said.

Auntie nodded in agreement, already expressing the same opinion a few times prior.

"It just proves we have to be careful," her father said, peering at her in the rearview mirror. The troubled look on his face suggested great apprehension.

They turned back onto the main street of Sedona, passing Kayla's. Maybe she would miss the pastries, but her bear claw in the checkered bag back home had always been her favorite treat, anyway. They whizzed by the local juicery. Their smoothies were refreshing and healthy, but they were pricey, and she could make her own delicious smoothies. Saying goodbye to Sedona would have been bittersweet if not for the awful send-off. If she had only kept a moment's focus and acted on her aural reading of Trini. Most importantly, she would never perform an uninvited spell of good intention again.

Worst of all, her uncle had come, as predicted by Candace. She dreaded the rising signs of trouble. For distraction, she peeked at Royal, sleeping peacefully in the cat carrier with his favorite fur-ridden blanket. He felt no worry under the spell of his vet-approved natural cat sedative and would undertake the arduous journey without too much stress on his fragile, feline nerves.

"Wow! What's going on at Wholesome Foods?" Auntie asked.

"Looks like someone's in a lot of trouble," her father remarked.

Arista broke free of her musings and looked at the plethora of red and blue lights flashing as they had on the drive home from Ash Fork. Had the cops acted on her tip that fast? Probably not.

She let all thoughts fall from her mind and journeyed inward to watch the scene unfold. She envisioned the melee within the store. Trini's coworkers had been involved and even Kristi had sprung into action. Trini's stalker was there too—a cumbersome man simply stating the facts.

Beep. Beep.

"Come on," her father said, griping at the captivated rubberneckers.

She came present. "They caught him."

"Who?" Auntie asked as they proceeded through the light.

Arista craned her neck until the very last sight of Wholesome Foods faded behind them. She faced front. "The bad man."

Chapter 26
Stalking Cats on a Wee Mouse

"Where'd they go?" Stevie asked, fresh from the restroom.

"They had to leave. Don't worry, it was nothing personal against you. Just more family drama."

"Well, I got my little goodbye hug," Stevie said. "I'm going to miss my little drama queen. I wish I didn't have to be the one who told her about Trini."

"We must keep them in our prayers, Stevie." Grand-nan gazed out the window, then snapped to attention. "But business must go on."

She handed him resumes collected for Arista's replacement. After agreeing on a few, they took turns calling the potential new hires and scheduled interviews for the following week. With all business matters attended to, Grand-nan Pearl announced her departure.

"Okay, sweetpea. I've got to get on the road. I'll be back in a few days. If you need me before then, give me a ring." She paused, puckering her lips in contemplation. "And be aware of strange men." She grabbed a wad of his cheek in a gentle pinch.

"We get a plethora of strange men ... and women. How will I tell them apart from typical customers?"

"Use your intuition. If it feels right, go with it, and stop cold if it doesn't. Anything else?"

"No ma'am, Grand-nanabanana! Day's halfway done anyway," he said with assurance. He adored her to pieces, but the upcoming break from her micro-managing felt too perfect.

Business hours elapsed more quickly than thought. He had plenty of customers to keep him busy and, in between, texted friends in hopes of a fun night's agenda.

In an unexpected lull near closing time, Stevie picked at his sparkling blue cat's-eye nail polish, hoping one interviewee would be the perfect match because until they found Arista's replacement, he was full-time, every day. Unexciting and stressful. Either way, a rut in which he refused to groove.

As the shop's interior seal of serenity broke, two men entered. He shuffled sales receipts and paperwork, attempting to look busy. "Good day, gentlemen. Let me know if you have questions."

They split up, slowly rounding the shop, one in each direction. The tall, thin one, who had ventured right, stopped at the eighteen-inch Cernunnos statue perched upon the highest shelf. He sized up the stag-horned Celtic god known as protector of flora, fauna, and all things wild. Extending a pinky to touch the golden alabaster workmanship at its base, he could not reach any further. After clearing his throat, he asked, "Excuse me, how much for this piece?"

"I'm sorry, that Cernunnos is not for sale, however I can order an eight or ten-inch version for you, and it should be here by end of week. And size will *not* hinder fertility." Stevie smirked and shimmied at his own clever humor.

Without reaction or eye contact, the man continued on to the orbs and candles.

Jilted. He chalked up the lack of response to an uptight personality. How uncomfortable that man must be in his skin.

The burly one eyed the adult section, also high upon the wall in a locked cabinet to avoid the notice of younger kids shopping for cool rocks with their allowances or vacation money. Momentarily fixated on the sleek, six-inch Obsidian phallus, he moved on to the variety of feminine pieces behind the glass, lingering quite a while.

"Let me know if you'd like to see anything." Stevie jingled the keys.

The burly ape with his pageboy haircut snorted and proceeded to the incense and herbs.

"Okay," Stevie said under his breath, but loud enough so that *Rude Customer Number Two* could hear. He loathed these unfriendly shoppers with their poor attitudes, especially close to closing time. He put the keys in the drawer and turned to take a sip of water, wondering how long they would stay. Annoyed, he turned to find them merged in front of him at the counter.

"Uh, heya." Surprised by their sudden presence bearing down upon him, he felt a tinge of intimidation.

"A really nice girl works here," the tall one said, blinking his eyes in reflection. "Uh … Arista! Yes, her name was Arista. She helped me last week." He scanned the shop. "Those Amethyst wings … I've got a big budget, and I want to give her the sell. When will she be back?"

"No worries. We don't work on commission here, so I'm more than happy to help you."

"Ah, no. You see, she worked long and hard for the sell, and I want to give it to her … you know, give her that sense of accomplishment. I don't mind coming back."

"Well, that's impossible because she's gone back to her hometown."

"Oh, Ash Fork."

That was an odd guess.

"Or is she headed back to Felton? I know she loves it there."

"Close. Boulder Creek. It looks like you *have* been talking to her." At least the self-important man knew her, as Arista would not give that info to just anyone.

The tall man looked at his brutish friend, winked, then back to Stevie. "Yeah, she's a real sweet girl. Real family person."

"Yeah …" Stevie paused, remembering her abrupt departure only hours ago. Further, *family person* is not how he would best describe her. In reality, she had just met her family, and the drama of it had caused her a total meltdown. He eyed the two men and realized Grand-nan's advice of watching out for *'strange men'* may have been literal. Hopefully, he had not said too much, and now that he thought about it, though they were stylish dressers, their vibe sucked. "Sooo, anything else I can help you two with?"

The tall man pressed his lips, shook his head, and consulted with his cohort. "Conn?"

An ugly grin crossed Conn's face as he pointed to the locked cabinet. "Yeah, how much for the shiny pussy?"

So ridiculously blunt. Stevie yanked open the drawer and snatched up his keys. He had already offered to help this goon, and now he just toyed with him, but for the rep of Grand-nan's shop, he put on his best professional front. "Let me check that for you."

He strutted to the cabinet with the pride of a freshly groomed standard poodle, unlocked it, and looked for something an ape would classify as shiny. He looked back over his shoulder at Conn. "I'm guessing you mean the Opalite?"

Conn neared, glaring at him.

Stevie took the glass trinket of milky-yellow and hints of pink iridescence and held it up for Conn's perusal. He could feel his own condescension, but the more he thought about it, this ape did not have online reviewer qualities. Doubtful he could write when he couldn't iterate an intelligent sentence. "Is this the one you're referring to?"

Conn eyed the piece but made no movement nor uttered a word.

"I'll take that as a yes." He flipped it over. "This piece is forty dollars."

Conn reached out to take it, but Stevie swung around and walked back toward the register. This chump was not going to intimidate him. "As you may know, Opalite is good for communication. It emanates *joy* and *positivity!*" He demonstrated with grand gestures while rounding the counter and reached for the wrapping supplies. "And it should improve your relationships, with self and others, as well as bring inner peace and tranquility."

"Nah, man, you just keep it," Conn jeered, still standing by the case.

"Not a problem," Stevie snarked, setting the piece down, then looking at them with his chin high.

The tall man gave him a pleasant smile while removing his wallet. He placed two twenties and a five on the counter. "We don't need a bag."

"Would you like it wrapped?"

"No, thank you." The tall man lifted the risqué stone carving from the counter, turned, and walked toward Conn.

"Would you like a receipt?" Stevie asked, watching the tall man hand Conn the piece, whereupon the goon eyed it with a grin before putting it in his pocket.

Without response, they headed for the door.

He punched in the calculations, and the register drawer shot open. "You have change."

The tall man turned back to him. "You keep it. And thank you so much for your invaluable help."

He watched the men until they were out the door and out of sight. He looked at the clock—ten minutes to close.

Ding.

"Weirdos."

He grabbed his cell and read the text invitation. He answered aloud with a resounding, "Yes, I'm dying to see that movie!"

Thrilled by the invite, he responded and readied the shop for closing.

It was going to be an amazing night!

CHAPTER 27
AWAITING THE COMMAND TO ILLUMINATE

After a halfway stop with a good night's sleep, the traveling trio made it to Santa Cruz County at noon the following day. As they weaved through the mountains of Highway 9, the motion of the highway itself brought Arista her return of spirit. She would weather her sadness. She cracked the window and let her lungs fill with the fresh, cool air. Her eyes drank in the lush evergreen upon the rich, dark red bark. Majestic like the monuments of Sedona, yet so full of life, their branches waved at her with the help of the autumn wind in a warm *welcome home.*

As they pulled into her crunchy, pea-gravel driveway, her body eased at the familiar homey sound of arrival. She left Auntie and her father gabbing in the car, grabbed her main duffel and Royal's crate, and walked up to her treasured cottage. At the door, her excitement turned bittersweet. She remembered moving in with Auntie after her ordeal with the killer and, shortly thereafter, to Sedona. Now, as she turned the key, she looked at her paned front door and visualized the busted glass from the killer's hand. The jagged pieces had been replaced with a fresh new pane, and the door held a new knob and locking mechanism in place of the one the sheriff had demolished.

She opened the door, noticing the lack of a rustic creak, her aged metal hinges replaced by new silver plates to match the knob. She missed the creak. Stepping through the front door, cat crate in hand, her nose instantly objected to the unaccustomed synthetic smell of new flooring. And it had an unpleasant shine, much unlike her comfortable, original hardwood.

"You good, dear?" Auntie asked, coming up behind her.

"Yes … great!" she said, disguising her trepidation. She set her duffel down but kept Royal's crate in hand.

"Your dad is taking me to my place."

"Of course."

She watched Auntie hop in the car and took a deep breath to lighten her wistfulness. She looked down at the new boards that led into the kitchen and thought of the bright side. This new footing took away one huge pet peeve—stubbing her toe or snagging her bootie sock whenever she forgot to avoid the slightly lifted edge of one board.

She carried the bulky crate full of feline to her bedroom and shut the door behind her. Strategizing with Royal, she set it on the floor by her bed.

"I know you're full-on freaking out about now, so we're going to keep you in my bedroom for a day or two. When you've re-acclimated, you'll have free rein."

No *mew*, only a wide-eyed stare of shock.

She unfastened the barrier and popped open the door, allowing Royal to slink out to his freedom. He stealthily began his cautious inspection of old scents, heading toward his cat post.

She plopped onto her bed and gazed at the ceiling. It remained the same, allowing her contemplation. While anyone would appreciate new hardwood floors, how would she be able to tell when Great-Great was around? That is if all went well with the releasing ritual. She rolled to her side and gazed at her sunflower lamp, flipping it on for sheer principle. She drank in the sentimental accessory almost as old as she, a gift from her mother and dad that accompanied her from L.A as a child. How valuable it had become to her now. She turned it off.

She relished in the unchanged. Her lamp to shine in times of darkness, and her ceiling, always willing to engage her thoughts. She looked at her window, appreciating her sheer curtains, meant to cut down glare but not entirely eliminate the view. She snuggled into her pillow, scanning her room at all the long-missed familiarities. Ahh, yes. Her standing altar. She looked forward to embellishing it with stones, scents, and character.

While life remained a mountain of ambiguity, she looked forward to the future. She opened herself to the idea of a *new normal.* So much had changed in the months she had been gone—the loss of her mother, her father now in tow, another friend lost to violence, and Shane. Now there *would* be a chance of running into him, though she did not know if that was favorable or not. And the uncle. Was it too much to wish that he just head back to Spokane? Finally, there was the matter that prompted the return. Hopefully, the ritual to entice her great-great-grandfather's spirit out of her would be a success.

"Enough musing." Energized, she jumped up, dispersing the jumble of thoughts, and rattled an inspecting Royal, causing him to freeze in alarm. "Aw, I'm sorry. It's okay." She wiggled her fingers toward him.

When his body relaxed and his assessment continued, she left the room, shutting the door behind her. She walked through the small hallway and into the kitchen. Her garden fairy still hung, its crystal as clear as the day she left. "I know, I forgot you. But here you are, and I can't wait to see your light show in tomorrow morning's sun."

The countertops sat stripped of clutter and wiped clean, and she hated to admit it, but they looked much nicer. "Maybe so, but you still need personality." She imagined rose buds and sunflower petals drying on a cloth, a new collection of herb jars and cannisters, and a solitary, celestial teacup sitting by her sink.

She took a deep breath. Around the corner lay something more intimidating. The site of her showdown. "Okay, let's do this."

First, she saw her dining table. Her Ouija board, in its practical form, stood as imposing as ever, but it also served as a grave reminder. Luckily, there were only a few specks of Henry's blood spattered on the front leg. She and Auntie had decided not to buff them out, instead wiping them with soap and water, then letting them serve as part of the table's history. But as she approached the stained leg, a mental image of Henry's dead body atop a slick of dark red gore consumed her.

"Not going there." She took a breath and ran her hand across the table's surface, feeling the kindred spirit of the artifact. It had solidified its legend, and its authenticity set a significant contrast to the fresh floor. In fact, they still needed to ink the initials provided during their Ouija session. "You'll get the credit for that long after Auntie and I are gone."

Her gaze ran along the outline of the table's frame, down toward the floor. Another recall—the close up of Henry's face, his eyes empty of a soul, his body covered in blood, and her athame prominently protruding from his solar plexus.

"Let it go," she said to herself, allowing the vile, deathly mental image to dissipate.

But the thought of her athame remained. Fergus had it, and with his arrival in Sedona, Candace's foresight had proven correct. His thirst for her blood remained.

Mewwww.

The plea of her beloved came forefront from behind his closed door.

"You're o-kaaaay," she said aloud with a whine of compassion.

The crunch of pea gravel announced her dad's arrival, and within minutes, he stood at the door, balancing a large box.

"Hold on!" She rushed to open it.

"What do you have in this thing? Bowling balls?"

With a chuckle, she directed him to the counter. "It's my crystal collection and spell books."

Together, they finished the remaining two trips from the small, rented trailer.

He took a satisfied swig from his water bottle. "So, we're sticking with the plan of me staying at Bethie's. You sure you're comfortable alone?"

"I'm all for you staying here, but not in the cramped back bedroom. You take the master."

"Riss, that's your room. There's no way I'm kicking you out."

"I insist."

"And that's why we'll stick to the plan of me at Bethie's. Just remember this is all because you've lived here danger-free for years, and we are of mind to think that the location is still unknown. One scent of trouble and I'm here … in the back room."

He held out his hand and raised his eyebrows as if testing a pooch's friendliness, then came forward with a hug. "I love you, Riss."

"Love you," she said in a peep, more effortlessly than before.

He walked out onto her porch, down the steps, and over to Auntie's car. "Looks like you're going to have either a yellow Volvo or this Outback to sport around town. Do you have a preference?"

She laughed at the mental image of her driving a bright yellow, rectangular wagon. The vision seemed as cheerful as a sunflower, but the Volvo had always been full of Auntie and her tight red curls, so she would probably choose the Outback if given a choice. "I'm fine with whatever."

"Yeah, that Volvo of hers is bright."

The two laughed while he lowered into the car. "See you at dinner."

As he backed out of her driveway, she looked over at her lavender in dire need of a trim, its scraggly grayed flowers well past their prime. She scanned the trees, eager for a customary sight, but instead found only plump, little, flighty birds playing. She hoped Margaret would visit her soon and hooted out a soft, inaccurate bird call. She stopped, remembering Auntie's remark of Margaret in Shasta. It mattered not. She was finally home!

CHAPTER 28
START WITH THE OCCULT

The sweat dripping from his forehead made the chill of the late hour even worse, and his leather jacket proved inadequate to shelter his equally damp tee. Fresh from the RNA, Mike ambled toward his house, still enlivened by a night of drinking and dancing. He wiped his forehead, then ran his fingers through his sticky hair, remembering the chick who had danced with him most of the night. Definitely a future hookup, but some other time since her cock-block circle kept distracting her. Luckily, the number had checked out when he immediately dialed it in her presence, and a sweet goodbye kiss proved even more convincing.

An unusual sound brought him present from the night-time daydream of a swelled cleavage and luscious lips. He scanned the darkened streets, peering into the shadows for any sign of danger, but the more he listened, instead of a potential wandering late-night druggie, it sounded like a whimpering child. He walked faster, not wanting to get involved. All he wanted was to be home, taking a hot shower.

Suddenly, a man's scream sounded out from the cemetery, blending with the urban soundtrack of sirens.

He flashed a look and was certain he saw her, the same young girl in white, with no parents in sight. Out this late, she *must* be homeless like his friend had said. Maybe he should check it out.

As he crossed the street, he squinted to see what she stood over just inside the cemetery's entrance. The closer he got, he could see it was a man sprawled on the ground.

He ducked behind a parked truck and peeked through the double-windowed view.

"What the *f*..." He considered his next move because he couldn't just leave her there. It was almost midnight! What if the guy on the ground was her dad? What if it wasn't?

He checked the area again—no foot traffic, sporadic cars, and most windows were dimly lit, if at all. As he crept across the street and drew nearer, he saw her shirt covered in blood—a solid glob, mid-chest, surrounded with spatters, and the guy on the ground, only a small bloodstain on his abdomen. Had someone sniped him? Further, he had absolutely no resemblance to the child.

Nervous, he checked in all directions as he settled at the rear bumper of the car closest to the girl. He ducked down and beckoned with a whistle and snapping of his fingers.

The girl quieted her whimpering.

"Hey," he whispered to her and continued his gestures, making eye contact. He reached into his jacket pocket and removed two packs of candy—one, his edibles stash and the other, a miscellaneous grab from the club. He kept the latter—a bright green packet of sealed Hi-Chewies.

She stared emotionlessly at him while he waved the noisy packet. He rustled its wrapper, then tossed it to her. When the sugar nugget landed at her feet, she looked down, then back at him.

That got her attention! "They're good. Try 'em," he said in little more than a whisper while nodding his head. Again, he checked his surroundings.

A flash of realization. How must the shady scene appear to a passerby? He ducked behind the truck, cringing at the irony—a grown man using candy to lure a child on a darkened, quiet street. He should rethink this.

A movement out of the corner of his eye caused him to look again. She was within feet of him, chewing the sweet apple-flavored treat.

So much for the questionable scenario.

"Hey … you okay?"

She reached out her hand for another.

"Yeah! Sure." He tossed her another individual packet. "They're good, huh? Hey, where's your mom or dad?"

She said nothing, just inched closer toward his treat-bearing hand.

"You got a grandma … *halmoni*?" He knew this term by his own grandmother's moniker from his mother's side, and the child looked a lot like his cousin in her youth.

She shook her head with caution in her eyes. "Soonsil," she said, putting her hand to her chest.

Her voice flowed out angelic and soft. Blended with her soulful eyes, he realized why men became fathers. "Okay. Soonsil, let's get you someplace safe." He would protect this child. He gave her two additional candies, cupping them in her hand, then stood. "We need to go, okay?"

Soonsil diligently nodded.

The precinct sat only blocks away. He'd report the downed man, but most important, was ensuring the child was in custody. Surely, they wouldn't question him much on the blood. He glimpsed her white shirt, the stains now only a fraction of what he recalled. How the night created such dreadful shadows, he did not know.

After a few blocks, the brightly lit county building came into view. At the late hour, people milled within as if a weekday afternoon.

Soonsil noticed their aim, looked at the cop cars parked at the front curb, and froze. Her eyes widened, and she shook her head, her face contorting in fear. She released his hand and ran back in the direction they had just come.

"Hey!" he yelled, surprised by the departure.

He chased after her through darkened alleys, with walking dead men and ragged women in their cardboard shanty homes. Past the open back door of a Chinese food eatery discarding its refuse and farther across the residential lawns.

Arriving at the cemetery, Soonsil collapsed to the ground whimpering again.

Mike plopped down beside her, panting from the rigorous pursuit. He stared up at the sky. What the hell to do?

"Hey now, whadda we got here?" said a slurred voice.

The group laughter that followed did not bode well. He knew the late hour could bring trouble. Mike sat up and found four men standing in front of them.

"Got us a pedo here and a sweet young girl," said the gangly man, his face weathered and in layers of grubby, oversized clothes. "Aw, can I have your candy?"

The man extended his hand to Soonsil, who froze, her eyes locked on him.

"Hey, man, we've been through some crazy stuff tonight. Can you just give us a break?" Not wanting to sound desperate or fearful, Mike wondered if reasoning could work?

"Oh yeah? Had a rough night, huh?"

Soonsil emitted a low growl at the drunkard as he turned his attention back to Mike.

He squatted down to their level. "*Doink!*" He laughed, shoving Mike's forehead with his forefinger. It smelled sour from cigarettes and filthy skin, and a strong odor of alcohol emitted from his breath.

Soonsil's growl became louder.

"Is that kid growling?" the drunkard asked, trying to focus with a steady sway of his inebriated body.

"Man, I'm telling you. Please, just let us be."

"Outta here," said the troublemaker's friend. A round of agreement from the others followed.

With his three buddies already retreating, the drunkard took one last look at Soonsil, whose growl had lowered. He gestured his fist toward each of them. "That's some weird ass kid ya got there." He spat to his side and hustled off in an awkward sideways jog to catch up to his group.

Mike considered the effect Soonsil had on four thugs. For now, he had to get them to shelter. "My house is just over there. Let's clean you up and decide what to do next. Okay?"

Soonsil nodded.

When they stood up, she held out her palm.

"Oh. Yeah, for sure." He dug out two more chewies.

After unwrapping one, she plopped it in her mouth with her jaw cranking down for the first chew of the firm candy, then used her free hand to hold his, hastening her steps to keep up with him.

During the quick journey home, he wondered if there was more than met the eye with this unusual child. Maybe even supernatural. He would call Fergus in the morning. Hopefully, he had the same number from the old SoCal days. The whole deal—blood, cemetery, odd child over a dead body—held an eerie aspect, and Fergus specialized in those matters.

•   •   •

Fergus looked at his ringing phone but hesitated at the caller ID. "What does he want?" He scoffed and re-pocketed it. Mike had been the coven's biggest flake during his SoCal heyday, and he had no desire to rekindle the acquaintance. "It's Mike."

Conn grunted.

A ping alerted Mike's voicemail, but they had more important things to do. After three days of delays—travel, lodging arrangements, and yet another shipping journey for the athame—Fergus and Conn arrived at the Boulder Creek Post Office, twenty minutes from the upscale hotel they had booked in Scotts Valley.

Entering the tiny semblance of a governmental office, Fergus took a small key from his pocket. Ol' pal, Henry, had a father in the area, and when he called him, Frank gladly let him use his post box address in exchange for a few errands during Fergus's visit to California.

Approaching the wall of varietal metal doors, Fergus found the oversized post office box and inserted the key. He removed his self-addressed package and a stack of single-page ads, ammunition catalogs, and a utility bill. Passing Frank's mail to Conn, he placed his own package in the crook of his arm and relocked the box. He pocketed the key and, head held high, strolled through the glass doors.

Conn stalked out behind him. "Easy."

"Yes. We're closer than we've ever been. I'm giddy with glee," he said, oozing drollness while getting into the SUV. "No hesitation when the time comes." He looked Conn dead in the eyes. "And that time nears."

Fergus held up the cardboard box in front of Conn and nonchalantly looked out his passenger window.

Conn stared at the box, unmoving.

Fergus looked back at him. "Is there nothing but crickets chirping between those ears of yours?"

Conn looked at him, puzzled by the remark.

Fergus jolted the box. "Open, please."

"Oh." Conn took the package and punched it.

"Hey! My athame's in there!"

"Sorry." Conn mightily ripped open the loosened flaps and handed it back to Fergus.

Fergus narrowed his eyes in irritation. "Thank you, I think." He removed the wad of tissue paper, revealing the athame wrapped in its crude sheath to examine it. "Maybe her maturity will make for a greater power." He dazed at the blade and imagined the carnage while rotating it, then ran his finger over the smooth Moonstone at the butt of the blade. "This should have been Obsidian."

He re-wrapped the athame, placed it in the box, and gently laid it at his feet. "Now we truly search. We'll start with the occult. There are only two crystal shops in these mountains, one here in Boulder Creek and another in Felton. We'll start here tomorrow."

CHAPTER 29
EXCLUSION OF OTHERS

Arista felt a long-missed buoyancy arranging her new interior garden, inspired by Candace. She had brought a little more greenery indoors by placing a small black-wire shelf by her kitchen window. Upon it, she arranged a variety of florae in miniature pots—a double-petal, purple African violet, a green-and-pink-leaved hypoestes, a vibrant light-green maidenhair fern and one agave, as a gesture to her unforgettable date in Arizona. She used her mister to give them all a generous spritz.

A recognizable knock—*one, one-two, one*—beckoned her.

Joy blazed from within as she ran to find three cheerful pirates—Maddie, Evan, and Bree—at her front door. Flung open, she gave Maddie a grand hug, almost knocking her cumbersome hat off her head.

"We know you're swamped with unpacking and all, but couldn't wait to say *hi*," Maddie said as the trio of swashbuckling-clothed friends swept into her entryway.

Next up for a hug was Evan, but she released when he locked up from her generous squeeze. *Maybe Bree is a bit possessive.*

"It's great you're back!" he announced with enthusiasm, making up for his lack of physical affection.

The hug from Bree felt genuine, and she looked gorgeous with her kinky blonde hair cascading down from her tightly-knotted, red-velvet bandana.

"You guys look amazing! Where's the party?"

"Nor-Cal RenFaire," Maddie said. "Pirate weekend. You want to go?"

She stuck out a pouty bottom lip, then said, "I wish, but next year, for sure!"

"Nice floor," Evan said, deliberately stepping with his showy silver-buckled, black pleather boots. "No creaks."

"Thank you. Tea, you guys?" Arista asked, leading the group into her kitchen.

They declined, hot to get going, but offered a round of small talk at her counter.

"Heads up, I told Shane you were back—and I also told him you know about the dating *B.S.*," Maddie said matter-of-factly.

"Whatever." She shrugged it off, but inside, felt the jolt as if an ice cube dropped down her top. Had Maddie always been so brash?

"Yeah … I'm not so sure that—"

"Evan, I saw them, and so did you," Maddie said, her insistence drowning out his words.

"Okay, guys, I'm sure Arista doesn't need to hear all this right now." *Thank you, Bree!*

"*I'm* just trying to protect you."

The words felt hurled at her, but she knew Maddie meant well, and gave her an appreciative smile. "I know."

With Maddie occupied on justification, she watched Bree roll her eyes, causing Evan to grit his teeth. Bree's assertiveness felt dodgy. She had come a long way in speaking up for herself since Arista had left for Sedona. Even though Maddie had been her bestie forever, Bree kept things on track this time. Maybe Bree was her shrewd, snappy *Pearl*, as the behavior rang similar to Auntie's friend.

Evan twisted his mouth. "I just don't think—"

"Enough, you guys!" Bree reprimanded, her rigid palms held up.

A little too *Pearl*-ish. "I'm super happy you *all* stopped by!" Maybe Bree and Maddie were headed for a showdown, but not today. Genuine appreciation directed at *all* quelled the power trips.

The pirates jangled and clanked down her porch steps, then loaded into Evan's car, headed off to pillage the booths, a large food court of turkey legs and pizza, and medieval games in distant Hollister.

Royal peeked out of her bedroom.

"Hooo! Exhausting," she told him, followed by an exasperated giggle.

Royal and she both strolled into the kitchen. Him, to his water dish, to ding his little bell upon the stainless steel as he drank, and her, to return to plant fussing and kitchen countertop arranging.

Dingledeedo. Dingledeedo.

She momentarily froze at Shane's ringtone. She sent him straight to voicemail. If only Maddie would have kept her mouth shut a couple more weeks about her return. She could not imagine running into him … much less talking on the phone. Too much going on and too much hurt. Could he just leave things alone for a while?

•   •   •

The sheriff shot a look at his incoming call. Their conversations had become more frequent than ever. "Sheriff Michaels."

"Hi, Sheriff, Bethie here."

"Heya, Bethie! How's my favorite babysitter?"

"Ha! You're a real hoot, Pete Michaels."

"I always liked you better than Mavis, you know."

She cackled. "I can picture her now. My nemesis in babysitting during your childhood years."

"No contest whatsoever."

"My, my, my, full of flattery today, huh? Anyway, I'm just letting you know that Arista and I are back in Boulder Creek."

"Ah! Welcome home."

"I don't suppose you've gotten any updates on our missing athame?"

"Well …" He drew out his response, remembering that during their last call, she had been less than forthright in matters related to Fergus.

"I will say that we talked with Spokane Police, who paid a visit to our *detested man* a week ago, only to learn from his landlord that he had left for Arizona."

"Yes, we're aware he's in Arizona."

"Does he know you're back in Boulder Creek?"

"We hope not. We have lived here many years without his knowledge."

"Well, if you see or hear from him, just give me a call. I'd like to talk with him. Any other information?"

"Not today."

"Who are you talking to?" said an unfamiliar male voice in Bethie's background.

"Hang on, Sheriff," she said, then talked to the anonymous male without muting. "It's the sheriff. Can you give him a description of Fergus?"

"Sure." The man's voice came forefront. "Hello. This is Ian Kelly."

"Nice to meet you, Mr. Kelly. How do you have the pleasure of knowing Miss Bethie?"

"I'm her nephew."

"Wait a minute! Are you Declan's boy?"

"I am."

"Dang! My father worked with Declan back in the seventies on a few murder investigations."

"You don't say."

"You need to tell him what Fergus looks like," Bethie said, now in the background.

"Yeah … so Fergus is tall and thin, like 6'5". Fine features, chiseled jaw, thin nose, clean shaven, designer clothes… slacks and button-down shirt. He can also appear very feminine, if you know what I mean."

"No. I don't know what you mean." He would never presume to know what anyone means, and the more detail given, the better.

"I think he may wear women's … well, one time Keira walked in …" Ian stopped.

"Go on."

"Uhhh, I'm not sure it's necessary. It was a long time ago. Anyway, fine-featured man, dark hair, though graying now. That's about all I can think of."

The sheriff looked at his computer screen, which displayed an enlarged arrest photo of Fergus from a DUI in Spokane, two years prior. A fine match to Ian's description, less the women's clothes. "Okay, thank you for that information. As I told Bethie, please contact us if you happen to run into him."

"We will. Thank you. Do you need to talk with Bethie?"

"Not unless she—"

"Hi, Sheriff. Bethie again. Just wanted to say *bye.*"

"Okay, Bethie, you take care."

He snickered to himself. She brought him an amusement that he could not quite explain. One of those people, who you're not laughing *at*, but their every gesture, expression, and move is joyfully comical in some unusual, quirky way.

The mugshot of a very unhappy man brought him back to reality. He studied Fergus's arrogant eyes on the screen while sitting back with his arms across his chest. He had dealt with these self-important, type-A's before and knew their MO—better than everyone else, and the rules did not apply to them. With what he had learned of Fergus thus far, his inevitable next move seemed obvious. "I'm betting you're already here."

CHAPTER 30
OLD, BORROWED GRIMOIRES

A week after returning to Boulder Creek, Arista had regained the normalcy of her long-missed mountain living. Well into morning, she drank a blend of dandelion and vanilla-bean black tea, chilled to room temperature after overnight steeping. She felt the refreshing cool current flow into her chest, hydrating her body.

Across the room, her lumbering Siamese re-acclimated to his kitty wheel bought just before they had left for Sedona. Purchased at the local thrift shop, it had cost a fraction of the original price, and he had mastered it with the help of a dancing feather bounced upon the running pad. It also provided a source of great amusement for Arista, watching him run in place like a twelve-pound Siamese hamster, chugging away and going nowhere.

"Look at 'em goooo," she howled, spurring him on faster. Sheer entertainment at its finest.

However, studying took precedence. She turned her attention to a stack of borrowed grimoires from Auntie's collection. Plenty of spells and recipes. First, she reviewed pages for ingredients pertaining to *possession reversal*—scents, herbs, crystals, or any other magickal item. Without the specific term noted, she needed to read between the lines.

This year's ritual held more value than just releasing her great-great-grandfather. It would be the first time she contacted a deceased loved one. So desperately, she hoped she could feel her mother's presence again, and since her passing had been recent, the odds were quite favorable. With just over two weeks remaining before the ceremony, she studied to ensure her contribution played a part in the overall success.

Royal's wheel thundered in the background, disrupting her. But it pleased her to hear him enjoying himself, and she worked to better focus. She jotted down ideas, ingredients, and instructions from Auntie's leather-bound black grimoire, adorned with a hand-painted large sea-foam-green moth—its antennae, feathery yellow, and the border of its expansive forewings, sangria-purple. Arista also had the Lunar Moth on many of her possessions because of its symbolism of trusting intuition, expecting inevitable transformation, and seeking true love. Since her current love life lay in shambles, she focused instead on embracing life regardless of circumstances. And for the first time, the death aspect attributed to the moth applied to her.

"Black thorn or rowan? Hmph. Not in Cali … that I know of. What other tree could we use? Hmmm … maybe Auntie will do the tree." She turned the aged pages with care, some so worn that a lackadaisical flip could render them torn. "Crystals! Now *that* I can do. For grief, we'll use Amethyst … Rose Quartz, or maybe we'll mix it up with Rhodonite … and Black Onyx, too. Have to keep that protection factor. And we'll need a little container of water. Easy." She jotted down the items and drew little square boxes beside each line to better check off the inventory during her shopping trip. "… to break a string of bad luck … blah, blah, blah …" She scanned for expected keywords, raising her voice over the rumble of Royal's workout. "Protection. Sea salt, of course."

After perusing all spell books, she drew her last checkbox and looked up in time to see Royal dismount his wheel. It rolled to a stop as he sat up tall beside it—relaxed, poised like a pear, with his tail neatly wrapped in front of his paws. His eyes fixed upon her as he awaited comment.

"Is your heart rate even up?"

Mew.

Even Royal felt the thrill and comfort of being back home.

While she had gotten used to the new flooring, she missed a couple effects. There had not been an ounce of supernatural. No creaks, no breezes, and no crazy stunts. Surely, because Great-great's spirit remained stuck within her, but it left her with a sense of loneliness and a little disappointed. Also, Margaret. Still absent from her evergreens. Truly, she needed more magick to balance out the mundane.

"Okay, I'm not complaining … because it's *great* to be home, but—"

A loud rumbling of Royal back on his wheel interrupted her ungracious observation. She flung her head around to see him dig into the foam pad lining, forepaw claws gripping, allowing his limbs their full range of motion.

"Okay, I get it! Instant karma. I'll keep my complaining to myself. At least you're happy. No more Wally trying to hump you while you sleep."

Her gripe had been wiped. She still loved her home, and moving forward was the only way.

Back to studying. Now a good recipe or two. "*Magickal Recipes & Whimsical Treats.*" This lovely brown leather journal had an Anna's Hummingbird with its iridescent green body feathers and a brilliant crimson crown, front and center. Encircling the delightful avian were embossed vines. She unlocked the vintage clasp and opened to the first cotton-paper page.

"Ooh! Cocktails, huh? '*Witches Brew.*' Blackberry and blood orange juice, splashes of ginger and lemon shaken with vodka … and muddled berries. Yummy. Next time I drink, I want one of those!" Auntie had taken a simple, unflattering Polaroid picture of the drink and adhered it to the page. The photography advancements of the smartphone era were sharply missing. Maybe she could help her with that … or maybe Auntie liked the unfocused, nostalgic look better.

"'*Birth of Venus.*' Vanilla-infused vodka, elderflower liqueur, almond milk, and muddled strawberry '*blended to a creamy perfection.*' Good Gaia! That sounds amazing! Well, I've never seen these, so she must save them for the Sedona crowd."

She bypassed the remaining alcoholic recipes and carefully turned to side dishes. She remembered Auntie making the witch hats shaped from refrigerated crescent rolls during grade school. One page after another until she arrived at 'Main Courses.' "Creamy cheese fondue within a fire-safe cauldron. That sounds cute!" Who would have thought Auntie had so many ideas tucked within her journals?

She turned the page to find desserts. After a few kitschy, green-dyed ideas—a hard 'no'—she landed on the pages of authentic ancestral treats. "Soul cakes! Of course, we do the soul cakes. No mummers, but my mom and Great-Great may appreciate the gesture." She sighed, envisioning waving goodbye to Trini on their final walk. "Maybe Trini, too." While the search for food in the aged grimoire provided a moment of light-hearted fun, the underlying sadness still existed. She let it flow upon her, breathed through it, then released the burden.

Back to her grocery list, she noted the components for her soul cakes—eggs, almond flour, cinnamon, and nutmeg.

"No raisins. Gross. Sorry, dear ancestors, I just cannot do the raisins. How about pecans instead?" She penned the last line. "I'm betting if you had access to the buttery flavor of plump pecans, you'd have preferred them, too."

Satisfied, she closed Auntie's grimoire, took one last glance at her list, then readied for her first solo jaunt to town.

•   •   •

Arista pedaled through her neighborhood and felt an amazing vibe. For a moment, it felt like the carefree days that preceded all her drama. Sure, she could have taken the car, but she would have missed inhaling the ambiance of her neighborhood—the chirping choir of birds, familiar children's voices giggling together, and neighbors mowing their grassy lawns. Blending the sensations of the mountain-chilled air on her face and the sun, with its luminescent shine upon her back, she felt a rewarding day ahead of her.

Upon arrival at the main strip of Highway 9, the town's festive presentation hosted a plethora of bright orange pumpkins of varying sizes at many storefronts. Cardboard cutouts of scarecrows and black cats were taped to store windows, and drying corn stalks embellished the stoops and posts. With the countdown to late October ticking, the display offered much in the way of fall colors and local events to come—costume contests, pumpkin festivals, and trick-or-treating. They all served one purpose—to commemorate how one's kin is not forgotten, even in death.

Earth & Ocean would be her first stop. She wanted her old job back and felt confident Analina would agree. She parked her bike by a planter crammed with tight-petaled gold marigolds and blood-red cosmos, then walked through the door, setting off that oh-so-distinguished chime.

Analina looked up from the register and brightened. She walked from behind the counter, arms open wide. After plenty of appreciation and welcoming banter, she launched into the down-low on a few of the shop's new artists.

"Mrs. Keller is making bone jewelry now. Check out my earrings." Analina pulled back her thick mane of dark auburn hair to expose a dangling thin column of shiny clear-glass beads, two abalone shell fragments, and one long sliver of the colorful shell hanging at the end. In the middle of it all, framed in gold spacers, sat one small, spiky vertebra. "These are rattlesnake. Pretty ironic with our current situation at the school." She raised an eyebrow in jest.

Arista *eeked* at the news and surveyed the earring. Ever-dazzled by the abalone. The vertebrae, not so much. Especially since Shane's ordeal with the same species. The thought brought on a full shiver of the eeber-jeebers.

"I know. I thought that at first, too. But! She humanely harvests the little bones from many different animals, sterilizes them, and puts them straight into jewelry. Who could believe our quiet little shopper was so creative?" Analina walked her to the full display of earrings embellished with raccoon claws, elongated wing bones, and cat teeth.

Arista nodded in trepidation, imagining the gruesome task of harvesting from decaying animals—the prying, plucking, and snapping of organic tissue.

Analina read her well. "Seriously? You don't like them at all?"

"A bit macabre?" If being honest, downright gross, but she would stick to subtlety.

"Not really." Analina fondled her earring. "I kinda like these rattlesnake and abalone. Think of the protection factor and transitory assistance. We all go through changes."

Arista desperately wanted her troubles to pass and considered the totem animal. "You know, when you put it that way … yes … they're kinda cool." She withheld anything less than admiration this time. And that keyword—transitory, could be useful in the ceremony.

"I get it, though. It took me a day to warm up before I agreed to the inventory. You think she put a spell on me?"

"Of course not. How about Miss Zoelly? How's she doing?"

"She's good." Analina stretched her smile until it became a concerned expression of grit teeth. "Actually, school's been tough. Last year *and* it's already starting again. Between the snake attacks and a few run-ins, I'm thinking of homeschooling her."

"Uh-oh, what's going on?" She wondered if Shane knew about this and hoped that he looked out for Zoelly.

"There's been a few bullying incidents. Zoelly swears she's fine with it, but she's having night terrors that could raise the dead. Running through the hall … she threw her music box one night … in her sleep! Scared the hell out of me. And the clincher is, she remembers nothing by morning."

"Poor thing."

"The doctor says kids outgrow them. As for the bullying, it's still an age of name-calling like *'jerk face.'* So, there's been no physical harm, but I know it bothers her. And me!"

"Of course it does."

"I just tell her to keep her confidence strong and not everyone in life is going to like her. It doesn't matter if you're rich and pretty or poor and homely. It doesn't matter ethnicity, glasses, body type, or whatever … someone's gonna have a beef with you."

"Redhead or witch … or both!" Arista added with eyes bugged, remembering her own run-ins with jerk faces.

"Yes, I'm sure you had to develop some grit growing up, just like I did."

"What doesn't kill us …"

"… makes us want to whoop ass," Analina said, her voice in a growl.

Arista laughed.

"So, you want your old job back?"

"Yes!"

"Start next week?"

"I'd love to!"

"Deal!"

They shook on it.

"Any chance I can get my discount today?" Arista asked as the chime of the front door rang.

"Of course. Just round up your items while I go help the customer."

So began her reintroduction to the magick within Earth & Ocean. Though she had plenty at home, she gathered fresh new crystals and packets of black salt for her upcoming ceremony. Next, she selected a string of Green Aventurine beads as an offering for Fortuna's fountain. Maybe the beloved Roman Goddess of good fortune and healing could sprinkle a little her way.

Finally, she walked over to the new bone jewelry, giving them another chance. While the price was a fraction of what they would be in Sedona, it ran too high—discount included. Some other time.

With Analina busy with her customer, Arista rang up her own transaction. Then, with subtle goodbyes completed, she set toward the door. She stopped at the gurgling Fortuna fountain, said a brief prayer of appreciation, and draped the newly purchased milky-green beads over the statuette's shoulder.

"Oh, Arista."

Analina's abrupt bellow in front of the customer startled them both. She apologized to the man and offered Arista a warning. "If you're riding your bike, be careful. There's an SUV that's been loitering across the street for a couple days. Not sure what they're up to, but … yeah."

Arista looked out the door. Across the street, two stores up, sat the vehicle in question. "Got it. Thanks for the warning!"

She stepped outside to her bike at the planter box. She remembered seeing her old friend, Michelle, at this same location, which seemed a lifetime ago. For Michelle, it surely was.

With caution, she straddled her seat, took heed to Analina's warning, and stared at the cumbersome SUV, its tinted windows keeping secrets. It not only looked out of place in their laid-back town, but an ominous sense emanated from beyond its dark glass.

She got on her bike, glimpsing over her shoulder just once to catch that license plate. Easy to remember. When she heard its engine start, she picked up pace to get back home.

CHAPTER 31
NO-NONSENSE SASS AND DIPLOMATIC RAILROADING

Bethie knelt on her pink foam pad, clearing all the dry underbrush of her lavender bushes. With Arista fetching the ritual ingredients from town, she had plenty of time to tend to home maintenance.

Snip. Snip. Snip.

The generous trimming exposed a small, pasty nodule, and she wracked her brain, trying to remember the context of this … egg sac. "Okay, which little buggy does this hold?"

But for the life of her, she could not recall, and no use wasting time on guessing games, as there was much to be done. She trimmed around the sac, and even put a little layer of fresh green sprigs above it, hiding it from hungry birds.

Snip. Snip. Snip.

From the corner of her eye, a light green object caught her attention. She looked down to consider it sitting atop the fresh-cut trimmings, but with her vision not so clear, she leaned in closer for a better view. It moved.

"That's it!" she said, peering at the three-inch-long Praying Mantis. "It's—"

In a burst of energy, the large insect flew at her, a battery of effective insect wings having a real go at her face. In a panic, she stood up, sputtering, screeching, and flailing about, sending the mama-mantis on her way.

Safe from the garden creature's assault, her heart raced from the encounter. "Good heavens! You don't fly up in people's face like that!" Her insulted scoff became an enjoyable belly chuckle at the very grounding moment. Thankfully, mantises eat lizards, mice, and even small birds, but they most often will not attack a human. "No sting. No bite. But a helluva fright!"

Enough gardening for now. With her achy joints already standing, time had come for refreshments. She would gather the loose debris later, since the she-bug probably wanted to return to her sac.

Once inside, Bethie poured herself a glass of ice water, and into it, squeezed one wedge of a fresh-cut Meyer lemon. She used her fingernail to pluck the floating seed into the sink and took a generous swig. Chore number two came to mind whilst extinguishing her thirst.

The first thing she had noticed on her return home was how utterly drab her floors looked compared to her Sedona home. When she espied Arista's updated flooring, it became even clearer.

In full skirt and frazzled hair, she had her mop out in no time, pushing and pulling in long strokes over the aged floor of her cottage, applying her special, homemade polish of olive oil, vinegar, and essence of lemon.

To release the energy of ills gone past,
To squelch and banish them with each stroke cast.
Cleanse this space, shine its face,
And any harm that was, leave no trace.

While she had already done this before she and Arista had left for Sedona, a freshener never hurt. She gave three additional vigorous swipes for good measure.

"There!" she declared, energized by the exertion.

More than anything, however, all this rambunctious hard work aimed to quash the rising angst within her. Something felt wrong, and she couldn't shake it. "I better check in with Arista."

As she reached for her phone, Pearl's ringtone sounded in her hand, causing her to jump. She settled in relief, knowing if anything could counter her anxiety, it was Pearl's no-nonsense sass and diplomatic railroading.

"Bethie, I'm afraid I have terrible news. I just got back from the gem show, and Stevie mentioned a couple men stopped by the shop in my absence inquiring about Arista."

She braced herself for the details. "When?"

"The day you left. You know I was leaving for that artist's show at the South Rim. He did not realize the danger. It's been about a week now."

Bethie felt a flush of cold plummet through her. "What did he tell them?"

"Well, they had said Arista had helped them with a pair of Amethyst wings. They said she had told them all about Felton ..."

Bethie cringed.

"... and he ... " Pearl paused, hesitating to deliver the news. "He corrected them ... to Boulder Creek."

Her breath left her as if punched, and she doubled over, sickened. With all her exertion from mopping and the instant drain of energy from the horrible news, she sat down on her floor and cupped her hand upon her forehead. "Well ... I felt trouble brewing. And here it is."

"Bethie, I'm so very sorry."

She stared out into her yard, visualizing the terror to come until Pearl's words seeped back into her consciousness.

"... he knew nothing about Arista's history. I knew the secrecy and had kept it from him. He's so sorry."

"What else did he tell them?" The more she knew, the better.

"Nothing. As they lingered, he said it didn't feel right, so he clammed up. He said one was decent, but the other was awfully crude."

"So ... a week ago?" Bethie asked, calculating their drive and the potential for air travel.

"Yes. Stevie is really sorry, too."

Bethie pictured scenes of death and destruction, then remembered the terror of Henry's notorious visit inflicting violence with long-term symptoms she dealt with to this day.

"I have a description," Pearl said. "He said one is quite polished and tall, while the other one is a big ape-type … blonde hair and a repulsive scar on his face."

"Okay, at least we know they're coming, and yes, they are coming." She applied Arista's silver lining. "There *is* strength in awareness. Don't think for a minute that this is either of your fault, as it's the typical havoc that follows this awful person, and I await the glorious day when we are rid of him forever."

"Tell me what you need from us?"

"I'm not sure. Let me talk with Ian and Arista, and then … *phew!* We'll just address it head-on."

"Okay, Bethie, we can fly out there … the whole coven. I will ready them for the trip. Please let us know."

Alone with her thoughts, Bethie remained on the floor, imagining herself in an amazing story. The ideal of watching Fergus fade into nothing, his being no longer in existence, and the nightmare of perpetual pursuit behind them. She held it until she felt at peace with it.

But it would be quite another task to see it to fruition.

She had to get to Arista's and rushed out the door as the inevitable consumed her. Their encounter with Henry was just the trial run of battling the despicable sadist to come.

•　　•　　•

Impatience trickled within Fergus. Another day of the same uninspiring scenery—a large red sign with its sawing lumberjack, stacks of wood for the locals' colder seasons, and erect, green-handled rakes, hoes, and shovels gracing the store entrance. Even worse, the stark grey dashboard of their rental framed the non-changing backdrop. He tugged at his constricting collar. Plane rides and car stakeouts had gotten the best of him, and now, on their third day of loitering across from the Boulder Creek crystal shop, he had reached his wit's end. Tomorrow, they would try Felton.

"I need a vacation after this, Conn. Nothing tropical. Everyone goes tropical. I want to go somewhere that holds mystery … somewhere secluded … maybe Machu Picchu. All the sacrifices made there, including children, you know." His mind drifted to the bloodshed and beheadings before a blood-thirsty ruler bedecked in a gold crown and jeweled earlobes that hung to his shoulders.

"Yup."

"You want to go with me?" He eyed the presentability of his devotee.

"Nah."

"Come on. My treat."

"Maybe."

A burly guy walked past the store and grabbed a bundle of wood, prompting him to wonder if he had already paid for it. But it didn't matter. "It was by chance we ended up here, you know."

Conn grunted.

"Fallon was leading us in a ridiculous direction."

"Yup."

"Conn, I had to get rid of her regardless of the bankroll she manifested. Have you communicated with the members?"

Conn looked at him without response, eyes shifting in reluctance.

"So, we left them hanging?"

Conn turned back to the window.

Fergus released an incredulous snort. "Well, that's a fine how-do-you-do. Couldn't you have emailed them or something?"

"Jameson does that stuff."

"Did you let Jameson know?"

Conn scrunched his face and shook his head.

He dropped his chin in disbelief. "Conn, they're going to think we left the country! What's it been … almost two weeks, with no notice or communication?" He felt flustered. The fact Conn's eyes looked elsewhere increased his irritation. "Conn!"

Conn swung around to face him.

"That's not responsible. Why must I remind you of these things? I'm the visionary … not the Operations guy. I can't always—" He stopped, catching sight of a pretty young woman walking out of the crystal shop. A rush of energy shot through him. "It's her!"

They watched Arista futz with her bike.

"I didn't see her go in. Did you?"

Conn sat unblinking and alert, like a guard dog held back only by a restrictive leash. "Nope."

Arista looked in their direction and held her stare.

"We're made," Conn said.

"No way she can see us with these tinted windows," Fergus said, motionless.

Arista got on her bike, smiled at a passing pedestrian, and rode off in the opposite direction with a blissful expression.

"See? She was just looking around. Not a worry to be found on that happy little face of hers." He smirked at her ignorance.

Conn started the engine and U-turned.

Arista pedaled along the highway's bike lane and disappeared behind the store.

They took the same route and kept an inconspicuous distance behind her.

She made a turn, then another.

Conn sped up, taking the last turn, just as she disappeared into a hedged driveway. He slowed as they approached the site.

Seeing Arista's bike by the porch, Fergus pinned the location on his cell. "Got it!" He felt the adrenaline of victory. "This could not get any better."

Onward they drove to the end of the street, when an aged yellow Volvo rounded the corner and met them head on.

Fergus's eyes met with Ian's, and he saw a look of recognition flash across his face, turning his expression to a rage he remembered well.

"Go!" he told Conn, who gunned the engine.

Looking back, he watched Ian speed toward Arista's house and disappear behind her hedgerow.

"Do not stop. Do not slow down!" His victorious adrenaline surge converted to dread and anger churned within him. "Fucking Ian! What the hell is he doing here?"

•   •   •

Arista heard the abrupt entry into her driveway, rushed to the door, and felt relieved to see her father. Then, she noticed his expression.

"Riss!" He ran to her and grasped her in a hug. "Thank God you're okay! Did you see him?"

The thought of Analina's warning and the SUV that she lost from her strategic maneuvering flashed into her mind. She had not been quick enough.

"He's here! I'd know that piece of shit anywhere! I locked eyes on him, and he saw me, too."

In a rush, Auntie appeared in the driveway with her own troubled expression. With no hesitation, she confirmed the news. "I already know. They found us. It was Stevie. He gave them our location by mistake, and he clarified their Felton comment to Boulder Creek."

"Oh no, Stevie," Arista said, squeezing her eyes shut as her shoulders dropped in defeat. She pressed her eyebrows until a tinge of discomfort distracted her from reality.

Her father looked at Auntie. "Over a decade of safety, and now we're exposed. Dammit!" His face soured. "Our biggest concern is how we're going to handle the hell-storm that's coming."

"First, we're getting the sheriff involved!" Auntie spoke with renewed energy, her hands flailing about as if directing a grand orchestra. "We can talk of spells and protection … fret and plan all we want. But with *this* relentless bastard, we need firepower."

CHAPTER 32
I WANT HIM DEAD

Sheriff Michaels pulled into the driveway of his ragtag team of serial killer catchers. Judging by their faces, a bit more information about Fergus had come to light. They scattered out of the cruiser's way, allowing him to park, but once out of his car, their information poured forth.

"Sheriff, DM is in town." Bethie paused and rolled her eyes. "Lest there be no mistake, I'll just say his awful name … Fergus! Fergus is here. Ian just saw him. They were in a white SUV."

"It was a white Expedition with tinted windows," Ian added.

"Right." The sheriff fumbled for his pad, unprepared for the urgency. "Okay, did you get the plate?"

"I didn't. I just wanted to ensure Arista's safety," Ian said.

"*9-5-R-O-Y-A-7.*" Arista rattled off the plate by memory. "Analina warned me of an SUV across the street from the shop, so I glanced at the plate." She turned to Bethie. "Anyway, I'm sure you see why it was so easy to remember."

Bethie blinked in confusion.

Written, the message came clear. "*9-5-ROYA7.* Flip that 7 upside-down, and you have Royal. If I remember correctly, that's your cat's name," the sheriff said.

Arista nodded.

He eyed his notes, then closed the pad. "Very astute of you, Miss Kelly."

"My cat's name and my birth year, so I think the universe is working with us. Plus, my boss warned me."

"Isn't that something … great work, Arista!" Bethie said.

"Good work, Riss." Ian rubbed her shoulder.

"Yep. We want to question Fergus in relation to a car accident that led to the demise of a staff member and disappearance of your heirloom. As I mentioned to Bethie earlier, it's interesting that he seems to be affiliated with our nemesis from last year, too."

Bethie turned to Ian. "He's referring to the serial killer."

"I am indeed. In the meantime, ladies and gent, I'll commit to patrolling your street a couple times a day during my rounds. The deputy will do likewise. Don't want any hardship coming down on the Kelly family."

"Thanks, Sheriff," Ian said. "This was a drive-by. They're casing the joint." He turned to Arista. "I'm taking that back bedroom, with or without your approval."

"I know," she conceded.

After a few more precautionary tips, the sheriff set to leave. "Okay, you folks seem to have a plan. I'm going to head out unless you have anything else for me."

"This is a good start, Sheriff. Thank you for getting here so quickly," Bethie said, reaching out to squeeze his arm.

He raised his eyebrow, amused by the gesture, then looked at her hand. "The last time you did that, I think you put a little whammy on my back pain."

Bethie's face brightened, and she surrendered a jovial cackle.

·   ·   ·

Fergus sat at the small desk in the corner of their spiffy hotel room, an expense he found necessary as he could imagine nothing less than luxury. He also blended well amongst the mid-to-upper-class civilians walking the sidewalks with their latte cups and haughty attitudes. The only caveat—he had to share the space with Conn, who hovered over him, smelling like a smoke lounge and sweat.

"Conn, please back up a little."

Conn did as told.

"Looks like we won't have to wait until Samhain, after all. I say we do this tomorrow. I need you to take out Ian. I want him dead. I hate that guy!" He twisted around and looked up at Conn. "Dead!"

"Yup."

"No hesitations. I have baggage with that one."

"I got 'em."

"Thank you." Fergus snorted out his tension and returned to his thoughts. "The old biddy will be easy to off, as will Arista. I mean, she can't weigh, what … a hundred pounds? And it's going to be brief. No dragging her back here. I'll do the ritual right there … rip and gut her in her own home."

Conn nodded, unfazed by the brutality.

"This will *not* be another fail, Conn. I've waited for this moment almost two decades."

"Yup."

He stared into Conn's eyes, unwavering, to drive his point home. "Count this as our only chance. You've been my right-hand man, and I will always take care of you, because you've taken care of me. You *must* have my back on this."

"I got it."

"Alright. Mondays are low-key, and Tuesdays are workdays, so few people stay up late. And did you see the neighborhood? A bunch of worn old houses that are simple to break into, and my guess is our sweet, white witch nor the rest of them have any actual weapons. Just be wary of random sharp objects." Considering Conn's facial scar, he already knew that.

"Yup."

"But … she *is* a witch. I mean, we wouldn't be here if she wasn't." He looked away, imagining the possibilities. "I wish I knew more about what powers she has." He tapped on the desk. "Keira could attune to me, but my guess is she didn't pass it on … out of spite." He sneered. "She killed Henry, and that man was a brute … so there's something fierce within her." Fergus clicked his tongue and pondered her source. Then, he shook his head and waved off his rising insecurity. "I'll be ready for it, whatever *it* is. I am manifesting this outcome if it kills me!"

Conn backed away as he arose. "I need to work on my invocations. It would be ludicrous to use a cheat sheet while performing a crucial ritual with blade, fire, and a live sacrifice. Can you get lost a while?"

"Yup."

Conn grabbed his cigarettes and lighter and stalked out for a smoke break.

Once alone, Fergus scanned the tidy room with nary a crease in the white coverlets on the beds, still fresh from the maid's diligent morning cleaning. He walked out onto the small deck, waiting for Conn to emerge in the below parking lot. He considered his goals—the trip to South America, the black Maserati two-seater awaiting his signature in Spokane, and the reward of fulfilling this long-term ambition.

Conn came into view, heading toward the Expedition. The cloud of smoke rising from his lips made him look like a steam train headed for destruction.

Fergus stepped back inside and shut the door. He grabbed his notes and a towel and secured both locks. He undressed, then positioned his clothes with precision on the bed, fussing at their seams. With nothing remaining but his black spandex boxer briefs, he set the towel on the floor and settled upon it. Notes on his right.

He closed his eyes, imagining the gash he would bestow with the acerbic blade. Her scream would die out long before she did as her lifeblood flowed from her body.

An intrusive thought. What if she put up a strong fight?

Perhaps he should drug her first for an orderly sacrifice.

No, too time consuming. Just plunge the athame to immobilize her, and collect the blood.

Further, his mind drifted. He stood in front of his coven, given honored esteem and an endless stream of wealth that he would spend on fine suits and expensive watches. And yes, he would throw a little in the coven's direction. And for Conn, he would allow more lighting and a warmer office temperature come winter.

He opened his eyes and absorbed the most appealing aspect of this entire ordeal … ending the Kelly lineage, a compulsion he held ever since Ian had walked into his sister's life.

CHAPTER 33
FAUX CASTLE OF OUTLANDISH STRANGERS

Sheriff Michaels drove his squad car up the small incline toward the Scotts Valley hotel with its scaled-down castle theme—three stories of stone masonry on rounded walls with a matching entrance and gardeners always snipping away at the landscaping. It held an unusual grandeur for the unassuming suburb.

He parked beneath the bulky front overhang, ready to follow up on his hunch that Fergus chose the deluxe hotel, only twenty minutes from the Kellys. This, based on his posh residence noted on the Spokane DUI arrest.

When he entered the building, the friendly front desk attendant greeted him with a warm smile, sweet eyes, and a ponytail as pert as her welcome.

He held up his badge. "Sheriff Michaels. I just called and verified a patron. I'd like to speak with him."

"Of course," the bubbly woman said, dressed in her pressed, logo-ed jacket. After a quick call, she announced, "He'll be right down."

The sheriff thanked her and settled on the leather sofa in the lobby. The posh surroundings comprised a simple color scheme—bold black and crisp whites against warm tans and ecrus. The shiny, jet-black sweeping staircase added dimension and geometry to the lobby's striking presentation.

Atop the stairs, a man of distinction appeared, and upon his descent, he walked with the poise of an aristocrat. While he recognized Fergus as the disheveled drunkard from the DUI photo, his current appearance was nothing but impressive. He stood up to greet him.

Off the last rung, Fergus stuck out his hand and bid the sheriff a congenial hello. "To what do I owe the pleasure of being visited by a lawman today?"

The sheriff shook his hand and introduced himself while eyeing Fergus's sturdy black metal watch, standing almost a half-inch up from his wrist, with a small silver crown on its face and opaque dots and lines in place of numbers. "I understand that you're familiar with the Kelly family."

"Yes, a Kelly member married my sister quite some time ago. Sadly, I just lost her to cancer." Fergus bowed his head in regret.

"I'm sorry to hear that. I wasn't aware." He wondered if he spoke of Arista's mother, with his relation as her uncle.

"Yes, sadly, we must endure losing loved ones as the years pass."

"This is true. I'd like to ask you some questions and thought rather than the formality of the station, we could keep it civil, here in the conference room. Does that work for you?"

"Of course."

The sheriff nodded at the clerk, who led them to a small meeting room. Once inside, he waited for Fergus to select a seat, then sat down opposite him. He ran a visual inspection of this out-of-towner who deeply aggravated the Kelly folks.

Fergus remained silent and offered a confident smile with an upturned chin. However, after a brief silence and enduring the obvious scrutiny, he spoke. "So, Officer Michaels ... you said you have some questions. I'm all ears." His eyes flashed in amusement.

"Are you familiar with a tattoo ... an inverted pentagram that sinks into an image of a red slit?" The sheriff placed his forearm on the table and opened his hand. "Right about here ... on the palm."

Fergus released a subtle smirk. "I do know that tattoo." He gazed above him as if reminiscing good times. "In the past, I knew some guys with that tattoo, but you know how time moves on, and we lose contact with old friends."

"You mind if I see your hands?"

"Not at all." Fergus raised his palms—clean and callous-free.

How disappointing to see no sign of the tattoo. "At one time, did you have that tattoo?"

"Yes, I must admit it. There was a time I kept company with … let's say … *despicable* people, but those days are far behind me."

"Did you know a Henry Wallish?" He watched Fergus, looking for shiftiness or any sign of discomfort at the topic.

"Ah, yes. A very disturbed man. Horrible man, in fact. Never liked him. The things he would do to women …" Fergus shook his head, grimacing. "No, I've not heard from Henry in … jeesh, close to twenty years."

Oh, the games he will play, but no need to pursue that avenue right now because he'd need a lot more evidence to order phone records. Instead, he switched topics to Dustin. As he did, Fergus made a subtle movement in his seat.

"Yes, I know Dustin. Him, I saw about a year ago. Nice kid … had a good job … came from a respected family." He eyed the sheriff, his neck rigid.

"Well, his car cartwheeled into a canyon, killing him. Were you aware of that?"

Fergus animated. "Oh, no! That's just awful news. Yet another loss and I did not even know."

"What was your relationship to Dustin?"

"Friends. Well, more like acquaintances."

"*How* did you know him?"

"He was a relative of a friend in my group. You know … self-help crowd, trying to stay sober."

"Right. Dustin also had the pentagram tattoo."

"You're kidding me. I didn't know. Our contact was by phone."

"Maybe he was paying homage to a classic understanding of you?"

"Maybe he was." Fergus shot a subtle glare to the sheriff, then averted his gaze.

He quieted and studied Fergus. He longed for him to squirm and crack in spontaneous admission. He felt the rise of a grin and let it break free.

The expression caught Fergus's attention, prompting him to sit up straight. "Any other questions, Sheriff?"

"No. But I've got to say … you have quite a confidence about you. Mmh! How does one go about acquiring that?"

"Live a good life." Fergus flashed a full smile of glistening, bleached-white teeth.

This guy was a complete sham. "Well, I'll surely remember those words." He stood up, offering him the lead to the lobby.

In the hotel's grand foyer, the sheriff said goodbye to the epitome of a narcissistic sociopath and exited the lobby, only to be greeted by a humongous cloud of secondhand smoke. Beyond the cloud, he threw an irritated look back at its owner, an ugly brute of a man.

The brute gave him a smirking, single nod, then let his neck sink into his broad shoulders, daring him to make a move.

"Hooo-wee, that must've hurt," the sheriff said of the scar across his face, hoping it was a cruel reminder. He did not wait for a response and continued over and back into his cruiser.

While situating his radio and seatbelt, he observed the thug in his mirror. Between the smarm he had endured from Fergus and the cloud of smoke coating him, he craved a shower, but relief would not come for hours. The positive note was that he had met the mystery man and his charming act of a high-class elitist did not fool him. Fergus was just another felon in fine clothing—and the bully at the door, his henchman.

CHAPTER 34
YOU MAY HAVE MISSED SOMETHING

The night brought an unprecedented chill. Striking Arista to the bone. Not just the cold. A big confrontation lay in wait, and what was usually the perfect time to cuddle up in plush fleece had moments of nauseating nervousness. To pass the time and distract themselves from the inevitable, she and her father reassembled the Ouija board to its more practical use after a full presentation of its history, including the previous year of identifying the lair of a notorious serial killer. A serial killer who ended up dead beside it.

"What a trip down memory lane. I only saw it a few times as a kid. My grandparents insisted me and my mitts stay clear of it." He offered his best grumpy old man impression, saying, "*Git on, laddie! Leave that table alone.*"

His mocking of their elder's voice brought a welcome comic relief.

"And look at you and Bethie! Making it work … very impressive." A broad smile crossed his face. Then his expression softened. "Riss, I know I can never make up for the lost time, but I'll do my best to be there for you now. I want to see you grow and get married … if that's what you want … and I hope to be a grandpa someday. I'd like to see it all."

"I'd love that." His sincerity struck her heart, and she teared. With many casual conversations behind them, she realized she actually liked him. He was fun … and funny, and he brought a sense of masculine security.

"You ready for this chaos?" he asked, staring into her eyes to convey the seriousness.

She took a huge breath. "Yes." Honestly, she was terrified, but she would be strong for him.

"I love you." He hugged her.

"I love you … Dad." She did it, called him *Dad*, though muffled by her face buried in his shoulder. She took in that familiar scent of pine, cedarwood, and bay leaf from his freshly showered skin. "Actually, give me one sec!"

"Sure."

She ran to her bedroom and came back in a jiffy with her phone. "I want a selfie. I don't have any current pictures."

His smile beamed, and he opened his arm in invitation.

She stood up close to him, and he cupped his hand around her shoulder. Posed together, she absorbed the image on her screen, then froze it in time. "Thank you."

"You betcha. Make sure I get a copy."

"You will. As will Auntie." Walking to her bedroom, she basked in the renewed relationship.

But once alone in her room, the nervous chill returned. This night had just begun, and she hoped their plan held strong. She left her door ajar and climbed into bed.

Her dad finished up business, the sound effects recognizable— flipping off light switches, setting a glass by the kitchen sink and closing her small pantry door. His footsteps went into the foyer, and she heard the unbolting of her two front door locks.

Arista reached out from under the covers and turned off her light. Between the anxiety and the crispy cold sheets against her bare skin, she curled into fetal position.

Her dad walked down the hall to the back bedroom.

The sudden illumination of his small lamp shined in through her cracked door. After a bit of rustling, he dimmed it to a lower setting, a small beacon surviving the darkened hallway. Almost shutting his door, the beam narrowed even more so.

Silence followed.

"Oh!" She bolted out of bed over to the cat post and scooped up a sleeping Royal. His furry muscles tensed as he frantically looked around the room. "Sorry, Royal." She gingerly set him down in her tiny master bath and gave him a loving stroke before closing the door.

From his bedroom, her dad called out, "Arista?"

"Just putting Royal in the bathroom." She hustled back into bed.

He grunted in acknowledgment.

Under covers, she listened to the soft howl of the blowing wind and heard the occasional hum of light traffic from the main strip in the distance. They were close to help if needed. Still, she endured the worry and her thumping heartbeat.

*   *   *

Fergus watched the glow disappear from the other side of Arista's hedge. "Okay, lights out. Let's give it an hour."

"Yup."

"I'm going to give you the athame. Hold it until I ask for it."

"Yup."

Fergus worked to control his heightening anxiety. The moment felt precarious … and perfect … and laden with potential. It was too good to be true, kindling unease. But he had to stay focused on the benefits— a new man, restored to dignity, wowing his congregation. He would give them accurate messages from their loved ones from the Otherworld, and channel spirits of good fortune and prestige. Maybe. Who knew? At this point, he did not care which powers he acquired because he knew something big, supernatural in all its glory, was coming his way. He could feel it!

A short time lapsed, and he spotted a county cruiser coming up the street.

"Get down!"

He and Conn ducked into the cab of Frank's truck, having turned in the already-made SUV. Fergus heard the lawman's engine slow as it approached Arista's driveway, and he waited as it crept past the entrance, picked up speed, and turned toward the highway.

They sat up and bided their remaining time, until finally exiting their vehicle. With a calculated stealth, they slinked across the street, and set upon the small cottage that housed a cache of possibilities.

"Keep a lookout. In fact, go check the street again. Make sure the neighbors didn't hear our doors and come outside. I want to see the house layout. I'll check who's in there and where they lie."

Conn nodded.

Fergus walked up to the door and found it unlocked. He flashed a look to Conn, who shrugged and began his walk to the hedge. Slowly, Fergus opened the door, free of creaks. The unusual noise-free entry for such an aged house made the onset even better.

Once inside, he realized the interior was darker than the outdoors, except for the light coming from the back room. He walked toward it, passing the kitchen on his left, a wall, then an unlit living and dining area. At the ajar door on his right, he peeked inside the darkness, hearing only one effect.

Mew.

He'd check this room later. At this moment, the subtle movements and light were his primary targets, and those came from the last room down the hall.

With his eyes adjusting to the dark, he arrived at the door and slid his head to the side in order to peek in, expecting to see her.

BASH!

The door slammed into the side of his head and sent a ringing deafness into his ears. In a flash, Ian lunged at him. Pounding on him, one punch after another, they landed on the floor. He flailed for a moment before bringing his forearms up in front of his face, attempting to guard himself against the repeated blows.

Ian hooked his arm underneath the defense. The right jaw! The left! Again and again.

Fergus tried to push him away, but the blows kept coming, pummeling his senses. He tried pushing himself from the floor. There was no use as the barrage of grueling blows rained upon him. Now, he merely fought to stay conscious.

Ian tired, and his punishment lost steam.

As the beating slowed, Fergus drew every ounce of his will to propel himself upward and rose to almost standing.

Ian fell to the side, flipped around, and dove at Fergus's legs, taking his stability and causing him to crash to the floor again.

On the descent, Fergus landed an elbow dead-center of Ian's ribcage, provoking a pained groan.

A pause in the beating. They panted for a moment, each regaining their strength. There would only be one survivor.

Ian thrust himself upon Fergus again, straddling him, and launching another assault. But only a fraction of his previous fury.

Fergus accepted the force. No fight left within him, he absorbed each punishing blow in full surrender.

Ian added one last humiliating, open-handed bitch-slap upon his aching face, then sat up tall. The victor. He heaved for oxygen as he straddled Fergus's thrashed body.

Fergus struggled to open his eyes through his swollen flesh. His skin burned, and his vision was tinged in red as Ian's silhouette became a blur in the dim lighting.

However, all was not lost. He just needed to keep Ian distracted. "How'd you know … it was tonight?" Fergus asked, his question forced out though the pain.

"How do you think? You … fucking … piece of shit."

Fergus snorted, choking on the blood in his throat before it bubbled out of his severely busted nose. Of course, he knew. Not only had he seen them driving in the neighborhood, but he also had that ability. "Dreams."

"That's right, and it only took one! Just like before." Ian inflicted a last patronizing slap and rose, grabbing a hunk of Fergus's cheek for leverage.

"But …" Fergus released a pained laugh as Conn stalked up behind Ian. "I think you may have missed something."

The athame's blade caught a ray of low lighting and glimmered as Conn lifted it with ruthless intention.

.　　.　　.

Her dad had insisted she stay put, remaining in the room until everything was safe. But Arista struggled to endure the fight between her dad and uncle from the shadows. Thankful for her dad's control of the situation, she watched him overpower Fergus with no sign of faltering. With 9-1-1 already called, she dialed Auntie. But as she did, she noticed a horribly fierce man tromping up her porch steps. Petrified, she backed into the darkness of her room and sought shelter at its furthest end. Did her dad know about a second guy? He had not mentioned him but kept details brief, his words easy to remember— *'You stay hidden. No matter what!'* With her call dropping to voicemail, she dialed Auntie again, hoping she had kept her phone charged.

As the brute opened the front door, she prayed her dad realized he played a part. Regardless, he was now sandwiched between the two of them. She came back to her door and held her breath, watching the scene unfold with an excruciating desire to help. She crept to her altar and grabbed her modest witchblade, came back to the door, and readied herself.

Suddenly, she saw the steel of her long-lost athame. In the intruder's hand, the blade rose, reflecting the low light.

The gasp stole her scream as the athame plunged down, lodging deep into her dad's back.

A flush of sheer horror washed through her. Her scream of unbearable distress released throughout the house, reverberating off the closed quarters.

The brute yanked the athame out of her dad's back, and he crumpled to the floor.

A flush of sensation came upon her. The onset of colorful shapes and neon colors filled her vision.

"No!" she screamed to her great-great-grandfather's attempted interference. She solidified herself in the moment. "Stop it! I don't need you! I want you gone!!" Her sobbing words thrust forth in strong defiance as her anguish turned to fury.

Upon the demand, a sharp pain shot through the center of her skull, leaving her dizzy. She felt his retreat as if a part of her had diminished. As her coherence returned, she flung open her bedroom door, and with witchblade in hand, and full rage intact, she faced the brute. She pointed her weapon at the ugly beast. "You!"

He sneered at her, her athame and her dad's lifeblood in his hand.

She shot a glance at her uncle as he struggled to his feet, then over to her dad, deathly still on the floor. She seethed, watching Fergus push him aside as he stood and felt the intense burn of her hatred. "I hate you! You're a fucking monster!"

Fergus laughed, his swollen, bloodied, and bruised face making him a grotesque caricature of his finer self. "You only know the half of it."

She longed to reach her dad, but now they both stood in her way. "Why are you doing this?! Losers!" she shrieked, alternating her revulsion between the two of them. "I hate you both!" How else could she release the damage within her and turn it loose upon them?

As Fergus and Conn closed in on her, she continued backing toward her front door. "You will get nothing from this night!" She grasped for her next step, eyes scanning her possibilities. With no further interference from her ascendent, she stood alone.

With her eyes fixed on Fergus, her courage returned. "You will disappear into oblivion and remain the **nothing** that you are—that you've **always** been!"

Fergus smirked and tilted his head. "Conn …"

Conn kept an unflinching watch upon her and awaited Fergus's command.

"Get this bitch."

Conn lunged at her.

"FREEZE!"

A rushing beam of luminous red radiated past her and became a small dot on the brute's forehead. With the lawmen's orders disregarded, a blast of bright white illuminated with an ear-deafening pop from behind her. A small hole opened up just above Conn's right eyebrow. His eyes blanked, and he dropped to the ground with a mighty thud.

The deputy arose from his crouched position and firmly shoved her aside. "Get down!"

She fell to the ground at her bedroom door, watching the deputy run to Conn.

"Freeze, Fergus!" Sheriff Michaels yelled from the entry.

"Yes, I hear you," Fergus said, slowly raising his hands.

Arista's eyes stayed fixed on her dad at the back of the hallway. She had to get to him.

Fergus locked eyes with her, then looked at the sheriff as he approached.

"Fergus! I *will* shoot you!" the sheriff warned. "Arista, stay down!"

She edged herself closer toward her dad.

Fergus stopped, his hands suspended in the air. "Sheriff, please help me!" His voice became a whimpering plea. "Please! They lured me here."

She heard the ploy, but her pathway became clearer. Carefully, she proceeded toward her dad. Passing Fergus, she felt his looming presence, his spirit desperately wanting to clutch her. She tightened her grip around her witchblade and hurried past him.

One last glance behind her, confirming the sheriff had Fergus, and she fell to her knees at her dad's side. All other worries diminished. In desperation, she cried out for him, draped across his body, hugging him, and begging him to be okay.

His eyes fluttered and opened to only slits.

"Dad! Dad, please just hold on." She hugged him and screamed to the sheriff for help, but he had just seized Fergus.

Her dad found just enough strength. "Riss … take … my hands."

She grabbed the hand closest to her and brought it to her heart—squeezing it against her cheek, kissing it, and drenching it in tears.

"Both," he said, struggling for breath.

Every millisecond now filled with dire intention, she took her dad's hands into her own. She felt him trying to lace their fingers.

"Come … my head."

Hands sealed together, she lowered her forehead onto his. With feeble words, he chanted in a low, incoherent murmur. She held tight, frozen in the merging of their spirits, trying to discern the meaning of his words but swept into the crushing reality that overtook her. He was dying.

A moment of distraction eased the pain as a euphoric rush coursed through her body. But it was fleeting.

"Riss … I love—"

His head and hands fell limp, and his grasp slipped from hers.

She wailed out in anguish. Her body trembled, and she draped over him. Her head flushed in a consuming heat, and her eyes burned from the flow of endless salty tears. She cuddled into him, nuzzled under his chin, her head trying to shake away the harsh truth.

·   ·   ·

Despite the tragedy, the sheriff felt an honored victory to crack the layers of this corrupt degenerate. He slapped the cuffs on Fergus. But losing Arista's father would haunt him for years to come.

With the ambulance blaring its sirens a few blocks away, Sheriff Michaels jostled Fergus onto the porch as Bethie barged past them through the front door. Crying out Ian's name, she ran to Arista's side and fell to the ground beside her, keening as witches do.

"We need a second ambulance," the sheriff told Hendrickson.

"On it."

Giving them time to grieve, the deputy made his call while the sheriff marched Fergus down the steps of the small, unassuming cottage that had become the most active source of violence in the county's four closest towns combined. With Fergus's thug dead, he would not be any trouble, but he still hated leaving the body with the women in such a saddened state. He needed to get this criminal secured in the cruiser so he could return to them.

As he approached the county car, Fergus snickered, bloodied snot trickling onto his lip.

"What's the matter? Things didn't go your way?" He wrenched Fergus's handcuffed arms a little higher up his back.

"Can't you see they lured me here to assault me? It's ludicrous that I'm the one being arrested!"

"Tell it to the court."

An ambulance careened into the driveway, its sirens blaring. The EMTs hopped out and rushed to his deputy, guiding them to Conn and Ian's bodies.

The sheriff diverted his attention back to Fergus, opened his cruiser's door, and shoved him inside, letting his head hit just above the doorjamb.

Fergus boiled in contempt. "What you don't know is—"

He slammed the door in his face, robbing him of his final word.

Chapter 35
Most Extravagant Dracula Costume

Slouched back against her navy corduroy reading cushion, Maddie lounged on her twin XL bed in sweats and a pink-and-black flannel shirt, flipping between her various apps. Lyrics from a song claiming to not *'practice Santeria'* belted out of her speaker as her fingers milled about a napkin of cheese puffs. A knock at her bedroom door interrupted the laid-back vibe.

Uncle Pat appeared. "Shane's here to see you."

"Weird. Okay, thanks."

Hearing Shane's name reminded her she had not heard from Arista for days. Maybe she was acclimating to her dad. She braced herself and set down her phone. Amazed after all these years, Shane granted her his first-ever solo visit. She knew the topic—Arista.

When she walked into the front room, he gave her a half-hearted smile. "Hey, can we talk for a few minutes?"

"Sure, come in."

With his subdued greeting, no doubt he came to talk about the notorious sighting. She peeked at Uncle Pat, reseated at the kitchen table with his checkbook, bills, and pen, and directed Shane into the small sitting room by the front door. Unfortunately, Uncle Pat would hear the conversation.

She gestured for him to take a seat on the sofa, then plopped down on a small, velvet bucket chair. "What's up?"

"Well … about that gossip you spread about me to Arista …"

"Not gossip. I saw you there." She would keep her patience in this matter but refused to be gaslighted into a different perspective.

"I was *not* on a date. We were there with our fathers, who are good friends."

She rolled her eyes, not buying what he had to sell.

"Maddie, I'm not BS-ing you. I have no interest in anyone but Arista, and I want to re-connect with her. You spreading an erroneous rumor has put me in a terrible light." His irritation softened. "We've *all* been friends a long time. You *know* how much I love her." He held the gaze. "I'd appreciate if you undo the damage you have created."

Though she felt defensive, Shane seemed genuine. Still, why should she have to defend her actions when she was just protecting a friend? "What do you mean *I created*? I saw—"

"You saw nothing more than two people out with their dads. Nothing more!"

"I don't know, Shane. She's going through a lot right now. She just reunited with her parents, then her mom died of cancer and she's a bundle of emotions."

His eyes bugged, and he struggled to get words out fast enough. "Well, that makes me want to see her even more! Jesus!" After sputtering forth his declaration, he clenched his jaw and settled. His voice came out firm and deliberate. "Maddie, please make this right."

"Just call her yourself."

"I have. She sends me straight to voicemail!" A swing of his hand settled to a controlled calm. "Look, I love Arista … more than I have ever loved anyone, and I *especially* want to be there for her now. I'll keep working at it from my end, but it would be great if you did your part by fixing that … *narrative* you told." His eyes held clear and steady on her. "Please."

Uncle Pat's nonchalant whistle preceded his entry into the living area. "Hey, guys. Everything okay?"

Shane stood up. "Yes. Sorry, Mr. Hilgard. I'll take my excitability elsewhere." He gave Uncle Pat a reverent nod as he passed him and looked at her once more. "Maddie, please." Then, he exited and shut the door with a respectful ease.

Miffed, she now second-guessed herself, and worse, the conflict had played out in front of the amused stare of Uncle Pat. She knew she had to give him something.

"What was that all about?" he asked.

So predictable. "I saw Shane with some chick in Capitola, and they were having a good ol' time." She clammed up, wishing in vain that would suffice.

"And?"

"Well, of course, I told Arista. She's my best friend! If he's going to see other people, then he needs to let her go. Not string her along in a relationship he's already ditched." She felt her own defensiveness rising as if he had dumped her.

"What is he saying?"

"He's saying it wasn't a date." She hated to admit it, but he sounded pretty convincing, and the possibility of misconception ate at her. Once sure of what she saw, she now questioned her judgment. Worse, *Uncle Knows Best* had involved himself and kept asking thought-provoking questions.

"Why did you assume they were dating? Was it a candlelit dinner between the two of them?"

"No."

"Were they holding hands? Kissing?"

"No, and no." She rolled her eyes, irritated by how innocent it sounded.

Uncle Pat sat down on the edge of the sofa. "Details?"

His finesse at gaining facts irritated her, and she growled in frustration at his smooth persuasion. "The supposed premise is they were at lunch with their dads. I didn't see the dads, but then Evan ran into Mr. Stoddard as we left."

Uncle Pat smirked and peeped out a bit of laughter.

"Ugh! They were totally having a good time."

"Cheater!" he barked out, followed by a dropped chin and wry expression.

She grunted in disdain and dazed out the window, beginning to picture her apologies to both of them. What could she offer to Arista as the rationale for her bold mistake?

"I'm just harassing you. However ... I think if you started that *fire* ... it's your responsibility to put it out."

"Thank you for your wisdom ... Master Yoda," she said with a beleaguered eye roll, perturbed by his interference yet humbled by his counseling.

"My pleasure," Uncle Pat said, in contrived cheer, before whistling his way back to accounting.

•　　•　　•

The light rain dappled the windshield while motoring through the mountainous curves. An offer of consolation from the brooding slate-gray sky as they rode in silence. The fitting sentiment from the universe gave little purpose to Arista's loss. As they returned from securing her dad's place alongside her mother in the sanctioned area of innovative burial, the cremation process would not be complete for a couple more days.

Amidst the sadness, Arista breathed in a strange sense of tranquility. There was nothing left to lose. Sad, but also a relief that Fergus was in jail. Still, the rawness and ripped-open feeling of the loss came in emotional waves. At first, she found them unbearable to withstand, but realized that if she faced them and grieved, her despair would ease and then wane. After all, how many tears can you weep from exhausted eyes? How many headaches can you endure from hard cries? She had to go on.

She had kept her father's death, now three days behind her, to herself. In time, she would call Maddie, but for now, she retreated inward. She reconciled the meaning by creating a fairy tale ending of her parents rejoining in the Summerland. They'd be reborn at the same time and place, would meet, fall in love and, through their love, have children. And this time, experience every moment.

They emerged from the depths of the mountain onto Bear Creek Road, catching sight of the horse stables. The usual low foot traffic now teemed with exuberant people cheering costumed children on horseback. From the looks of it, a contest, and she longed for a reprieve. "Auntie, can we watch the horse show?"

Auntie hesitated. Then, a decisive answer. "Of course!" She punched the brakes harder than expected and made a hard right into the parking area.

HOOOONK!

"Oh, be quiet," she sassed to the alarmed driver passing them.

They bumped and bounced across the rutted dirt parking lot and found a space at the farthest end, making for quite a trek to the stands. Along the way, Arista raised her face to the light sprinkles. Tender from crying, she took pleasure in the fresh, wet, coolness on her skin. "I hope the weather stays mellow."

"Either way, we won't melt," Auntie reassured.

As they approached the arena, she kept her face lowered, knowing the stark look of sadness fixed upon it. So many times over the past few months, it held the effects—mottled, red, and scrunched.

Upon seeing the energized contestants, her mood lifted, and her appearance no longer mattered. Auntie, too, looked engaged in the escape. They found space at the arena fencing and leaned into the festivity.

The first contestant they saw was a young girl with dark brown hair, dressed as a Monarch. Donned in black leotard and tights with a set of brilliant butterfly wings around her shoulders, she fondled her bouncy headband of black-sequined antennae tucked behind her ears. Her father paraded her and her brown-and-white Pinto in true showgirl fashion.

Arista remembered her own horseback ride with Dakota, and the paradox of the costume brought humor. "That's a bit ironic," she said, releasing a quiet laugh, picturing her own experience of horse-meets-Monarch. She looked at Auntie for agreement, but the joke missed.

Next up was a cowgirl with luminous coily hair dressed in a bedazzled pink leather fringed vest and chaps. Her giggles twinkled like fairy laughter throughout the arena for much of the ride. The horse she rode had a flaxen chestnut coat, just like the one Arista had ridden with Dakota. They drew much applause.

After the cowgirl, in trotted a stark white horse and, upon it, a boy with spiked honey-blond hair dressed in a bright orange jumpsuit, complete with a puffy, white collar and swaths of blue at the shoulders. Upon his black headband, a shining silver plate with a squiggled rune.

"What costume is that?" Auntie asked in a whisper.

In her frame of mind, she struggled to remember the name. "Nuri … um … it's a popular anime character. Evan and his little brother always had t-shirts and figurines of him. Naruto! That's it."

Auntie nodded.

After three more equally amusing entrants, the final ride belonged to a young boy with a close-cropped buzzcut dressed in the most extravagant Dracula costume she had ever seen. Ghost-white makeup covered his face, and he had a hand-drawn widow's peak at his hairline. A ruby-red vampire's cross dangled from a black velvet ribbon tied around the collar of his white frill-lapeled dress shirt. He completed the outfit with skinny, rectangular-shaped, purple-lensed specs and a tall-collared black satin cape that reminded her a lot of the one Auntie owned.

"Oh, this one … he's something," Auntie said, amused and pointing.

Arista agreed, her heavy eyes lifting from sadness.

Nothing disrupted this little gent's attitude. A dog barking, he strolled onward. A baby crying, he sat taller. And even when his horse spooked for a second, his father handled that. He *expected* everything to be a-ok.

"He's so confident," Arista marveled and felt teary. It was nothing the boy did, instead, more of what he represented—facing challenges head-on with unwavering determination. No, he probably didn't just lose his mom and dad, but still.

When he passed, the boy threw a momentary look her way before returning his gaze to the ring.

She let out a small gasp. "Did you see that?"

"I did! I think you're the only thing that distracted him this whole ride."

They observed him, looking for another blip in focus, but none came. He remained stoic, sitting tall, and undistracted until his father led him out of the arena. Upon his exit, the crowd erupted into a bombastic cheer. Moments later, they were called to the center after victory by *applause-o-meter* and given the first-place prizes—a blue ribbon for the boy's neck and an extra-large blue sash and rosette for his Bay mare.

"You ready?" Auntie asked in a hushed voice.

"Whenever you are." Walking toward the car, Arista further processed. "You know, he didn't bat an eye the whole time. Even when he looked at me, he didn't break character. He had a job to do and did it. Now he's taking home first place, and I don't even think he realizes what a great show he gave us."

"He may know," Auntie said in an amused tone as they arrived at her car. "However, in all my years, I have found that if you have the gift of bringing a smile to someone's face, you are blessed … as are they."

After sinking inside the cab, Auntie started the car.

"Auntie, can we talk for just a minute?"

"Of course."

"I'm sorry you lost your nephew."

"And I'm ever so sorry you lost your dad, Arista."

They wrapped each other in caring hugs and shared the tears.

Pulling away, Arista said, "I know my sadness will ebb and flow. I had already started reading about it when my mom died. Just know the in-betweens … those spaces, I know I'll be okay. I'm serious. I think I'm doing pretty well. How about you?"

"We must all carry on. I'll be fine, too," Auntie said with a reassuring smile.

"So, not sure about you but I think I'm good to go for tomorrow's releasing ritual of Great-Great. I almost popped a blood vessel keeping him subdued the other night but, in the same breath, I'll say he may already be gone."

"I wondered about that!" Auntie blurted. "I wanted to wait until you were ready to talk, but I truly wondered why he didn't emerge during that horrible moment!"

"Well, he was definitely a-percolatin'," Arista joked, still teary-eyed. "I was just so enraged that I told him to leave. Then, I got this shooting pain … like a hollowing out … I don't know how else to explain it …"

"So, by controlling your fear, you controlled the possession. Astounding!"

"Actually, it's kind of the opposite. I had *no* control over my rage." She relived the intensity. "I felt the emergence, screamed at him to leave, then felt … like … a slice right through my brain." She snorted at the painful memory.

"You poor dear," Auntie said with a wince.

"Anyway, after all that, he didn't try again."

Auntie hummed in fascination.

"You know, I've been meaning to ask you—what keeps someone from going to the Summerland … or Otherworld? Why do you think he lingers?"

"I've always heard that a haunting is unfinished business."

"That's what I thought. So, what is your grandfather waiting for?"

Auntie held her pensive look, and her reaction heightened the ambiguity even more so.

The silence simmered amongst them.

"Well, that certainly begs the question, doesn't it?" Auntie said, tapping her index finger on her lips while gazing out the window.

"A bit."

"Hunh!" Auntie said, then relented to the mystery, putting the car in reverse to back out of the space. "Something to ponder later."

Arista blew it off, too. "We should compare notes for the ritual. I found some interesting things in your grimoire collection."

"Not just mine. Some of those entries came from my grandmother."

"I noticed the different handwriting."

As they discussed old family recipes, the focus on other matters helped her grief. She knew it would resurface but that was to be expected.

"Arista, tomorrow, I'd like to run by my old friend's house. With Margaret in Shasta a few more days, I may recruit Iris to help us with the releasing ritual."

"I heard you mention that to Pearl."

"Yes, while we have mutual respect, things never clicked with her as they did with my coven sisters. And Pearl has clashed with Iris on more than one occasion," Auntie said, gunning her engine to exit the lot.

As they left the festivities behind them, Arista replayed the scene of the little vampire on his horse. She remembered the calmer moments of her own ride with Dakota. Amidst the stress in her life, it could be an outlet for grief. "Auntie, do you know how much it costs to own a horse?"

CHAPTER 36
PSYCHOS DO NOT GIVE A DAMN

With fond memories of giggling children and their sleek mounts from earlier that morning, Auntie and Arista sat in reverent silence, enjoying the calm of each other's company.

As threatened at the horse show, the skies opened up and watered Mother Earth, creating a white noise that filled the otherwise quiet room. The falling rain, and drips dropping from the eaves, came forefront as Arista's own tears rested.

An enticing aroma of cinnamon and pumpkin persisted from the kitchen.

"I'll check on that," Auntie said, getting up to gauge the cooling timer.

From late August through November, enjoying Auntie's pumpkin bread at least ten times rang true to custom. And even with Arista's appetite lacking, Auntie insisted on baking the treat for her.

Out of habit, Arista checked her cell. With her ringer off for days, she found a few missed calls—her psychologist, two from Shane, and a voicemail from Maddie. She selected Maddie's message.

'Hey, Arista. Soooo … about that thing … with Shane … I think I owe you both an apol—'

She could not deal with that right now.

Auntie made a subdued announcement. "The pumpkin bread is ready. You want a slice?"

Arista looked up and saw the compassionate, sweet smile on Auntie's face. Of course, she wanted a slice. While her stomach disagreed, how could she say no? She nodded, hopped up, and went to help.

Auntie's demeanor lightened, and she hummed a little tune while prepping the refreshments. Together, they created an array of rhythm within the kitchen—shutting of cupboard doors, clanking of appetizer plates and teacups, and fluid pouring—all contributing to an upbeat tempo.

In a jiffy, two dishes, each holding a thick slice of moist bread, and two cups of ginger tea, sat upon the table. With enthusiasm, they dug into the afternoon treat. Arista found that the warmth of the cinnamon, nutmeg and allspice within the fresh-baked bread soothed her heartache, and the ginger tea comforted her stomach.

"A tinge of ginge," Auntie said after a sip.

"That's what Kenny used to call me."

"Ugh. Glad that one moved."

"Aww. He teased, but he didn't mean it."

"I think he was a bad influence on Shane," Auntie said with a sensible nod.

Interesting, she brought up Shane. "Think so?"

"Yes, I believe Shane is better off without his influence."

Not that it mattered, but very odd that Auntie brought up Shane. A new insight that whatever she sensed about him must be positive.

Auntie continued, with no eye contact. "I wouldn't count that relationship done just yet. And forgive me the boldness, but—"

The sound of tires on pea gravel prompted Auntie to peek out the window.

Arista awaited the visitor information while savoring a chocolate chip, smooshing the melty morsel to the roof of her mouth, and sucking back its flavor. She chased it with a sip of spicy tea. Delicious!

"It's the sheriff," Auntie announced and made haste out the door.

Arista wiped the corners of her mouth, slipped on her shoes, and headed out the front door in time to see Auntie's jaw drop before she lit into a tirade.

"Bailed out! You've got to be kidding me!" Auntie shook her head, resisting the news.

Arista stepped down from her porch. She could see the sheriff's frustration, his typical stoicism replaced by a clenched jaw and compassionate eyes enduring Auntie's outburst.

"We cannot hold him if he posts bail ... which he did. Currently, it's your word against his, and Conn was the only confirmed murderer who possessed the weapon. Fergus says he did not know his friend would resort to killing, and—"

"Good grief, Pete Michaels! That is the biggest bunch of lies I've ever heard in my life!" Auntie paced in a tight circle like a nervous chihuahua.

"He told the DA that Ian lured him to Arista's house to beat him to death, and Conn was just protecting him. We all know it's crap, but ..."

"No, no, no," Auntie whimpered, shaking her head and pinching the bridge of her nose.

Arista stood speechless, staring at Auntie's angst and listening to the sheriff's voice of professional reason on the most awful news. She put aside her sadness. No more time for that. She remembered her false sense of security only hours earlier—the criminal *had* gone to jail. Now, he roamed free. Only survival skills would benefit her as their inevitable showdown endured.

"I'm sorry, Bethie. We all know it's a crock, and I want to put him away as much as you do, but under our state laws, he's got his rights, and we are obliged to release him."

The sheriff sounded regretful and had plenty of empathetic looks, but it did little to settle their loss of security.

Auntie took a huge breath. "Sheriff, this is the worst possible news. That man is a danger to Arista ... a terrible, terrible danger to her! And now, we have everything to lose." She quieted, her eyes shifting in mental calculation.

"What about the car accident … the person from your staff? Didn't that account for anything?" Arista asked.

"Speculative, and still in the investigation phase. We have search warrants and the like but have to work with Spokane Police, and the interstate process complicates matters. For what it's worth, you can file a restraining order."

"Oh, that sounds effective!" Auntie's words mocked in derision. "*I have this paper here that says for you to stay away!*" She slapped her hand on her hip. "Please! Psychos do *not* give a damn about restraining orders."

"I'd suggest you do it for formality's sake. It will represent the valid fear you and Arista carry toward him. It will play better for you in the court system."

"Sheriff, I am beside myself right now, and I have to go back inside." She flung around and trudged toward the porch.

"I understand. We'll stay close. I know it doesn't mean much … but we will."

In the distance, Auntie fidgeted, twitched, and sputtered with anxiety as she climbed the stairs. "… cannot believe this!"

Arista watched the door slam behind her, then looked at the sheriff. His offer did little to reassure her. Their good timing for *her* life had not saved her dad.

The sheriff's eyes fixed on the slammed door before he looked at Arista. "I wish I had better news."

She didn't blame him but had nothing else to say. She backed away and gestured toward the house. "I'm going to go check on her."

He gave a respectful nod and walked to his cruiser.

She exhaled in disappointment, feeling the frazzled effect of her own nerves. As she walked toward her house, a sobering awareness struck her. She knew only one way to stop the madness.

Inside, she found Auntie at the kitchen window watching the sheriff drive away and rested her head on her wise one's shoulder. "You okay?"

"Yes, and I'm sorry. I should be the one asking you that. I didn't mean to lose it, but I cannot fathom how the courts do that." She stared out the window, still dazed by the shocking update.

"I know." Arista paused. Should she verbalize it? Yes. "It feels like we have to get rid of him ourselves." She listened to the incriminating words come out of her mouth, bypassing her usual judgment.

Auntie's eyes bugged, and she flung around, startled by the proclamation.

"I know. I'm surprised I feel that way, too, but he will not stop coming for me. How long has it been? Two decades, and here we are again. He must be driven by something … maybe, something we don't even understand. Desire … greed, hatred, who knows? As a rational adult, he should realize he cannot just kill me and take my so-called abilities. Dad said something to the effect of it being my birthright, so he's trying to kill me for something that he cannot even have. Who thinks like this?" She shook her head. "What drives him—other than freakin' insanity?"

"I don't know," Auntie said, gazing out the window.

Arista felt her anger burn. "And me … and the ones I love, pay the price over and OVER again! And for what?! Reading auras? Having an occasional vision or an intuitive insight? My spells don't even work. My apple spell for Shane … kerplunked to the floor in a mess. My spell for Trini …" She flinched, unable to voice her conceivable blame, and her voice broke. "Nothing! No fire from my eyes! No manifesting! I'm lucky to make ends meet."

Auntie faced her, listening intently.

"And that's thanks to you!" To insinuate was not enough. She calmed and brought forth the unspeakable. "Auntie, I have to kill him."

"Oh, Arista! I won't let you do that. First, I don't want you that close to him, and second, it's not healthy for your spirit. Why do you think your father never killed him? As far back as my grandparents, our tenet is that taking a life is never the answer. It taints the soul, no matter if it's for self-defense or not."

"I don't want it to come to that. I hope the law busts through the door at the right time, but if they don't, I'm ready to face him. I know what it's like now."

"We will find another way."

"No! I'm serious." She felt the confidence harden within her, stoking a newfound rise of destructive fury that had overtaken her woe and helplessness. She wanted to end him, the one who had repeatedly taken from her. "The running, the hiding—all this *fear* has got to stop."

Auntie shook her head in frustration.

A flash of Arista's carefree past came upon her. The lackadaisical days of yesterday seemed so ignorant now. So clueless about life's harsher realities. Michelle's friends in high school had been right about her being a sunny-side-up bore, denying the existence of darkness, and never had her world been so dark. "I'm going to kill him, and this time … I don't need your grandfather's help."

Auntie jabbed her index finger toward her with a fitful warning. "I will say this … to protect yourself … Fine! I give you free rein! We must defend ourselves at all costs. But the way you are talking, it's as if you're plotting it, like you want to cross that line. Don't get me wrong, I want him dead too! However, to cast that sentence with your own hand will only damage you. Please remember this."

"I've already killed someone."

"No! You were merely the hand. That was not your intention nor your spirit behind the deed. There *is* a difference."

"I don't see it like that."

"Arista—"

"My decision is made. I want him to come." She gazed out the window as the soft raindrops became a dowsing shower. More than just symbolism of her tears, rainfall nourished the earth and cleansed the air. Most of all, it brought forth new life. "We're not running or hiding anymore. We're going to stay right here and perform the ritual, whether or not your grandfather is gone. And if my *dear uncle* comes—which I guarantee he will—we'll deal with him accordingly."

"There's got to be another …"

Auntie's voice trailed off as Arista turned and walked toward the cabinet above her oven. She reached up, grabbed it, and brought it down to her chest.

"Arista?"

She turned and walked toward Auntie, holding it out. The long-lost athame secured in its original sheath.

Auntie's fretting turned to pure shock, and her mouth gaped. "How did you get that?"

"When they took Fergus to the cruiser, I took it from that … *thing* on my floor. I switched it with my old witchblade."

"I remembered you getting up but was so deep in my grief that …" Auntie calmed, stroking the athame. She pursed her lips, deep in thought, and settled into a relaxed posture, shoulders dropping to ease. Releasing a breath, she grabbed her phone, pecked at it, and waited.

One ring and Pearl's voice sounded through the speaker.

"Pearl, we need you here. We need *all* of you here tomorrow."

CHAPTER 37
A MAN OF HIS STATURE

Fergus sat beside the small metal desk, staring at his reflection in the window. His background comprised canned laughter of an old sitcom and the sound of oxygen pumping into Frank's lungs who laid on the couch wrapped in a worn, tan cable-knit blanket.

He studied his face, the extensive destruction muted by the sunlit window. Disappointing how low he had sunk, and the sting of Conn's death brought him an isolated loneliness. Maybe he liked Conn more than he thought. He numbed for a moment before appreciating that, because of his account of Ian's entrapment and the state's laws, he was a free man. Now, since he had nothing else worth his time, might as well dig into Plan B.

"Love that bail bond system," he mumbled, tapping the puffed, bruised skin beneath his left eye. Thankfully, Jameson answered his call and wired one million dollars to the court since the lawmen knew, from Arista's admission and their own eyes, that he was not Ian's murderer, and since Ian had beaten him bloody and bruised, the court entertained his account of self-defense. Therefore, it would be up to a jury to decide the outcome many months or years from today, and that day would never come with a well-hatched plan.

He swiveled his chair and rolled over to the desk, wedging himself in place. He fiddled with the knickknacks of the serial killer who had sat here before him—personalized cheap pens, an age-old army-green Swingline stapler, and an old photo of little Henry sitting on Santa's lap in the eighties. In it, his face fearful and crying, as he pushed away the jolly man's head.

His foot twitched while he scanned the bare wall, its faded wood paneling full of thumbtack holes. The outdated style felt demeaning. This was no place for a man of his stature, so with a list of numbers to dial for recruitment, he got to business. The sooner he executed his plan, the sooner he could get the hell out of there.

"Jim, it's Fergus."

"Fergus? Hmph, haven't heard from you in a while."

"Yeah, not much time to talk. Trying to get a group together for a job."

"I gotta tell ya, man … I'm not into your crazy stuff anymore. I'm married now … got a couple kids … just living the straight life. Ya know?"

Curbing useless small talk, he bid Jim adieu and dialed the next possibility.

"Russell. Hope I can count on you, my friend. For old times' sake …"

But Russell was living a better life, too, as were his other options.

He had one more shot, and his best bet since the bozo had left him a recent voicemail. He selected Mike's unanswered message.

'Hey, Fergus! Been a while, man. So, I got someone I want you to meet. Really wild. Give—'

Message deleted. He remembered how Mike always had a new lead, and all his newness, as predicted, would amount to nothing. However, he needed recruits.

"Fergus! My man! You got my voicemail."

"Hey, Mike. Yeah, but I'm calling for something else. I need help on a job, like old times. Good pay, my friend."

"What ya got, and what's the dollars?"

A willing participant at last. "Great. You're still doing the occult?"

"Oh yeah, I'm hooked in with the real deal now. That's what I called you about. Did you listen to my message?"

"Yeah … no. I've been a little busy. So, real deal, huh?" Here came the newness. Fergus tapped his nails on the desk as the thought of Mike's story-to-come grated on his nerves.

"*Really* real!"

"Great. Bring them."

"I don't know if that's a good idea. We're in early stages and she's a little unpredictable."

"Even better, I'd love to meet her."

"Alright, man, you asked for it. So, what's the payoff?"

"How about 2K for both of you?"

Mike laughed. "Nah, that's way light. I know you've got *big* bucks now."

It irritated him that this flighty bastard thought he had any negotiation power, but, in this instance, desperation played a hand. Still, having to compromise ached throughout his recovering body. "Five."

"How about ten for each of us?"

"I'm not paying you twenty grand!" He flinched at his own exertion and calmed. "I just had to post a million-dollar bail bond, and the account is *light*."

"Jail, huh? Couldn't find someone else to do your dirty work this time?"

Fergus faked a chuckle. "Eight for you, doled anyway you want, and that's the last offer." He missed Conn. Dull as a post but as obedient as they came, and the cost for his loyalty was simple living expenses, and a lifted, loaded truck replaced every three years.

"Fine. Deal."

"Good. The job's in Boulder Creek Sunday night, and I need you ready to go!"

"Samhain, huh? Not a problem, buddy. I'm just up here in Frisco, so easy commute for me."

"What's your girl's name, and why's she so special?"

"Soonsil, and I kinda just stumbled upon her."

"Hunh. She'll kill if necessary?"

"Who knows?"

"Is she gifted in the arts or something?"

"I'm guessing so."

Enough games with this idiot. "Alright, I *greatly* look forward to seeing you both. Come early so we can go over things. Got it?"

"I *got* it," Mike said with a hint of touchiness.

Fergus dictated Frank's address and disconnected. With an ally secured, he felt the soreness of his wounds as his pain meds wore off. He also needed to redress his stitches and doctor his nose.

"You need anything, Frank?"

"Huh?" Frank jolted, his expression alarmed by the sudden question.

"Can I get you anything?" he asked, much louder.

"Nah … I'm … good … Thanks," Frank said, gasping out the words with the help of his oxygen tube.

He gave Frank a firm slap on his shoulder and headed to the rundown bathroom, passing the pressboard walls of the claustrophobic hallway. He walked into the small space with its rusty, water-stained sink and looked forward to leaving this impoverished lodging behind him. He had to get back to his Spokane poshness, and the day after tomorrow was his last chance at victory. If he had to lie with dogs to get his prize, so be it. He refused to go to jail and would be long gone by the time his court date arrived. And assuming another identity would be easy, as he had been down that road, and it worked out smashingly. If all else failed, he'd head to Peru, making good on the plans he discussed with Conn.

Hateful of his image in the bathroom mirror, he dabbed the white cream on his busted, stitched, and bruised flesh, running his finger along all these new flaws, wincing at their vicious bites. All minor setbacks. His drive to kill Arista had only magnified with Conn's death, and the more he thought about it, his obsession with sacrificing her had taken on a life of its own. Jealousy. Powers. Revenge. It mattered not. He just knew whatever existed before had intensified even more so.

CHAPTER 38
DID SHE JUST GROWL?

An exuberant bark from the closest neighbor's Doberman carried up the road, announcing Mike and Soonsil's arrival.

"Will holy wonders never cease?" Fergus said, spitting out the droll words from behind grit teeth, arising from his new perch at the old metal desk. He resisted the urge to preen. Who cared what Mike thought?

He walked past a couch-bound Frank and peered out at the inconspicuous gray four-seater parking in the yard. He saw no passenger and settled for the fact Mike came alone. However, Mike lingered, talking with someone. Probably a phone call. Then, a subtle movement in the backseat caught his eye.

Mike emerged from the driver's side, went to his back door, and popped the handle, allowing a small arm to hand him a snowy-white plush toy with big black orbs for eyes. He held it in the crook of his elbow while assisting a child with shoulder-length, jet-black, straight hair out of the car.

"What the—" Stunned, he watched as Mike handed her the toy, which she brought in snug to her chest. She flashed a knowing glare at Fergus while he watched from the shadows of Frank's house.

"Are you frickin' kidding me?" Fergus muttered. "Why would he bring a kid? Idiot!"

"Huh?" Frank bellowed.

"Nothing, Frank. Just talking to myself," Fergus said in a loud voice, knowing the man, half-deaf.

He shook off the audacity and exited the house, oozing smarm. "Well, Mike, who do we have here? Is trick-or-treating on your agenda for the night?"

A smirk crossed Mike's face. "I knew you'd react this way. But looks can be deceiving." He stopped and gazed down at the child clutching her pointy-eared plushie. "Fergus, this is Soonsil. She doesn't talk much, so no offense meant by her silence. Soonsil, this is my old friend, Fergus. I haven't seen him in a while, and the fact we are here holds substantial reward."

Soonsil looked up at Fergus. When their eyes met, she clutched her plushie more tightly.

"Did she just growl?" Fergus asked, keeping steady eye contact with her.

"I don't think so." Mike squatted down to Soonsil's level. "You okay?"

Soonsil blinked and looked away from Fergus, leading her expression to soften as she met Mike's eyes.

He arose. "Nah, man. I don't think so."

Fergus flashed a miffed look at the child, then led them into the house. "We'll talk more about this later. What the hell is she holding?"

"I think it's a fox with a bunch of tails. You know how those hybrid anime characters can be. Anyway, you'll be glad to know that Soonie takes long naps. Right, Soonie?"

Soonsil nuzzled her nose deeper into her plush toy.

"Yeah, you're more of a night owl, huh?" Mike rubbed her head with a gruff appreciation.

She tucked her lips into her mouth, looked up at him with trusting eyes, and nodded.

"Okay, we'll find you a cozy bed." He looked at Fergus. "Can you accommodate that?"

Fergus rolled his eyes, then bared his teeth in a forced smile. "Whatever *she* needs."

•   •   •

Waiting for Mike to emerge from his self-inflicted childcare duties, Fergus scrutinized the grayed, splintered remnants of Frank's old fencing. Soaked from rain, it looked like you could mash it with a fork. Beneath it lay rusted cans with bullet holes that could give someone a case of Tetanus with the wrong move. He allowed himself to kick one of the rusted tins since his year-old Jimmy Choos were ready for Frank's garbage from all the desert and mountain wear-and-tear.

At last, Mike emerged from the house.

Fergus's impatience simmered as he stood with arms crossed. "Okay, Mike, you have my interest piqued. Why the child?"

"First, let me tell you how I met her. I'm strolling down Dolores at almost two in the morning, and I hear this guy scream … I mean, high-pitch terror. Of course, I was going to ignore it because I hear that stuff all the time, but then I see this little girl with him, and I will not turn my back on that! She's got this bloody mess all over the front of her … major crying. So, I give her some candy, and she's been at my hip ever since."

"Why didn't you just take her to the cops?"

"I did! We walked to the station, and she ran off at the sight of it. Maybe a dirty cop killed her family or something."

Fergus snorted. "Nah, this isn't shady at all."

"I'm not lying!"

"Oh, I believe you, but there's something more to this story. She's playing you. So, what's the secret power you mentioned?"

"Later on, we had some jerks harass us. I could have run, but that would've been a total dick-move for her. So, while I'm thinking of our best move, she just glared at them and … growled."

"*That's* what I'm talking about." How did this idiot not see the obvious? Another reason he had unacquainted himself with him years ago.

"No, listen. That little girl's growl sent four thugs packing. In the opposite direction!"

Fergus shook his head and smirked. While the details validated his suspicion, neither he nor Mike would find out the extent of her ulterior motives. Once the night had passed, he would sever ties again, and there was no way his haphazard associate had the wherewithal to take care of her. Not unless she could live on beer and beef jerky.

"They didn't even look at me after that. Anyway, I got us both out of there and she's been with me ever since. Like two weeks now. I know I gotta do something with her, but when you called, I figured I'd take care of it later. Plus, I have an ex in Santa Cruz, and she can help me figure out what to do with her."

"That kid needs to be in school and sent to a home, and I don't appreciate you bringing her. Hardcore shit is going down tomorrow night, and you said she would kill. You made it sound like you had some badass warrior who could contribute."

"I said *maybe* she would kill. Come on! She has something. She scared off four goons, and I found her over some dead guy in the park— who, by the way, I never heard about again, not in the news or anything. Also, she's not afraid of blood because I had to coax her out of her bloody clothes, and that was only after I promised her a new dobok. That's her taekwondo scrubs she sleeps in."

His army of two felt anemic, at best. "So, it's you and me."

"And Soonsil."

"Soonsil will stay here with Frank."

"Come on, Fergus. At least let her wait in the car. She freaks out if I take off without her. Her shrieks could bring the law, and from what it sounds like, we don't need that sort of attention."

He brought his finger up to his lips as he pondered the possibilities. He savored the diversionary tactic swirling in his mind. What could be more disarming than a child? "Maybe she *could* come in handy. Alright. She better do what's she's told."

"She will, as long as it comes from me."

Fergus felt a lift of possibility. "Okay. You, me, and Soonsil. I guess this could make a perfect setup."

CHAPTER 39
THE SILVER BOUGH

Arista's troubled mind flurried with imagined scenarios. Never had her life felt so muddled. Destroyed by heartache and loss, energized by a newfound demon of vengeance within herself, yet still trying to hold on to a semblance of the happiness and normalcy she hoped to rekindle in her life. She kept the contemplations behind a wall of silence as Auntie drove them to Iris's house for a renowned magickal instrument. Later that night, the long-awaited ceremony would ensure Great-Great's release, and she hoped the experience would also prove successful in her contacting her parents.

"Arista?"

Going to the Summerland felt intimidating and rife with consequences, considering all she had learned regarding Margaret's and Mr. Tessay's pasts. Not a mere spell, Margaret had a prolonged visit with her departed cousin during a Samhain ritual and emerged unable to speak. Over the following month, her new ability to shapeshift into a great-horned owl gradually exposed itself. Likewise, Mr. Tessay was still a child when he almost drowned, saw the spirits of his ancestors beneath the lake and re-surfaced with their help. Minus his hearing but plus an ability to commune with the deceased at whim.

"Arista."

Now, she dabbled with this afterlife. Could she lose one of her senses? Come back as a shapeshifter? Maybe it could be another power of her supposed magickal future, but it would depend on the animal. For that matter, what if she couldn't get back?

"I can smell your gears burning, Arista. Are you okay?"

"Yes." She remained entrenched in her musings, shifting to her malevolent uncle. With all considered, was it so wild to think her end neared? So, what if it did. She had become accustomed to death, and it no longer scared her. Not even her own.

"Are you sure?" Auntie's head swiveled front and side to gain her attention.

"Yes, I'm good." She remembered herself and added a token smile. "Thank you for asking."

Turning right onto Bear Creek Road, they drove deeper and deeper into the misted mountain air, the wipers set on low. The leaning shroud of trees felt precarious, as if they had entered a magickal realm, and the branches would reach down and pluck them up at any moment. Leaves had fallen en masse, creating a thick border of vibrant yellow shake along the roadside. Fewer cars passed and, when they did, disappeared just as quickly in the twists and turns of the mountain. And the slick sound of their own tires on the rain-soaked pavement created a potential to skid with one wrong move. Hazardous, like her oncoming night.

"I checked the moon cycle, and it's waning crescent tonight," Arista said, using small talk to distract herself from another spiral into obsessive thought.

"Don't worry about that. A full moon would be ideal, but the night is more significant."

She bit at her lip, remembering that Auntie taught her to place much importance on the lunar cycle. Then again, this was their first time working together on a complex Samhain ritual, which held significant potential for communicating with the departed. The liminal aspect having as much pull, if not more, than the moon's full glow.

"It will be fine," Auntie reassured her.

"What if it's unsuccessful? New is good for new beginnings. That would be ideal. Full moon, of course, excellent for ritual, but we get a waning crescent."

"Well … waning crescent is about letting go. What are we doing?" Auntie looked over at her, then back to the road. "We're letting go of the spirit within you. So, it works just fine."

She surrendered a grin. "Are you making that up? I mean, *yes*, I know it's about letting go, but I thought that was more for forgiveness or obsession."

"True, but now that we're in this position, I see a whole new meaning."

Typical Auntie logic. Bent at whim, but valid.

Seeing the sign for Mountain Lion Road, Auntie sputtered, "Crap. We've gone too far. It's just before this one. That's what happens when I'm yacking and not paying attention." She wedged into a small turnout and executed a precise three-point turn.

The road to Iris's house further warned of trouble. Bumpy and unpaved, they bounced within their seats, the shocks of the old Volvo lacking in low-back-sparing spring. The sun shining through the tree breaks above them served only to illuminate the oily, crimson-leafed threat of plentiful poison oak bushes along the incline.

"There it is!" Auntie gestured with her nose.

A slate entryway marked their turn ahead on the left, a garden of color at its base. Making the turn, four witch hazel shrubs lined the driveway, their dark pink centers surrounded by petals shaped like tentacles in bright yellow. Just beyond were four magnificently large, globe-shaped bushes of neon-pink florae with yellow centers—the Sansaqua Camellia stood impressive in its fall vibrance.

"Wow, her thumb is quite green," Auntie said, eyeing the shrubbery before parking at the weather-beaten solar panel propped against a prominent redwood, looking like the start of a dump run pile.

Out of the car, Arista eyed the superb health of the shrub nearest her at the head of a cobblestone pathway aimed toward the house.

"Oh, gracious!" Auntie said like an excited child in the toy aisle.

Arista looked toward the source of her enthusiasm. The scarlet-orange blooms of a large California fuchsia had attracted a small, ruby-throated hummingbird. It zipped about the flora until noticing the approach of humans, then whizzed off around the farthest corner.

"We're on track." Auntie said, her eyes sparkling as they followed the bird's path.

"You love those hummingbirds." She could only be amused … every time.

Nearing the sun-parched, wide, wooden steps, five lounging cats sat up alarmed, then darted in all directions.

Arista studied the age and wear of Iris's house, its natural wood siding splitting and grayed. The home's most notable feature ominously hovered—a huge circular window on the second level that reflected the surrounding redwoods with mirror-like clarity. With each step closer, the mirroring effect faded, and she saw a person peering down upon them.

"Well, look at that!" Auntie marveled. She walked to a workbench area, her delighted outburst aimed at a row of potted flowers, one specimen within each.

Arista looked back up at the circular window to find the silhouette gone.

"Look how her mandrakes are thriving!" Auntie pointed at the green rippled leaves hosting a five-petal violet cup of yellow-anthered stamens.

"Wow! We haven't grown those before, but I know you've always talked about them." She humored Auntie's excitement, as Auntie had always done for her.

"They are finicky, and I just don't have the patience. But Iris seems to have the magick touch!"

Together, they admired the plant's ovate leaves arranged into a rosette with yellow berries. With barely a stem, they appeared similar to a head placed directly on stout shoulders. She wondered what the root's presumed human shape looked like beneath the loose, deep soil.

"Good morning, ladies," Iris said with a voice that struck precise in articulation with a hint of arrogance.

"Oh, Iris! My goodness, it's been too long!" Auntie said, charging the lady dressed in a silk leopard-print caftan who waited with arms open wide.

"Bethie, much, much too long." Her poise was nothing short of perfection, and her voice, a purr of imposing wit.

After a genuine embrace, Iris turned to her. "And this must be the lovely Arista. You are quite the legend in these parts."

So *not* a legend. Here it was again. Her belief in herself never matched the fawning from Auntie's friends, and she wondered how much this lady knew.

Iris delivered a kind and knowing hug while peering down at her. The woman's genuine smile mixed with piercing eyes felt unsettling, but politeness was necessary. "Nice to meet you, too."

"Well, ladies, I understand you will perform a transitory ritual—journeying to the Otherworld if all goes correctly?"

"More or less. Arista prefers the term Summerland. Anyway, I hear there is a notable success with your apple branches."

"Of course, follow me. Don't worry about your shoes, as there is minimal mud if you stay the path."

As Iris led them toward the backyard, spooked felines of all colors ran out from beneath a variety of worn chairs that lined the walkway—a fluffy gray-and-white from behind the faded lounge, a tabby from under the broken rattan, and a flame-point Siamese from beneath the sturdy wrought-iron. The latter shot across Arista's path, almost tripping her. Her clomping to regain balance caught Iris's attention.

"Don't trip on my lovelies. We get few visitors, and my children are quite anti-social."

Arista tittered at her own clumsiness. "I have a Siamese, too."

"Oh, you must have seen Rupert. Truly, my favorite. Those beautiful blue eyes set on his orange markings."

"Yes, my Royal has quite the blues too, but his are set on satiny black."

"My Wally has blues, too," Auntie added with a little hoot.

"Yes, my babies mean I have fewer nature critters—mice, lizards, snakes—though I get to enjoy an encounter once in a while. I guess it's better that way. I could have rattlesnake problems as they do at the school. Another one Friday, don't you know?"

"Another one?" Arista asked, reminded of the mystery she had set aside for all her issues.

"Yes, but it was Elijah. Never have I met such a heathen. Though I suppose no child should have to endure such an injury."

Arista flashed a look at Auntie. "That has *got* to be witchcraft. Don't you think?"

Auntie twisted her mouth. "Could be."

The thought of reptilian encounters dissipated as Iris cleared her throat. "And here we have it," she said as they rounded the corner, and a small apple orchard came into view.

A sickening sweetness inundated Arista's sense of smell. There were healthy trees near the end of their seasonal cycle, the plump green apples still hanging, yet also plenty of fruit had already fallen, the base of the trees reeking of rot. A jumbled combination of scents—fruitful life and decaying death.

Caw!

"Good morning, Mr. Pitch," Iris purred.

A jet-black raven popped out of the nearest tree and coasted to the small metal shed off the last aisle.

Caw!

"Don't be concerned with Mr. Pitch. He means you no harm, just coarse on the call."

"Oh, we're quite friendly with birds. And he is so sleek," Auntie said, staring at the corvus with its inky, black sheen.

"Yes, he most certainly is," Iris agreed with pride in her voice. She gave the raven a reverent nod.

"How do you know it's a *he*?" Arista asked, feeling quite clever with her question since Evan had trumped her with the same one about owls.

Iris turned to her, eyebrows raised. Her mouth slammed shut. She stared at her for a moment and then slackened her jaw. "Well, Arista … because *he* is quite large when compared to all the females I see him courting. And the feathers at his neck." She pointed and called out to him. "Mr. Pitch!"

Caw!

Mr. Pitch ruffled his feathers, the ones at his neck becoming extra scruffy.

"Do you see the ring of scruffy feathers at his neck? The hackles?"

Both she and Auntie nodded, absorbed in Iris's ornithology lesson.

"*His* hackles are another sign that he is indeed a male." Iris stared at her, awaiting more questions.

Nervous, she smiled, feeling the woman's piercing eyes were upon her once again. Her stare, coupled with the slight breeze blowing her loose, leopard-print loungewear, made her look like a wild cat swishing its tail and considering a pounce.

With questions answered, Iris led the ladies to a tree midway down the aisle. "This is the Mutsu apple, also known as the Crispin. The former owner planted my little orchard soon after the Mutsu's arrival in the U.S. in 1946. While this particular tree is quite young … 1992 … you will find the flesh is firm, and the taste offers a palatable tartness. Though for your purposes, I suppose taste isn't necessary." She plucked a ripe apple from the tree, took a small bite, and motioned an invitation.

They both declined.

She took another nibble and pointed to a different branch. "Now … I find this a fine specimen, as it possesses all three components. First, there are three floral blooms, quite unusual for so late in the harvest season. There are also two small apples and one fully ripened piece of fruit—flawless of flesh and brilliant with a colorful luster. That's three, two, and one. Birth, growth, and maturity at death. All components representing the flow of human life." She looked at them, her expression presenting pride in her horticulture results.

Arista studied the small branch. It was a work of pure and natural art. No flaws, bug bites, or scale.

"This is marvelous," Auntie said.

"Shall we do it, then?" Iris asked.

After Auntie's confirmation, Iris tossed her apple to the ground and walked toward the shed. "In this orchard, not an ounce goes to waste. From humans to birds to the grounded critters, all apples are consumed. Even the ones rotting will till into the soil, thanks to the worms."

Arista stared at Iris's discarded apple while the eccentric woman fetched a yellow-handled, semi-rusted branch cutter from the shed.

Mr. Pitch peered down at her. He flapped his wings, jarred by the opening and closing of the door, but stayed perched on its eave. He released a clicking noise from his slightly curved black beak.

"Yes, Mr. Pitch. I know." Iris held up the branch cutter while approaching them. "Who shall have the honor?"

"Arista?" Auntie posed while looking at her with an encouraging smile.

Arista took the bulky shears in hand. "So, no different from a new crystal or tarot reading … my hands alone." She swung the cutter up, wedged the jaws of its blades around the tree's limb, and squeezed … harder … and harder until the handles met. The branch sagged, held by only a few slivers of wood.

"Be ready to take it in hand," Iris said, raising a small set of garden shears to make the final cut.

Arista took the branch with reverence, surrounded by approving eyes.

After heeding Pearl's misgivings about Iris, the visit had turned out to be less threatening than Arista had imagined. All she could smell was the sweetness of apples. The scent of decay, now overshadowed in the victory of attaining Iris's version of the Silver Bough, an ancient symbol of the Celts, and her night's passport to the Summerland.

CHAPTER 40
THE INCONVENIENCE OF HER

Auntie had just missed the call, being out of service range. Arriving in their neighborhood with bars plentiful, she tapped the voicemail. Pearl's message blared out of her speaker. *"Bethie! We're grounded. Give me a ring asap."*

"Oh, great," Auntie grumbled, returning the call.

Pearl delivered the news of a postponed flight out of the Phoenix, followed by already-discussed Plan B. "We'd hop in the car and drive, but that would put us too late. And there's still a chance we board soon."

'*Curses!*' Auntie mouthed to Arista, then offered Pearl her acceptance. "Well, it can't be helped, and yes, please let us know."

Auntie disconnected. "I didn't invite Iris because of her and Pearl's past differences. Now, unless I can get her here, we're going to go it alone. Given our suspicions that Fergus will interfere, I am concerned. We need another set of eyes."

"Do you think she'll come?"

"This is a huge night for many. With her expertise, she may already be committed, but let's try."

Hustling to the door as the raindrops began to fall, Auntie dialed the number as they entered Arista's cottage. She left a desperate plea on Iris's voicemail. Once finished, she sat down by Arista at the table, examining the Silver Bough. "We were just there. Where the heck did she go?"

"Tincture time?" Arista asked, figuring Auntie's question rhetorical.

"Yes."

Arista set about the kitchen, readying the ingredients for their pre-ceremony tonic. "She could be outside without her phone. I do it all the time," she said, glancing at her yard and seeing little, plump birds playing amongst the slick, wet outdoor furniture.

With drinks poured, she walked to the table and set down two petite cordial glasses before taking her seat. Still hours before sunset, they sipped their first cup of the calming tincture that Auntie had created.

"So, what's in this?" Arista asked, the taste usually not as desirable as she'd like.

"Swamp vervain. I traveled an hour and a half for the live version … no store-bought dried crumbles for this event. I processed it over the past week, so the drying of the plant's aerials played in correct timing to the macerating process."

They raised their delicate glasses to clink a toast to success. "Slàinte," they said in unison.

Auntie smacked her lips from the zing of the alcohol.

"It'll be okay … with or without Iris." Arista said, absorbing the earthy taste. She could not tell if her reassurance aimed more toward Auntie or herself.

"I agree. We may very well surprise ourselves with our capabilities."

She knew Auntie held a strong front, as did she. It came down to courage for both of them.

• • •

Mike walked out of Frank's house with a nap-refreshed Soonsil trailing behind him.

"I told you, she stays here," Fergus said, irritated that he had to repeat himself.

She scuttled closer toward Mike, eyeing Fergus with caution.

Mike clutched her shoulders as a protective guardian. "You changed your mind. Remember? You said, *'perfect setup'* or something like that." His voice grew firm. "Look, I can't leave here. She'll raise holy hell, and Frank doesn't need that."

To have this kid around went against all his principles, especially something so crucial as tonight. But as he glared at her, the previous brainstorm of her being useful seeped back into his hazy realization. He emphasized a pained sigh and walked to Mike's car.

"Nice." Pleased, Mike looked down at Soonsil.

Fergus felt a pang of insecurity, realizing his memory had become stunted since Ian's attack. At least Conn killed him. He would never bear the brunt of one of his beatings again. Still, he hated to admit it but, the poisonous hooks of depression had embedded into his psyche, just as before his creation of Fallon. He was sick of his face, his weakness, and now his damaged mind, and a part of him was horribly sick of his own insatiable obsession with this promised one he relentlessly pursued.

He sank into the passenger side and slammed the door, resentful of having to deal with Mike, a degenerate from his past. Further, it irked him watching Mike kowtow to the kid—guiding her through the dark yard, helping her situate in her seat, and always holding that stupid toy for her.

Once Soonsil buckled in, he shot a glare into the back seat. She cowered at his stare and clutched the stuffed animal. He hated the inconvenience of her. Yet another female child fast becoming the bane of his existence, and if she truly had a force that repelled punks, maybe he would add her to the night's sacrificial list.

He faced forward as Mike plopped down behind the steering wheel.

"You ready?" Mike asked.

"I—" Fergus stopped, realizing that Mike's question was directed at Soonsil. "Just drive!"

Mike eased out of Frank's driveway. Motoring down the road, they came upon the noisy Doberman enjoying yet another session of incessant barking. This time, at their passing vehicle. A long chain on his neck allowed him out into the streetlamp's spray of lighting. The beast snarled with fangs exposed, serious about doing bodily harm if given half a chance.

"I hate dogs," Fergus muttered. For as long as he could remember, he had detested the loudness and dissonance of a dog's effect. Be it bark, growl, howl, or pant. As did Keira. He snorted, dismissing the thought of his deceased sister.

As they drove past, he noticed the owner sitting on his porch's top step, lipping a cigar with a glowing orange tip. Apt for this special night. For a second, he wondered how he could sit there and endure the noise without reaction. What strength of sanity did this man possess? He narrowed in on the owner's hostile glower and realized it was nothing more than a sadistic enjoyment of letting everyone—wildlife, neighbors, and even his wife in the kitchen window—suffer the unending racket.

CHAPTER 41
DIMINISHING OF ALL RIGID MATTERS

"The neighbors are away tonight, so we can freely chant and wreak all the havoc we want," Auntie jokingly said, approaching the brick-encircled fire pit they had temporarily constructed in Arista's driveway. Small enough for measured safety, but large enough to emit a pleasurable heat as the last night of October drew to its close.

Arista studied the pit and visualized herself lying beside it. Hopefully, Auntie could lead the ritual, fan away flying embers, and watch out for Fergus, all at the same time.

In the meantime, she would keep the athame inconspicuously near for utmost safety. She also hoped that maybe … just maybe, Fergus had gone back to Spokane, skipping town to avoid prosecution. In an ideal world …

Auntie handed her the matches. "The honor is yours, my dear."

She took the box with reverence and struck the flame. First, she lit a small bundle of Mr. Tessay's rose-petaled sage and set in on the rim. Next, she let the remaining flame kiss the kindling beneath the medium-sized manzanita logs.

Bethie nodded, pleased with the successful lighting on a breezy night. "I figure we'll have this beauty well-stoked by midnight. We've got about an hour and then we'll begin. I think—"

Auntie's phone gave a distinctive ring from inside the house. Her eyes lit up. "That's Iris! Hopefully, she can make it." She rushed off to retrieve a timely answer.

Arista stared into the growing flames, rearranging the kindling to allow the fire to breathe. She watched them flicker as they consumed the wood, then released into a mesmerized state. Never had she experienced the night with such meaning, but never had she lost so many dear to her.

Auntie hooted within the house. "Oh, that's wonderful!"

Arista felt the relief. They would have the seasoned witch's help. And her extra set of eyes. She tucked her athame beneath the closest chair cushion. Then, she relaxed even more so into ritual, as the fire lapped at the night air, its heat stroking her face.

Continuing preparations, she brought out the gifted chicken foot from Candace. She symbolically scratched at the air, crisscrossing toward the ground and upward, creating a web of protection about her perimeter. Immersed in her ritual, she took to trance, letting her head sway while she waved the claw, her motions growing larger and larger. She imagined a polyphony of ancient stringed instruments guiding her in the dance while confronting her fear of death and letting it become ethereal. What once made her feel despondent now drifted beyond her like a soft winter wind. Frigid, yet of no strength to knock the last withered leaf from its dormant tree.

A faint weeping begged her attention.

Absorbed in the breath and movement of her pre-ritual reverie, she did not oblige it. Focusing, she felt the lightness of her body as she moved in harmony with her spirit.

Again, the faint cry seeped into her ears.

She slowed her dance and cautiously opened her eyes. It came from beyond her hedge.

Auntie jabbered on her phone within the house, overwhelming the effect that came from the darkness. The fact the effect sounded child-like concerned her. In her gut, she knew this served as the onset of her night's ordeal with Fergus. However, she heard Fergus hated kids and had only ever been interested in one—her.

She considered that it could be something unrelated since trick-or-treating wrapped up only hours prior. Maybe this child became separated from their parents. She had to look.

The cry settled into a whimper. It's source still unseen.

Hearing Auntie finish her call with Iris, she knew she would rejoin her soon. Vigilantly, she walked toward the hedge. "Hello?"

She heard the pitiful whimper more clearly.

Everything within her gut knew Fergus played a part in this charade. But even if he held the child as a decoy, she would help. She wished she could have acted sooner to help her dad. And Trini. She would not let another chance die. She looked back at the blade peeping from beneath its cushion, then peered around her hedge.

In the darkness, a child in white. A young Korean girl, about the same age as she, when she first came to live with Auntie. She had to get her over by the fire. "Oh, my goddess, sweetheart, come here." She motioned for the girl to come, warily scanning for signs of Fergus.

As the girl stepped from the darkness into the firelit yard, her crying stopped. She looked at Arista, then back to the street.

"Iris is just down the street. Hey, who is that?" Auntie bellowed, from inside the house.

"Are you lost? Where are your parents?" Arista asked the child, letting compassion overrule caution.

The little girl brought her hand to her mouth, fingers insecurely grabbing onto her lower teeth.

"You're afraid." Arista guided her toward the firepit and the safety of an effective blade.

Auntie yelled from the porch. "Arista! Who is that?!"

"It's a girl. I'm worried about her," Arista responded.

The child grew rigid from their interaction and halted. She looked up at Arista, and her eyes narrowed, bringing a sudden sense of creepiness.

"Hey, Arista. Happy Halloween!"

The sickening, recognizable voice came from behind her.

"It's okay, Soonie, he's got your toy," Fergus said to the child.

Arista turned as Fergus walked into view, another man close behind him. The child quickly ran toward the man and latched on to his waist as he handed her a stuffed animal.

Auntie screeched, carefully navigating the porch steps. Her eyes widened with anger, and her finger wildly slashed. "You stay right there! The police are on their way!"

Fergus beamed with a huge smile. "No, no, Betsy. Oh wait—Bessie, I think … or Betsy. Whatever. I just watched him drive by. He checks on the hour. So, we're going to give this another go."

Fergus grabbed the chicken foot from Arista's hand and chucked it into the fire, causing a loud pop and a brief blue flame to shoot skyward. Immediately, he countered her physical reaction to hit him by grabbing and pulling her into his body.

"He's one call away," Auntie said with conviction. "And the neighbors!"

Arista head butted at his chest behind her and kicked at his shins. He held strong, tightening his grip.

"You know, you're quite the legend with that Hummingbird Spell. And one hell of a noggin' on you." Fergus laughed. He looked at his colleague and explained. "That old gal withstood a *pounding* from Henry—and just look at her. The epitome of spryness."

Arista's thoughts raced as she stilled for a strategy. She wanted to kill him, wanted to watch him die in agony, her hand the executioner. But his strength held firm. She eyed the cushion that hid the athame by the fire. Maybe she could push him into the fire.

Reaching the bottom step, Auntie ran at Fergus with her arm raised to strike.

"Mike," Fergus calmly said.

Mike shoved the child aside and jumped in front of Fergus, giving Auntie a mighty shove to the ground. He hovered above her for a moment, then returned to the child's side.

"Tsk. Tsk. Tsk. Now, Bessie, that's not very hospitable of you. I suggest you stay put, or you're going to get someone hurt. Dare I say … killed?"

Arista stomped his foot and flailed.

His grip eased only a moment before he grabbed her neck. "Knock that shit off!" He re-secured his hold. "The last time we were together, you were full of spiteful things to say. But tonight …" Fergus held his index finger to his closed lips, then whispered in her ear. "Quiet as a mouse."

From the ground, Auntie looked at Mike, then Fergus, and judging by her agitated expressions and shifty eyes, her mind ran wild with reckless ideas. Hopefully, she would just stay put. "Auntie, please," she said. She could not bear to lose her, too.

Fergus rotated her toward him. "Arista, there is no reason to fear me."

A burst of resistance came from her repulsion.

He dodged any damage and squeezed her in a gripping embrace, and while the direness of her situation became clear, all tension released from her body. In full surrender her fear diminished, and she found herself waiting to see what happened next.

"Arista, I am—"

Fergus's voice faded as her thoughts cycled through the previous year. Shane's beautiful smile by the Grand Canyon, a crazy horseback ride in the Sedona desert, the short friendship with another murdered friend, and the gauntness of her mother's face on the pillow.

His muted mumblings almost distracted her, but now she could only see her dad—the congenial smile he kept through her abrupt questions, his patience while she adapted to their reunion, and the way he pulled her close, chanting in his last dying moment.

The horrible memory of his violent death brought her present with the one who bore responsibility. She hated him!

"Ah, yes! There you are," Fergus said, snapping his fingers in her face with an amused smirk.

The anger erupted from within her, and she struck at him.

He read her intention and caught the blow in his open palm. He enveloped her fist with his long, tentacle-like fingers and flung it back toward her. "Nice try, little one."

CRACK!

A pained human grunt grabbed everyone's attention.

Mike crumpled to the ground, Iris standing above him with a firm grip on a shovel. "One down," she said, her chin held up in defiance.

The child let out a blood-curdling scream. She dropped to Mike's side and cradled his head in her arms, the blood from his head staining the front of her white shirt.

Watching her weep, Arista felt a strange kinship to the child, recognizing how she must feel to watch the man she loved, possibly her father, fall to violence.

Iris approached the group as Auntie picked herself up from the ground.

"You must be Fergus," Iris said with a droll sneer. "I've heard much about *you*."

"Really? I'm not familiar with you."

"I'm—"

"Oh, wait—I don't care," Fergus said, grabbing Arista. He flipped her around and squeezed her tightly up against him, bringing her feet off the ground. He took a couple steps forward and executed a solid, thrusting kick from his long leg, shoving Iris to the gravel. Then, noticing Auntie fumbling at the cushion, he put his foot to her behind and sent her tumbling over the chair. "Ah! My athame!" Cheerfully, he seized it.

Watching him grab her athame triggered another attempt. Arista pulled hard on her arms, trying to break free. She kicked at his shins and screamed.

He covered her mouth and cranked her neck upward so tightly she thought it would snap. Quickly, he brought the sheathed blade to her neck. "I will kill you right here!" His words whispered, but strong in her ears.

She could scarcely move within his grasp. His arms wrapped around her like pythons, ever-tightening. He spun her around to face him while simultaneously removing the sheath. His cavalier expression had turned to intense hatred, the whites of his eyes bulging. Holding the bare blade against her neck, she became lost in the soulless void of his stare. A human as frightening as the most monstrous nightmare. And as his target, she felt eight years old again, unable to stand against him.

A ruckus to her left brought her present, and she looked over to see her fellow witches struggling to stand.

"I'll kill her," Fergus warned, causing them hesitation.

In his overpowering presence, the alternative worked, too. Auntie and Iris could be spared if she let everything go. Her mother and father had already faced it, each in their own agonizing way. To think of it now, her parents had robbed Death of her when she was eight. Now, Death had come for recompense.

But as she felt the ceding of all previous ambitions, an eerie ambiance stole her away from the surrendered moment. More impending than losing hope, an iciness swept in amongst them. Bigger than Fergus, the looming arrival of an all-encompassing force interrupted all thought.

Everyone felt it. They stilled. Scanning the yard, the oncoming warning of chaos threatened all present.

Fergus briefly studied the scene, then yanked Arista back to attention. Suppressed, he dragged her through the yard while waving the athame and threatening Iris and Auntie to stay put.

Cautiously, they edged toward him.

Arista remained focused on her changing environment, zeroing in on the sound of the crackling fire and grounding herself in this present moment that held something extraordinary. More intimidating than Fergus, the presence stealthily filled the air.

The lights of her house flickered. She saw Royal bolt from the windowsill. Then, all went dark.

The night air strengthened to a tundra-like cold. The opaque breath emitting from her mouth proved her read, accurate. And now a hint of rotting scent permeated through the brisk air.

Fergus eyed her unlit house. Securing her tightly, he looked toward the flames struggling within the pit, just as they reduced to nothing. A wispy plume of smoke billowed skyward. He blinked, eyebrows pinched together in concern, nervously studying the yard. "Don't try any—"

Arista launched an effective palm strike at his chin and broke free.

Immediately, he jerked her backward, delivering a brutal counterstrike.

Stunned, she dropped.

"Last warning, Arista."

"There is something awry here," Iris announced, slow and hypnotic, voicing the unspoken fear of all present.

Ignoring the pain from Fergus's strike, Arista looked at the girl. She saw it. A dark haze rising from the child as her sobbing ceased.

"Oh my," Iris said in sobered realization. Her gaze also set upon the child, who slowly rose from Mike's side, her chin lowered and her eyes dilating beyond full black irises.

Soonsil's head rotated left, then right, surveying her scene, her expression free of emotion and her movement, robotic.

"She's gwishin," Iris announced, her voice cracking.

It sounded dreadful. But the translation fell lost as all eyes settled upon the strange little girl. Her evil scowl fixed on only one person— Iris.

A roiling jet-black fog materialized around Soonsil. An aura of absolute death. The front of her white, blood-spotted shirt transformed—slick red saturating toward the seams until a large bloody hole sat dead center of her chest. As her height grew to that of a petite woman, her skin turned a ghostly, ashen white. Her hair lengthened, becoming straggly, hanging down in front of her face. The odor of rot filled the air, and a brooding moan was the last sound before her mouth entirely disappeared. She advanced toward Iris.

Fergus kept the blade to Arista's throat, but the gwishin held his attention.

For safety, Iris pushed Auntie aside and backed toward the hedge, saying, "This one is the ghost of a young, murdered woman … unable to fulfill her life's path, and resentful at being trapped in this realm."

The gwishin glided up to Iris and hovered before her, inches from her face.

"Now, you listen to me, young lady," Iris said, reprimanding like an indignant schoolteacher. "You … you …" Iris gagged, trying to finish her sentence. Her eyes bulged in horror as she began clutching at her throat, struggling to speak.

"Oh! So that's the *real deal*? Nice job, Mike!" Fergus looked over to Mike in a heap on the ground and hummed an approving tone as he watched the damaging effect of the gwishin's power. With his mouth at Arista's ear, he whispered, "Yes, Soonsil is a definite keeper."

Iris fell to the ground, clutching at the earth one last time before her body stilled.

About to descend upon Iris, the gwishin unexpectedly turned toward Auntie when she cried out for Iris.

The severity played on Arista's deepest fear. Harder, she tried to break free. But futile. "Wait!" she shouted.

Fergus covered her mouth and dragged her toward her porch as she desperately tried to keep her balance.

Auntie grabbed the chair and hurled it at the gwishin.

No effect. It efficiently righted from the jarring blow and closed the distance between them.

Fergus lost his grip, allowing Arista to break free and rush from his side. She stopped short of the gwishin. Clearly, Soonsil had harmed Iris because she had hurt Mike. Now, Arista had to keep Auntie safe at all costs. "Please! We're *not* your enemy."

The gwishin closed in on Auntie, who defensively held up her bony fists.

"Soonsil. Please!" Arista neared her, dodging Fergus's swiping attempts at control. Leery of the dark spirit, he put forth only half the effort.

The ghoul hovered before Auntie.

"Enough of this trifle!" Fergus yanked hard on Arista's hair, sending her to the ground, then haphazardly dragged her toward the house.

"Soonsil!! He's going to kill me!" She held Fergus's grip on her hair within her hands, trying to lessen the pull while keeping her footing as he dragged her alongside him. **"Just like you!!"**

Soonsil's head rotated toward her, the slivers of a deathly pallid face between the straggly hair, devoid of human features.

Fergus picked up Arista and flung her over his shoulder. The ground looked miles away, and her equilibrium faltered. The blood rushed to her head as she punched on his back. But the blows landed ineffectively and only caused more pressure within her own skull.

"Please." Her plea came softly. With her energy entirely spent, she held out her hand, fingers spread toward the gwishin, reaching for the horrifying semblance with a thread of hope. Seeing her only as a young woman who had fallen to violence.

The gwishin floated backward from Auntie and turned toward Arista with an ease of haunting grace.

"Arista!" Auntie yelled out to her, an anguished look on her face, wanting to help so badly. Quickly, she hustled to the edge of the property, disappearing behind the house.

Arista hoped she would not go into the house. Fergus would hurt her! She could not bear it. Not Auntie!

On the porch, Fergus tossed her toward the door.

Momentarily woozy, she looked up at him.

A sudden strike of terror as his body contorted. He arched backward with a violent thrash, and an agonizing pitch shrieked from his mouth.

Arista gathered her wits and ran to her door, seeing Soonsil rise behind Fergus on the reflection of its glass panes. Inside, she slammed the door and locked it.

A figure ran up the hall toward her.

"Arista!" Auntie frantically whispered.

Her stomach sunk in relief. As suspected, Auntie had gone around to the side entrance. They grabbed onto each other in encouragement before looking out the door.

Outside, Fergus had fallen to his knees. His head sagged backward, and his mouth gaped as if it would split apart at the jawline. From his throat came a guttural sound of torment. Dire agony emanated from within as Soonsil loitered behind him, her body jerking in a broken rhythm to his. An effect of his death.

"What is she doing to him?" Auntie whispered.

Then, Arista saw it. A speck of blood staining the front of his shirt at the abdomen. Tiny from her point of view.

From behind him, Soonsil raised a chunk of meat. Taken from his back, she brought the deep brownish-red organ to a mouth that materialized—its gums black and teeth plentiful, fanglike-thin, and needle-sharp. Opening wide, the gwishin bit down on the displaced liver, puncturing and chewing the meat, bit by bit.

His lower back would have held a gaping wound from this loss.

Now, he would die.

Arista turned away from the gore, but only briefly. As the most nauseating thing she could have ever imagined, she immersed herself in Soonsil's carnage. No remorse, no empathy. Not for Fergus's horrific final moment.

He fell to the ground, his face crunching on the jagged edge of the large tourmaline stone that graced her front porch. A final gashed insult to injury.

The women stared in silence while Soonsil finished devouring the last gory chunk. Then, the mouth sealed shut and disappeared entirely before her long, straggly black hair covered it once again.

They kept deathly quiet. In awe yet mortified.

The gwishin slowly turned and descended the steps, floating with no aim.

In the distance, Mike stirred, drawing the ghoul's attention. She picked up pace toward him, morphing slowly back into the semblance of an innocent child.

"What an odd fascination she has with him," Arista said, her gaze holding steadily.

They watched Soonsil's every movement with the curiosity of children.

Her small hand stroked Mike's face while the bloodied hole in her shirt slowly closed and whitened, leaving only the initial blood spots from his shovel-inflicted head wound.

Mike blinked to awareness and slowly sat up, prompting Soonsil to whimper and nuzzle into him.

"Astonishing," Auntie remarked, then her attention fell to other matters. "We need to get to Iris."

She was right. All the chaos seemed to last forever, but in truth, only minutes had passed. Hopefully, they could save Iris. They quietly opened the front door.

Mike stood and took Soonsil's hand while scanning the property. He looked over at Iris, then to Fergus's bloody carcass on the porch. "What the … uhhhh, I don't know what happened here, but we'll just go now." He looked at Soonsil. "No place for a kid. I'm so sorry you had to see this."

He backed away, keeping aware of the scene. Nearing the hedge, he turned to the street and griped. "There goes my money." He tightened his grip on Soonsil's hand. "It's okay though."

Arista cringed that a friend of Fergus could have such power at his command. "Wait!" she yelled, stepping over his body and rushing down her stairs. "Soonsil, you don't have to go with him."

"She's right. You *don't* have to go with me," Mike said in a sober admission as she peered up at him. He gave her a genuine smile and released her hand.

"We're doing a ritual tonight that can release your spirit." Arista stepped closer and softened her voice. "I'll give you the Silver Bough. You can be free."

Mike's face blanked, and he looked down at her.

The child's eyes glimmered in the moonlight. She shook her head, adamant in her decision, before grabbing Mike's hand and tugging him toward the street.

"Oops. Hang on." Mike hastened a couple steps away, bent down, and picked up her plush white fox. He dusted it off on his pants and handed it to her. With one last look at Arista, he shrugged, and the two of them walked into the obscurity of the night.

CHAPTER 42
THE VEIL IS THIN

Auntie rushed over and knelt down at Iris's side, tapping her cheek. Arista followed, noticing the changes around her. The air had cleared, and the temperature rose to that of a usual cold autumn night. A flickering of light within her cottage preceded the kitchen window, shining like a beacon, breaking through the malevolent mood.

Putting her ear to Iris's mouth, Auntie grew frantic. "She's not breathing! I've got to do the compression thingies!"

"I'll call 9-1-1!" Arista launched up to grab the phone. But as she approached her porch, the blatant reminder of a disemboweled Fergus came forth. If the police came, they would ask so many questions.

She hesitated and looked back at Auntie, seeing her arms rigid and straight while pumping on Iris's chest. She had to call for help!

"Arista!" Auntie yelled.

"9-1-1 Operator, what's your emergency?"

Arista flung around toward Auntie.

"Hang it up!" Auntie said as Iris choked to consciousness.

"Oh … uh, I'm really, really sorry. No emergency, after all." She ended the call and ran toward them.

Iris sat up, her wooziness akin to a partier's drunken episode. She took a deep breath, trying to steady herself as Auntie gasped from her exertion.

Arista squatted down beside them and looked at Iris. "Are you okay?"

Iris pushed herself up to sitting. In a confused stupor, she blinked, considering the question. "I believe so." A faraway look came to her face. "I remember the child … the gwishin." Concerned, she scanned the yard.

"She's gone. You'll be okay." Auntie said, patting her arm.

Iris relaxed and blinked forth another thought. "There was something else. A terrible struggle … I was fighting with someone." She rubbed at her head, squinting in confusion. "My mind."

"Was it the gwishin?" Arista asked.

"No. Male … and overbearing." Iris blinked, gathering crumbs of her memory. "If I'm not mistaken, it felt a bit like your Fergus character. Yes … his demeanor, and his voice. Also, there's a superb familiarity that I did not pick up before. It's quite odd."

Auntie held a momentary look of dread, her eyes shifting. She flashed them over to Arista. Then, let it go. "Well, it's a good thing we woke you!"

Still weak, Iris laughed, sat up taller, and, broadening her chest, gave a wide-armed stretch. Two snaps sounded from her back. With her strength and coherence returning, glimpses of her prudent character returned. "In dreams of fighting, it is said you are fighting aspects of yourself. Perhaps Fergus and I share certain aspects."

"Oh heavens! Cancel that thought!" Auntie said, then stood and offered her hand.

Helping Auntie hoist Iris, the woman's words struck Arista. This was no 'dream'. This was their supernatural world, and Iris had just died near a somewhat gifted psycho. He could attune to her mother. Who's to say his gift of attuning affected only one person?

"You must see a doctor first thing tomorrow. Maybe even tonight," Arista suggested, then offered her kudos to Auntie. "And Auntie can add reanimation to her repertoire of abilities. CPR or not."

Auntie blew it off with a snort and modest wave of her hand.

"Indeed," Iris said, stretching her neck and jaws. "So, where is—" She froze upon seeing a bloodied Fergus on the porch. "Oh dear. Looks like I missed a *big* to-do. Is that human pile who I think it is?"

"Yes, another matter we need to tend to," Auntie said in exasperation.

Iris gave a single nod of awareness. "Noted. Where did the little girl and her … handler, for lack of better words, go?"

"Let me just say it's concerning what's roaming our neighborhood right now." Auntie looked into the obscurity beyond the hedge. "Anyway, we'll go over all of that later."

"Whatever you ladies say. And yes, I'm sure you're worried about *the body*. Just know I'll gladly help with that, but we need to get it in my car. Thereafter, I say there's no time like the present for the ritual."

The body comment sure begged a question—actually, several—but Arista kept them to herself.

"Are you *absolutely* sure you're up for all this?" Auntie asked Iris.

"I'm not sure my strength is at its full potential. That was quite the shenanigan your uncanny guest pulled. But I'll do my best."

•　　•　　•

After many minutes of strenuous effort, Fergus's body landed in Iris's trunk. A final shove of his remaining leg and Iris sealed the deal with a firm slam.

The bloodied porch came next—hosing it, salting it for an overnight sitting, and lighting three sage bundles. They set the smoldering herbs in jumbo abalone shells at the points of a triangle covering the area where the gory spillage had occurred. Hopefully, no malicious remnant of spirit remained.

"I think that might do," Auntie said, wiping her brow. "I'd suggest widdershins a few times over the next week."

Arista nodded, thinking of her besom's counter-clockwise spins to undo all the turmoil from the porch.

"Lucky for us, it's outdoors, and his diseased mentality is not stuck within your house," Auntie added.

Iris sat with a blank stare. Auntie must have given her little information about the previous conflict, or else she would have had an opinion as well. Unless her return from the dead still hampered her wits.

Ritual time. The fire reignited without issue, though smaller. Yet, it burned bright enough to cast a renewed warm glow upon her yard, free of all chaos and murder.

"Iris, I don't want to raise a red flag if unnecessary, but ..." Auntie pursed her lips. "Is there a chance Fergus will be in the realm of Arista's travel? Especially since he may have crossed your path in the in-between."

Oddly, in her gut, Arista felt rid of him but listened.

"There is a possibility. It would depend on his gift. What are his talents in the craft?"

"The only thing we're aware of is his ability to attune to Arista's mother."

Iris blinked a few times, determining the possibilities. "The veil is thin, so we cannot know for sure. Who you see is usually prompted by your intention. Though surprise visits are possible."

Looking at Iris, Arista, and then back to Iris, Auntie awaited the verdict.

Arista tossed up her hands asserting herself. "It doesn't matter. I want to go." She looked at Auntie. "I really want to see my parents again. So, I'm willing to take the risk."

Auntie gazed into her eyes and sighed. "I understand."

Back on track to original plans, they unpacked the totes full of plush blankets while Arista solidified her new intentions with Iris. After facing the gwishin's prodigious freeze, the night's seasonal chill felt hospitable.

A rustling in the bush caught her attention. She figured it to be a neighborhood cat or small rodent. Whatever they were, they stilled when the night raptor screeched.

Arista flashed an inspired look at Auntie.

"It's not Margaret. She's still in Shasta. And I'm pretty sure that was a barn owl."

"That was, indeed, a barn owl," Iris said without looking up from her organizing.

Almost. "So, my visit is to see my mom and dad … I'm pretty certain there's no more Great-Great … and I know to be careful of a nasty, roaming uncle." She felt a bit intimidated by the undertaking but capable.

Auntie gave a half-hearted smile while straightening the blanket. "Iris, are we sure we let this one take the journey?"

"Rest assured, Arista will see who she is meant to see," Iris announced with proud confidence. Unexpectedly, she teetered and lost her balance.

Auntie and Arista rushed to her sides.

"Whew! Just a bit dizzy," Iris said, wavering a moment before readjusting back to her prominent posture. "I do believe dying can be hard on the system."

With Iris's well-being confirmed, Auntie began the ceremony by creating a black-salted circle around their vicinity.

Back in her rightful possession, Arista seconded the procedure with an imaginary boundary drawn with her athame. Circling clockwise from north, she pointed it east, south, west, and north again, extending the protection just beyond her yard.

Casting the circle strokes have been drawn,
The thinning veil reveals humanities gone,
May their love in this circle be born anew,
And only love shall leave, faithful and true.
So, may this be.

As she blessed her own boundaries, she drew a perpendicular circle from above to below and above again, repeating her chant. Then she laid prone on the plush pallet with Auntie and Iris situating on either side of her in lotus position.

She closed her eyes and felt Auntie anoint her forehead with a diluted oil that smelled of many autumn scents—cinnamon, orange peel, allspice, and apple. Thereafter, Auntie placed the smoke-cleansed Silver Bough, primed with the same oil, longways down her chest and solar plexus. Next, she placed her hands above Arista's crown and heart chakras. Iris mumbled to Auntie, then held her palms above Arista's third eye and root chakras.

In reverence, Arista inhaled, then exhaled. This journey held discovery and nothing to fear. She willed it to be that way—*Nothing to fear.*

Iris began an incoherent chant while Auntie hummed in a low undertone. The voices, in their staggered unison, brought a soothing resonance.

Inhale. Her body lightened.

Exhale. Her eyelids grew heavy. Neck relaxed.

Lightweight.

Nothing ... to ... fear.

Peace.

Nothing ... to ... fear.

And a drop into the unknown.

A steady fade-in found her walking in a vast, dark realm of timelessness. From above, a warm glow began to shine down upon her.

In a monumental burst of activity, the scene unfurled. From the dizzied rush came stability, and she found herself in the center of an emerald-green lea. Immense patches of sourgrass covered the landscape, highlighted by yellow sunbeams, and the rolling hills that surrounded her were dotted with mature oaks, and lush, overgrown fescue. The smell filled her with an early summer spirit, cheerful and untroubled. Above her, a scream of freedom, as two red-tailed hawks soared on the wind. A lyrical wave of tranquility all around her. This idyll shined pure perfection—natural, vibrant beauty as far as the eye could see.

Onward, she walked.

Before long, her first encounter came into view—a woman with a female toddler, their playfulness abundant beneath the pleasant blue sky of sporadic billowy white clouds. The little girl's pigtails bounced in delight as she ran, arms reaching out to her mother. As Arista drew nearer, she could see it was Trini just as she scooped up her daughter with a joyful ease, held her close, then set her back to the earth. She turned to Arista and smiled before fading from view.

A breath of excitement escaped her, but no volume came forth. Instead, she felt the buoyancy of her body and spirit, a feeling of burdenless pleasure, a child herself and her parent with her. Unseen, the loving, watchful eye of her own mother brought her an ease and devotion she had long forgotten. Carried by the rising summer wind, her mother's voice traveled along with it, touching her face and gently blowing her hair. *'So … much … love.'*

Arista felt emotions flowering within her, expanding her chest in utter happiness. Feelings of undying dedication. Adoration. She drank in her mother's tenderness as the spirit journeyed onward, traces of her voice drifting with the wind.

Arista followed, meandering the hillside's path, becoming desperate to keep up. But onward, her mother's spirit traveled, leaving her farther behind.

Only a moment of discontent as her mother's essence lightened, then another sensation came forth. As she approached a sprawling aged oak tree, she inhaled a scent of pine, cedarwood, and bay leaf. She could not see him nor hear him, but his loving spirit flooded her awareness. She closed her eyes to better focus. The breeze fanning the scent all around her. Transcendence from grief. Her father still existed, in a form she did not know but could feel. The understanding steadied her angst of whether the pain he endured at death remained. It did not.

She wanted to better comprehend their presence. To see them. To further understand by their own words. But as grasping at a sage bundle's rising smoke, their spirits swept into the uprising wind, combining scent and sound. Entwined and becoming one, higher and farther, they drifted away from her.

She felt a whimper leave her lips without volume as she gazed skyward. She wished to be with her parents just a little longer. However, as a fleeting dream, she found herself alone again in the beautiful Summerland. Looking around, she understood that even her visit to this utopian realm was temporary, lest she decide to take her last mortal breath.

Chapter 43
No Touching Truth

Bethie held her hands above Arista, continuing to drone in a pleasant hum, the white noise for her grandniece's journey. She kept an undistracted, soft, peripheral gaze upon her.

Arista's eyelids fluttered and rolled. She had moments of smiling, followed by the cinching of her eyebrows and small whimpers.

Iris opened her eyes and offered direction. "Keep the placement of your hands, but let her go. You can cease the hum and simply think of courage. Think of liberation. Think of her return."

Bethie gave a soft blink and nodded, expressing her understanding, but kept her low hum constant. She could not, and would not, abandon Arista entirely. The intonation served as her lifeline out of the Summerland. Necessary in case she came across *him*. After all, Iris knew only a fraction of the trials she and Arista had endured from Fergus's long-time ambitions. Depending on the degree of distress she saw in Arista, she would end the ritual, with or without the blessing of her friend with superior magickal prowess.

A peep arose from Iris.

Feeling a tinge of guilt for her inner resistance, Bethie lowered her hum. She glanced at Iris and caught her shaking her head as if trying to stay awake. Worried, she whispered, "Iris—"

In a firm gesture, Iris held up her hand, dismissing concern.

• • •

Arista walked onward, entering an area of grass that stood at her waist. Meadow katydids trilled in a staccato song. While a sound associated with the most miserable heat of summer, she felt only a soothing temperature upon her skin. She grabbed wads of the bristly strips of tall grass in her swinging hands, letting them slide out of her fists, the undersides smooth. What else was there to find?

Ahead, she saw movement. Something rushed toward her. The grass parting at its rapid pursuit.

She stopped. Even if she had wanted to feel alarm, the emotion did not exist here.

Closer it came, picking up speed. With hints of fur becoming visible, it looked canine.

She held her breath in anticipation.

The notion confirmed when a coyote appeared from behind the tall grass, stopping many feet away from her. Its luxurious coat, mottled in natural-colored hues, gleamed in the day's sunlight, and the bushy tail of dense fur gave a slight wag.

Recently, she had seen a coyote but could not remember where.

Its wet, jet-black nose glistened, but the eyes struck her most. It stared at her with knowing, vibrant yellow orbs, a tight black circle in each of their centers. The coyote dropped its tail and raised its nose, releasing an extended series of yips. It stopped and looked at her again, its eyes no longer feral. A teacher.

In an instant, she understood and drew in the lesson of this spirit. Survival and tenacity through the most troubling of times and managing the wild ride of uncertainty.

The coyote blinked, gazed into the distance, then looked back at her. With its ears high, and eyes intent upon her, it whimpered and took a few steps toward her.

She breathed in its message of adaptation and harnessing energy.

Another yip, louder and firm.

She must continue honing her ever-growing wisdom while being aware of those around her—especially the tricksters.

When she held out her hand, the coyote looked back at the grass, sounded two more short yips, then whined an amusing yawn.

The last bit of clarity—laughter, an underestimated necessity of life.

The creature backed toward the grass where it had emerged. Its time grew short.

She walked closer, reaching out to touch the clever beast. But with each step, the distance grew between them. Further she tried but could not satisfy the effort.

The coyote's last glance at her revealed the meaning. There was no touching truth, only heeding its message. And when she understood this, it faded from view.

Arista looked around her. She did not want to leave this pastoral haven so full of unfulfilled memories, people she loved, and lessons of wisdom. But a humming voice captured her attention, and she knew someone waited for her.

The beautiful meadow blurred into a swirl of color and dissolved into blackness.

Within the dark passage, she traveled toward the hum.

It was Auntie!

.   .   .

Arista awoke to find Auntie's and Iris's inquisitory eyes looking down at her. Memories of the soft call of her mother's voice and her father's scent came rushing forth. She released a breath of awe.

Auntie raised the Silver Bough from her chest and handed it to Iris. In a soft tone, she asked, "Arista, do I have your permission to open the circle?"

It took Arista a moment to digest her authority over the action before duly consenting.

Auntie opened their circle with the athame's reverse sweeping motions that Arista had used to create it.

Arista sat up, gathering her energy, with Auntie and Iris helping her to her feet.

Iris handed her the bough, and said, "Into the fire, it goes."

Arista took one last admiring look at the bough's prominence, felt its natural essence within her hand, then set it into the flames.

They gazed at the igniting branch. The death of an apple's complete life created a sweet, woodsy scent that completed the night's ritual.

While the last remnants turned to ash, they kept a reverent silence, tidying the area—mixing the salt line into the pea gravel, shaking out and folding the blankets, and extinguishing the fire's last glowing embers with moon water from the previous full moon phase.

Auntie and Iris tended to the post-ritual tea pouring while Arista took her athame inside to her altar.

At last, they made small talk while sipping one celebratory cup of tea before Iris had to leave.

"Ladies, it has been a pleasure working with you, but I truly must get home. I feel like I've hiked the Skye Trail." Iris looked down at her bare wrist and said, "I'm actually quite miffed that my favorite Lapis bracelet slipped as I left home."

Auntie scanned the ground. "Are you sure you didn't drop it here?"

"No. I heard the tinkling of it hit my front step, but it did not dawn on me until I was already in the car. I'm sure you will agree there were more pressing matters."

Auntie winced. "Iris, about that other matter … the one in your trunk. Should we follow you home? How can we help?"

"It's no matter, Bethie. My friend's pigs love a special treat once in a while." Iris mischievously smiled, her teeth bared.

The horror of the visual made Arista cringe. She flashed a look at Auntie, who held an expression of shock upon her gaping face.

Auntie caught her glimpse and quickly eased. "Well, once in a *great* while is probably okay." She nervously chuckled at the outlandish statement.

Iris walked toward the hedge. At the street, she turned and gave them a final elegant, cup-handed wave, and departed.

Auntie turned to Arista. "Shall we?" She threw a look toward the cottage.

"Yes," Arista said as her exhaustion set in.

Once inside her cottage and cozily dressed for bed, Arista debriefed the individual encounters with Trini, her parents, and the coyote with its spiritual messages.

"Ha! Coyote totem!" Auntie blurted. "Wouldn't that be a hoot if Mr. Tessay just barged in to play tricks with you?"

"Maybe their family totem played fresh in my mind. Either that or the crazy one on the highway. Funny that its message is totally relevant, though."

"That, and as Iris said, you saw what you were supposed to see. Any other time, it could have been a fish, wildcat, or even a dragon."

Arista imagined the upheaval that a dragon would have brought to the landscape's serenity. Then again, the goddesses Rhiannon was sometimes associated with dragons. "Anyway, thankfully, no Fergus … but no Great-Great either."

"As for my grandfather, I'm thinking that means he's back to his old stomping grounds. Though no visits yet?"

Arista shook her head. She looked toward the hallway formerly frequented by Great-Great, prompting Auntie to do the same.

They startled as two orange orbs floated toward them from its darkness.

Mew.

CHAPTER 44
OH BROTHER, POOR YOU!

Two nights following her visit to the Summerland, Arista sat on the edge of her bed, finding an unexplained peace forming in her psyche. She had wondered if she could recover after losing her parents again. Who could endure trauma after trauma?

However, she considered her improved mindset a blessing of her Summerland visit and knew it had changed her for the better. Day by day, throughout the past couple years, her ignorance-is-bliss persona had tempered. She also felt what might have been her first-ever encounter with rage watching her father killed. How could she not?

Now, after feeling so many emotions, raw and unpleasant as they were, she found herself in a grounded inner calm. The possibility of happiness, returning.

Anyway, she had posed it that way to her psychologist earlier in the afternoon. And the professional thought-sorter deemed it reasonable. No, she had not gone crazy. Yes, onward life flows.

She admired the lump of fleece blanket slung over the top tier of Royal's cat post. How cozy he must be underneath it. With the nights growing colder and longer, the throw paid colorful homage to the time of year—latte cups, pumpkin pies, and maple leaves in gold, orange, and red. Because of damage, chaos, and loss, she found an innocent pleasure in its simple design.

She approached the blanket and peeked inside, prompting two small slits of Royal's awareness. He upturned his chin, teeth jutting beyond his whiskered chops. Stroking his chin, she said, "I still have you and Auntie."

She re-covered him and turned back toward her bed, knowing why she held such tremendous calm. Because at long last, Fergus was dead. No fear remained of his scheming. While the initial plan of killing him, the one she discussed with Auntie, had not included a gwishin, the scariest of allies proved quite effective.

Knock. Knock.

She looked at the clock—nine p.m. That pivotal time of stranger danger or just a friend forgetting bedtime boundaries. A friend would have called.

She approached the door with caution. "Who is it?"

"It's Shane."

She would not have answered *that* call. Her stomach dropped, and she groaned, her defenses rising to protect her.

"*Who* is it?"

"It's—"

She opened the door. "Hey," she said, in her most monotone effort, hurt by the sight of him. Since she had addressed every other difficulty in her life, she might as well bear this one.

"Hey," he said in a subdued cheer. "Did you hear from Maddie?"

She remembered the snippet she heard of Maddie's message—the awkwardness in her voice, the hesitation, and the possibility of it being an apology for the dating rumor. Regardless of the quick fix and it sounding promising, she kept her excitement level on low and her expression unaffected. However, the longer she stared at him she realized it was difficult to not love the same beautiful guy who kept invading her memories. "Yes. But I haven't listened to it yet."

Shane's face softened. "I'm deeply sorry about your mother, and I know things have been tough. So, if this is a bad time, I understand, but if you're able, I'd like us to talk."

Without word, she walked to her living room, leaving him at the door. Where could she even begin? Her mother was but a fraction of her drama. Gobs of trauma, which she would probably need years of counseling to neutralize, though he would hear none of it. Not tonight.

Shane walked past her, standing by her kitchen counter, his expression sheepish. He sat down on her sofa, then looked up with a compassionate smile. "Riss, I want to support you. Please know that you can talk to me. I know you're going through a lot, and I'll stay in that friend zone for as long as you need, but I hope we can be together again."

She dazed out the window, ready to hear what he had to say, but kept her glances few. While Maddie's voicemail could exonerate him, why had he been in the gray area?

"So, you've been back awhile now?"

"A few weeks."

"Right." He looked down at the floor. "It's real fresh in here …the floor looks great."

"I miss my old floor. It was authentic and *lasting*, *not* shiny and new." She made sure the statement dripped of insinuation and made no eye contact.

"I know, it was the original-original, right?"

She sucked in a breath and tilted her head with impatience. "Shane, what are you doing here?"

"I miss us." His eyes fluttered, the statement sounding like a plea.

She rolled her eyes and crossed her arms.

"I mean it. You don't think we'd end like *that*, do you?"

"What do you mean? We broke up. I've heard nothing from you since … like, May."

"Riss, our last call was in June … June 13, and the parting was as much, if not more, your call than mine. We agreed to that. On amenable terms, I thought."

She dreaded opening up, worried she would have no control and could look like a raving lunatic as she attempted to verbally demolish this person whom she still loved. Worse, it could be rife with rampant tears, and she refused to let him see her cry.

Shane stood up and walked toward her.

She bristled and thrust her palms toward him. "Stop … please … just sit back down."

He conformed without hesitation, but his congenial expression hit a serious note. "Maddie told you I was dating. It's not true. I've tried calling you, but you don't pick up. So, I tried giving you space. She agrees she made a mistake, and if you listen to the call—"

"I don't know, Shane." How could she think about a relationship when her emotions were such a pile of muddled goo? What kind of girlfriend would she be?

"Are you willing to listen to me? And I mean fully … with your heart?"

She scoffed in contempt. More so toward her predicament than his request.

"You know I will not lie to you. Anyway, I hope you believe I will always tell you the truth … no matter what." His gaze stayed fixed on her.

She looked away from him. "I'm waiting."

"My parents saw how mopey I was when we broke up! In fact, I was miserable, and I'm not exaggerating. So, they pushed for me to go have fun."

Oh brother, poor you.

"I out-fumbled them for months, but last month, they had me go to their friend's barbeque. Little did I know, they were trying to set me up."

"How cozy."

He ignored the remark. "She'd just had her own breakup, and that's all we talked about. How much we missed *you* guys!"

"Yeah, and what happened next?"

"Nothing! Nothing happened except for the fact I met another person."

"Right."

"I'm telling you the truth. Nothing happened. Not even a kiss … not even the *thought* of a kiss. In fact, we were both irritated that we were being forced upon each other."

"Hmph." *Do I dare believe this?* She looked into his eyes, searching for the shiftiness of a lie.

"Honest to God," Shane said. "Honest to witch's goddess."

A small laugh escaped her at his choice of words. He was trying so hard. She studied him, waiting for him to look away from her scrutinizing stare.

He held his gaze.

His sincerity felt genuine, leaving the rumor unclimactic. Where was the sex? The betrayal? "So, how long did you two date?" she asked, a final shot at finding the flaw in his story.

"Not a date. Once more our dads unknowingly set up a lunch for all of us. We spent that time strategizing a plan for her to get her boyfriend back, that's when I saw Maddie and Evan." Shane's demeanor changed to a slight impatience. "I tried to go find them and explain the whole thing, but they left. Maddie knows this to be true now. That message will tell you she made a mistake … a *big* mistake! And as stubborn as she is, you know she would not cop to that unless it was truth."

It sounded legitimate. Maddie had a tendency of jumping to conclusions and misconstruing comments and deeds that seemed like slights. Eventually, all would come clear, leading to her humble apology.

"*Everyone* knows how much I love you, Riss," he said, staring into her eyes.

To hear him call her Riss brought a sense of security. While her dad was the first, Shane had called her by this name the longest.

"So, I respect your best friend trying to protect you." He stood and moved closer. "As for us, the only reason for our breakup was the distance. That, and you getting mad at me for hounding you to come home. So, I won't rush you into anything, but when you're settled … if you want … maybe we could have tea together?"

There he goes, speaking my language again.

"I can also protect you from rattlesnakes and all."

"Oh, no! Another episode at the school?" Engaging in the non-emotional topic felt safe.

"No, just too many this year. I'll catch you up on all of that, too … over tea."

She twisted her mouth and looked away from him. "Maybe so."

He smiled. "Okay, I'm going to leave now, and I'll check back in a couple days. Of course, if you want to talk before then, I'm totally game!"

He walked to the door, taking his time, probably expecting her to run and hug him. But no … this was all too fresh.

He stepped outside and looked back at her.

She gave him a half-smile.

He reached for the doorknob and pulled.

"Shane, wait!"

As he peeked back in, she ran to him and threw her arms around his neck.

They clutched one another, and for just a minute, her heart and mind comforted into a nourishing, recognizable bliss where safety, intimacy, and happiness reigned.

But that was enough for now. One talk did not fix everything, and she was a little miffed at herself for giving in too soon. With a comfortable five feet re-established between them, she looked him in the eyes and crossed her arms.

He smiled and shut the door.

After his truck's rumble faded, she walked out onto her porch in the chilled November night. The kindling of revisited love warmed her, and her spirit felt light. She could find happiness again. Despite all her drama, she would not stop living.

Suddenly, a movement from the far right. On the needled branches of her farthest pine tree, she could just make out the silhouette of a horned raptor and the reflective flash of its eyes.

Hooo. Hooo.

She eked out a controlled high pitch of excitement as the owl spread its wings and flapped skyward. She watched in awe. No barn owl this time. That *was* a great-horned owl! It had to be Margaret, back from Shasta. She could not wait to tell Auntie.

Ecstatic from all her familiarities returning, she walked back inside, contemplating life as normal again, with Shane's hug serving as the greatest encouragement.

Glancing at her kitchen windowsill, she caught sight of her coppery Raku medallion from Sedona sitting by her miniature agave plant. Remembering one wrinkle, she said, "Great. Now I'm the bad guy because I *did* kiss Dakota." She harrumphed in dismissal. "It was only a peck."

CHAPTER 45
WE NEED TO TALK

With her spirits still high from Shane's visit, Arista nestled into bed.

Alert from her activity, Royal emerged from beneath his high perch and blanket to take his place atop the covers in the fold of her stacked knees. She rubbed the backs of his ears while he kneaded cotton dough, then tucked her chilly hands at her chin to gaze at her bedside lamp. Its sunflower, a semblance of her happiness returning.

'It will take time.' The counseling tidbit from her morning came to mind. It had been accompanied by plenty of gentle guidance that parents are our strength, our heritage, and our role models. They can also fall short of perfection, whether through words, deeds, or even leaving us too soon. She said something else that resonated. *'Parents can give us philosophies to fall back on as we grow. These traits come forth the more we mature. Sometimes, helping us. Sometimes, helping us to help others.'*

She reached over, turned off her light, and snuggled tight under the covers. What had her parents left her in their short time together? Acceptance that we all eventually face our death? Sacrifice at all costs for your children? Yes, and yes. But what else?

She thought of her last moment with her father—having her close at his forehead, their hands linked, and the strange sensation that followed. He had talked about it before, that a parent could pass their gift upon death. Could her dreamworld now hold influence?

When Shane mentioned the rattlesnake problem, she remembered her previous impression. It carried undertones of witchcraft, and she had missed too many chances to help. She would not let this black magick go unaddressed.

She felt a heavy sleepiness alight upon her eyelids and readied for a fresh experience.

. . .

Midway down the unacquainted hallway, a light emitting from beneath a small bedroom door beckoned Arista. Within her narrowed visage, only the very center showed sharp enough to determine what she would find, the outer edges blurring to the deepest midnight blue. Pictures with blurred faces hung within the space, and scents of cinnamon, lavender and a hint of rose became apparent. A pleasant combination known for creativity.

She neared the door, hearing faint murmurings from within. How lightweight they felt. How innocent they sounded.

Once inside the warm glow of the room, she saw six black and white votive candles placed on pink crackle-glass holders forming a circle around a white shag rug. Upon the rug, looking away from her, a small, hooded person clad in a bright yellow cloak incanted in whimsical rhyme, swaying, serpentine-like.

As Arista floated closer, the muted speech became clearer. The voice, youthful, and possibly a girl. With attentive listening, she deciphered the words, repeated over and over.

> *Sssss, for the meanies I do send,*
> *Sssss, for friends who just pretend,*
> *Sssss, for the heartless that bully boys and girls,*
> *SSSsssssss, is my serpent sent into their world.*

The figure held her small hands outward, writhing a wooden handcrafted snake meant to mimic the flexibility of a true serpent. Her sporadic hums filled the room before transferring the snake into one hand, then reaching into an open-mouthed jar with a small vertebra tied to its rim. She pinched a portion of pulverized and powdered snake dust, brought it to her lips, and blew it into the air.

Arista rounded the figure to determine identity, and as she did, the revelation hit her in the boldest way. The girl's hair. Her voice. And her nature.

·   ·   ·

With Earth & Ocean opening soon, Arista had an urgent stop before work. She had overlooked the meaning of all those little talks.

Energized with her message, she drove across the busy strip of increasing weekend traffic, past the Navarros' homey abode, and onto the terraced residential hillside. She rolled in front of a small white house with black trim, parked in front of its coral-colored rose bushes presenting their last seasonal blooms, and exited her car.

Instead of listening to the various songs of delighted birds, her mind rushed with all the signs she had missed since spring of the previous year. As if her own ruing of Shane in bed with a snakebite was not enough, Zoelly had told her mother many times—*"That was not supposed to happen."*

Arista opened the small gate, appreciating the black, chunky feline with a splashed white bib, enjoying his view from the interior bay window. Again, she flooded with memories of all that Analina had shared about Zoelly's school life—stories of name-calling, two-faced friends, and the potential for home-schooling.

Now, with her dad's gift of dream-travel, all came to a logical answer for Arista. Thankfully, at a pliable, young age, when the lessons of right and wrong in witchcraft are creating their very foundation.

She knocked on the glossy, black door and waited while footsteps came to greet her.

Upon opening the door, her unexpected home visit brought a worried look to Analina's face. "Hey, Arista, what's going on?"

"Is Zoelly home?"

Zoelly's head of lavish hair poked out from behind her bedroom door mid-way down the hall. The same hall from her dream with the hung pictures now crisp in family detail.

"Of course. Why?"

"I already know you saw me," Zoelly said in a humbled sass. Rolling her eyes, she walked toward them.

Analina swung her head to her daughter, then back to Arista.

Arista smiled with gritted teeth. "We need to talk."

CHAPTER 46
OF LAPIS AND MOUNTAIN OPAL

"It's just not matching up, Sheriff," Jo said.

"What do you mean it's not matching up?"

"The wound is more extravagant than the weapon on file."

"Uh-huh."

"In fact, Ian Kelly's wound holds similar damage to our serial killer last year."

"You don't say."

"I do say. The murder weapon on file for Mr. Kelly's death is three-point-two inches long with a straight, thin blade, whereas his wound shows a substantially longer … two-point-three inches longer … depth-wise, as well as significant damage to surrounding tissue, suggesting a thick, curved blade. I'm tellin' ya, Sheriff, it looks a lot like the damage Wallish sustained."

He let out a long, slow breath but would play this cool. "Interesting data, Jo. Thanks for keeping me informed."

"You bet, Sheriff. Oh, and be careful on the streets. You hear about that story of some kid that turns into one of those white-clothed, drenched-lookin' ghosts you see in the movies?"

"Can't say that I have."

"Yeah, it's all over the internet. A couple different sightings from door-cams. Likely to be a hoax, though … Halloween night and all. But that'll keep you up at night, huh?"

He grunted.

"Anyway, let me know if you think of anything regarding this wound dilemma."

"Will do." He hung up his phone. "Trickery," he said aloud, envisioning AI ghosts, before turning his thoughts to the wound discrepancy. "Lots of trickery." Arista or Bethie had switched the weapon that night, likely when he took Fergus to the cruiser, and this left him in an unfortunate predicament. They had every right to keep their heirloom, especially after the station had allowed it to be taken. Even more so since the weapon used to kill Wallish ended up in the hands of another murderer, killing Arista's father. He groaned at the layered irony.

Still, he would pursue investigation.

He phoned Bethie, surprised at the immediate answer. "Hey there, Miss Bethie, I'm wondering if I could have a moment of your time."

"Of course."

He laid out his findings and awaited a response.

"Hmmmm. Strange," she said, offering nothing further.

Again, a face-off … who would crack first?

The road noise from Bethie's speakerphone hummed in the background.

Though delayed, she offered an explanation. "Sheriff, not sure what to say. I'm no forsenics person—"

He found humor in her miswording of *forensics*.

"I *surely* don't mean to refute your coroner's word, but you know you were looking for our family heirloom. Remember? I asked you about it several times over the past year. So, it's quite the head-scratcher."

The tangled web one weaves. "Weren't we considering that Fergus had the athame? If you recall, I had suggested you call him and see if he had it."

"You did suggest that."

Again, hushed posturing. As with every smoldering fire, he threw more kindling. "Also, I want to alert you that Fergus seems to have skipped town. He's not checked in as instructed."

"Hunh. Let's hope he stays away for good this time! I can one hundred percent assure you, I don't know where *he* is."

Where was her fright? Where was her usual scattered confusion and bustling anxiety over the lurking absence of their nemesis? Enough was enough. "Okay, Miss Bethie, I wanted to check if you had any information. Or if you had, in fact, found the athame … and so on."

"Thank you, Sheriff. We appreciate you letting us know to be on the lookout … since he's skipped town and all."

This was getting nowhere fast, so he cut his loss of wasted time, bid Bethie adieu, and released her from the discomfort of his lawful awareness.

• • •

"He knows," Arista said, ending the call for Auntie so she could be hands-free at the wheel.

"Of course, he knows. He's as smart as they come. It works well for him to have both—professional knowledge and his own intuition. He let me go … for now." Auntie twisted her mouth in contemplation. "Where was I? Oh! So, when Pearl called, she said to relay a message to you. I know it's a tender subject, but it may set your mind at ease."

Great, here we go.

"They announced Trini's death in the local news, and Stevie said the manager had killed her upon leaving work, which would have been around nine p.m. on the night of your love spell. Stevie mentioned you two did the spell much later because of inventory. Correct?" Auntie asked with a quick glance.

Arista nodded and considered the data. It provided a bit more relief, but not as much as seeing Trini happy with her daughter in the Summerland.

"So, let that go."

"Thanks, Auntie."

"In the meantime, I'm dreading what we find at Iris's."

"I know. Three unreturned voicemails since the ceremony, but that's why we're going to check on her."

"Carting around Fergus's body … several bouts of wooziness … and she mentioned that inner struggle."

Arista hummed in agreement, worried for Iris's safety. No time stood more susceptible than the liminal space between the lighter and darker halves of the witch's year for contact with the dead, and Iris had left with Fergus dead in her trunk.

Auntie pulled into Iris's driveway. While the colorful landscaping remained lush from the moist weather, an absence hung in the air. The loitering felines startled at first but did not altogether disappear.

"Oh dear, it's quite strange," Auntie said, killing the engine.

"I feel it, too. The stillness," Arista said upon exiting the car.

Approaching the house, Arista peered up at the large circular window. No silhouette hovered.

The cats lingered around Auntie's feet, meowing. "Unusual for them to be so—"

"The dishes," Arista said as panic set in. "There's no food and little water!" She picked up the stainless-steel dish, showing a dried, crusty white rim of its usually-filled level, and rushed to the spigot. "At least they had a little rainwater."

"Yes, that worked for her mandrakes, too," Auntie said, grabbing the watering can for the deeper soil.

As Arista tended to the felines with food from their sealed plastic tub, Auntie busied herself with potted plant care.

Once finished, they saw it at the same time.

"Oh dear!" Auntie said, rushing over to the front door mat.

Arista, at her heels, bent over to pick up the pretty sterling silver bracelet with Lapis and Mountain Opal beads lying at the doorstep. "This has got to be the Lapis bracelet she said had fallen as she left the house."

"Yes, she knew she had dropped it, and there's no way she would have walked past this day after day." Auntie's eyebrows pinched in worry.

Holding their breath, neither wanted to say it.

"Auntie … I don't think she made it home."

CHAPTER 47
AN AVALANCHE OF CHURNING FOAM

A vast, grayish-white sky crowned Riverfront Park, and the equally stark carpet of fresh-fallen snow at his feet enclosed him within the frigid landscape. Swallowed whole by Spokane's ether, the crisp air and striking cold, hollowed sharply into his throat.

But it was good to be back.

He leaned against the cement bridge railing, watching the largest U.S. urban waterfall violently descend as an avalanche of churning foam rushing forth on its northwestern journey to the Columbia River. Moving onward … as he must. Fergus ruminated on his former shell. That tall, aging, handsome man with great inner turmoil no longer held him. Instead, he had overtaken *her* in a fierce battle that self-actualized his truest power, that of possession. Attuning to Keira all those years, anemic, producing nothing of merit. Only incessantly taunting him of her daughter's soul that he could never attain. It no longer mattered.

Now, he had possessed another being, taken over her mind and body, and as of today, walked amongst the living … as Iris.

He looked down at the aged, feminine hands encasing his spirit. If winning over his members as a trans-goddess proved simple work, his potential just rose exponentially. At this very moment, he fully assumed his new identity as Iris.

She imagined a ceremonial flinging of that former body over the railing, watching it disappear into the agitated river. It did not matter that the pigs had already partaken with great enthusiasm. And the greatest part, he had achieved this possession without Arista's blood, her athame, or her unattainable death. The promised one held no reign over his success, after all. Freedom from another bondage—his obsession since her birth. The saying was true—the most agonizing trial of death can bring forth a magnificent rebirth. Literally. Now, as Iris, a wizened crone, this body could hold for quite some time. Thankfully, the coven responded well to a woman's poise and authority.

"Beautiful, isn't it?" a young man in his late twenties commented. He had a slim frame with close-cropped hair and a slicked-up forelock. His wispy mustache hovered above a genuine smile of pearl-white teeth.

"Yes, love, it surely is. It's the perfect place to help me sort my thoughts and strategize next steps. How about you?"

"Yeah, me too." His eyes animated, and he moved closer.

"Such a friendly young man. What's your name?"

"I'm Antonio," he said, holding out his hand for a shake.

She looked at his hand but offered none in return. "Antonio, I'm Iris, and it's a pleasure to meet you. Are you a local?"

"I was a law student at the university, but the pandemic derailed my plans. Then, I lost motivation and just … trying to find my new path to normal."

"You don't say. A young Catholic man, huh?"

"Yeah, for sure. You?"

"No, love. Not quite."

Iris saw Jameson's stout body hurrying up the street toward them. Dapper in his heavy, black, double-breasted wool coat and tweed herringbone flat cap. She waved him over, knowing he would not recognize her, then looked back to Antonio. "One moment, love."

Jameson hustled to cover more ground. Given this was his first gander at her, she thought a natural setting would be a gentler approach. Plus, she did not want to run into any other coven members at the Rec Center before their formal introduction. Giving him fair warning over the phone did not take much persuasion for her assuming the position as leader. For proof, she rattled off confidential bank information that only the two of them knew. Next, she promoted him to her right-hand man and explained that he would be granted all the perks that Conn had enjoyed. Finally, it proved exceptionally helpful to disclose his deepest dirt lest she need to bury him in it. After all, Fergus had not killed nor arranged any killings regarding his foes. That was Jameson's job.

As Jameson neared, she refocused on the young man beside her. "Antonio, I'm going to host a meeting this afternoon right after I pick up my new vehicle. I'd love to have you come. It may very well change your life."

"Sorry it took so long," Jameson said, interrupting with a breathless pant. He removed his cap out of respect.

She watched him size her up, trying to decipher the authenticity of her account. She gave him a wink. An apt gesture since Fergus had frequently winked at him when asking for illegal favors.

"Jameson, please meet Antonio. I think he would enjoy our community, don't you?"

Jameson gave Antonio a friendly smile and shook his hand. "Absolutely. Nice to meet you."

"Well, Antonio … would you like to be a part of something life-changing?"

Antonio shrugged and took out his phone to check the time. He put it back into his pocket. "Yeah, I got a few hours till I need to be somewhere. Where we headed?"

"The Rec Center."

THE END

I hope you enjoyed book number two in the
Murder, Tea & Crystals Trilogy!

For Reference and Inspiration

Air & Fire, https://www.airandfire.com/home.html - Many returned blessings, Emelia ☺

Better Place - https://www.betterplaceforests.com

ASL / Sign language , www.lifeprint.com and a shout-out to Mr. Duncan, ASL Teacher at Bellarmine College Preparatory, San Jose, CA

Andrews, Ted, How to See and Read Auras, Llewellyn Publication, 2006

Robert Zemeckis and Bob Gale, Back to the Future, 1989, 1991

Echo and the Bunnymen, The Killing Moon, 1984

El Tovar Lodge, https://www.grandcanyonlodges.com

Elvira, Cassandra Peterson, www.elvira.com

Engels, Shawn & Nichols, Steven, Witch's Brew, 2021, Sterling Epicure

https://www.familyeducation.com/baby-names/surname/origin/native-american

https://landscapedesignbylee.blogspot.com/2016/07/desert-flora-and-landforms-of-sedona.html

George R.R. Martin, A Game of Thrones, 1996, New York :Bantam Books

https://tribaltradeco.com/ and
https://us.tribaltradeco.com/blogs/medicine-wheel/medicine-wheel-
teachings-native-medicine-wheel-system-
explained?_pos=3&_sid=9f75be880&_ss=r

https://irishcentersf.org

Eddie Vedder, Jeremy, Ten, Pearl Jam, 1991

Hilton Santa Cruz / Scotts Valley, Santa Cruz, CA

https://kpopjacketlady.com/2018/08/10/korean-ghosts/

https://en.wikipedia.org/wiki/Kumiho

George Lucas, Star Wars, 1977, Lucas Film

Northern California Renaissance Faire, San Juan Bautista, CA
https://norcalrenfaire.com/

Raku Pottery Works - https://www.rakupotteryworks.com/home

https://www.skyetrail.org.uk

Spirit: Stallion of the Cimarron, Dreamworks Pictures, 2002

Stevie Nicks, Sisters of the Moon, 1980, Fleetwood Mac

Sublime, Santeria, 1996

https://localwiki.org/santacruz/Robert_%27Umbrella_Man%27_Steffe
n

Ursula K. LeGuin, A Wizard of Earthsea, 1968, Parnassus Press

https://www.visitspokane.com/things-to-do/recreation/parks/spokanefalls/

White Raven, Felton, CA

The White Witch Podcast on Spotify – Huge shoutout to Carly Rose and her abundant information on all things witchy!

Wikipedia

Witch Jokes - https://upjoke.com/witch-jokes and https://www.boredpanda.com/witch-puns/?utm_source=google&utm_medium=organic&utm_campaign=organic

World History Encyclopedia

Yaima, https://www.yaimamusic.com/

101 Dalmatians, Walt Disney Productions, 1961

Witchy Dictionary

Áine - An Irish goddess of the Tuatha Dé Danann and is also a fairy queen. She is associated with summer, sun, wealth, and sovereignty. She is sometimes represented by a red mare. Her most-told story is exacting powerful revenge on the king who forced himself upon her. She bit off his ear, leaving him maimed. Since only flawless individuals could reign, he lost his throne.

Amethyst wings - Amethyst "Wings" come from Amethyst geodes cut in half with the two halves hung side-by-side on a very sturdy metal stand that complement a grand appeal. Usually costs thousands of dollars.

Ayam Cemani - An inky black chicken breed indigenous to Indonesia, known by many names: world's most bewitching chicken, Lamborghini of poultry, Goth chicken and Sith Lord bird. Jason Bittel writes for National Geographic, the Cemani is perhaps the "most deeply pigmented creature" found in nature. Every aspect of its appearance—feathers, beak, tongue, eyes, and claws—is jet-black.

Brigid – A goddess of pre-Christian Ireland. She appears in Irish mythology as a member of the Tuatha Dé Danann. She is associated with wisdom, poetry, healing, protection, smithing, and domesticated animals. Saint Brigid (of Catholicism) shares many of the goddess's attributes and her feast day, 1 February, which was originally a pagan festival called Imbolc. It has thus been argued that the saint is a Christianization of the goddess, or that the lore of the goddess was transferred to her.

Charcoal tablet – A form of smoke cleansing. Once the charcoal is fully lit and ash has begun to form (usually a couple minutes), a small piece of resin is set in its middle. As the resin begins to bubble and melt, its smoke and fragrance is released.

Chime candles – Four-by-half-inch candles used in spell work. Used with anointing oils, herbs, carved sigils, etc.

Cernunnos - An ancient Celtic god who represented nature, flora and fauna, fruits and grains, fertility, and prosperity. He is frequently depicted in Celtic art wearing stag antlers or horns and usually a torc around his neck. Associations to other religions include Cernunnos to Buddha because of their similar cross-legged sitting / lotus positions and stature of peace and poise. Because of his depiction with horns—hence, another moniker as "the horned one"—he may have been one inspiration for the imagery associated with the devil in Christianity. Also, considered to be *The Green Man,* the images of the Old Religion brought into Christian churches before the Reformation, and one of the most ancient, pagan symbols to be found in the Christian church.

Gaia - In Greek mythology, Gaia is the personification of Earth and ancestral mother of all life. She is the mother of Uranus (Sky), from whose sexual union she bore the Titans (themselves parents of many of the Olympian gods), the Cyclopes, and the Giants; as well as of Pontus (Sea), from whose union she bore the primordial sea gods. Her equivalent in the Roman pantheon was Terra.

Hurdy gurdy - A string instrument that produces sound by a hand-crank-turned, rosined wheel rubbing against the strings. The wheel functions much like a violin bow, and single notes played on the instrument sound similar to those of a violin.

Oud - A Middle Eastern short-neck lute-type, pear-shaped, fretless stringed instrument, usually with 11 strings grouped in six courses. Though, some models have five or seven courses with 10 or 13 strings, respectively.

Rhiannon – A major figure in Welsh mythology. She is a strong-minded Otherworld woman, known for intelligence, political strategy as well as beauty, wealth, and generosity. In her most-known story, she endures tragedy when her newborn child of royal blood is abducted, and she is accused of infanticide. Undergoing her undue penance, she demonstrates the powers of a giantess, and strength of a horse, by carrying travelers on her back. Eventually, all wrongdoing comes to light, and she is reunited with her son and regains her good name. Usually known as a Horse Goddess, she is also associated with songbirds, snakes, and dragons.

Samhain - Believed to have Celtic pagan origins, and some Neolithic passage tombs in Ireland and Britain are aligned with the sunrise at the time of Samhain. It is mentioned in the earliest Irish literature, from the 9th century, and is associated with many important events in Irish mythology. The early literature says great gatherings and feasts marked Samhain when the ancient burial mounds were opened as portals to the Otherworld. In the 9th century, the Western Church endorsed November 1st as All Saints' Day, and November 2nd later became All Souls' Day. It is believed that Samhain and All Saints'/All Souls' influenced each other and the modern Halloween. Most American Halloween traditions were inherited from Irish and Scottish immigrants.

Silver Bough – Writer, journalist, and scholar of old Irish, Eleanor Hull, drew parallels between the silver branch and the golden bough of Roman legend. A branch required for entry into the Underworld. In like manner, the branch (silver or otherwise) is an object given to a human invited by a denizen of the Otherworld to visit his/her realm, offering "a clue binding the desired one to enter."

Smudge – The burning of sacred herbs (e.g., white sage) or resins in ceremony. While the term is most often associated to some Indigenous peoples of the Americas, it bears resemblance to other ceremonies and rituals involving smoke, including the ancient Gaelic ritual of Saining and Australian smoking ceremony.

Tuatha Dé Danann - A supernatural race in Irish mythology. Many of them are thought to represent deities of pre-Christian Gaelic Ireland.

Irish Translation

Cad é sin?! / What is it?!
A Dhia dhílis! / Dear God! (in exclamatory fear)
Each ifreannach! / Damned Horse!

ABOUT THE AUTHOR

Sherri was raised in southeast Texas. Walking barefoot most days and catching crawdads as they swam the creek beds, she had a love for all things free and natural. Her childhood ran rampant with talk of ghosts, demons, and backcountry folklore. This inspired her first story for sale, about a poisonous flower that shot toxins onto children as they smelled it. Her classmate bought it for all the change in his pocket. Shortly thereafter, her mother packed the two of them up and headed to the central coast of California. Since that time, she has worked corporate, married, raised two sons, and now writes full-time creating atmospheric paranormal fiction. Her debut novel, *Murder Under Redwood Moon*, shot straight to #1 New Release on Amazon.

SHERRI L. DODD
MURDER UNDER REDWOOD MOON

Final Note from Sherri L. Dodd

Word-of-mouth is crucial for any author to succeed. If you enjoyed *Moonset on Desert Sands*, please **leave a review** online—anywhere you are able. Even if it's just a sentence or two. It would make all the difference and would be very much appreciated.

Thanks!
Sherri L. Dodd

We hope you enjoyed reading this title from:

www.blackrosewriting.com

Subscribe to our mailing list – *The Rosevine* – and receive **FREE** books, daily
deals, and stay current with news about upcoming
releases and our hottest authors.
Scan the QR code below to sign up.

Already a subscriber? Please accept a sincere thank you for being a fan of
Black Rose Writing authors.

View other Black Rose Writing titles at
www.blackrosewriting.com/books and use promo code
PRINT to receive a **20% discount** when purchasing.

www.ingramcontent.com/pod-product-compliance
Lightning Source LLC
Chambersburg PA
CBHW030759210726

48290CB00002B/337